INDEFINITE DOUBT

INDEFINITE DOUBT

Baker Street Legacy Book Three

GAIL R. DELANEY

Praise for Indefinite Doubt

"Seriously, this is brilliant work. The story is amazing and the characters are people you want to know and hang out with. Gail R. Delaney really has something special with these characters. Brilliantly done!"

Angela Roe, Reader

"All good things must come to an end—but WHAT AN END! Through sweet moments, devastating discoveries, and harrowing escapes the final chapter of the *Baker Street Legacy* left me satisfied and yet wishing I didn't have to say goodbye."

Angela Laverghetta,
Author of The Innisfail Cycle series.

Art
REQUIRES HEART
#SupportArtistsNotAI
www.GailDelaney.com

To Esther Mitchell: my alpha reader, beta reader, and treasure of a friend. Thank you for letting me bounce ideas, share snippets, and answer my questions Google couldn't provide but you could. I value you in my life, and appreciate your friendship.

To my beta readers: Esther Mitchell, Angela Canon, Angela Roe, and Amy Dewey. You helped me — each in different and invaluable ways — to make this book the best it could be.

To Niall MacDomhnaill ailias MacCuinn and Author Eilidh Miller, who helped me make Angus "Mac" Hennessey sound Scottish and not just an American trying to sound Scottish.

To a certain individual who inspired a character who took a turn. Thanks for being a good sport.

And to all the fans and lovers of the "Baker Street Legacy" series for waiting 8 long years. I never intended to make you wait, and your grace is appreciated.

Book Content Expectations

Due to the nature of the genre and the storyline, please be aware there are instances of terroristic violence that may feel parallel to real-world events, as well as personal danger, violence, gun violence, abduction, torture, and pharmaceutical abuse in an attempt to manipulate. The characters struggle with PTSD, grief at the loss of someone close to them, liars, deception, and trauma. There are discussions and ramifications of trauma, pregnancy concerns, and betrayal.

Please note that manual communication (based on ASL or BSL) is written in italics but within quotation marks to indicate dialogue.

Baker Street Legacy

Baker Street Legacy
Storytelling Style

Baker Street Legacy is a continuous timeline, in which any given book extends the story of the book prior to it and sets up for the next book while also telling its own story. The books must be read in order to have a full understanding of the saga.

This means each book has its own story arc, but also extends the greater story arcs.

There will be cliffhangers, but as the author, I will always provide you with a payoff within the book you're reading. Each book has its own plot, it's own storyline and its own resolutions. Each book (with the exclusion of the final book in the series) will have set up for the next book. These may or may not be considered cliffhangers by some. But, be aware, they exist.

If you have stayed with the series to this point, I'm glad you're here and I hope you found the journey worth it.

Baker Street Legacy
Spotify Playlist

Do you like having a soundtrack to the books you read? I've created a playlist for the Baker Street Legacy on Spotify.

You will likely notice Grayson and Kipling are inclined toward the legends of jazz along with some popular contemporary crooners. A little Frank Sinatra and Nat King Cole; a little Michael Bublé and Colbie Calliat.

I hope you enjoy.

"Any truth is better than indefinite doubt."

~Sherlock Holmes
The Yellow Face,
The Memoirs of Sherlock Holmes

Chapter One

"I've been doing some research, Kip. He's not marrying you on Saturday. Do you know that? He can't!"

Kipling Branson stifled her groan, but barely, and pushed her fingers through her hair before looking into the computer camera to meet her best friend's indignant glare. She looked tired, but whenever Kipling tried to ask if she was okay, Mina turned the conversation back on her.

And told Kipling all the reasons her choices were wrong.

"There you go again thinking I'm an idiot, Mina."

In the hallway outside the office, Grayson pulled along their luggage with the wheels thumping on the original hardwood floors. They were supposed to be on the road within the hour for Sussex, where they would spend the next three days in final preparation for their wedding on Saturday. Just the passing thought made Kipling's heart flutter with giddy happiness.

"Are you even listening to me? What is it going to take to convince you of the truth? That everything he's feeding you is a lie? He's a liar."

Mina's demand yanked her back and twisted her stomach. Her happiness was temporarily smothered by her lifetime friend's conspiracy theories and outrage that Kipling would marry a man she'd met six months earlier; especially considering the circumstances then, and since. But marrying an officer of MI6 wasn't exactly like marrying a commodities banker. Kipling knew what she had accepted when she accepted his request to become her husband.

"It takes weeks, sometimes *months* to get a marriage visa for a US citizen to marry a Brit. I'm not talking a *fortnight*, or whatever the hell Mr. Posh Thesaurus Mouth would call it. I'm talking weeks and weeks. That's *if* you're approved. You only agreed to marry him seven weeks ago, and who knows how long he dragged his feet to apply—"

"Oh, good grief. Here we go again. What is it going to take for you to believe he loves me? He wants to be with me?"

Watson, either attracted by her frustration or dodging the thought of a cat carrier as long as possible, jumped into her lap. She stroked the cat from head to tail, finding comfort in his affection.

"Kip, *I* love you," Mina said, her voice barely dripping with condescension as she pressed her hand to her chest. "You know I love you. And you're amazing, you've accomplished so much, especially considering your obstacles—"

Kip couldn't help the shocked widening of her eyes. "My obstacles?" Heat flashed from her chest up her throat to her face. Mina's insult was quite possibly the first and only time Mina — her friend since elementary school — had referred to her deafness as a hindrance.

Not once.

Not ever.

"But he's a frickin' international *spy*, honey. Seriously…"

"He's not a spy…" she mumbled but lost her steam. It wasn't worth explaining. Again.

Mina's words were cruel. Absolutely cruel. Mina threw back at her the misgivings and worries Kipling had shared with her in the early days of her relationship with Grayson Holmes. How could she not wonder what a man like Grayson would see in a pretty average doctorate student from Boston's South End? But even without knowing how she worried, Grayson had proved again and again how much he loved her. How much she meant to him.

She swallowed and licked her lips, focusing on a notepad beside Grayson's blotter to keep from looking again at her supposed best friend. Grayson's neat penmanship had written out a short list, each item crossed off, apparently a list of errands he needed to run in preparation for the weekend. One made her smile and she brushed her fingertips over the paper.

~~Call Mum Branson for the invitation list~~

With six words he probably never consciously thought she would read, Grayson Oliver Sherlock Holmes brought a smile to her face and lightened her heart all over again.

Kipling pulled her attention away from the list to look at Mina again. "Is your biggest argument against our wedding this Saturday that we couldn't possibly have a marriage visa?"

"No, my *biggest* argument is you're crazy to agree to this at all, but we'll start with the visa. Did he even tell you how long it would take?" Mina demanded, arms crossed with wide eyes.

She canted her head and squinted at the screen. "Let me ask you this, Mina. As an officer in the Royal Majesty's Secret Service, and someone owed some wicked favors by his superiors, you don't think he could make sure my marriage visa was approved and ready by this weekend?" She shook her head and huffed, annoyed with herself for even engaging in the argument. "The university had already submitted paperwork for a work visa, so marriage or not, I'd be staying."

"Aha!" Mina cried, pointing a finger at the screen. "That's another thing! You said you're having the ceremony in their garden." Her derision made the word garden sound nasally.

"We were going to, but—" She already knew the next argument Mina would throw at her and braced herself against it. She didn't have a chance to explain the change in plans.

"*That* can't happen either!" Mina's voice pitched up a level of volume with every declaration. "Kip, listen to me. He's gaslighting you, and I'm trying to help you see it because I'm apparently the only one who sees through his lies. Unlike in the good old USA, where anyone and their cat can be ordained and marry anyone else in the automotive aisle at Walmart, it doesn't work that way in England. I spent *hours* going over marriage requirements."

Kipling gasped and sat back hard in the desk chair, covering her mouth. "You mean he intended to keep me living in sin?"

"How can you joke about this, Kip?"

Siting up again, Kipling leaned in to be closer to the screen. She lost all desire to explain. "Because you're being ridiculous."

"Ha! See?" Mina pointed again at the screen, pulling a smug face. "Sure looks good but means *nothing*."

"We aren't getting married in the garden—"

"What the hell, then, Kip? Are you not marrying him?"

Kipling shook her head. She was done justifying. Done explaining. Done giving Mina more than she deserved. Grayson had immediately agreed to a ceremony in the garden back in June, but the short time just didn't allow it. Mina was right; in the UK a ceremony in the Holmes garden wouldn't be binding by the church, or anyone else. His sister Shirley had married in May in the garden, but it had been for the event only. The location. The sentiment. She and Daniel had been legally joined at the parish by the vicar the Monday following the ceremony before they left on their honeymoon. Not wanting to wait on arrangements, Kipling and Grayson decided together they would marry in the Sussex parish on Saturday, and the reception would be in the family garden. It wasn't about where they married, it was that she would be his wife.

"No answer?" Mina taunted.

"What do you care, Mina?" she asked with a sigh, her heart squeezing with a sudden heartbreak. "You're not coming anyway, right?"

Not waiting for Mina to answer, she set her hand on the mouse and clicked closed the video call window, ending the connection. The act felt final and painful, and her gut told her she might have just lost her longest, closest friend. She pressed her lips together and swallowed hard against the sudden lump in her throat and burning in her eyes. She set her elbow on the desk and hunched forward, bracing her head in her hand.

The chair squeaked as Grayson turned it toward him, and Watson jumped to the floor. Kipling didn't fight when he took her hand and drew her to her feet, wrapping her in his arms. The sob attacked her, tearing at her chest. Grayson cupped his large hand around the back of her head and held her close, kissing her hair.

"I'm sorry, my darling. Would if I could fix this."

She wrapped her arms around him and pressed her cheek to his chest until she felt the rhythmic thump of his heart, pressed closer until her hearing aids squealed with feedback, but she didn't care. His embrace was home, was peace, and she'd be damned if she let Mina Russo take that away from her.

Langdon Howell huffed and tugged his suit jacket into place, dusting the lapels with his fingers. "It would seem I am destined not to enjoy dinner."

"More's the pity." Grayson's mocking tone drew Kipling's glance, and despite the situation, she found a sense of calm and normalcy in the angry curl of his lip. He spared only a brief sidelong look her way before focusing again on Howell, the man who had nearly killed them both, and who had threatened to carry through with the act if things weren't done to his satisfaction.

Their waiter arrived, setting the same meal before each of them. Chicken Piri Piri with spicy Portuguese rice and grilled vegetables. She'd had it once back home in Boston, and any other day, she might be enticed. Her stomach twisted at the aroma. The thought of food, the act of forcing it down her restricted throat, made her feel ill. Howell retrieved his utensils, laid his napkin in his lap, and motioned with the end of his knife that each of them should begin as he cut into his own meal. Kipling met Grayson's gaze across the table, and offered a small smile, hoping he'd seen her silent command to 'be ready.'

"It troubles me greatly neither of you believes me to be a man of my word," Howell said, cutting through the chicken. "Doctor Branson has succeeded, and as stated in our negotiations, you both will leave here alive."

Kipling snapped her attention to Howell. "Negotiations?" she croaked, her voice lifting upward in pitch.

"You bloody bastard—" Grayson began, but Howell's choked cough interrupted him.

Gregory McQueen's stealthy delivery of the poison had gone unnoticed, and now it had Howell in its grip. Even though she wouldn't mind watching Howell die — an acceptance that made her blood run cold — Greg had assured her the effects were immediate, intense, but temporary. Suddenly red in the face, and perspiration bloomed in large beads on Howell's forehead and he slapped a hand against his chest. He swayed but gripped the edge of the table with his other hand to keep from tipping over. His jaw worked in an attempt at speech, but nothing more than a gargled sound came out.

The plan from there required immediate action. Kipling stood and gasped, ready to call out for help. He was having a heart attack. But before she could draw the attention of all the restaurant patrons, Howell lunged to his feet despite his choked features. Howell pulled a handgun from inside his dinner jacket.

"No!" Kipling screamed.

His hand shook, the muzzle swaying, but Howell stood so close he couldn't possibly miss. The gunfire cracked in the air and Grayson's head snapped back, gore and blood spraying behind him as the bullet ripped through his skull. The spray hit Kipling, hot and searing and she screamed again.

Kipling sat up in bed, gasping for breath, her heart threatening to crack through her ribs and break free of her body. A chill danced up her spine when the night breeze coming through the open bedroom window brushed over her damp, exposed skin. She pushed her mussed hair off her face and squinted in the dark, trying to orientate herself. Moonlight streamed through the one window overlooking the garden, giving her just enough light to allow her to reacquaint herself with the still unfamiliar bedroom. She'd slept here half a dozen nights in total — spread over two months — but it didn't help in those first moments of panicked confusion when she escaped a dream.

At least Kipling hadn't cried out in her sleep and woken Grayson's sister like she did the first time she and Grayson had stayed at the Holmes cottage weeks earlier when she arrived in England.

Too awake to even attempt sleep, her nerves still aggravated and her pulse still jumping, Kipling eased the soft cotton quilt off her legs and sat on the edge of the twin bed. She raised her cell phone she'd plugged in to charge overnight, and tapped the screen to see the time. Just after two. She needed to be up and ready to begin her hectic day in five hours, and this was not the day to wake up with bags under her eyes. Using the illumination from the phone screen, she found her hearing aids, then closed the battery compartments and slipped them into place. Seconds later, each chimed to assure her they were on and active before the sounds of the still house came into sharp focus.

Jo's deep breathing from the other bed.

The rustle of the tree leaves outside with the night breeze.

Birdsong of some nocturnal bird she couldn't identify, and seconds later a response.

All a gentle mingling of sounds not heard during the day, either because they belonged to the night or would be lost beneath the jumbled noises of living. If she were home on Baker Street, she wouldn't bother with the hearing aids to get up during the night; but here, she didn't dare move around too much for fear of waking the members of the Holmes family. She didn't know if she was being quiet if she couldn't hear.

With a glance toward Jo's bed to assure herself Jo was asleep, she stood and winced at the small creaking noises of the old frame. Barefoot and not daring to stop for slippers, Kipling walked with as light a step as she could manage to the bedroom door, eased it open, and stepped into the hall before closing it again. It wasn't until she was in the hall at the top of the straight staircase that she heard the piano music drifting up from downstairs, muffled by the closed library door where the antique upright piano was kept. She'd seen the piano tucked into the corner of the library but had never seen or heard anyone play it.

A glance toward Grayson's bedroom door confirmed the door was open, the room beyond dark. Alerted by her far from cat-like stealth, Watson came slinking from the bedroom into the moonlit hall, rubbing along the doorjamb before he jogged to her, and rubbed similarly on her calf before preceding her down the stairs. She smiled, following the cat with a more ginger step since she wasn't nearly familiar enough with the Holmes cottage to navigate with confidence in the dark.

At the bottom of the stairs, she paused, glancing into the rooms she could see to confirm no other lights were on except for the one shining beneath the library door. Grayson still played, because there was no real doubt to her he was the pianist, the music gentle and soothing but wholly unfamiliar. She was, by no means, knowledgeable on music other than she could differentiate Beethoven from Gershwin, and some of the most commonly known classical pieces even if only so far as to know it was well known. Without the ability or technology to enjoy music as a kid, her love of reading had bloomed instead. Regardless of her lack of knowledge, the piece soothed her. This music was delicate, flowing beautifully from note to note. She stepped closer to the door, leaning to listen with her ear close to the wood, but her curiosity won and she carefully pressed down the antique lever, pushing the door into the room.

The comforting aromas of leather, pipe tobacco — despite the fact Emerson Holmes had been restricted from smoking in the cottage for many years — and wood oil greeted her. Built-in shelves lined every wall, interrupted only by windows on three of the four walls, with Father Holmes' ornate antique desk occupying the middle of the space facing the central fireplace, currently dormant. The piano was tucked in the corner of the library in an alcove deep enough to keep the instrument clear of regular traffic. It only took a few steps into the room for Grayson Holmes to come into view, seated on the piano bench in his blue flannel pajama pants and gray tee shirt, his head bowed as his long fingers drew beauty from the heirloom.

He stopped playing when she reached him, extending his arm to reach for her. A slow, sexy smile curled his lips at one corner when he looked over his shoulder at her.

"Don't let me stop you," Kipling said, taking his hand before she slid onto the space on the bench beside him, her back to the keys in a position that made it easier to see his face. "I didn't know you played, but somehow it doesn't surprise me at all. "

Grayson chuckled, the sound low and rumbling in his chest, and brought her knuckles to his lips for a kiss. He lowered their hands to rest on his thigh, his thumb stroking her fingers. She loved this man, beyond limits and beyond description; she loved him so much it sometimes made the simple act of breathing difficult.

"Why are you playing piano in the middle of the night?" she asked, keeping her voice low in reverence for the stillness of the cottage surrounding him. She tried to look affronted but doubted she fooled him. "And why isn't there a piano in Baker Street?"

He drew in a long, deep breath, and heat rose up her throat at his study of her bordering on arousing scrutiny. "This piano *was* in Baker Street," he explained, switching the order of answer. "It's where Mum first began my lessons, teaching me herself with Dad helping. He learned from Mrs. Bertrand. You met her——"

"At Shirl's wedding. I remember," she finished with a smile and wink. "She was very sweet."

He nodded, canting his head in the general direction of the rest of the cottage. "When we moved back here to Sussex it was one of the few things my parents brought with us." Not releasing her hand, he brought his other across to lay his palm against her jaw, stroking near the corner of her mouth with his thumb. "If you would like a piano, I will see one is waiting for us upon our return."

"After our honeymoon," she said softer, her heart beating faster, but for a far better reason.

He raised his chin, his expression easing into a smile. "After our honeymoon."

"I suppose it would be rude to flee the church as soon as we are pronounced," she said, not asking a question, and with the attempt of a serious expression.

Grayson laughed, ending the rumble with a kiss that added fuel to the warmth in her blood and made her stomach tumble. She moved into the kiss; Grayson never kissed her casually, not even when parting. His kisses were never distracted, but always distracting. But just as they had been for the last four days, both were aware of where they were, and all their kisses — stolen or otherwise — had only left her needing him. He held her face in his hands, keeping her close with their brows touching and their rapid breath mingling in the space between them.

"Now, my darling," he said and gave her another kiss at the corner of her lips. "Would you like to tell me about the dream?" His question was gentle, yet insistent.

She shook her head, but only enough to serve as a reply and not enough to separate from him. "No."

"Kipling—"

"I want to ignore it tonight, Grayson. Is that okay?"

"You've had one each night since we arrived, and I can't help but wonder if your difficult conversation with Mina has a part. You understand it helps when you tell me."

"No," she cut off, but barely and adding a laugh. "What helps is sleeping beside you. What helps is feeling the beat of your heart against my back and your breath on my shoulder. You are better than anything else. How much longer?" she asked, just as she had many times each day since they arrived, and each time he had known exactly.

"Eight hours, thirty-five minutes until…" He tipped his chin so it touched hers, and his lips brushed her lips without indulging in another kiss. "…our wedding."

A delicious chill danced over her skin. "Then you'd better do something other than kiss me or we'll break that unspoken promise to your mother."

He made a low, frustrated noise in his throat and leaned away, but not so far he let her go. "I have never known torture equal to being in the same house with you, and not making love to you."

Kipling let her eyes flutter and she tipped back her head, groaning in frustration. "Please distract me, Grayson," she both begged and teased. "I desperately need a distraction or I'll never go to sleep again, and no one likes a haggard-looking bride."

He laughed and lowered his hands, shifted to face the piano again. So she could watch him play, she pivoted around the end of the bench to face the keys as he first played a single note with his right hand, then a short series with his left. It sounded close to what he'd been playing when she found him, but not exactly.

"You never said why you were up in the middle of the night playing piano," she said, glancing quickly at him before returning to her study of his hands.

"Distraction," he answered simply.

Kipling chuckled and leaned her cheek on his arm, swaying with him a moment before righting herself to watch him play. After what seemed to be test or warm-up strokes of the keys, he slid with an apparent effortless ease into the same melody she'd heard from the top of the stairs. It was delicate, and soothing, and made her think of a gentle breeze or a ballet dancer. If watching him play didn't have her so entranced, she would have closed her eyes and swayed with it. He finished the piece, and the final notes eased away as he dropped his hands into his lap again.

"It's beautiful. What's it called?"

Grayson shrugged and cleared his throat, a thoroughly un-Grayson-like move. "I don't know."

"Who's the composer?" He didn't answer, giving her a sidelong look, his fingers laced in his lap with his thumbs rolling slowly over and around each other. He didn't answer but arched a single eyebrow. Kipling squinted, a niggling realization skimming up the back of her neck. "Grayson, did *you* compose this?"

"Yes," he said, then cleared his throat and shifted on the bench, tapping on a single key, the note resonating within the antique body of the piano. "It's rough, I suppose. Needs work."

"How long have you been working on it?"

He sighed and bobbed his head back and forth, wrinkling his

nose as if considering some extensive timeline. "An hour and a half."

Kipling gasped, staring at him with her jaw hanging open. "An hour and a half? Grayson, that's amazing. When did you begin composing music?"

He chuckled; a deep, low rumble in his chest that seemed louder in the stillness of the cottage. "An hour and a half ago."

Kipling couldn't form a response, only able to stare at Grayson with her hand pressed to her chest. Just when she thought perhaps she had a good understanding of the complexities of this man he shocked her with another aspect of himself.

He plucked the note again, holding down the ivory key to stroke it from hinge to edge. The note slowly faded. "I came down seeking a way to distract myself from your absence, and even in your absence, you inspired me."

"Grayson," she managed to whisper, her throat tightening with a surge of intense emotion that threatened to leave her completely mute. She swallowed and grabbed his hand. "I love you."

He smiled slow and warm and leaned toward her to press a kiss to her brow. "You are my world."

Chapter Two

How does love speak?
By the uneven heart-throbs, and the freak
Of pounding pulses that stand still and ache...

Grayson's world was silent, except for the thumping rush of blood in his ears. Pachelbel's Canon in D slipped away from his conscious awareness, despite the way the organ music embraced the acoustics of the vaulted ceilings of the centuries-old parish church. Nothing existed beyond the breathtaking beauty of the woman walking toward him, her hand hooked in the bend of her father's arm.

Kipling...*his* Kipling...raised her chin and her gaze met his, a slow smile bowing her lips.

Her hair glowed with the sunlight streaming through the three four-meter tall lancet windows of stained glass in the pulpit alcove behind the bema where he stood waiting. No veil hid her face, but a ribbon and pearl headband woven into the loosely twisted and braided style that left wispy curls around her face and down her throat. Perfect for his Kipling. Simple and classic, timeless and beautiful.

Perhaps it was the princess-cut beaded bodice that accentuated her form, or the way the sheer tulle of the skirt flowed around her, or perhaps it was because she had chosen him — *him* — and the love she had gifted to him that made her the most beautiful woman in all of existence.

In a rush, his world compressed and released and everything came rushing back; his stilled heart galloping forward to catch up.

"Take it easy, Ollie," Gregory said behind him, bringing his hand down on Grayson's shoulder with two thumps. "No passing out on us."

Kipling's smile bloomed, and he knew she'd witnessed his undeniable reaction to seeing her; her pleasure in his reaction coloring her cheeks. Grayson acknowledged he was far from the first man left entranced, enthralled, and awestruck at the beauty of the woman they loved walking toward them but he truly doubted any bride could be as beautiful as Kipling Branson.

Sandra Sookoo reached them first as the matron of honor and winked at Grayson before moving to her left to allow Kipling and her father to reach Grayson. Jack Branson offered Grayson a smile strained behind a wealth of emotion dancing in the big man's eyes. There was no doubt — now or ever — how loved Kipling was by her parents. Grayson dipped his chin, touched his right-hand fingers to his lips, and offered an unspoken "Thank you" to the man whom he deeply respected. Jack pressed his lips together and nodded, small and silent, and kissed Kipling's cheek before turning to join his wife in the first pew of attendees on the bride's side.

Grayson had to grip his own hands in front of him to keep himself from reaching for her, a visceral, undeniable urge very nearly overwhelming him. Instead, he looked into her gleaming eyes for a second longer than proper before taking his spot beside her so they faced Reverend Anderson. Grayson drew in a long, slow breath through his nose and released it just as slowly through parted lips to still his thundering heart.

Reverend Anderson smiled at them both, a *Book of Common Prayer* open in his hands. Grayson had known this man his entire life, and Reverend Anderson had been the one to marry Emerson and

Annalise Holmes forty years before. After today, he will have officiated the marriage of two of their children.

"The grace of our Lord Jesus Christ, the love of God, and the fellowship of the Holy Spirit be with you," he said in his practiced, hearty voice that filled the church interior.

"And also with you," echoed the friends and family in attendance.

"In the presence of God, Father, Son, and Holy Spirit, we have come together to witness the marriage of Grayson Oliver Sherlock Holmes and Kipling Marie Branson, to pray for God's blessings on them, to share their joy and celebrate their love.

"Marriage is a gift of God in creation through which husband and wife may know the grace of God. It is given that as man and woman grow together in love and trust, they shall be united with one another in heart, body, and mind, as Christ is united with His bride, the Church."

Grayson knew he should focus on the vicar's words, but instead, he was hyper-aware of the beautiful woman beside him. The heady, mingled aromas of freesia, hyacinth, calla lilies, lily of the valley, and chrysanthemum, all the flowers of her bouquet drifted to him. Beneath them was the citrus scent of the shampoo she had begun to use since living in the UK; the scent he woke to each morning drifting from her hair as it spread over their pillows and her bare shoulders.

He watched her in his peripheral, tilting his head toward her just enough to see her profile. She glanced at him, and smiled, casting down her gaze as a new flush of color bloomed in her cheeks.

How does Love speak?
In the faint flush upon the tell-tale cheek,
And in the pallor that succeeds it; by
The quivering lid of an averted eye —
The smile that proves the parent of a sigh:
Thus does Love speak.

"Grayson and Kipling are now to enter this way of life," Reverend Anderson continued, his speaking of Grayson's name pulling him back from his thoughts with a sharp mental jerk. He quickly ran through the ceremony script to ensure he hadn't missed a necessary response or action and had not. "They will each give their consent to the other and make solemn vows, and in token of this, they will each give and receive a ring. We pray with them that the Holy Spirit will guide and strengthen them, that they may fulfill God's purposes for the whole of their earthly lives together."

Each moment made it harder not to look at her, not to reach for her. Instead, he gave in to his longing to study her and she tipped up her chin to look at him, her smile blood-warming. As Reverend Anderson inquired of the congregation whether any had cause or reason they couldn't be wed, he silently mouthed the words "I love you."

"Grayson, will you take Kipling to be your wife? Will you love her, comfort her, honor and protect her, and forsake all others, be faithful to her as long as you both shall live?"

In a single tick, his throat was dry and his heart galloped again. He had to lick his lips and swallow before answering with a confident, "I will."

"Kipling, will you take Grayson to be your husband? Will you love him, comfort him, honor and protect him, and forsake all others, be faithful to him as long as you both shall live?"

"I will," she said barely in a whisper. She smiled, the honest expression lighting her eyes as a single tear slipped free. Unwilling to allow even one tear to fall without wiping it away, he brought his bent finger to her cheek and smoothed it from her skin.

"Will you, the families and friends of Grayson and Kipling, support and uphold them in their marriage now and in the years to come?"

All in attendance spoke, "I will," and the joined voices wrapped around them.

The Church of England held firm to the structure of the ceremony and very seldom allowed a variance, but in this instance, Reverend Anderson had given his consent. He looked to Grayson and said, "Grayson and Kipling, I now invite you to make your vows, in the presence of God and His people."

Kipling held out her bouquet for Sandra to take as Grayson

took a fortifying breath to steel his nerves. The traditional vows required they join hands, but for this, Grayson had practiced daily to ensure his technique was flawless; or as flawless as he could manage now with the tremble in his hands. He'd faced murderous criminals, dangers, and possible death and had never so much as wavered. This was not fear, not anywhere near. Grayson never knew excitement could bear such a physical reaction.

This moment was purposefully silent and between only the two of them and anyone who understood Kipling's silent language.

"I, Grayson, take you, Kipling, to be my wife, to have and to hold from this day forward; for better, for worse, for richer, for poorer, in sickness and in health, for love and to cherish, till death us do part; according to God's holy law. In the presence of God I make this vow." He ended by pressing his open hand over his own heart.

She returned the vows, and the absence of any nervousness in the delicate, elegant movement of her hands gave him a slight pang of jealousy; but the fluid beauty of her silent language kept him mesmerized.

As they finished, Greg stepped forward enough to place their rings in the binding of the book of prayer, and in turn, Reverend Anderson held the book toward them.

"Heavenly Father, by your blessing let these rings be to Grayson and Kipling a symbol of unending love and faithfulness, to remind them of the vow and covenant which they have made this day through Jesus Christ our Lord."

Grayson reached for the antique yellow gold ring with three oval opals and four diamonds — the ring his great-grandfather had used to wed his great-grandmother — and took Kipling's left hand in his right to slip it on her finger. "Kipling, I give you this ring as a sign of our marriage. With my body, I will honor you, all that I am I give to you…" His voice faltered, giving in to the effervescent happiness bubbling in his chest. He had to stop, but when she curled her fingers to hold his he met her amber eyes, and his control returned. "With my body, I will honor you, all that I am I give to you, and all that I have I share with you, within the love of God, Father, Son, and Holy Spirit."

Kipling took his ring from Reverend Anderson's book and her gentle, delicate hands held his as she slid the ring over his scarred knuckles. "Grayson, I give you this ring as a sign of our marriage. With my body I honor you, all that I am I give to you, and all that I have I share with you, within the love of God, Father, Son, and Holy Spirit."

Although not part of the ceremony in the strictest of sense, Grayson wrapped her hand in both of his and brought it to his mouth, pressing his lips to her soft, fragrant skin.

"In the presence of God, and before this congregation, Grayson and Kipling have given their consent and made their marriage vows to each other. They have declared their marriage by the joining of hands and by the giving and receiving of rings. I therefore proclaim that they are husband and wife. Those whom God has joined together let no man put asunder."

Grayson closed his eyes, her hand still to his lips, before opening them again to turn with her to the altar. Together they knelt, hand in hand, as Reverend Anderson addressed those gathered.

"Blessed are you, O Lord our God, for you have created joy and gladness, pleasure and delight, love, peace, and fellowship. Pour out the abundance of your blessing upon Grayson and Kipling in their new life together…"

Little else registered because the words had been spoken and nothing would change it. Joy and gladness…pleasure and delight… love…

Kipling was his, and he was hers, and no man could pull them asunder.

Wise men say only fools rush in
   But I can't help falling in love with you.

As the soulful, jazzy melody played and Harry Connick Jr crooned his love ballad, Grayson raised Kipling's hand above her head and turned her in a twirl that let her tulle skirt flair away, wrapping around both of them as he brought her into his arms. Kipling smiled — or smiled wider because she hadn't stopped smiling since she stepped into the Church of the Holy Comforter in the center of Grayson's little village.

When he released her hand, she draped her arm across his shoulders to brush her fingertips on the back of his neck. His hair had grown since the unfortunate events that had forced a cut that removed much of his curls, and the new soft waves slid through her fingers. Grayson pressed his hands to her bare back, his palms warm in contrast to the evening cool. He'd made it very clear he appreciated the open back of the wedding gown, leaving her spine exposed for his touch from shoulder blades to the small of her back for his caress.

That, and his stunned look, had been worth the purchase price. And then some.

He hummed with appreciation and leaned down to press a kiss to her shoulder, then the side of her throat, and finally her lips as he swayed them together to the music.

Like a river flows surely to the sea.

Darling, so it goes.

Some things were meant to be.

"This is a perfect song," she said, her chin tipped back so she could watch his face. Like her, he had been smiling all day.

"I thought so." He winked, and again spun her away from him, and back again.

"You picked it?" she asked, coming against him.

He'd shed the cream linen jacket, wearing his shirtsleeves rolled halfway to his elbows, and leather braces over his shoulders. His tie, the same slightly lighter cream as his shirt, was still around his throat but loosened with the top button at his collar undone. Just when she thought she'd settled on how Grayson looked sexiest, he added to the list. But perhaps the sexiest of all was his "he's my husband now" look.

"I did," he admitted, and chuckled, glancing back toward the gathering of their friends and family who still remained. Her parents sat with his family, outnumbered six to one, but they looked perfectly at ease. "Your father told me you've always liked this performer, and as I listened to his work, there seemed none other more appropriate to sum up our last six months."

Kipling hummed her agreement and nodded. "Will you sing it for me, Grayson?"

"Oh, no," he said immediately, shaking his head, but not so much as to break away from her fingers again in his curls. "Our marriage is far too young to risk you leaving me on the spot for my lack of a proper singing voice."

"Nonsense, Grayson." She stopped dancing, forcing him to stop as well, and raised her eyebrows with a cant of her head. "Please?"

He took in a breath, and growled low, looking past her again as he urged her to dance once more. "But please, can we leave this out of the divorce agreement?"

"You'd better hurry, Mr. Holmes. The song is nearly over."

Grayson slid his hand up her back beneath her arm, and cupped the back of her head so he could bend forward and press his cheek to hers. With his breath warm on her cheek, Kipling closed her eyes to listen to him sing. He wasn't nearly as bad as he thought himself to be, but she expected a baritone singing voice like when he spoke, but his voice instead had a smooth tenor tone. It wrapped around her, weaved through her. His words rang as true as any love sonnet or poetic letter he'd ever recited or written.

"Take my hand, take my whole life, too. For I can't help falling in love with you." He pressed a long kiss to her cheek, just in front of her ear, before drawing back. She didn't realize tears slid down her cheek until he smoothed over them with his thumb. "I told you I was rubbish."

"No," she managed only to mouth, no sound slipping past her restricted throat, so she shook her head and laid her hand along his jaw. "No, you are beautiful and wonderful and I love you, Mr. Holmes."

"And I love you. I adore you. You are my world, Mrs. Holmes."

Chapter Three

MADRID, SPAIN
THREE WEEKS LATER

"Oh..."

Kipling's response was simple in words and far from her usual eloquence, but the light in her eyes and her wide smile spoke volumes to Grayson. She reminded him of his sisters when they were young and had been given the exact gift they'd asked for from Father Christmas.

"I hoped you might enjoy this excursion as one of our last in Spain," he said, taking her hand to lead her up the first of several wide steps of the sweeping curved, front staircase to the ornate neoclassical entrance, with massive windows and baroque influenced statues outside the National Library of Madrid.

Kipling glanced at him, but only briefly before her intense study returned to the statue of Miguel de Cervantes Saavedra who stood guard over the library entrance. "You take me to all the best places, Mr. Holmes."

He stopped their approach, and she was so lost in her awe she didn't realize until his hold on her arm stopped her forward movement. She turned to face him, one step up from where he stood, and the pure wonder in her eyes made his chest squeeze. He wasn't sure what made him happier, that she was so happy or that he had a hand in bringing that sort of light to her face.

"Now, we could do this the ordinary way," he said, dipping his chin to look toward the grand entrance from beneath arched brows. "Take the tour. See the public areas. Or…"

She moved to the edge of the step closest to him, and he swore he heard her breath hitch before she asked, "Or?"

"Or…" He dragged out the word just long enough to see the spark of anticipation in her amber eyes. "You can be Doctor Anthea Foster, special consultant to the British Embassy here in Madrid." Since the flight of stairs was extensive, he started up them again, drawing her with him. "It would seem a certain collector of ancient antiquities has made a claim to hold the oldest known copy of a particularly rare text. So rare, in fact, he has petitioned the British government to purchase it for the sake of posterity. At the cost of nearly £3 million."

He turned his head just enough to study her enthralled, wide-eyed gaze. Smiling at the fun of her pleasure, he looked forward and canted his head, continuing in the explanation of the legend he'd worked up for this day. With a little help from River House and Sandra Sookoo's amazing skills. "As one of the world's leading authorities in antiquities and ancient languages, after a thorough review you conducted in London, you have agreed to assist us with authenticating *Septem contra Thebas*—"

Kipling gasped and stopped short, turning into him again. "*Seven Against Thebes*, third in the *Oedipodea*," she said on a gush of air, and excited color bloomed in her sun-kissed cheeks. She looked over her shoulder toward the nearing top of the staircase. "They have a copy here?"

"Not officially, no." He took the step needed to bring him beside her, and started up the stairs again, releasing her hand to touch her back. "Certainly not on any published archive list, but Señor Cardozo and I have worked together previously, and he is quite willing to provide any assistance possible to the throne. He's a bit of an anglophile."

"Hmmm," she said with an innocent tilt of her head. "I can appreciate that. I've found I'm becoming one myself."

He chuckled and then sighed. "I do hope your Greek is strong."

"Not as strong as my Latin, but I get by a bit better than most tourists." She smiled and winked.

He laughed and returned the smile. Her answer mirrored a response he'd given her — nearly word for word — when she'd asked him about his fluency in Italian while they were in Rome the week before. "I suppose I should have told them you wanted to read *Attic Nights*. How embarrassing."

She made a sound somewhere between a snort and a laugh, dismissing the idea with a toss of her hand. "Oh, please. I read Aulus Gellius years ago. What antiquarian doesn't? Aeschylus, on the other hand, is a rare find." Kipling paused their ascent and looked at Grayson, her eyes slightly squinted as she took in his face. "Is that why you're wearing colored contacts? To disguise the heterochromia?"

"Tends to be something people remember."

Kipling nodded with a low "hmmm" of acceptance.

They reached the top of the steps and he dropped his hand from her back as he opened the door with the other, letting her lead the way into the grand entrance. "If I ever harbored any doubt you might convince the library curator of your qualifications, they have been thoroughly and completely assuaged."

"*Did* you harbor any doubt?" she asked, giving him a teasing side-eye.

"Never."

Her steps slowed and her head tipped back, eyes wide and lips parted, as she took in the grand, elegant entrance to the library that looked more like a museum. Swallowing his chuckle, but unable to suppress his smile, he pressed his hand to the small of her back once again so he could guide her across the marble floor. The expansive space and staircases, marble floors, and arched cathedral ceiling had her head tipped back so far he was afraid her neck would snap — or she might break it by stumbling, trying to take in everything.

"Ah, Señor Sheffield," called Marcos Cardozo, the library's antiquities curator, as he crossed the entrance lobby with his hand extended while he was still several yards away.

Grayson stepped away from his wife to meet Marcos, first taking his hand and then enveloping it in both of his own for a firm shake. He had "worked" with Marcos several times — both alone in appearance, and in collaboration with Grayson's team — and liked the man. He was advanced in years, probably well past an age most men would have sought retirement but had always expressed a sincere love for his profession.

"Marcos, my friend," Grayson said, adjusting his speech enough to apply emphasis to his r-sounds, mimicking the Dorset/West Country accent he'd adopted in his past interactions with the curator. "Please, remember to call me Callum."

He realized too late he hadn't told Kipling his assumed name, nor had he defined his plan to rely on sign while they were at the library to avoid any necessity on her part to either attempt an accent impression or feign understanding if Marcos lapsed into Spanish. She'd already admitted, early after their arrival in Madrid, that her Spanish was weak at best and while most who spoke *Español* could get by in Madrid, she had faltered. Ancient languages were, by far, her greater strength.

Which made her all the more attractive to him.

Knowing she wouldn't flounder, Grayson motioned toward her to approach them and once she took a step, brought his hands before him to sign. *"Doctor Foster, this is Mr. Marcos Cardozo. He is the antiquities curator here at the library."* As he signed, he spoke so everyone was equally part of the conversation, fearing he stumbled over the spelling of 'antiquities curator' since his manual language education was not nearly that advanced.

Marcos nodded and made a small sound of understanding, taking Kipling's hand before bowing his head and offering her a wide, friendly smile. In Grayson's experience, most people did not have common knowledge in the proper respect to be granted a hearing-impaired person. They didn't intend to be rude but didn't know proper etiquette. Rather than speak to Kipling, Marcos looked to Grayson for "interpretation."

"It is our pleasure to have someone of Doctor Foster's knowledge and skill visit our archives."

Grayson smiled and nodded, providing the interpretation even though it was fully without necessity. Already keen on the plan, Kipling remained silent but offered the sign for "*Thank you*," which he again interpreted.

This could be dizzying.

"If you follow me, I will take you to the archives. Have you explained to Doctor Foster the need for protective attire?"

"Yes," Grayson answered, glancing at Kipling, who walked with them but took in every angle, corner, and bit of architecture.

He hadn't, but he also knew despite her outward distraction, she likely heard everything they said on the walk to the back of the library to an elevator bank to take them down to the archives. Once inside the elevator car and Marcos entered the security code to give them access to the lower vaults, she blinked and looked to them both, smiling silently.

Marcos linked his hands in front of him and spoke to Grayson. "Has Doctor Foster had a previous opportunity to experience our library?"

"No," Grayson answered. "She works primarily out of the Museum of London, and this is her first trip to Madrid. I thought perhaps there might be time after she completes her task." To continue the façade, he relayed an abbreviated statement of the same to her, and she smiled, nodding. "There are few libraries on the scale of yours."

"Gracias, Señor Sheffield," Marcos said, nodding his head fervently. Then he smiled with a self-deprecating wince. "Gracias, Callum."

Kipling waited until Grayson looked directly at her before signing, slowly, with a single arched brow. "*You are going to be one very lucky man later today, Mr. Holmes,*" she signed, offering a wink since Marcos wasn't looking at her anyway. With full intent, she curled her lower lip between her teeth, holding eye contact with him.

He had spent a decade in the field, trained to keep his cool under a variety of stressful situations, from facing death in combat to convincing the worst of the world his intent was on their side without flinching, and yet his wife's wink, smile, and promise was enough to heat the back of his neck and force him to look away from her without response.

"She looks forward to it," he managed to say without having to clear his throat.

"What about this one?"

Kipling ran her fingertip along the raised scar that began a few inches over his left scapula, beneath his arm, to slash along his upper ribs. With his arm down, the scar was barely noticeable, but he was stretched out on their bed with his arm over his head, his hand tucked behind his neck. The sun was setting, but its glow filled the room.

Grayson raised his head off the pillow enough to look down his chest at her, and she smiled back, loving the view of her husband reclined beside her. He looked to where she touched him and drew in a long breath through his nose as she ran her finger over the dots like braille left behind by the staples used to seal the wound once upon a time.

"Outside of Istanbul. Weapons runners trying to make a run for the border back to Syria. We ran them off the road. Got to most of them before they could draw weapons. Turned into hand-to-hand. That was a serrated fixed blade but dull as hell."

"How long ago?"

"Six years, almost seven."

She scooted further down toward the foot of the bed, the sheets rustling with the movement, and slid the covers away to expose more of his torso to just past his hip. Grayson drew in a long, deep breath and she caught a glance in her peripheral of him licking his lips as she ran her palm over his abdomen to the top of his thigh, his muscles tensing beneath her touch, as she sought the next mark. Kipling had silently cataloged them whenever she saw one she'd not seen before, waiting for the right time to ask.

His thigh had several scars of varying sizes, depths, and severity. She wasn't a doctor by any means, but her gut told her they were the same age. The worst was a dimple her fingertip could fill and was closer to the inside of his thigh than the front while the other scars peppered an area of about six square inches.

"Were these all from the same time?" she asked, not sure if knowing they were all from the same time would help the knotted twist in her gut she had to force herself to ignore when she thought of all the times he might have died and she would have never known him.

"Yes," he answered. "Shrapnel from an IED. I can't tell you where. Even the details of the location are GSC Top Secret."

"Did anyone die?"

"Our people?"

Kipling nodded, circling her finger around the skin surrounding the dimple, digging deep in her reserves to hold his gaze without flinching. It had begun as a game, a tease, asking him about one of the other scars on his arm that she didn't know about. The burns from Howell's bomb had masked the scar, and as the angry red of the healing flesh had eased the scar had stood out with stark contrast. But she'd continued to ask, and the more she asked, the more she wished she hadn't.

It was a two-edged sword. She both wanted to know, to understand, but she also appreciated the phrase "ignorance is bliss."

"Yes," he answered, and raised his other hand from the bed beside him to smooth her hair away from her cheek. "Three. From another Six team. And Greg was in hospital for three weeks. Those," he said with a tip of his head toward his thigh, "were minor."

Kipling looked away from his direct gaze and scooted up

enough to lay her cheek on his stomach, angling her head so her hearing aid didn't press against his skin to cause feedback. Grayson inhaled deep and let it out, shifting on the pillows so he could bring down the hand behind his head to smooth his fingers over her hair. Outside the open balcony door, a roll of thunder rumbled through the city, and a suddenly cold wind swept in from the street. With a flick of his hand, Grayson tossed the rumpled coverlet over them, covering his legs and up to her shoulders, leaving his upper body exposed.

"Darling," he said after several minutes of silence.

She shook her head against him, her hearing aids squealing momentarily with feedback. "I love the sound of the thunder." In truth, she didn't want to talk anymore about the scars and marks on his body.

Her logical, academic mind knew she'd been living a sort of fairytale. Except for a few terrifying days shortly after she'd arrived in London when Langdon Howell had nearly killed him and threatened them both, her time in London had been unrealistically blissful. Days together spending time, planning their wedding, learning everything about each other; nights spent together in each other's arms. It was destined to end — would have to end — when he returned to his position at River House and she began her teaching position at Westminster College.

But the likelihood of serrated knives and shrapnel weren't really a problem at the well-honored institution of higher learning.

Thunder rumbled again and she closed her eyes when the rhythmic pelt of rain began on the balcony and the street below, large drops pinging off the windows.

"Give me your hand," he said after a few more minutes.

Kipling opened her eyes, and in the few moments she'd been still the evening had taken over in full force and the room was in near darkness except for a light they had left on in the sitting room. Grayson laid his open hand on his stomach, palm up, near her nose, and wiggled his fingers.

"Come on. Give me your hand."

She slid her arm free of the warm blanket and rested her palm on his. Grayson tugged her arm further from the blanket and turned it to touch her fingers to his right side above the defined, corded muscle along his hip and pelvis. Beneath her fingertips, she felt the dip of another scar, very shallow, but well-defined.

"Appendix," he said. "When I was fourteen. Come on. Come here."

He curled his hands around her arms and gently tugged to get her to rise over him and move closer to the head of the bed. She settled against him again, draping herself over his chest to rest one hand over his heart, her chin on her hand. Grayson smiled at her and turned her other hand so he could kiss her palm. Then holding her gaze with his, his eyes appearing darker in the dim light, he angled their arms down until their hands slid below the blanket again and he placed her palm around the curl of his hip, her thumb resting very close to temptation.

Kipling's blood flushed hot beneath her skin, and her heartbeat jumped to high speed. She licked her lower lip and pulled it through her teeth, stroking with her thumb. A low rumble shifted through Grayson's chest before he eased her hand further down his thigh, as far as she could reach without moving. But far enough, she felt the familiar spot on his lower thigh where the skin lacked a patch of crinkled hair and other spots of hair hid a long scar.

"Do you know the scar there?" he asked, his smile more of a smirk.

"I do," she answered in a whisper.

"Greg convinced me I could ride Old Mr. Elton's mule bareback and failed to mention he had heard that Riley — that was the mule's name — was foul-tempered and not inclined to being ridden. More than that, he failed to mention he'd heard rumor Riley was inclined to bolt back to the barn when perturbed."

"What happened?"

"I jumped on. Riley ran. Riley jumped the fence. I didn't quite make it. The fence broke. And so did my leg. The spot is where they had to perform surgery to return my femur to its proper place."

Kipling hissed. "How old were you?"

"Eleven. My point is, darling, that not every mark was a brush with death. In fact, and in as much as I realize it hardly seems the case, generally speaking my job is done at a desk. We are an intelligence organization. Yes, sometimes the gathering of that intelligence can be dangerous, but events of the last few months are… atypical."

She thought about telling him she knew, but if she'd known he wouldn't have told her. She thought about providing some argument but had none. Instead, Kipling tossed the blankets out of her way and slid over him, kissing him before either said anything else.

Chapter Four

I told you I'd have it there. When have I ever let you down?

No, don't answer that.

Yes, it's there.

You owe me BIG time. Not an easy job to accomplish.

Thank you.

Of course, Ollie. Welcome back.

Let me know when you're ready to get back this damn cat.

I'm not sure which is worse...the fact Watson is a bloody pain in the arse to live with when he thinks he's been wronged, or the fact Esther is talking about getting a cat.

G rayson chuckled and slid his phone into the breast pocket of his shirt. The cab crossed through the intersections of Bickenhall and Porter. They'd be home in less than five minutes.

"What's funny?" his wife asked.

His wife.

They had been married a month — had traveled through Italy, to Spain, to Greece, and back to England — and the warm bloom of happiness still took him over whenever he let reality wash over him. A year ago, marriage was less than a non-consideration. It was a ridiculous thought. Without effort, she changed his life and his heart. He reached across the space of the backseat and took her hand, bringing it to his mouth so he could kiss her fingers.

"Greg is distressed. It would seem watching over Watson the last month has inspired Esther to want a cat."

Kipling smiled and laughed, a low and enticing sound at the base of her throat. It was likely Watson had decided the best way to express his distaste for the situation would be to force his company on the one person responsible for his care who possessed the least natural affection for felines. That was definitely Greg.

They reached Baker Street and the cabbie stopped in the roadway, the parking spots along the kerb most convenient to 221 blocked with other vehicles. Grayson opened his door to slide free of the cab, offering Kipling his hand to help her out as the cabbie went to the boot to retrieve their luggage. With the bags set on the pavement, Grayson took two £20 notes from his wallet and paid the cabbie, then joined Kipling where she stood waiting. She had her back to the street, her head tilted to take in the front façade of 221. Dusk approached, and the lights inside the downstairs guest parlor and upstairs hall greeted them, already on as part of a computer program Mac had written to ensure the house never looked empty. Even when Grayson spent weeks away at a time. The fact the parlor lights were on was perfect. He stepped beside Kipling and set his suitcase on its wheels so he could touch his hand to her back.

Kipling angled her head to look at him, smiling. "I've loved the last few weeks of travel, but a very large part of me is happy to be home again. I feel like we've been away forever."

"Then let's get inside." He gripped the handle of her luggage in his other hand and pulled them both toward the front stoop. "Unless Greg had the forethought to stock the cupboards, we've not much to eat, but I'm fine with takeaway for tonight. How does that sound?"

"Perfect." She sighed and leaned her shoulder against the brick façade while he worked the lock. "I'm looking forward to our bed, too."

Grayson looked over his shoulder at her and grinned, winking when she grinned back, pulling her lower lip through her teeth. With a chuckle, he disengaged the lock and opened the door, stepping clear on the premise of allowing her entrance while he disengaged the house alarm. Tapping the keys, he held his breath and waited.

Her gasp was his reward.

Trying to keep the amusement from his voice, he pulled the luggage into the foyer and shut the door as he called out, "Is there something wrong, darling?"

"Oh, just get in here and stop acting like you don't know," she called back, and he smirked, hearing the smile in her voice.

Leaving the luggage at the bottom of the stairs, he joined her in the guest parlor where she sat at the bench of the most elaborate surprise Grayson had managed to date. "I promised you a piano would be in Baker Street when we returned."

She turned enough on the bench to face him, her eyes glistening and her lips pressed together in an intense smile. "I don't know why I'm surprised," she said, her voice rough. "How did you manage this?"

"Late night online searches while you slept, and a great deal of assistance by Greg here in London. Apparently, maneuvering an antique grand piano into the parlor was a bit of a challenge," he said, sitting beside her.

He ran his hand along the rich, deep cherry-polished wood that seemed to naturally hold warmth. The images representing the rare

Erard of London piano on the seller's website paid no justice to the beauty of the instrument. "The greatest challenge was finding a piano I felt worthy of its new home and its new mistress. Pianos, if not meticulously cared for, don't always age well. I consider myself lucky in finding this one."

"It's beautiful," she said, barely above a whisper, and ghosted her fingers over the antique keys. "How old is it?"

"This one is from around 1834."

With a gentle, appearing hesitant touch she pressed on a single key — the Center F — and the sounding board rang clear and true and rich. Greg had seen to the final tuning as well. Kipling closed her eyes, and he watched her profile, mesmerized by how she sank into the simple sound.

"If you keep spoiling me like this, Grayson, we'll end up in the poor house within six months," she said with a small smile, before opening her eyes again to look at him.

Grayson laughed and set his fingers over the keys, keeping his touch gentle so the sound didn't overpower, and played a simple warm-up melody. "Have no fear," he said, crossing his right hand over his left to add a playful kick to the piece. "We are in no danger of being cast out on the street."

She made a small sound in her throat, low enough he almost didn't hear it, but it was enough to make him stop playing to look at her. She stared down at the piano, her forehead drawn into thoughtful lines. "That is an expression of deep contemplation," he said. "What are you thinking?"

"Of something I should have thought before, I guess." She raised her head and looked at him. "Now I feel silly."

Grayson rubbed his lips together and went back to playing the piece. "Don't feel silly. I've never implied finances were something you should be concerned with, so why would it come to mind?" He spared a quick glance at her, never stopping the music.

"Because *most* people would probably think to broach the subject prior to getting married. Isn't that the adult thing to do?" She sighed and dropped her hand from the keyboard.

"Perhaps." He shifted into the expanded version of the piece he'd begun composing the night before their wedding, feeling confident once his fingers had warmed up and recalled the lessons from his youth. He held far more faith in his playing skills than his composition abilities. "And I would be inclined to agree more if such a thing as paying utilities were the foremost concern. In a span of weeks, you have relocated, we've had some…excitement…" His sarcasm earned him a single chuckle. "And we've planned and executed a wedding and honeymoon."

"Precisely," she said, pointing a finger at him.

He smiled, understanding her point. "To answer the question you have never asked, I am in no dire need of funds. The Holmes Family Trust, created by Sherlock based on his keen and exceptional understanding of investment ventures, has done well to take care of all of us. And unless one of us along the way should prove to be a very unskilled gambler, the Holmes line will be taken care of for generations to come. The money is well protected via ironclad legalities tied to the very bloodline. We have no mortgages and minimal expenditures. Add to that the sizable financial settlement reached between Sherlock and a certain author we need not name for the use of his name and likeness."

Finishing what he had composed of the piece, he turned toward her enough that his knee pressed against hers and he leaned an elbow on the top of the pianoforte. "The majority of my salary has also been invested since my bachelor lifestyle required little in the way of luxuries. Basically, mad money. So, my darling, I shall be able to surprise you in a variety of ways with no end in sight."

Before she could offer any counterargument, he leaned in and stole the next words from her lips with a press of his own. He raised his hand and slid his palm along her jaw, holding her so he could deepen the kiss, and she rewarded him by leaning into the touch and pressing her graceful fingers to the sides of his neck.

The first vibration of his mobile he ignored, intent instead on the focused pleasure of kissing his wife. But when the mobile took off in a series of alerts, followed by the different and more rapid pattern of a call he reluctantly gave up his endeavor with a low groan and took the mobile from his pocket. The caller — Greg —

had ended the call, but his texts were clear on the screen. All relaxation Grayson had felt prior to that moment was gone, and he frowned.

> Ollie, Cooper is looking for you.
>
> Have you heard from him? He called me to ask if you were home yet. I said I hadn't seen you. Not an outright lie. But he's adamant. Brace yourself.
>
> Who knows what the bloody hell he wants. He refused to tell me.

"Is something wrong?" Kipling asked as the phone screen lit up again with Jeffrey Cooper's number and name.

Grinding his teeth against the interruption, he tapped the screen to send the call directly to voicemail. Nearly three months before, Grayson had informed his Six director he would be on a leave of absence, and *he* would tell *them* when and if he would be returning to Six. He had yet to make a decision. As he'd just told Kipling, he didn't do it for financial stability; he had committed his life to the Royal Majesty's Secret Service out of a deeper desire to feel he offered more. But the last few months, stretching back even further than that when they had tricked the entire Holmes family into believing Greg McQueen was dead, had shattered Grayson's opinion of the agency.

He wasn't over his anger.

"It's Cooper," he answered. "I've no interest in what he has to say."

He opened Greg's text message and responded.

> He is attempting to reach me. I've no interest. I'll contact him when I'm good and ready. I'm turning off the phone for the next couple of hours.
>
> If you need me, text, and I'll see it when I am back.

Greg's response was immediate.

> Understood.
>
> Talk to you soon.
>
> I have to go to the pet charity...

Grayson held the power button on the side of the phone until it shut down and slid it back into his pocket as he stood from the bench. He offered Kipling his hand, and she took it, letting him draw her to her feet.

Deep concern lines creased her brow, and he leaned in to press a long kiss to them.

"None of that. I am on holiday. He will have to bloody well get over it. Let's go out for dinner, shall we?"

"If you want..."

"We'll stop at Tesco's on the way back." He led her toward the door, around the luggage he'd left at the bottom of the stairs. "I'll tell Allan to deliver the usual staples tomorrow. Unless you'd like to venture out to the market."

She braced her feet and stopped them so Grayson had to turn to look at her. "Grayson, if you need to speak with him, you need to speak with him. Regardless, you're still an MI6 officer."

"An MI6 officer who has just returned from his damn honeymoon and deserves a few more days of peace," he said, fighting hard to keep the tension from his voice.

She canted her head only a couple of degrees, her eyes shifting to his lips as he spoke, then drew in a slow, long breath through her nose.

She released it just as slowly before she spoke. "It will be over eventually, though, won't it."

It wasn't a question.

"Entirely depends on your definition," he said, suppressing the next wave of anger clawing in his chest. "The *if* is still in question, and the *when* is most definitely not today. Now, let's go have dinner."

By London hours, they left their newest favorite Hong Kong Chinese restaurant a couple of blocks from home at just past eight in the evening. By Kipling's inner clock, it was past ten and after the nearly five-hour flight from Athens, she was exhausted. The closer they walked to Baker Street, the more oddly excited she became about sleeping in their bed.

In the middle of a yawn that threatened to crack her jaw, Grayson chuckled and brought their joined hands to his mouth to kiss her knuckles.

"Not long now, darling. I feel the same." The last word was lost in his own impulsive yawn.

Kipling shook her head, widening her eyes. "Who knew a month-long vacation would be so exhausting?"

"Ah but exhausting in the best possible way."

They made a short stop at the Tesco on the way, but only long enough to grab a few things for breakfast and leave instructions for food to be delivered. It was a throwback to Grayson's bachelor days when Allan Tremain and his wife maintained a standing weekly order for Grayson, and while Kipling found a satisfying joy in shopping for "them," in a domestic way she hadn't really considered just a few months before, the idea of not needing to leave Baker Street for at least the next forty-eight hours appealed to her.

With their sack of groceries in one hand, and the fingers of his other laced with hers, they walked the last block toward home. Just as 221 came into view, the first hint of a cold drizzle hit the back of her neck and Kipling tucked her chin into her shoulders. But the chilly rain was nothing compared to the icy shiver that raced up her spine when she saw MI6 Director Jeffrey Cooper standing in the shadow of their lintel, tucked as deep into the shallow recess as he was able to fit to avoid having the drizzle hit his bald head.

Grayson spotted Cooper at the same moment she did, his steps stiffening. The streetlight cast angled shadows around his mouth when his lips straightened, not a frown but far from any smile, and his hold on her hand firmed for a moment before he released her to remove his house key from his pocket. He didn't verbally acknowledge Cooper and the frigid buffer around them was palpable. Rather than making room for his director to pass into the house first, Grayson opened the door and ushered Kipling inside with his hand at her elbow. Inside, she moved deeper into the foyer to make room while he disarmed the alarm and Cooper came through the door, already shrugging off his overcoat.

Kipling stood at the bottom of the stairs, her stomach in a knot, and watched Grayson. She had to mentally tell herself to blink when her eyes burned. Still silent, Grayson slapped shut the cover over the alarm system, swerved around Director Cooper, and headed for the kitchen, catching her hand as he went to bring her with him.

"Did you leave your manners in Greece, Holmes," Cooper grumbled, following them at a slower pace, his advanced years and expanding waistline probably just as much in play as the hostility between the two men.

As far as Kipling was aware, Grayson hadn't communicated with Jeffrey Cooper in any way in weeks; not since the day he and Greg went to Vauxhall and MI6's headquarters to confront Cooper head-on about Six's deception and manipulation in faking Greg's death. Grayson's rage had reverberated like the hum of a tuning fork that day, but when he returned with Greg he'd left the explanation shallow. He and Greg were taking an extended leave of absence, Six would pay restitution as much as was possible for stealing a loved son and cousin from the Holmes family, and Grayson guaranteed nothing more in service to Six. He was still technically an officer, but the betrayal had cut deep.

So deep Grayson had refused to invite Director Cooper to the wedding, despite the fact he'd told Kipling — before all the lies and manipulations became evident — that he considered the man a friend. Grayson didn't want Jeffrey Cooper to have any contact with the Holmes or McQueen families, whom he'd had a part in deceiving, even though he claimed he was following orders.

Still silent, Grayson rounded the edge of their U-shaped counter and set the sack on the counter, removing the few provisions they'd picked up. Needing to do something, Kipling gathered them as he unloaded and put them in their small refrigerator, fighting the tremor of her insides that threatened to make her ill.

She didn't need a diagram and explanation to know Cooper showing up at Baker Street meant something both significant and troubling.

Director Cooper cleared his throat. "How are you, Ms. Branson?"

"Are you intentionally pretending to be dead from the neck up, or are you actually that much of an arse?" Grayson snapped, slamming a glass jar of jam on the counter.

Kipling jumped, looking from Grayson to Director Cooper and back again. When Grayson ignored the call earlier, she'd naively thought the evening would be salvaged, but her gut gave an angry scream otherwise.

"Apologies," Cooper said, without much conviction in his voice. "I was attempting to be sensitive to the trends of society." He shifted his focus to Kipling, and she fought not to duck behind the counter. "Will you remain a Branson, or will you fall to archaic patriarchy and change your name to Holmes?"

"That's hardly my issue," Grayson snapped off.

Finally finding her balance again, Kipling laid her hand on Grayson's forearm, and his clenched fist eased. She licked her lips and leveled her gaze on Director Cooper. "I'm proud to accept the name of Holmes, Director Cooper."

"*Doctor* Holmes," Grayson ground out. "You've been corrected before, so unless you are experiencing a memory defect your oversight is entirely intentional."

Cooper made a mocked expression of understanding when Grayson's true source of ire was clear but failed to acknowledge the accusation. "Ah, yes. Of course. Again, my sincere apologies. But as joyous an occasion your recent marriage may be, I didn't come here to wish well the newlyweds—"

"I never for a moment held on to such an illusion."

"Enough, Grayson!" Cooper hollered, his face blooming bright red until his ears looked sunburnt. He huffed and looked away, setting his lips firm before focusing on them again. "Enough of this. You're being ridiculous."

Grayson's first response was a slow smirk — no, a sneer — before he straightened his shoulders and crossed his arms over his body. "Far be it for me to ignore an education on etiquette. Please, Director, without further delay tell me what requires you to show up on our doorstep within hours of our return to London."

The red glow subsided, but only slightly, and Cooper pressed his lips together until the edges were white before he finally spoke. "You are required in Boston." He leveled his gaze on Kipling. "Immediately."

Chapter Five

The air inside Kipling's apartment was stuffy and stale after four months of being closed up and uninhabited through the moist, warm, and humid season of the year. As soon as they were through the door, she dropped her pocketbook on the table and headed for the heating and a/c control on the wall, turning on the system and immediately dropping the wanted temperature to sixty-five. It would cool the apartment quickly, and they could adjust later.

Even though it was early afternoon, she hoped she could manage to stay awake long enough to adjust the temperature again so they didn't wake up in a five hundred square foot, three-room, walk-in freezer.

Grayson dragged their luggage into the bedroom, setting them against the inside wall, and came back to the kitchen, his hands on his hips as he glanced around. "I'm not entirely sure why, but I expected it to look different."

"It feels different," she said, going to the refrigerator. Opening the door, she confirmed her hopes. Mom and Dad had stocked them with some essentials so they wouldn't starve. She smiled at the foil-covered casserole dish with the sticky note that read *"375 for 40 minutes. Love you."* A peek under the edge confirmed it was her mom's seafood casserole and she smiled.

"How so?"

She shut the refrigerator door and opened the top freezer door. And smiled wider. Three quarts of Gifford's ice cream, her favorite flavors — Grapenuts with Vanilla, Coffee Fudge, and Black Raspberry Chocolate Chip — lined the back of the space, surrounded by more healthy options like chicken and vegetables. Mom knew her well. Shutting the door again, she looked back at her husband. She kept losing track of their conversation.

"How so what?"

His grin was teasing, lopsided. "I said I expected your apartment to look different, but it's the same. You said it feels different. How so?"

"Oh. Sorry. I guess flying from Athens to London, then London to Boston *by way of Reykjavik* in a span of a couple of days has muddled my brain." She pressed her palm to her forehead as she looked around. "I'm not even sure what day it is," she mumbled before finding at least some focus. "I don't know if I can explain. I've had this apartment for years, but just now it felt like I walked into the apartment of a family member I haven't seen since I was ten." Kipling sighed and crossed the compact kitchen to the small table and sank into one of the three chairs. Grayson matched her, sitting diagonally to her.

"It's Wednesday," he said, extending his arm along the empty table, palm up.

She took his hand and rested her head on the wall behind her, making the mistake of momentarily closing her eyes. "Thank you. Do we need to head downtown today to see Agent Flannery?"

"He asked we attempt to meet him, yes; however, he also understands we have been traveling and may need a day to recover."

"Oh, good…" she mumbled, the tug of sleep overpowering.

"No no," he said, the chair legs scraping as he stood, tugging on her hand. "No sleeping at the table. We'll have a lie-down and consider food later. Looks like Mum has taken good care of us there."

Kipling groaned in exaggerated protest, smiling at the same time when he called her mother Mum. She let him pull her to her feet and leaned into his chest without protest, their joined hands linked behind her back. She opened her eyes to look up at him. "Do you remember kissing me in this kitchen?"

He hummed a low rumble that moved through his chest and into her. Despite her exhaustion, her heartbeat jumped when his gaze slid down to focus on her lips. "A morning that irrevocably changed my life, and for my misplaced faith in my own ability to leave without tempting fate I will forever be thankful."

Kipling arched one brow and smiled. "Misplaced faith?" Grayson released his hold on her hand so he could wrap both his arms behind her, pressing his palms to her back. She raised her arms and brought her hands behind his neck so she could push her fingers through the tangled mess of curls and waves the Boston humidity had inspired. "What do you mean?"

"I believed I was capable of parting with a simple kiss of farewell." He leaned in and did what he had done that morning, pressing his lips to her cheek. With his skin still against hers, he said softly, "And then you turned into me, and I was lost."

Kipling's body responded as it always did with her husband's touch, kiss, or voice. Her skin flushed and her heartbeat jumped. She didn't need to be reminded how that kiss had taken over both of them. Just as she had that morning, she turned her head into his touch until the corners of their mouths skimmed against each other, and she parted her lips in welcome. That morning, the fire and the intensity had overpowered and shocked them both. That morning, he had left.

She moaned when his hands moved from her back to her hips, pressing her bottom to bring her closer to him. Breathing hard, Kipling tipped back her head to see his face. "You don't have to leave me today, Grayson."

"I would never wish to be accused of disinterest, but we are both tired and I suspect you are still sore from your fall."

Kipling snorted a chuckle — being barreled over by another traveler in the Logan Airport International Arrivals Terminal hardly constituted a "fall" — and ignored his attempt at diverting her attention by rubbing her palms over his shoulders and down his chest to the first button of his camp shirt.

"Just think how well we'll sleep," she said, unbuttoning the first button before she leaned in to nuzzle against his exposed chest. "And if you're worried about bumps and bruises, I think you need to conduct a thorough…" She kissed his warm skin, smiling when he drew in a sharp breath. One more button undone. "exhaustive inspection of my body."

To push aside any final arguments, Kipling bared her teeth and ran them over his tight pectoral muscle as she undid the final buttons. His growl was hungry, flooding her with the satisfaction she had the ability to inspire the reaction in him. Grayson took her head in his hands and covered her mouth in an open kiss long enough to steal her ability to think before he scooped her up and carried her to the bedroom.

Grayson raised his head off the pillow and squinted, trying to orientate himself in the unfamiliar room when the insistent tone of his mobile yanked him from sleep. The blinds were drawn so the room was dim, and it was absolutely frigid. The mobile's tone sounded again and he sat up, careful not to jostle the bed and wake his wife who slept on her stomach with her face turned away from him.

By the time he located his trousers and removed his mobile from his pocket, the tone had stopped. He flipped over the phone to see the screen, squinting at the unfamiliar number identified as the Federal Bureau of Investigation and the area code within Boston. A second later the tone sounded again and the screen lit up with the same number. He scowled, wondering who would be calling him on an unknown number. Grayson slid his thumb across the screen to pick up the call and brought it to his ear.

"Hello," he said simply, not ready to offer up his name.

"Hey, bud. Glad I caught you."

Grayson scowled again. "Flannery? What is this number you're calling from?"

"Oh, yeah right. My cell got wet. Our tech guys are dryin' it out. Got a spare until tomorrow. Sorry for the confusion there. You got a few minutes?"

"Emm…" He glanced toward the bed but knew a conversation wouldn't disturb Kipling. Her hearing aids were on the table beside her. "I do." Grayson switched his phone to his right hand so he could turn his wrist and check the time. It quickly approached seven in the evening, well past Patrick Flannery's usual end of day. "I assume at this point we will meet tomorrow. I fear travel has worn us thin."

"Oh, yeah. Tomorrow in the office is fine, but look, I got something I'd like to talk to you about outside the walls of the Bureau if you get what I mean."

"What are you proposing?"

"I'm gonna be down your way in a few minutes. There's a pizza place a block down from your wife's building. Manos' Greek Pizzeria. I'm swingin' in there for a pie and a couple of grinders for the kids. Can you meet me there in twenty?"

Grayson was familiar with the spot, having walked by it with Kipling the last time he was in Boston. "Yes, I can meet you there. Do you require Kipling—"

"Nah, just you. Nothin' you can't tell her when you get back."

Grayson rubbed the corner of his eye with his index finger, pushing through the tired. "I will see you there."

He tapped the screen to end the call and set his phone on the bureau beside him so he could find his pants and trousers. Wouldn't do to walk down the street starkers. Mostly dressed, he moved around the bed to Kipling's side and crouched to eye level. She was asleep, her features serene, and he considered not waking her. But if she woke while he was gone, it would likely upset her. Grayson ran his finger along her brow and temple, easing a long lock of her rich brown hair from her cheek.

She inhaled, smiled, and opened her eyes. Grayson waited until he had eye contact to pull back his hand so he could sign. *"Agent Flannery has asked to speak to me for a few minutes."* Her brows drew together and she lifted her head off the pillow, providing him a brief and tempting view of her bare breasts. He forced himself to focus. *"Nothing to worry about, darling. He is meeting me at a local restaurant. I won't be gone more than thirty minutes. Would you prefer I bring back something to eat rather than cook? It's getting late."*

She let out a long sigh and collapsed back on the pillow. "Yes, that sounds good."

He smiled and leaned forward to kiss her forehead. *"I will be back soon. You're beautiful. I love you."*

She smiled back, her eyes already drifting closed again. "I love you, too."

He pocketed his mobile on his way out of the bedroom and retrieved the apartment keys from the table. After a pause at the thermostat to change the air conditioning setting, he left the apartment and locked the door behind him. Despite the late hour, the air outside was thick and heavy and warm, the moisture saturating the air a cloying cling on his skin. He'd thought Boston in winter had been excessively miserable, and while he wasn't likely to trade this sticky heat for that biting cold, thus far Boston hadn't done much to endear itself on him.

The walk to Manos' Greek Pizzeria took less than five minutes, placing him there a few minutes before Agent Flannery's expected arrival. It gave him time to review the available menu and place an order for their large antipasto salad with the thought that if Kipling didn't wish to eat immediately it would hold well in the refrigerator.

Ten minutes passed and the salad was ready, but Agent Flannery hadn't arrived. When the other agent hadn't arrived another ten minutes later, Grayson left the restaurant to walk back toward the apartment building. He opened his call log as he walked and tapped the previous phone number. Before he could put it to his ear, a recorded message played saying the recipient was not available and to leave a voicemail.

"This is Grayson," he said, reaching the stoop to the apartment. "I waited, however at this point I say we should speak tomorrow. The day has gotten away from us. Kipling and I will see you then."

He pocketed the mobile again once he reached the proper floor but pulled up short at Kipling's door.

It sat open by three inches.

Grayson set the carry-away bag on the floor and put his back to the door, using his palm to push it open, silently cursing his lack of a weapon. Of course, why would he have suspected even for a moment it would be needed here? The apartment was as silent as he'd left it; he heard nothing but the hum of the air conditioner.

Except for the pounding of his pulse in his ears.

The sun was setting, and nearly all the natural light was gone. Thankful the apartment was small, he easily saw all of the kitchen and parlor at one glance and found it empty. With the door fully open, he left it that way and moved to the bedroom door.

The bed was empty.

"Kipling!" he called, taking two long strides to the attached bathroom door. It was open and the room was also empty.

His gut clenched and a cold sweat hit the back of his neck. Grayson slapped the wall switch to turn on the bedroom light, taking in the details of the room in one quick sweep.

Her hearing aids were gone.

The clothing she'd worn on the flight was gone.

She was gone.

On the bedside table was her mobile, and on her pillow...was her wedding ring.

Chapter Six

10 MINUTES

"Whoa, whoa, whoa! Ease up, chief. Wanna run that by me again?"

Grayson stood in the center of the kitchen, head bowed, eyes closed, pinching the bridge of his nose in an attempt to somehow find both focus and calm whilst avoiding contact with anything in the flat that might have forensic evidence value.

"It's a simple question. Did. We. Speak. This evening?"

"No," Agent Flannery answered, and Grayson heard the confused expression in the man's tone. "What's this about?"

"I need you at Kipling's flat as soon as possible and bring a forensic team. The best you have."

"Grayson, what's going on." All joviality had vaporized from Patrick Flannery's voice. "What's wrong?"

"Kipling has disappeared."

"I'll be there in less than thirty."

The call ended, and Grayson let his arm drop heavy and limp at his side. He wasn't sure what had flamed his anger more, the fact he had instinctively called Flannery's number as saved in his contacts

— and not the number from which he'd received the call earlier that evening — or that Agent Flannery had immediately answered. Proving how easily Grayson had been duped. He wanted to tear through the flat, go running down the street calling her name and find Langdon Howell in his detention cell and demand answers. All in the same heartbeat. The same painful, pounding heartbeat. Instead, he sucked in sharply through his nostrils and raised his head, determined to do what he could before the FBI forensics team arrived.

He dared touch nothing.

But he could observe.

Grayson closed his eyes and drew in a deep, inquiring breath once again through his nose, this time for discernment rather than calming. The stale smell of recycled air assaulted his honed senses first, the air conditioning having been on for the last two hours. With that, he caught the smell of the *Flota* brand laundry detergent they'd used before leaving Spain; enough of a contrast to the Ariel brand at home that it stood out. It overpowered any scent Kipling herself might have left, whether it be her shampoo or her soap.

The antipasto salad he'd purchased was still in the hall beyond the open doorway, its pervasive smell of peppers, onions, and prosciutto leaking into the space.

He inhaled again, pushing aside his awareness of the former to seek anything new or out of place.

The lingering, stale smell of tobacco. Cigarette. Menthol. Not the pernicious coil of secondhand smoke, but the cloying stench on a smoker's clothing and skin. And some obtrusive, fabricated male cologne intended to smell like the mountains and fresh air but only stank of cheap chemicals. A man had been in the flat.

His blood heated, but he pushed aside his sudden rage to maintain his focus. Unable to discern anything further with his olfactory senses, he opened his eyes and scanned the room.

Nothing was amiss on the cramped counter space allotted to the small kitchen. He looked from the counter along the interior wall separating the kitchen from the sitting room to the bank of counters and cabinets against the wall separating her flat from the next.

Kipling hadn't taken action yet to remove her personal effects from the flat, so her canisters and tchotchke were all where she had likely left them. It had been too many weeks for him to effectively recall all the items, and his few visits to the flat had been for purposes that distracted from any intent to memorize what he saw.

Regardless, everything appeared in order.

Kipling's handbag still rested on the table, the zipper still closed and appeared undisturbed. The chair he'd occupied, on the side of the table facing the hallway wall, was just as he'd left it when he'd stood to encourage Kipling to rest. Her chair, however, was not against the wall where it should have been. It had been turned at an obtuse angle from the wall, one side against the side of the table, and at a haphazard angle as if hit or perhaps tripped over as someone passed the table, not knowing to adjust their gait due to unfamiliarity with the room layout.

He crouched to examine the lino, seeing a black scuff coming from the direction of the door. It confirmed his thought. Someone had hit the chair leg as they entered. Grayson rose to stand again and went to the bedroom. He'd already tainted the scene himself by turning on the light but determined not to affect possible evidence anything further. Standing at the foot of the bed, he did the same as in the kitchen. Taking in the details and how they differed from when he'd left to supposedly meet Agent Flannery.

The blankets that should have covered her side weren't laid back in her usual manner when she left their bed but pulled back with enough force to completely expose the mattress where she'd slept with most of the coverings on his side. Her phone was likely in the same position she'd left it in when she set it down after texting her parents briefly to say they had safely arrived in Boston. She had removed her hearing aids, as she did whenever they retired to bed, and opened the battery compartments to effectively turn off the devices before setting them beside the phone.

The aids were gone, as he'd noted before.

On her pillow, resting in a dip as if it had been pushed down, was the ring Grayson had proposed with and the ring that had been anointed as their wedding band. The ring his great-grandfather

Sherlock had given to his wife. An antique yellow gold engraved band set with three oval opals accentuated by four diamonds. She had loved the ring, and Grayson could not fathom an instance in which she would willingly have left it behind.

Which could only mean her departure was unwilling.

"Holmes?" came the familiar voice of Agent Flannery from the hallway.

"Here," Grayson said, mentally shoving aside his emotional turmoil to force himself to take the first steps toward finding his wife.

He strode into the kitchen, taking in first the concerned lines on the face of his ginger American counterpart and friend, and then the man and two women who followed, each carrying their kits. He firmly shook Agent Flannery's hand and nodded to the three forensic specialists.

"Focus on the kitchen and the bedroom, through there," he instructed, pointing over his shoulder to the open doorway he'd just come through. As they divided to begin gathering evidence, he turned his focus again on Agent Flannery. "Thank you for coming so quickly."

"You're good, Grayson. What the hell happened?"

Grayson set his hands on his hips and inhaled through his nose, focusing as he pushed the breath out again. He needed to ground himself here so he could recall everything — *anything* — important, even if it seemed utterly inconsequential.

There is nothing so unnatural as the commonplace.

Where to begin…

"Unless she disappeared off the plane, why don't you start in Logan? If we need to go back further, we will."

Grayson hadn't realized he'd spoken aloud. He knew he had to, at least for now, insulate his emotions; a task he would have found even more basic than second nature to accomplish a year earlier, now a task he feared monumental.

"Our flight landed shortly after one; a relatively uneventful trip other than being exceptionally long and exhausting. It was nearly four once we completed the Customs process, retrieved our luggage, and called a cab…"

"Yeah, and?"

Grayson raised a hand and closed his eyes, replaying their journey to the line of cabs waiting along the kerb. He described the scene as he played it again in his mind. He'd commented on the wall of humidity and heat they hit as the automatic doors from the luggage claim opened. Kipling had laughed, drawing a chuckle from him when she teased him about how his hair would misbehave. The partially enclosed space reeked of cigarette smoke and car exhaust. Grayson had looked over his shoulder at her, and at that moment, a man coming down the walk slammed into Kipling, knocking her to the ground as he fell with her in a tangle of limbs and luggage.

He'd left the luggage and gone to them, pushing past the brute to his wife.

"She said she was fine," Grayson explained. "The man mumbled a half-arsed apology and took off again, dragging his bag with him while I assisted Kipling to her feet."

"What did he look like?" Flannery asked.

Grayson opened his eyes but squinted because in retrospect the man's appearance in an investigative scenario would have struck him as suspect. He made no attempt to mask his frustration in himself. "Entirely nondescript. Possibly tanned white, possibly light-skinned Latino or Hispanic, Mediterranean, Spanish, or even Portuguese. Mustache. He wore a ball cap so as to cover his hair and mirrored sunglasses despite being in a garage space. Entirely without consequence had he not knocked my wife to the ground."

Another enraging realization slammed into him when the unpleasant olfactory memory mingled with his recollection. Menthol cigarettes and cheap cologne.

"Was she hurt?"

"She mentioned only an ache in her shoulder and upper arm, and I witnessed only a minor abrasion. With the man gone and our bags collected again, we obtained a cab and came straightway here. We arrived near five, and shortly after went to bed."

"Did you have sex?"

The officer in him knew the question was necessary, but the man in him bristled at the crassness of the words. He paused only long enough to let the analytical mind prevail. "Yes. Then Kipling called her mother to let her know we had arrived safely, and we would speak with her tomorrow, and we fell asleep."

Realization sank into his gut like a ball of ice. He would need to tell his in-laws something — even worse, he had no idea what exactly — had happened to their only child. He swallowed the bitterness burning against the back of his throat.

Grayson continued to answer Agent Flannery's questions, despite the black fog smothering his mind and choking his heart.

"How long did you sleep?"

"Perhaps half an hour before I was awoken by my mobile."

"Who called?"

"You."

2 HOURS 47 MINUTES

"You sure you're good, chief?"

Grayson sat in the passenger seat of Agent Flannery's sedan, staring at the quaint New Englander cottage where Jack and Jane Branson lived and had raised their daughter. The last time he'd been here the yard was blanketed in snow and icicles hung from the gutters. Now the grass was green and flowers hugged the front of the house facing the street. A blue, flickering light in the front window indicated they were likely in their parlor watching television.

"I am impossibly far from anything I would define as good," Grayson answered, not looking away from the house.

"Yeah, bad choice of words there. Sorry. I guess I mean you sure you wanna go in there."

"I have no choice. To do less would be cowardly."

"Well, I don't envy you none."

Grayson turned from the window to look at Agent Flannery. "I appreciate the sentiment. And your help."

Agent Flannery pressed his lips together and nodded. "I'll keep you posted. If I hear something—"

"Anything."

"Anything, I'll get aholda you."

Grayson drew in a long, slow breath through his nose and use the exhale to pull the door handle and open the door, climbing from the car. Patrick waited until he reached the door before pulling away from the kerb. Beside the door still hung the slate sign reading "Book Lovers Welcome. All others enter at the risk of your illiteracy."

He glanced through the small window in the door that gifted him with a view of the foyer staircase leading to the upper floor. With a deep ache in his chest, Grayson remembered the first time he'd stood in the same spot and looked through the same window.

Jane Branson appeared through a doorway at the back of the foyer, the glimpse of a counter beyond indicating it was likely the kitchen. She smiled when she saw Grayson looking through the window, wiping her hands on a dishtowel as she approached. She opened the door and ushered him inside. Tantalizing aromas permeated the air in the small house, making his mouth water immediately. Vegetables and potatoes and meat, fresh bread, and spices created a tantalizing combination.

"We started to think you were really stuck," Mrs. Branson said, shutting the door behind him. "You can hang your coat there." She indicated a row of pegs on the wall. "Kip just went to wash up. She's had her hands in pie crust since she got home." She gasped and attempted to look contrite. "Oh, I wasn't supposed to say she made the pie. Don't tell her I told."

"I won't," Grayson said, finding a moment to slip in a word while he hung his coat.

"She'll be right down." She motioned up the stairs and headed back the way she came. "I must check on the biscuits. Jack is in the front room if you'd like to take a seat."

"Thank you," he called after her retreating form.

Before he could take a step toward the room off the right side of the foyer, which he assumed to be the front room and where Jack Branson was likely to be based on the sound of the television, he heard the closing of a door at the top of the stairs and moved to the bottom step to see if it might be Kipling. A shaded light hanging from the ceiling at the top of the staircase cast a glow behind her as she bounded down the first few steps, her hand on the polished wood railing, her feet — covered in thick, pink stockings — thumped on the wood.

As her head cleared the edge of the ceiling leading into the stairwell, she raised her chin and looked down, seeing Grayson for the first time. Her steps stilled and her eyes widened, and Grayson smiled. He set one foot on the bottom step and rested his hand on the rounded top of the baluster.

"You looked surprised to see me."

She rushed down the stairs so quickly a rush of panic hit Grayson that she might fall and fall she did — or leapt might be more appropriate — into his embrace, her arms wrapped around his shoulders. His arms around her, Grayson took a step back so her feet were on the foyer floor, but she didn't ease her hold and he had to bend a bit so she stood. Kipling kissed his cheek, and again, before she kissed his lips, her hands sliding around his neck to rest on his jaw.

Grayson hummed into the kiss, drawing his palms up her back to pull her closer, ever mindful they were in her parents' home and propriety of some kind had to be maintained. But barely.

When she drew back to look up at him, tears made her amber eyes shine. Her gaze shifted, studying him, the soft pads of her thumbs stroking his cheek.

Grayson sucked in a sharp breath, steeling himself against the inevitable, and raised his hand to knock on the door. It took only moments for Mum Branson to appear in the foyer beyond the door, and her smile widened when she saw him. He tried to smile, but knew he failed miserably when her expression faltered and she called out "Jack" as she reached the door.

I am weary from grief; strengthen me…

Chapter Seven

5 HOURS 6 MINUTES

"Where are you now?"

"At Kipling's parents' home," Grayson answered Greg. "In Chelsea outside the city."

He sat on the edge of Kipling's double bed in the bedroom he had only seen once before, hunched over with his forehead in his hand, rubbing at the headache behind his eyes. It felt like a lifetime ago since he'd seen this room. It approached midnight, if not later, and the stillness of the night in Chelsea had settled on the quiet neighborhood. One bedside lamp cast light through the small room. Soft yellows and pinks, with touches of white, made the room welcoming and soothing even though everything in him was in turmoil.

Telling Jack and Jane Branson he'd effectively lost their only daughter, with no presumption as to her whereabouts or safety, had been one of the hardest things he'd ever done. The pain in Mum Branson's eyes was nearly his undoing, and while they'd embraced him, he accepted the blame of the situation was his.

"Agent Flannery asked I not stay at the flat until they complete processing any evidence. I agreed, though reluctantly; I harbor the hope she might return there from wherever she has gone."

"Involuntarily…"

Anger flashed hot through him, but he just as quickly tamped it down because he knew Greg was doing no less than they would with any situation they investigated. Just as Agent Flannery had done upon arriving at the flat. "Yes," he managed to say. He knew he didn't hide his emotions from his cousin, even from across the ocean.

"Howell," Gregory said simply.

"That is my assumption, but how? He serves at the Crown's pleasure 3,200 miles away with no casual visitors and no means to communicate."

"I'll call Sandra. If anyone can find out his way of communicating, it'll be her. She might even have an answer before I get there. Lynne is on a quick job but should be back soon. It's minor. If needed, I'll get her to Belmarsh and talk to people. You know she can be persuasive."

"That she can." Grayson released a long, heavy breath, his eyes closed. "I would attempt an argument stating your presence is unnecessary, but I've neither the strength of spirit nor fortitude of conviction. I welcome your support."

"I'll be there as soon as possible. Ollie," he said and paused only a beat. "Once everything is squared away, I'm on the next flight. We'll find her."

Unable to speak any further, Grayson let his hand holding the mobile drop to hang limp from his thigh. Exhaustion at a soul level pulled at him, but he knew sleep would be impossible. The effort to straighten, open his eyes, and toss the mobile onto the mattress beside him was nearly too much for him to manage.

He was powerless, effectively cuffed and muzzled. While the notification to come to Boston came via the FBI to MI6 and then to him, he wasn't in the States in any official capacity. He was here as a witness for the prosecution against Isaac Sheldon representing Six, but also, and far more importantly, as support for Kipling as she had to relive the events of months before when Sheldon kidnapped her at gunpoint and unsuccessfully attempted to kill her.

While he expected Agent Patrick Flannery would keep him abreast of the investigation, when deemed appropriate, he had no power to act himself. When he'd been in Boston last, he had done so as a representative of Six. Being on extended leave at his own demand had gifted him precious time with Kipling, and now in her absence, stole his authority.

He uncurled the fingers of his other hand, focusing on the ring that had been left on her pillow, her wedding ring, halfway down his proximal phalange.

On the bedside table nearest him was a small stand holding an assortment of necklaces, some earrings, and bracelets probably worn by a very young Kipling based on the novelty and cartoon designs on some of the earrings specifically. Grayson took from the stand a simple chain in rose gold with no other adornments. Working open the clasp, he threaded the chain through his great-grandmother's ring, closed the clasp again and slipped it over his head. The ring settled in the center of his chest. Where he determined it would remain until he placed it again on his wife's finger.

A soft knock at the door and Jane Branson calling his name forced Grayson to pull himself from the fog. He stood and took the few long strides needed to reach the door. Kipling's mum stood in the hall, the single light in the small landing a halo behind her, dressed in a fluffy purple robe despite the warmth of summer.

"Did I wake you? I'm so sorry," he said, but she shook her head and held up her hand.

"I doubt any of us will sleep tonight. But I did hear you talking and wanted to check on you. If there was any word…"

"No. I was speaking with Greg."

"He's coming to Boston."

She didn't ask a question, but Grayson nodded in affirmation. He raised his arm to rest on the door jamb and rested his forehead against the back of his wrist. "Likely the beginning of the week. He is tasking members of our team with ways to assist, and then will be on his way."

Mum Branson tilted her head, and while the light behind her shadowed her expression, he felt her study. "Grayson, we need your honesty."

He let his weary head fall forward and closed his eyes. "You deserve nothing less."

"Come downstairs," she said, turning to descend the stairs.

He retrieved his mobile, unwilling to be without it should a call come in. The foyer light at the bottom of the stairs wasn't on, but light from past the foyer cast enough glow to see. Leaving the small light on in the bedroom, Grayson followed her a few steps behind. The light came from the small kitchen and Dad Branson already sat at the table. Grayson wondered if he'd been so loud they heard him in the stillness of the house, or of Mum Branson just happened to be upstairs. Jack looked up from the cup in front of him, a haggard strain around his eyes and a jolt of guilt twisted in Grayson's chest for being the cause of their distress.

"Would you like tea?" Mum Branson asked.

"Thank you." He sat in one of the two empty chairs.

Without casual conversation, she retrieved a mug and poured hot water, bringing the cup with the steeping teabag already in it. Dad Branson said nothing, just looking into his mug without drinking. Mum Branson poured her own tea and sat across from him. He stared into his mug, watching the water change color with the tea straining from the pouch.

"Tell me what you want to know first. I shall share absolutely everything I can," he said, finally raising his head.

"Who took our daughter?" Dad Branson asked, slowly pulling his stare to Grayson, the scrape of his voice raw and painful.

"Physically taking possession of her, I do not know," he answered as honestly as he could. "It is my firm belief until proven otherwise, whoever took Kipling" –he choked on the words and had to pause and swallow– "operated under orders of the same man behind the bombing at the college where Kipling and I first met, her abduction in February, as well as the bombing of my car and my abduction in London. His name is Langdon Fairfax Howell."

Mum Branson sucked in a sharp breath and Dad Branson's eyes rounded beneath his bushy eyebrows. Grayson smiled though felt no pleasure or humor. Of course, they would understand the connection. Only two people so deeply engrained in classic literature could have raised a daughter equal to Doctor Kipling Branson Holmes.

He nodded. "Yes, as fantastical and fictional as the connection would seem to most, Langdon Howell is a descendant of Charles Augustus Howell known as Milverton in the fictionalized retellings of Conan Doyle. My ancestor and his ancestor despised each other, and the hatred continued through the Howell line. As did their criminal undertakings, which had them cross paths with Six. And myself."

"This is all because of a family feud?" Dad Branson asked.

"It began as such, and strictly on the part of the Howell family, but has grown far more personal," Grayson admitted. "I am the son of a brilliant engineer and grandson of an accomplished doctor, neither of which were professions to draw the attention of the Howell criminal organization."

Knowing they deserved the truth, as distasteful as it was and as ugly a light it would shine on their new son-in-law, Grayson took a swallow of the hot, still-weak tea and steeled his resolve. He began the explanation of where the tragedy began when Nelson Howell brought a building down around Gregory McQueen and left the Holmes family shattered. He'd felt smothering shame when he told Kipling how he had beaten Nelson Howell to death with his own hands in a blind rage but facing her parents with the same truth after all they already knew heaped shame and guilt on him with a weight he'd never before carried.

Nelson Howell had gone after Grayson and Greg very specifically that day because of the blood in their veins. Grayson had killed Nelson as retribution for killing Greg, though ultimately it was Six who had wronged the Holmes/McQueen families the most. Langdon Howell — brother to Nelson, and while arguably more intelligent, also more mentally unstable -- devised a twisted plan to retaliate against Grayson, seeing Kipling Branson as the perfect foil. He had absolutely no idea how perfect. His machinations had failed, giving Grayson far more strength than he ever imagined. Explaining from that point was more about joining the dots that Jack and Jane Branson already knew, having lived the events of previous months.

When the bloodletting in the form of relaying information that felt more akin to a confession was complete, Grayson was left staring into his now cold, heavily steeped tea mug in the smothering silence of the kitchen.

DAY 2: FRIDAY

"How you holdin' up, chief?"

Grayson hunched forward in his seated position on the couch in Patrick Flannery's office, hands linked and hanging loose and head down. This was neither the circumstance nor the timing he had intended for his return to the FBI offices. His neck and shoulders were knotted and stiff, his head hurt, and his soul was beaten bloody. With a long, drawn sigh he ran his hand over his hair and sat up straight, looking toward the door Patrick had just entered.

"Crumbling beneath the weight, if I'm entirely honest."

Flannery crossed the office, one hand extended with a steaming mug as he reached Grayson. Tea or coffee, he didn't care as long as it was caffeinated. He stood and took the mug, confirming it was coffee just before taking a sip. Black, strong, and stale but he didn't care.

"How'd the in-laws take the news?"

"As well as one would expect if by well one expects heartbreak, anger, and confusion. While they have known since the beginning who and what I am, and how my identity has been responsible for events of the past few months, learning the full extent of the Machiavellian machinations of one who has declared himself some sort of archnemesis to the Holmes name was a bit more than they ever anticipated having to accept."

Flannery snorted a short laugh. "Deadass, chief."

Grayson's knowledge of American — most specifically Boston, because it was a language unto itself — slang failed him to know exactly what the man meant but based on tone and expression he presumed Flannery agreed with his assessment on some level. Flannery took another drink of his own coffee, ending with a loud "Aaah" as he went to his desk, setting the mug on the blotter.

"So, the lab has been right out straight with your suitcases and all, and they found nothin' to help. Also found nothin' that says we need to keep it, so they should be bookin' it up here wicked soon."

"Thank you. I appreciate your support in this."

Agent Flannery made a scoffing sound and waved off Grayson's thanks. "It's a hell of a situation, chief. No worries. You must just be drivin' yourself nuts over it."

Seemingly on cue, a young man appeared at the open office door, pushing Grayson's and Kipling's luggage one in each hand. The exterior of both had a film of fingerprinting dust and the broken seal stickers applied at the apartment before the FBI took custody of the luggage was still visible.

"Here we go," Flannery said as he waved to the kid, who raised a hand and slipped back out of the office without saying anything. "Junior lab tech," Flannery explained. "He's still getting the lay and all. From somewhere down south, like Brooklyn."

Grayson itched to dig into the case to see how thorough the investigation and examination of his suitcase had been, but instead nodded his thanks while taking another drink of his now lukewarm coffee.

"I'm here, either way. What is the status of the trials for Isaac Sheldon and Charles Malcolm?"

Agent Flannery sighed, long and deep, and rounded his desk to take a seat. He motioned for Grayson to take a chair across from him as he unlocked his computer. "I'm gonna be honest with you, Grayson, and know it has nothing to do with what happened to your wife, but I can't tell you too much about Sheldon's case. You may be called as a witness, I'll tell you that. But you're not exactly impartial."

"I concede the fact. Reluctantly."

"The judge will eventually have to make the call to either wait for Kipling to—" he stuttered off whatever he might have said and adjusted to say, "be available or to request closing arguments."

Grayson dipped his chin in acknowledgment. He knew a conclusion of the trial was a possibility. Kipling was a witness; however, there was likely sufficient evidence to proceed.

"Malcolm, though, is a wicked shitshow, I'll be honest," Flannery continued. "Sure, we've got him on tape and all at the university, but there's not enough to nail him to the wall. Burke probably could've, but we're workin' on hard evidence to get Malcolm for murder, too. His attorney is pushing for dismissal."

"I suggest searching every aspect of his attorney, from familial connections to any obscure link. Dig and you might link the dots back to the Howell family in some capacity."

Flannery clicked his tongue in his cheek and tapped his temple with a single finger before pointing at Grayson. "Right with you on that one. Like you said, it's not going to be easy to spot. Get this, though. The lawyer who showed up back in March after Malcolm's arrest? Yeah, he's gone. Poof. Malcom ain't talkin', either. Just says he has new representation."

Grayson slumped in the uncomfortable chair, slouching so the back of the chair hit him across the shoulders, and rested his elbow on the wooden arm. He squinted against the persistent headache, rubbing his finger across his mouth, drawing up from his memory the one time he had observed Malcolm's lawyer. Grayson realized he had never learned the man's name.

Beside Malcolm sat a man dressed in a well-tailored, dark suit with dark blond hair, carefully groomed, and a perfectly trimmed mustache and beard. Pockmarks scarred his cheeks, but disappeared beneath the facial hair, making Grayson suspect the marks were the reason for the growth. The only assumption was the man was Malcolm's lawyer.

"You have no justifiable cause for your illegal search and seizure," the lawyer said, his accent ringing strangely off as if a practiced or learned Bostonian accent versus natural. It was subtle, but Grayson heard the variation.

Cold fingers slid up the back of his neck. Perhaps his love for Kipling actually had affected his mind, like he had been accused. Fine details had escaped him. If such obvious facts were hidden from him, what else had he missed?

A sound from the bedroom, the distinct click of a lock being disengaged, had Grayson stumbling out of the bath to face his host.

Langdon Howell.

Though clearly younger than Nelson Howell who Grayson had encountered in previous years, Langdon was no doubt family to the dead criminal. Dark blond hair hung over his tanned forehead, the golden tone of his skin a testament to his Portuguese ancestry, and although Kipling had described him as having a mustache while in Boston, he was now clean-shaven, his otherwise smooth skin marred in spots by old pock scars. Not enough to diminish his appearance, but enough to be noted.

He was dressed like any proper English gentleman, in a light gray suit and polished shoes, his hands tucked behind his back.

"I'm pleased to see you are able to leave your bed," he said, and if Grayson hadn't known the lengths to which this man had gone, he might actually be convinced of concern. "Do be careful and refrain from doing anything foolish."

Grayson could excuse his lack of connection after the explosion, but he should have put the two together later.

"You still with me, chief? Need another coffee?"

Grayson rubbed his brow, the headache taking a stronger hold. "I feel the fool," he said before forcing himself to look at the man. "The attorney first here with Malcolm was Langdon Howell. He didn't appear again because he had returned to England. There is your evidence of a connection."

Flannery's hands stilled over his keyboard and he stared at Grayson, unblinking, before sitting back with enough force his chair swayed. "Well, Jeezus. How the hell did you—" He stopped himself and held up his hand. "I don't wanna know. How do we prove it?"

"I am unsure whether any proof I can provide would be admissible in court, but it may be enough to give your judiciary system some leverage with Malcolm. Sandra Sookoo is exceptionally skilled and can provide a digitally enhanced and rendered transition from images you have of the man who claimed to be Malcolm's lawyer to Langdon Howell. He is one in the same, and she can remove the layers of disguise."

Flannery nodded several times in silence before he squared himself in front of his computer again. "Sounds like a plan."

Chapter Eight

DAY 3: SATURDAY

"I'm not sure what's worse. The parky winters or the damp summers that feel like someone left the hot tap on," Greg said as he slammed shut the passenger door of Grayson's rental Chrysler 300, squinting up at the afternoon sun through his sunglasses.

"Twain is infamous for saying if one doesn't like the weather in New England, wait a few minutes," Grayson said, using the key fob to lock the vehicle before joining Greg on the sidewalk. "Since returning, I have found Boston to be either humid or more humid. Or raining," he added.

Greg had arrived from London that afternoon, and Grayson suggested food before dropping him at a hotel near Chelsea. Director Stanton had provided assurance Grayson would be allowed to return to Kipling's apartment on Monday, and until then it would be too much to ask of the Branson's to allow Greg to stay in their small home as well. As it was, Grayson felt the weight of his presence and imposition in their lives. Both were near should he suddenly have news to share, and a constant reminder to them of his failure to keep their only child safe.

Between Logan Airport and Greg's hotel, there were easily a dozen pubs, steakhouses, diners, and Italian eateries but with little interest in eating he'd chosen based on his knowledge of his cousin's taste and they now walked the pavement toward the restaurant whose online reviews lauded its steak and ale selections. The wait was short since they were only two versus the larger parties checking in and were given a small table near the bar within a few minutes. Nothing particularly appealed from the menu, but he ordered dinner to justify the bottle of red wine he ordered for the table. Despite the fact, Greg ordered a dark ale.

Waitstaff delivered the wine, beer, and a basket of bread with a slow smile at Grayson before she told them their meals would be ready soon. He registered the implication beyond her duties but felt not the slightest inclination to respond either way.

"Thank you," Greg said to her as Grayson poured his cabernet. "Does Flannery have anything yet?" Greg asked once she stepped away.

Grayson drank half the content of his glass, ignoring the bread. "Not a bloody thing," he said, the foot of his glass making a dull thud when he set it down. "Even when Sandra provides the needed rendition of Langdon Howell as Malcolm's pseudo-lawyer, it does little other than to confirm my ineptitude and failure."

"You didn't realize you needed to be paying attention—"

"Where exactly is the line between needing to pay attention and *not* paying attention," Grayson snapped, immediately pressing his lips together as the attention of several other restaurant patrons turned to look their way. Ignoring their curiosity, he poured more wine. "Imagine the entire course of events that may have been avoided had I simply *paid attention.*"

He flattened his sneer by lifting the glass to his lips again.

Greg watched him, his arms folded on the table in front of him, silent. He eventually sat back with a long sigh and picked up his mug, drank, and set it down again before he spoke.

"I don't need to ask how you're doing."

"Bugger off."

They sat in silence for several minutes, Grayson staring at the deep red of the wine in the dim ambiance light. The cabernet already burned a hole in his gut and his logical mind said at least eat a piece of bread. The part of him hating himself and his incompetence was louder and he refrained. Due punishment, along with the brutal headache he was likely to have in the morning.

They didn't speak until a different member of the waitstaff brought their meals. Greg offered the expected recognition and thanks, his words just enough to force Grayson to ignore his foul mood and offer a nod as well. Greg picked up his utensils, but Grayson found himself staring at the chicken and potatoes on his plate, lacking the motivation to attempt a bite. He dropped his hands into his lap and sat back, slamming his shoulders against the back of his chair with an exhausted slump.

DAY 6: TUESDAY

Grayson stopped in front of the flat door, swiveling his suitcase to set against the wall adjacent to the locked door. Greg was two steps behind him, staying slightly behind with his hand on the raised handle of Kipling's bag.

He took the keys from his pocket, bouncing them in his palm before maneuvering the correct key between his fingers. He'd studied enough psychology, including body language analysis and avoidance tactics, to be overwhelmingly self-aware of his actions. This was a space intrinsically linked to Kipling, and without her, he didn't belong here. More, she should be here with him.

"Let me do it, Ollie."

"No," he said, trying to keep the frustration from his voice.

It wasn't for Greg but for himself. They were a day later returning to the flat because of a delay on approval at the Bureau, and the delay both frustrated him and put off the torture he now faced.

Kipling's domain without Kipling.

The tumble of rotors drew the bolt. He withdrew that key and bounced the bundle in his palm to find the upper deadbolt key and unlocked it as well. The door opened and stale air once again assaulted him. The forensic team had turned off the air conditioning and taken the filters, leaving no possible evidence untouched. He had communicated with the building manager who had informed him the filters had been replaced, but the system had been left off.

A metallic tang of fingerprint dust mingled with the lingering acetone smell left by the ninhydrin. The chemical odor tingled the skin of his sinuses and he sneered. Rather than turning on the air conditioner, he set the control panel to fan and while Greg set the luggage he maneuvered out of the way Grayson went to the sitting room to open the windows. Rather than cycle the chemically tainted air he wanted it gone.

"What do you need me to do?" Greg asked from the kitchen. The refrigerator door opened and quickly closed. "Looks like a grocery run should be high on the list."

"I want the smell of their presence gone," Grayson said, not looking back at his cousin. "It reeks in here."

Grayson fought with the decades-old swiveling lock on the double-hung window, made resistant by layers of paint and weeks of humidity, heat, and lack of temperature control. It finally gave and his hand slipped. His wedding band pinged off the glass. Grayson clenched his teeth until his jaw ached and slammed the heels of his hands against the wood until the lower window moved. Immediately the volume of the street sounds below increased. The pull of air from the fan system stirred his shirt and he curled his fingers on the raised ledge of the window, resting his forehead on the glass.

He didn't know what to do.

He didn't know where to go.

He didn't know how to breathe.

He didn't know how to not know what to do.

"I'll go to the grocery we passed while trying to park. We circled the block three times; I'm pretty sure I can find it. Any requests?"

Alcohol…

But he stayed silent.

Greg tried to lift some of the load with casualness as if the absence of Grayson's wife was temporary. She was shopping and would be back soon with a new dress.

If only it were true…

"Buy what you prefer. I will make do," he finally answered.

Greg left the flat, and as much as Grayson welcomed the support and assistance and would never regret the presence of a cousin thought dead and found again, for the time being, he welcomed the solitude. Staying with the Bransons left him little space to breathe without being painfully aware of their worry and recrimination, though they never spoke of it. If not there, he was at the Bureau building waiting for some small crumble of hope and none had yet come.

Greg exited the building and turned right, rightfully opting for the walk to the closest convenience and liquor store. It was a short distance, and taking the car was unnecessary. Especially since the rental was parked a block in the other direction. Parking would prove to be a challenge.

He turned his back to the window and returned to the kitchen, confirming Greg's observation that food was in short supply. The casserole Mum Branson had made for them had remained in the refrigerator for too long to be consumed. Never having need or opportunity to explore Kipling's kitchen in detail, Grayson opened cabinets and took a brief inventory while searching for what may be available to clean. Nothing appeared particularly odd or out of place but very typical of a single woman's kitchen. When he opened the smaller cabinets over the refrigerator, he found half a dozen bottles of various wines. None the same mark or vintage and based on the dust on the bottles she had put them there and forgotten them. Grayson took down one and read the label. He didn't recognize the maker, but it didn't matter.

If he could accomplish nothing else, he could accomplish getting good and pissed. He opened the door closest to the sink and took out a tall glass. Yanking open three drawers found him a corkscrew.

By the time he heard Greg in the hall outside the apartment, his voice carrying the tone indicating to Grayson he likely spoke with

Esther, Grayson had finished one bottle and opened the second. He was slumped on the sitting room sofa, a stack of new bedding beside him that hadn't yet made it to the bedroom. The idea of sleeping in the bed without his wife had all but poured the chardonnay down his throat. Now his world was fuzzy, his head was heavy, and the pain he'd hoped to drown now sat on his chest with the weight of an elephant.

Greg set the bags on the table with one hand, holding the mobile to his ear with the other, and shut the door with his foot.

"Back at the flat, love," he said, the lightness of his tone in the hallway all but gone. Grayson felt his scrutiny and took another drink from the three-quarters full glass, nearly draining it. "I'll tell him. Love you, too. Talk soon."

"Don't hang up on my account," Grayson said, his tongue thick.

Greg came to the threshold between the small kitchen and equally small sitting room, his hands pushed into his pockets while he studied Grayson.

"Far from a vintage year, but passable," Grayson said, motioning to the bottle on the low table in front of him. "Does the job."

"I've never seen you like this, Ollie."

Grayson drew in a long breath through his nose, notes of vanilla, butter, and nuts from the wine filling his senses. He blinked slowly, willing the alcohol to finally do its job and render him either unconscious or utterly unaware.

"Of course not. Last time I was like this, you were dead."

Chapter Nine

Day 12: Monday Afternoon

"The only thing I can figure, Boss, is that whatever put the cogs into motion to stage Kip's abduction—" Sandra stuttered over the word, then stopped. Even though the silence was no more than two ticks, it was deafening. "I'm sorry, Boss."

"Avoiding the word doesn't lessen the fact," Grayson said in the direction of his mobile lying on the table, Sandra Sookoo's voice projecting from the speaker. He reached for the electrolyte beverage Greg had been shoving at him and drained the last of the sickeningly sweet "fruit juicy" whatever. "Please continue. The facts are what I need, and we have had precious little of them."

She cleared her throat, and he heard the tap of computer keys. "Mac helped me set up a program to rapid-scan absolutely all footage of Howell from the moment you took him into custody in Knightsbridge. He's had no visitors, not even legal representation. No calls. No emails. No carrier pigeons."

"Regardless, he is involved."

"Oh, he bloody well is. Get this, Boss. Wednesday two weeks

past, the day this happened at the same time you were waiting for Agent Flannery to arrive at Kipling's flat, this bell head *tosser* stood up," with each fact, her voice volume ticked up, but more than that Sandra's word choice amplified his attention. She wasn't one for more colorful choices unless called upon. "Walked to the door of his cell, looked at the CCTV camera aimed at it, and smiled the most disgustingly smug smirk I've ever seen!"

Her voice cut through his head, but her words cut through the pained fog and Grayson sat up straighter snatching up the mobile from the table. "You're absolutely certain of the timing?"

"Absolutely. I had to make sure it wasn't a coincidence. It was bloody *midnight* in London and this bastard stood from his bed and looked right at the camera." She made a sound akin to a growl and a groan and huffed. "I swear, Boss, when Mac saw the clip he wanted to go smack that damn smirk of Howell's face. Lynne convinced him that pleasure should be left to you."

The volume and clarity of Sandra's words decreased as if he'd left the room where she spoke, but the full weight of the information came into sharp view.

Howell had been playing the long game...

Yes, he had machinated the events that connected Grayson to Kipling. Yes, he had done so with the intent of doing more than killing a Holmes — he had done it as an act of revenge and in hopes of destroying Grayson from the inside. Crush him.

But his game had been dismantled when Grayson had done what Howell thought unimaginable...he'd fallen in love with Kipling.

How long had this twist of the knife been planned?

How could her abduction in Boston have been choreographed when Howell had been in custody without contact since weeks before their wedding and weeks before the date of their arrival again in Massachusetts could have been known?

What was the extent of his narcissistic, psychopathic Machiavellianism?

"Boss?"

"He has affiliates here in Boston beyond Isaac Sheldon and

Charles Malcom, obviously. They would have been well established well before the beginning of this year before the bombing." He paused in his thoughts, rubbing his brow to push away the dull hangover thud. "Bloody hell."

"What are you thinking?"

"Nothing I'm prepared to voice yet, as the ramifications — if I am correct — might go much further than any of us thought."

"What do you need?"

"As much information as possible and given my limitations I require your analysis expertise. Expand all search and correlation parameters to include anyone — *anyone* — he had contact with in any way while in Belmarsh. Guards. Janitors. Cafeteria help. Anyone who would have been within any proximity to him to speak or be heard. Or seen. Don't limit to conversation. Eye contact is sufficient. Anyone who was in a room prior to Howell. Cross-reference with all known associations even distant and seemingly inconsequential with Six personnel, affiliates, spouses or partners, *and* connections here in Massachusetts. Primary focus on Bureau employees of any level, their families, et cetera. While he's clearly no longer a cog in this machine, include Burke DiMatto. I have underestimated Langdon Howell long enough."

"This is going to take time. Even with Mac's mojo."

Unfortunately, the clock is ticking, the hours are going by. The past increases, the future recedes. Possibilities decreasing, regrets mounting.

Haruku Murakami spoke Grayson's truth.

"Time will pass either way. Even if we should be so lucky as to find Kipling, this information will be vital for a meaningful conviction. Better to begin the work now."

With her vehement assurances, they ended the call and Grayson stood to yank open the various drawers in Kipling's kitchen. Not finding what he needed, he moved to the small bedroom and scanned her bookshelves. *Surely she would have —*

He pulled from one of the middle shelves a spiral-bound notebook, already flipped open to a lined page. Grayson scanned the writing quickly, confirming within a few words they were notes likely from one of her doctorate classes or assignments. As having already earned her degree months before, the necessity to preserve the note-book seemed unlikely and he flipped the page to a blank sheet.

Grayson returned to the kitchen, retrieving a cup Kipling kept on the counter with a variety of pencils, ink pens, and a few bright-colored gel pens. Dumping the writing utensils on the table, he sat and began to write. Dictating his thoughts may have seemed to some to be faster, and typing into a computer more efficient, but Grayson's mind worked best at solving puzzles and tracing details when the exercise of thought was from mind to hand to paper.

His thoughts were a dervish of bits and snippets, at points forcing him to close his eyes to process images and events — details he had failed to acknowledge at the moments of occurrence but had been shuffled away into the dark corners of his consciousness to be retrieved later.

Except he had wasted nearly two weeks drowning precious details and potential clues in the bottom of a bottle of whatever he found handy at the end of the day. Disgust and disappointment in himself attempted to fog his thoughts, but he pushed the emotions aside to eat away at his soul should he fail utterly.

Like no other time in his adult life was the need to ignore emotion and sentiment greater than now. The stinging twist of pushing aside love and fear for impartiality and composure stood as a reminder of why he needed to solve this puzzle.

The apartment darkened as hours passed, and he rose from his chair only enough to flip the light switch near the door. He didn't acknowledge time until the apartment door opened and Greg returned, carrying a takeaway bag. The smell of food registered, but Grayson ignored it.

With little else to occupy time, Greg had offered his assistance in the development of the case against Charles Malcolm. Director Shah of Six had been quick to provide the necessary clearance and assurances to the Federal Bureau of Investigation to confirm his credentials.

"I brought back—" Greg halted short and lunged across the compact kitchen to leave the food on the far counter, coming back immediately to the table. "Mind mapping. What have you learned?"

"Learned, nothing yet," Grayson said, sitting up to toss the near-dry pen across the table. His back protested the extended position hunched over the table and his hand ached, but it was inconsequential.

He briefed his cousin on the information from Sandra, and Greg's eyes widened without further explanation needed. One seemingly inconsequential moment was the cornerstone to a massive infrastructure of manipulation. He didn't have the final architecture, but Howell's act of gloating began to form a primary blueprint.

"When will Sandra have connections?"

Grayson shook his head and flipped his wrist to look at the time. "She only began the process seven hours past. The scale and scope of correlating all the dots could well take days, delayed by my blind stupidity."

"Not blind stupidity, Ollie," Greg said, shaking his head. "Blind love. Blind fear, even. But not stupidity. For once, your emotional soul overrode your clinical mind. You're human after all."

"The cost of my humanity may be too high."

DAY 13: TUESDAY MORNING

Grayson's mobile chimed with a familiar tone as he stepped into the public lobby of the Boston Federal Bureau of Investigation building. He nodded to the receptionist and security guard, who smiled back, and brought the mobile to his ear.

"I am in the lobby," he said, approaching the bank of lifts.

"Good," Agent Flannery said on a huffed breath. "I've got a hell of an update for you and probably better you're here for it."

"I will be there momentarily."

He ended the call and stepped into the lift as the door dinged. The lift was otherwise empty and went directly to the appropriate floor. A few Grayson encountered in the hallway gave a nod of acknowledgment but none stopped him to speak. Likely his expression stated conversation was out of the question; he was not inclined to mask his focus. He wished to share with Agent Flannery his conclusions, at least in part, but his curious mind hoped the agent shared something to enlighten. As he neared Flannery's open office door, the sound of mingled voices came from inside and Grayson recognized them as Flannery's thick, non-rhoticity accent and Director Stanton's deeper, more defined tone.

"This is some wicked twisted bullshit," Flannery said. "He ain't gonna accept it and I sure as hell don't blame him."

"You know it's bullshit. I know it's bullshit. But until we figure out what the hell is *really* going on—"

"Let's refrain on the assumption I will or won't accept the information until you've presented it," Grayson said, stepping into the room.

Both men looked in his direction, Director Stanton pivoting to do so. His eyes were pinched at the corners and his nose flared with a grimace. Agent Flannery appeared equally vexed, his hands at his waist and his mouth a thin, straight line.

"Trust me, chief, you ain't gonna to like it."

"I've gathered as much."

Agent Flannery looked to his superior, who nodded, apparently leaving the revelation to him. With a huff, Flannery shook his head and made eye contact. "The trial against Sheldon started yesterday—"

"I am aware."

"Yeah, well, Fed prosecution has been tryin' to figure out what to do without Ms. Branson — Doctor Branson — Doctor *Holmes*—"

"I am hardly concerned at the moment whether you properly acknowledge my wife's appellation and cognomen, Agent Flannery," Grayson forced through clenched teeth.

"Sorry, chief. It's not like the trial comes to a screechin' halt like traffic on 93 North, but they gotta figure out how to deal with the gap in evidence. So this morning, a lawyer who says he represents your wife submitted a petition to the federal court. She's asking to testify remotely, not in the courtroom. And if the judge won't comply, she says she don't want you there."

Grayson moved forward, holding up a finger to give Flannery half a breath to allow his interjection. "Has her well-being been confirmed?"

"Chief, I just told you she don't want to see you."

"Which is entirely ridiculous, and thus not the priority in this conversation. She was taken against her will, and quite likely anything on her behalf is without her consent. My question stands: Was her well-being confirmed?" he asked again, stressing the weight of each word with a slow cadence.

Agent Flannery looked to his director, who nodded as he released a hard huff. Flannery made eye contact again and canted his head toward the computer monitor on his desk. "Come on around. They submitted a video as support."

Flannery stepped backward to round the far side of his large desk while Grayson approached the other way. The agent sat, his chair creaking as he shifted toward his monitor, and a few taps later a video player window opened on the screen.

Grayson's heart clenched to see his wife frozen in a moment of time as the video thumbnail. Frozen expression, her mouth tense and turned down in the slightest frown and strain wrinkled her brow beneath the fall of hair along her temples. She sat at a table, utilitarian and nondescript, with a monotone wall behind her in an ash color. A shoulder and arm emerged from the edge of the image indicating someone sat beside her, but nothing indicated who it might be. Kipling looked forward but slightly off-center, likely looking to whoever recorded the video.

"You ready for this?" Flannery asked. He didn't wait for Grayson's reply before clicking on the play icon.

The video came to life with Kipling shifting to take a deep breath and square her shoulders, nodding, as an offscreen voice asked, *"Could you please state your name for the recording?"*

"Kipling Marie Branson."

Grayson couldn't take a deep breath, his heart fluttering in violent arrhythmia. He pushed his clenched fists into his trouser pockets to hide their sudden tremor and clenched his jaw to the point of pain.

"You hold a doctorate in literature, correct?"

She nodded.

"Be sure to verbally answer for us, Ms. Branson."

"Yes, I hold a doctorate. I'm sorry."

"No problem, Ms. Branson. We want to ensure the information presented is as complete and understandable as possible. Are you married?"

She sat back a few degrees, her shoulders shifting, and she swallowed visibly before answering. *"Yes, I am."*

"What is the name of the man you married?"

"Grayson Holmes."

"He is a British citizen, correct?"

"Yes. Um" — she shook her head and closed her eyes — *"he has dual citizenship. British and American."*

"He is an officer for MI6, correct?"

"Yes."

"Does he frighten you, Ms. Branson?"

She blinked several times before looking down toward her lap. *"Yes."*

Something niggled at Grayson, something beneath the words and the tone, something pushing through the heartache from her words. Something off. Something wrong. Something alarming.

Deception.

Her deception?

No.

"Before I ask for clarification on your answer so we can accomplish the intent of this recording, can you confirm you have no desire to avoid testifying in the federal case against Isaac Sheldon regarding the events that occurred this past March?"

Kipling raised her head, staring straight to the speaker he couldn't see. *"That is correct. Isaac Sheldon did abduct me and attempt to kill me."*

"That is testimony for the trial. Let's return to your husband."

She looked down and away again.

What was it? What was it?

"Why are you afraid of your husband?"

Kipling raised her chin and shook her head, and her hair brushed back off her shoulders. *For a moment…*

"Stop the video."

Flannery did immediately, looking back at Grayson. "I knew it would be hard to listen to, not that I believe a word of it—"

"I need not listen. That is not Kipling."

Flannery squinted, deep lines digging between his ginger-tinted eyebrows, and his look shifted from Grayson to the screen and back again. "Look, chief, I get you don't want to believe—"

"Is there any point to which you would wish to draw my attention?"

"To the curious incident of the dog in the nighttime."

"The dog did nothing in the nighttime."

"That was the curious incident," remarked Sherlock Holmes.

"I assume the Bureau is familiar with Deepfake technology and the rapid advancement in Artificial Intelligence in the civilian sector."

Flannery's head tipped to the side like a curious pup and swiveled his chair to stare at Director Stanton, then back to Grayson still looking as perplexed. "Well, yeah. Intelligence has known about this stuff for years. These days unless it's a wicked bad programmer you can't tell just by looking at it. The AI technology is wicked convincing. The professional ones need tech analysis. You can't just look at a video for two minutes and spit out—"

"That's not my wife," Grayson reiterated while completing Flannery's argument. "You may wish to have your technology team analyze the digital file, or I can forward it to Sandra Sookoo who will likely be much faster and more accurate, but I need no further convincing. By completing the analysis you may be able to convince the judge to deny the request, however."

Agent Patrick Flannery leaned back in his creaking chair until the back of it bumped the edge of his desk, staring at Grayson. The look of confusion and doubt was gone. He might request an explanation how Grayson knew, but he was already fully convinced Grayson was correct.

"Go ahead," Flannery said, his smile ticking up.

"Admittedly, it is an admirable deployment of the technology; however, whomever created the video failed to incorporate idiosyncrasies very specific to Kipling. First, in the short portion of the video you played, Kipling looked down and away from the person speaking offscreen. She continued to look down even when he began to speak, only raising her head to answer when he finished.

"Second, her forward attention is constant, sustained eye contact with the individual speaking. Consider with scrutiny every conversation you have had with my wife."

Flannery's eyes widened and his brows rose.

"And lastly, until such a time I view the video in its entirety when I am sure I will find more incidents…" He stepped forward and reached past Agent Flannery to reverse the video for a few seconds. "She is not wearing her hearing aids."

Flannery snapped his attention to the video, leaning forward until his nose nearly touched the monitor screen. "Well if that ain't the balls."

"While the video creator paid exceptional attention to detail otherwise, at least in this frame, they failed to include that which would be obvious to anyone close to Kipling. Even if they had included the aids, her actions and responses are not appropriate. Kipling naturally looks to the mouth of whoever is speaking to her; it is second nature for her. Likewise, were she looking down or away and they were to speak, she would immediately bring her attention back to them. It's likely the video will be highly convincing otherwise, but this is not my wife."

Director Stanton snatched up the phone handset and entered an extension. "Damn it," he mumbled. "What a shitshow."

"When you have completed your call, I have my own theories to share."

Chapter Ten

DAY 19: MONDAY, EARLY AFTERNOON
JOHN JOSEPH MOAKLEY US COURTHOUSE

G rayson shifted on the wooden bench that felt more like a church pew than appropriate seating with its lack of cushioning. His back ached and if he didn't move every few minutes, his legs started to fall asleep. The logic behind such uncomfortable seating baffled him.

As Jo would likely say, the benches "fit the aesthetic."

The courtroom was large and elaborate, with massive arches and detailed wood trim with massive bowl-like chandeliers with smoky glass lighting the room. The architecture carried voices surprisingly well. He had sat in the courtroom from Wednesday through Friday of the previous week after the judge had denied the request of Kipling's supposed legal representation to avoid testifying in the courtroom. The court understood the request was questionable, but until any other step to deceive was taken they would not take action. They required she appear or be in contempt.

Grayson had sat in the courtroom observers' benches every day, with Greg joining him most days, should the trial progress to the point of reaching Kipling's testimony. Isaac Sheldon stood trial on several counts, only one of which being his abduction and attempted homicide against Grayson's wife. Quite literally, it was the only reason their presence was required in Boston at all. It was Grayson's understanding the prosecution had sufficient evidence, they believed, to convict Sheldon without Kipling's direct testimony but they wanted to close every gap.

Part of him hoped she would arrive, give her testimony, and they would simply leave together. Given her absence, and the belief her departure had been an abduction, his hope was without grounds.

Prior to the lunch break, the prosecution team had indicated it was their intent to question Kipling in the afternoon and anticipated her arrival with her legal team. Since the announcement, Grayson's stomach had been an acidic stone and his chest had been tight. Years of working in international intelligence and his nerves rarely affected him.

This was different.

This was his soul.

Greg sat beside him, the ancient bench creaking with the weight, and held out a takeaway cup with orange and pink writing. Kipling's love of Dunkin' Donuts coffee had rubbed off on both Grayson and Greg in the last few months.

"Here you go, Ollie. Any word?"

"No, and nothing indicating she or her supposed legal representation has arrived at the building. I see no one who hasn't been here throughout the testimonies." He popped back the seal on the plastic cup lid and the aroma of coffee and cream rolled over him. It was still hot and burned his lip, hitting the acid in his gut. "We should be called to order in the next two minutes."

On cue, the doors at the back of the courtroom opened. Grayson looked over his shoulder to watch the prosecution team enter. A middle-aged Black man with whitened hair and two women, one also Black and the other Latina. Thus far, Grayson had been highly impressed with their approach to the case, presenting the government's evidence against Sheldon with precision. The second woman was impressively aggressive and intelligent to the point Grayson felt the smallest twang of sympathy for the witnesses she'd questioned.

As they reached their table at the front of the courtroom, the door opened again with Sheldon's team following suit. Their team was led by a sloppy-dressed Caucasian man with short but thick hair that reminded Grayson of Kipling's father, except this man was unkept as if he'd just come in from a winter storm. A young man accompanied him, always neat and well-dressed, but clearly not long out of law school. Grayson contemplated whether the appearance of ineptitude was intentional as part of the grander ploys put in place by Howell, or whether Isaac Sheldon had been tossed to the proverbial wolves, left to someone assigned as a public defender.

More observers filed into the room, some of them press. It was a high-profile case since Isaac Sheldon was accused of the bombing at the university that had ultimately killed nine students plus Grayson's uncle, leaving two more likely disabled for life, and many more injured and scarred mentally for the rest of their lives. With affected families from all over the country, his ring of damages went far beyond Boston, Massachusetts.

The hair on the back of Grayson's neck prickled. He glanced toward Greg and knew his cousin's expression well. He felt it, too. Grayson leaned forward, resting his elbows on his knees to lower his profile, and glanced toward the group of people passing by their row. Two women stood just past the end of their bench, shoulder-to-shoulder, speaking. The ambient noise of the filling courtroom prevented Grayson from hearing anything they said. One angled her head just enough to look past the shoulder of the other...and directly at him. But he avoided eye contact. She obviously singled him — or Greg — out of the crowd, and he was more interested in why than in letting her know he was aware of their focus.

He could only see the full expression of the one watching him; the other woman staying turned fully away from him. In a painfully ironic twist, he wished Kipling were with him because she would be able to tell him what they said.

He'd tried to learn.

But two words did seem to roll through his head. *Find him.*

Activity at the front of the courtroom indicated the afternoon session was about to begin, and Grayson sat back as the two women went to the row immediately behind the government's council table. Moments later, everyone stood as the jury entered and the court was called to order by the Honorable Judge Tamara Sauvage. Within moments, Grayson understood why his nerves had sparked.

"Your Honor, it was the government's intention to call to the stand Doctor Kipling Branson-Holmes to provide testimony; however, we have been informed Doctor Branson-Holmes has defied the order to appear."

Grayson listened but simultaneously observed.

The two women who had stopped near them had knowledge as to where Kipling was. While other trial participants and attendees reacted to the statement, either watching in disbelief or speaking in hushed tones with whoever sat near them. But not the two women. They sat unfazed, with no reaction at all indicating the news was a surprise. Grayson shifted his attention from the women to the ginger hair of Patrick Flannery where he sat a row behind counsel but to the far side of the room.

The agent turned his head the slightest degree to look in Grayson's direction. With no outward indication that the two women were of interest, Grayson unlocked his phone and with his eyes forward and attention seemingly on the front of the room, he quickly typed a message.

> Behind the government counsel. Two
> women.

> Yeah. Got 'em.

> They know where she is.

> I'm on it.

Grayson was prepared to give more instruction, a requirement to explain his theory, but none was requested. The trial moved forward, and minutes later Agent Flannery stood and left the courtroom, not hazarding even a glance in Grayson and Greg's direction.

"He's on it," Greg said, no inflection of question in his tone.

"Yes. Wherever they go from here, we will know."

Grayson and Greg stayed in the courtroom until the judge announced a break, and they stood with everyone else. The two women hustled to leave ahead of anyone else wanting to depart the courtroom, and Grayson took caution not to watch them as they went. He wanted to follow but had absolutely no doubt they knew who he was, who Greg was, and would keep eyes on him while at the courthouse and he wanted no indication his attention was on them in any way.

"They will not return," he said, angling his head enough to watch the women leave the room. "I suspect their day has not gone as planned, which makes me anxious to know what has changed."

"You're confident in Flannery's ability to keep an eye on them."

"He is near as devoted to the truth as I am."

"So…just like the last three weeks, we wait."

"Patience is bitter, but its fruit is sweet. I hold hope in Rousseau's wisdom. We need to leave. To where I don't know, but I know we will learn no more answers here."

Chapter Eleven

After nearly two hours of walking in brand-new heels, Kipling's feet hurt, her legs ached, and her hair clung to the back of her neck. She had taken multiple side streets, despite the ache and exhaustion, because the panic in her chest wouldn't ease.

It was the same panic that had screamed *run* when she saw first the waterfront and then the federal court building came into view. The waterfront brought back a rush of cold and the visceral memory of being dragged down. Deeper and deeper.

And then pulled free.

Pull free. Get free! Run!

So in the bustle of people entering the courthouse towards the security staff, Kipling had slipped into the crowd, step by step putting more space between her and the women who escorted her. She watched the backs of their heads as they moved forward and she moved back. Kipling caught the moment one noticed she wasn't behind them, and she bent at the knees to bring herself below the shoulders of those around her. Once around a corner, she didn't slow and didn't pause for fear they would reach her before she had a chance to be out of sight.

She kept her head down and hurried down the steps, still not daring to look back. Looking back might be her undoing.

Run, Kipling! Run!

His voice and words chased and pushed her down Northern Avenue. She used the parking garage to hide her escape until she got to Seaport Boulevard.

Go home!

No, it's not safe!

If she went home, she was in danger. If she stayed where she was, she was in danger.

Both facts couldn't be simultaneously true.

With violently trembling hands, she had removed her aids several blocks from the courthouse, stomped them to pieces beneath her heel, and left them in shattered bits in an alleyway. Blissful and terrifying silence blinked out the chaos distracting her.

But why had she destroyed them? In the moment she had no hesitation. There had been a reason.

Now, she couldn't remember why. And her world was silent.

Don't let them find you!

Go home! You'll be safe at home!

The home she wanted was now still a mile and a half away, but with no ID, no money, and not even an MBTA pass she had no choice but to keep walking. Her apartment was close, but what could she do when she got there?

He will be there.

What if he's there?

He'll protect you.

Who will protect you from him?

When Peters Park came into view ahead of her on Washington Street, Kipling managed to find enough energy to speed her step until she reached shade. The day wasn't hot, but the air in Boston was thick and she sighed in relief once beneath the trees. She stumbled through the shade to a bench along the walkway, dropping hard onto the unforgiving metal. As soon as she stopped moving, a new pain set in. Her feet throbbed and tingled, the sting of blisters prickling on the back of her heels.

Kipling covered her face and curled forward, her head throbbing with dehydration and fatigue. She just wanted to stop. She wanted to sleep. She wanted a drink.

She wanted to find him.

He'll be angry. He'll take it out on you, Kip. You told me you needed to be away from him. Don't you remember telling me all the horrible things he did to you? Threatened you? Hurt you? It's why you left him. You told me you didn't want to see him. You told me you needed to get away. Why do you keep talking about him?

Kipling shook her head within her hands, trying to chase away the voices. They were familiar, and told her, again and again, they were the only ones she could trust, but her skin crawled with doubt. How could she feel both a need to run to something — someone — and run away at the same time?

I swear to you, Kipling. I am coming for you. I promise you. I swear on my life.

His voice, deep and urgent and honest, danced on the edges of her peripheral confusion. She sucked in several sharp breaths, struggling to push down the panic. Her chest hurt and tears burned her eye. Her arms and throat tingled with gooseflesh and perspiration made her dress stick to her back. She was so tired. So tired.

Adding insult to injury, the aroma of spices and roasted meat came to her on a subtle breeze, chilling her skin further but inspiring a hungry rumble through her stomach. She needed to go home. What she would do when she got there, she didn't know. She just needed to go home.

Pain stabbed the bottoms of her feet and the blisters from the shoes when she pushed herself off the bench to stand. Her legs trembled and she felt weak. But she had to keep going. There was no other option. Focus on the destination, not on each step to get her home.

Kipling gritted her teeth and breathed through the first several steps. She stepped out of the shade along the park edge and looked back the way she had come.

Her chest tightened and she gasped.

Salvation or damnation…run…but to who?

"I know it's wicked shitty, chief, but I need you to let us take the lead on this one. If these people abducted the missus like we all suspect, that's obstructing a federal investigation, kidnapping, witness intimidation, and probably a dozen more. We gotta be the ones to move," came Patrick Flannery's voice through the car speakers.

"I am well aware of my impotence in this situation," Grayson forced through clenched teeth. "Being aware doesn't diminish my frustration."

"I get it. But we're trackin' them and lookin' for her. I agree with you a hundred percent she was with them, and then she wasn't, because they're sure acting scared pissless. Haven't strayed much more than a block or two from the courthouse, but it looks like they're bringin' in reinforcements."

"Pictures of anyone and everyone suspected as being part of this should be sent to Sandra. She is still working on correlations and connections made with and to Howell while in Belmarsh Prison. Facial recognition would likely link the dots quickly." He pointed ahead to direct Greg, who drove the car. "There. Half a block."

Greg nodded, already slowing as he looked for a parking space.

"If anything changes, I'll be calling. You have my word. I know this is wicked hard on ya but try to just…be normal."

"We are aware we may very well already be under surveillance, and if not already I'm quite sure the flat is already being watched. We are stopping for food. Like normal people," he added after a pause.

"We've got your back, Grayson."

"Your support is appreciated."

He ended the call as Greg turned into the small car park for the Chinese restaurant from where they had pre-ordered food to pick up on the way back to the South End. The distance from the courthouse to Kipling's apartment was perhaps slightly more than three kilometers, but due to the day and hour, the drive had been slow. It was another kilometer at least. As soon as they stepped out of the rental car, aromas of deliciously seasoned food and spices greeted them. Logically, Grayson knew he needed to eat but even the savory smells didn't entice him.

"I understand what it is to feel helpless. Useless," Greg said as they approached the restaurant door. "When I couldn't do a damn thing to help you or Kip last winter. I hated every damn minute of it."

"Do you regret adhering to the limitations Six put on you?"

"Every damn day." Greg pulled open the door, and an even more intense wave of aromas hit them. "I wonder sometimes what the hell they did to my head to convince me I had no choice. I'm still not convinced they *didn't* do something to my head."

"Yet another reason I'm not inclined to return so quickly to their servitude. I didn't join Six to become a puppet."

Greg paid for the takeaway while Grayson took the brown bag from the counter. "You're not going back," Greg said without the slightest inflection of a question.

"I have yet to decide."

"I'll bet you my autographed Tom Baker 1980 *Doctor Who Weekly* magazine you're not going back."

Grayson paused at the passenger door of the car, feigning shock before he opened his door. "That may be the incentive I need to return."

Greg laughed and walked around the front of the car and stopped short. "Ollie…"

Grayson halted his shift into the car at the sudden shift in Greg's tone, moving free of the car again. "What?"

Greg didn't answer but motioned Grayson to come around to his side. Perplexed, he put the food in the passenger seat and walked around the back, nearly stumbling back from the sudden punch of reality to his chest. On the ground with her back against the car, and her head down with arms folded on her raised knees…was his wife.

"Kipling…" he managed to force from his throat and dropped

to one knee beside her. He touched his fingertips to her shoulder. "Darling."

She startled and gasped, her head coming back so quickly it hit the car side panel, and Grayson couldn't breathe. Couldn't blink. She was stark and thin, easily a stone lighter than when she'd first come to England and even then he had worried for her health. She was pale, her eyes shadowed, the makeup she wore seeming severe and heavy, but unable to hide the overheated flush in her cheeks.

Kipling stared at him wide-eyed, pressed against the car, terror and confusion — *why fear?* — radiating from her.

"Kipling, darling…" He reached for her again.

Her gaze dropped to his mouth and she raised a hand, but he was unsure if she intended to reach for him or wanted him to stay away.

Grayson took his attention from her gaunt features to her ears for the tick he needed to confirm she wore no aids. He shifted to both knees, near her but not touching her. He brought his shaking left hand to his chest, forming a cup with his hand, adding the sign for K with his right…the name sign he had created for her. It meant she was his soul. She watched his hands, then sucked in a breath as if she'd forgotten to breathe.

"Grayson," she finally said, her voice rough and raw. Then her features twisted into one of anguish and tears shined in her eyes. She completed the action of reaching for him, touching his jaw with her trembling fingertips. "I want to go home," she cried.

He moved to her and wrapped her shaking, desperately frail body in his arms to hold her as she cried. With her cheek to his chest, Grayson raised his head and looked to his cousin, whose face mirrored his own confusion and turmoil.

She was here. She was alive.

But what had they done to her?

Chapter Twelve

Darkness had overtaken the hotel room an hour before, with the only illumination being the light Grayson had left on in the attached bath so Kipling wouldn't be in complete darkness when she woke. Grayson hadn't left the chair he'd brought to the side of the bed, hadn't taken his attention from her, afraid he might look away and she would be gone.

They were in Lexington, Massachusetts an hour away from the parking lot where a power far greater than anything he could fathom gave him the one thing he'd begged for — pleaded for — for weeks.

Kipling.

He had yet to know what had happened to her. He only knew that when he knew who had done it, who had hurt her, who had *touched* her, they would know his wrath.

Having no doubt she was still in danger, and until such a time as her safety could be assured and the degree of danger evaluated, he and Greg initiated several steps to get them here without being noticed.

Despite the fact neither he nor Greg were active officers for MI6, they were never without sufficient resources should a legend be required. Mr. and Mrs. Jason and Kim Williams arrived at the historical, restored Victorian hotel as late check-ins in a vehicle he had procured on short notice at a rental agency away from Logan Airport. If someone did try to find information via CCTV, they would go first to the easiest and most obvious businesses, not a non-chain, four-vehicle fleet agency. As of yet, they had no clear knowledge of the resources held by their antagonists and until they did, they worked under the assumption of sophistication.

Greg stayed in Boston, coordinating with Flannery to both obtain necessary items from the apartment and remain unseen. As flustered and uncoordinated as the women at the courthouse appeared, it didn't seem likely extensive electronic surveillance had been applied to the apartment.

Not that it would have gone unnoticed. Surveillance would have been leveraged.

Once Grayson had the new, unknown vehicle and their destination of Lexington determined, Kipling curled into herself in the backseat of the car and fell asleep. Grayson checked on her frequently, both in his back view mirror and glancing over his shoulder, if only to assure himself she was still there. The tension in her body, and the wide-eyed apprehension when she looked at him, burned in his stomach as acid.

Greg stayed in Boston for the night at another location away from the apartment and would rejoin them the next day. The Chrysler 300 Grayson had driven since arriving in Boston would remain near the apartment while Greg obtained a different vehicle. Tomorrow, they would together determine the next steps. While Grayson was willing to leave some elements of the investigation to his FBI counterparts, he would not leave his wife's safety in their hands.

Not again.

Never again.

Kipling slept through the night, never fully waking though several times she became restless, fighting the blankets. He heard his name more than once and desperately wanted to lie beside her and bundle her into his arms to chase away the nightmares. But her trepidation and hesitation toward him made him leery of attempting comfort without her being fully awake and aware, for fear waking in his arms might frighten her.

The thought of his wife fearing him crushed his soul.

Exhaustion overtook him sometime before dawn, and he woke with a start to a room dimly lit by the rising sun. His back protested the slouched position in his chair and his neck protested the strange angle. Grayson blinked and raised his head from the chair back to find Kipling sitting up in bed, her knees drawn to her chest beneath the blankets, watching him.

Grayson shifted and sat up to face her fully. *"How are you feeling?"* he signed, feeling clumsy and illiterate after just a couple of weeks without practice.

Her attention shifted only slightly from his face to his hands, then back to him. "I didn't realize I was so tired," she answered, her voice strained and hesitant.

"Can I get you anything?"

Why was manual language so easy before, and now he struggled to make simple conversation?

Because she still looked at him with fear.

Three sharp knocks at the door interrupted them before she answered. Grayson signed to let her know, and when Greg called "Ollie," through the door, he added it was Greg. She nodded but hugged her knees tighter to her chest. He groaned as he gained his feet, momentarily glad she was unable to hear him. Grayson scrubbed his face with his palms as he crossed the room, opening the door to his cousin. Greg carried a variety of bags from at least three retailers and pulled behind him a large, new suitcase with Grayson's computer satchel balanced on top of it hooked over the extended pull handle.

"If you've ever wondered whether you want to shop at any of those 'Open 24 Hours a Day' stores, I don't recommend it. There is definitely a different sort of folk out in the wee hours of the morning."

"Says he who was just there himself."

Greg chuckled and moved past him to place the bags on a small couch set against the wall opposite the foot of the bed. He looked to Kipling and raised a hand in greeting. Her smile was tense and unnatural. Turning his back to her again, he asked "How did the night go?"

"She slept, thankfully," he answered, ignoring the twang of guilt for turning his back on her. "I just woke, so I don't know how long she's been awake."

"So you haven't talked to her yet."

Grayson shook his head, just the slightest tick to hide the action. "Let us show her what you have and let her decide what she needs."

Greg nodded and scooped up the bags again with a rustle of thin, recycled plastic to set them at the foot of the bed at the corner furthest from her. "You translate for me, Ollie. My hands are full."

"Greg went shopping for us," Grayson explained. *"We thought it best not to try to retrieve our things from the apartment as it would be too obvious."*

Greg started by pulling clothing from the greater quantity of retail bags. "I would have been clueless without Esther," he said and Grayson relayed, taking solace in the small smile that touched her lips. "She walked me through everything."

Esther had done exceptionally well guiding Greg, despite being thousands of miles and several hours ahead of them. Greg had purchased basic clothing appropriate for the season for both Kipling and Grayson. Perhaps not either of their usual styles, but in truth taking a step away from their typical appearances was the best approach. He included everything from small clothes to comfortable shoes and sandals. He moved on then to another variety of bags, producing everything from soaps and body wash to hair products to necessary first aid items to better treat Kipling's blisters and general care.

"Thank you, Greg," she said in a soft voice.

"Of course," Greg said with a nod. He moved on to the final grocery bags. "I hear the restaurant downstairs is amazing, but I thought snacks would be in order. Got your favorites." From somewhere in the middle of the bundle of bags he produced a simple brown bag with pink and orange letters easily recognized by any New Englander. "A dozen Munchkins, half glazed chocolate cake, and half blueberry."

Her smile widened, more genuine. "How did you know?"

"I paid attention all those times Ollie went down around the corner from Baker Street for you. I didn't get a coffee because it would have been cold by the time I got here."

Her gaze shifted from Greg to Grayson when Greg mentioned Grayson's every few days trek to the Dunkin' around the corner at home. He smiled, hoping her inclination to seek him out was a positive shift. "I appreciate it."

"*Would you like to shower and change?*" Grayson asked.

She nodded and slipped from the bed, the dress she'd worn the day before now wrinkled. Didn't matter. Grayson intended to burn it. Kipling hissed and stumbled, and Grayson took a step toward her but she straightened, shaking her head.

"I almost forgot about the blisters."

Grayson waited until her attention came back to him. She was close enough and the light was sufficient he believed she would be able to see his lips sufficiently. "I will tend to them when you're done."

Kipling nodded. When she was within reach, she raised her hand as if she intended to touch his arm when she passed him, but she withdrew with her fingers curled and picked up several items from the bed before going into the attached bath. Grayson released a long breath when the door closed and the click of the lock engaging echoed like cannon fire through the room.

Greg put his hand on Grayson's shoulder, squeezing firmly. "Focus on the fact that this time yesterday we had no idea where she was and if she was safe."

Grayson forced his focus to move from the closed door to his cousin. "My logic reminds me frequently of that fact, but my emotional heart doesn't quite agree."

"We'll get there. Speaking of getting there—"

"Strange segue."

Greg smirked and turned back to the couch where he had

deposited most of the items he'd arrived with, and brought from the mound Grayson's computer satchel, taking from it a familiar large envelope. He held it out to Grayson, who walked to the desk to open it. He pushed the desk chair out of the way and sat while working open the clasp.

Inside was everything they needed to adopt one of Sandra Sookoo's skillfully mastered and created legends, and then some. Included were passports and government-issued IDs, both British and American, a variety of credit cards and bank cards likely already activated to avoid any appearance of sudden existence and a substantial assortment of both American bills and British notes. Hidden in his wallet, no matter where they were, he carried sufficient alternative identification to protect both himself and Kipling, which they utilized the day before to rent the car and check into the hotel room. While in Lexington, they would be Jason and Kim Williams but if they needed to take further action, they would take on another identity.

He sincerely hoped it wasn't required and a resolution would come quickly; however, he was far too familiar with such situations and scenarios to truly believe anything would be resolved soon.

"Did you speak to them?" he asked, looking up from the documents to watch Greg's expression. It would tell him more than anything else.

Greg pressed his lips together and nodded. "I did. I asked to meet them away from the house."

"And…"

"Relieved to know Kipling has been found, though I suppose that's not the right word for it. They want to talk to her."

"Understandable."

"I told them we don't think the danger has passed but will let that happen as soon as you think we can. I also said for now they need to not let on to anyone they know. Not anyone, and not until we know the players. They're…they're upset. And angry."

Grayson drew in a long breath through his nose, letting it out as slowly to fight the knot in his gut. "I am fully aware I was never, at any point, the ideal son-in-law but this may very well destroy my hopes of a relationship with them."

"Bring them back their daughter, and then worry about it."

"The fact I must *bring her back* at all is the crux of the problem."

"Oh," Greg said with sudden enthusiasm and pulled a small, black case from his pocket to set on the desk. "I don't know if we should qualify these as serendipity, kismet, predestination, or just one hell of a fluke."

Greg had said he had the case when he arrived in Boston, but at the time Grayson's thoughts and concerns were elsewhere. *Serendipity, indeed.*

Grayson picked up the case and opened it, revealing the brand new, advanced technology hearing aids Mac had overseen the creation of in the weeks following the events in London. Mac had manipulated her original aids to make them communication devices to help and give support to Kipling in her riddle games with Howell. While he'd removed the adaptations, Kipling had occasionally had issues with them. They had been the same devices she wore when they jumped into a frozen Boston Harbor. In truth, whatever fate may have come to her aids they were very near the end of their functionality either way. Perhaps that was the answer; the aids had malfunctioned permanently and forced her to go without their assistance.

These units were smaller than her previous aids and carefully molded to fit her ears. Mac had assured the sound quality and functionality would be greatly improved. He had consulted with every resource available. In truth, Kipling had been excited about the upgrade.

"Thank you for bringing them," Grayson said, closing the case again.

"What's the next step?"

He shook his head and looked to his cousin. "In all truth, I have absolutely no idea. Today, my focus is her care beginning as soon as possible with a substantial breakfast."

"She looks like she's barely eaten since——" Greg stuttered off the rest of the sentence, but it didn't require completion.

"Agreed. I intend to learn what I can."

"Keep me informed." Greg headed to the door. "Tell Kip we're here for her. All of us."

"I shall. Thank you."

Greg closed the door behind him, leaving Grayson in his place with only the sound of the shower in the bath — beyond a locked door — to fill the silence.

Chapter Thirteen

Kipling stood in the hotel suite bathroom, fragrant moisture hanging in the air and steam fogging the large, ornately framed mirror over the double vanity, staring at herself in the glass. The plush bath sheet wrapped around her nearly twice. The reflection was a stranger with overly prominent clavicles, bony shoulders, thin arms, and a gaunt neck. She didn't know how long it had been since she saw herself but knew the woman she saw wasn't right.

Nothing was right.

She was divided; her thoughts and actions were at war with each other.

Grayson's study of her made her skin warm, and simultaneously her blood run cold. Her nerves sparked painfully. She wanted to reach for him and withdraw in the same breath. The same heartbeat.

How was that possible?

Kip, you're the one who told me he abuses you. You told me how cruel he became on your honeymoon. You admitted some of the bruises were from him, not whatever you told everyone happened in London.

Kipling closed her eyes and pressed her lips together, taking in deep breaths through her nose. When she closed her eyes and tried to find the events she was reminded of, other memories came to her, clear and vivid and far from frightening.

Grayson moved from the counter, hands cupping her face in the same second his mouth -- open and warm -- covered hers, stealing her breath.

For a moment, Kipling was so lost in the devouring intensity she couldn't move, but when he shifted the angle of the kiss and his tongue caressed hers, Kipling moaned a purr and wrapped her arms around him. Her hips hit the edge of the counter, and without breaking the kiss, Grayson scooped her up and set her on the counter edge, a firm pull of her hips bringing her hard against him.

Panting for breath, and aching for him, Kipling closed her eyes when he paused the kiss, his forehead pressed to hers, their breath mingling in hard bursts between them.

"Don't you dare ask me if I'm pleased," he said and kissed her again.

Kipling opened her eyes, her breath short and rapid. She covered her face with her hands, pushing hard against the twisting panic in her chest. When she convinced herself she again had control, Kipling lowered her hands and picked up the new hair-brush Greg had brought her along with all the other personal care items. She brushed her hair, finished drying off, and pulled over her head the simple sundress Greg had also brought for her. It was sleeveless and loose, with a slight elastic cinching at the waist. It hung on her.

He always insulted your weight. You said he called you chubby after the first time you had sex. Kip, how can you not remember this?

She picked up the brush again, dragging it through her hair with angry, frustrated strokes until her scalp tingled.

She combed her fingers through his short hair, the regrowing waves curling around her fingers, trying to catch her breath as Grayson kissed his way up her body from navel to breast, his tongue and lips hot against her exposed skin. His hand caressed her side to her hip and down her thigh until her heartbeat caught in her throat.

Grayson rose over her, his mouth in the curve of her throat. "I crave your mouth, your voice, your hair," he said against her skin. She was seconds from flying apart, fighting to breathe, pressing closer to him. "Bread does not nourish me, dawn disrupts me, all day I hunt for the liquid measure of your step."

"Grayson," she gasped and his hand left her, replaced by his body, pressed to her, in her, and she cried out.

Kipling slammed the brush down on the counter with such force it bounced back and out of her hand, landing on the floor. In frustration, she bent to retrieve it by one of the feet of the clawfoot tub that had reminded her of Baker Street the moment she stepped into the bathroom. An ache, deep and to her soul, set in around her heart.

She wanted to go home.

Not her apartment. Not even her parents' home in Chelsea.

She wanted to go *home.*

With nothing left for her to do but stand in the middle of the bathroom or open the door to the bedroom beyond, Kipling took a deep breath and released it as she turned the lock and opened the door.

Grayson was right outside the door, his brow drawn into deep furrows. *"I heard a noise,"* he signed. *"I feared you might have fallen."*

Kipling looked over her shoulder, momentarily confused. "I dropped my hairbrush," she explained, heat crawling up her throat to her cheeks. She turned back and looked quickly around the large hotel room. She'd barely noted much of it the night before, exhaustion being so overwhelming she barely made it to bed. Other than Grayson, the room was empty.

"He's gone back to Boston. We thought it best someone be there to watch the apartment should anything happen."

Kipling nodded, battling the war within herself. When had she become so timid around Grayson? She'd never — *You have to be careful about everything you say or he gets angry.* — No!

She closed her eyes for two seconds and opened them again to find him studying her, a deep line across his brow between his eyes. Then he stood and motioned toward the now-empty couch, the bags of items emptied and likely put away.

"Sit and I will tend to those blisters."

"I think they're okay…"

He laid his palm against his chest. *"Please."*

Kipling nodded and went to the couch, sitting. He went to the antique roll-top desk where basic first aid items were lined up, scooping them up before turning back to her. She expected him to sit on the couch, but instead, he sat on the floor at her feet, legs crossed. Grayson looked up at her and tapped beside his mouth, and she nodded.

"I have something else for you. Mac sent them with Greg," she read on his lips and he held out to her a small case.

Kipling took it and opened it, revealing two small devices inside. The evolution of her hearing aids had begun as large, bulky processors that hooked around her ears before being inserted into the ear canal. She had accepted the quality of sound since it was all she'd known. With each new, upgraded aid she obtained the devices became smaller and the sound quality improved. She knew she would never have the same hearing experience as someone with normal hearing but had appreciated each change. These were, by far the smallest she'd ever tried, partially because her audiologists said something so small wouldn't be as effective for her situation.

But none of them had Angus "Mac" Hennessey.

She smiled and picked up the right-side bud, trying to determine how to turn them on or load a battery. Grayson leaned forward and took it from her fingers, indicating a tiny slide switch. She nodded, turned it on, and slipped it into her ear. The first thing she noticed was how they felt, or really didn't feel, in her ear canal. Her aids had always been intrusive, but a necessary discomfort. This one, she barely felt at all. She heard three short chimes, and then sound clicked back into her silent reality.

It wasn't overwhelming. The room was quiet except for a low hum of the air conditioning vents along the ceiling and the ventilation fan in the bathroom she must have left on. She turned on the other and placed it as well, completing the loop.

"How do they feel?"

She jumped and gasped and looked at Grayson. *His voice!* She stared wide-eyed, both surprised by the sound and excited to hear him again. Grayson canted his head, watching her.

"Are they working?"

Kipling nodded. "They're…different."

"Different good or different bad?" The corner of his mouth ticked into the slightest hint of a grin.

"Just…different. You sound…different."

"First, let me tell you the case itself is the power source to recharge the aids, a contact charge, and Mac said he anticipates each charge to be good for over one hundred usage hours. Second," he said, curling his large hand around the back of her calf to bring her foot into his lap with a gentle touch. "Tell me how I sound different."

He met her eyes for a moment before focusing on the task of examining the raw spots on her feet from her trek through Boston in new heels. Many of the blisters had broken by the time she had hobbled her way into the hotel room the night before, so he treated them with an antibiotic cream and cushioning bandages.

"Not so different I wouldn't know your voice," she explained, and his glance shifted to her again. "But richer, deeper. Like… before it was two-dimensional and now it's three."

His smile was small but warm. "And your own voice?"

She shook her head. "Not very different. Still loud to me."

"I'm thankful Greg brought them with him since you are without your previous aids." He applied the last bandage needed for that foot and looked up at her. "Where are they?"

Kipling squinted and blinked, trying to bring the previous day into focus. Most everything was muffled. Blurry. "I crushed them not far from the courthouse."

He eased her foot from his lap with the same gentle touch and switched to the other foot. "Can you tell me why you did that?"

She made a sound similar to a chuckle being choked, deep in her throat. "No, I don't think I can. I just…knew I had to."

He looked away, applying ointment to the tip of a finger before he smoothed it over an angry spot on her heel. "Are the new ones comfortable?"

Kipling hummed and nodded.

"I'm pleased to hear that. Mac will be happy as well. When able, I will let him know."

"Is Mac here, too?" she asked. She'd been surprised to see Greg, his presence creating more questions for her. "Or anyone?"

Why did Greg come? How long—

"No, the rest of my team remained in England. They could be of more help there having access to all resources. Anything to find you." He looked up at her. "In the end, fate seemed our strongest ally." Grayson drew in a long breath through his nose, finishing the treatment of her second foot. "I thought it best to request our breakfast be brought to the room, partially because I'd rather not force you into shoes quite yet and partially because I think it's best we not be too obvious about our presence. It should arrive soon."

"You can't trust him, Kip. You told me that. I'm only repeating back to you what you told me."

She swallowed and fought the sudden, anxious charge beneath her skin demanding she withdraw from his touch. Back and forth. Yank left, yank right. Her mind and her body were in this endless tug of war with each other. How could that be true? "Thank you."

Grayson raised his chin and looked directly at her, holding her gaze long enough her pulse fluttered. "Of course, my darling."

Three knocks at the door made her jump again. Grayson leaned forward and kissed her knee — a warm bubbling of her blood skimmed beneath her skin at the kiss — before he rose with ease to his feet as a woman's voice called, "I have your breakfast, Mr. and Mrs. Williams," through the door.

"Grayson," she said before he stepped away from the couch, and he stopped to look down at her. "How long was I…" She couldn't finish the question.

He eased back his stride to bring him back to her, never looking away, and raised his hand to her jaw. She clenched her jaw, a brutal and intense need to withdraw shooting through her, but she didn't move. Grayson ran his thumb along her cheekbone, the back of his curled fingers against her skin. She held her breath as he worked his jaw before drawing in a slow, metered breath.

"Nearly three weeks," he answered finally. "Three of the absolute longest and worst weeks of my existence."

The knock came again, and Kipling swayed when he took away

his touch to answer the door. He thanked the woman pushing a cart with covered dishes and carafes of juice and coffee. Kipling scowled when he spoke, turning her head to face the door, and tried to school her expression. She had heard Grayson use different accents at different times for different reasons, and by far his American voice was already her least favorite.

Chapter Fourteen

He was doing his very best not to be obvious, but Kipling felt every glance — no matter how brief — he shifted to her while she poked at the food on her plate. It was delicious, and he had ordered several options so she had a choice, but her stomach wanted to fully revolt every time she forced down a bite.

She was hungry and repelled at the thought of eating at the same time. Everything felt that way, a clashing incompatibility between everything she thought and felt and remembered. Nothing made sense. Nothing lined up.

Anger twisted with what she could only describe as sorrow. She wanted to fight, but she didn't know what or who.

"I'm sorry," she whispered, everything inside her tensing. "It's all so good and I want to eat it. I—"

Grayson slid his hand across the small table where he'd laid out their breakfast and curled his fingers over hers. Kipling jerked, and in the same second he lifted his hand and her throat threatened to close. A ragged shudder clenched her spine and she closed her eyes.

"I'm sorry," she whispered, her voice lost in the bitter panic.

"Kipling." His voice was so low and rough, she swore she felt it shimmer gently over her rather than heard it. "Darling…please. Open your eyes and look at me."

She took in a deep breath, clenching her trembling fingers in her lap, and blew it out slowly through pursed lips. When she opened her eyes, tears blurred her vision and rolled down her cheeks, but she couldn't raise her hands from her lap to wipe them away. Blinking to clear her vision, she raised her chin to look across the breakfast spread at her husband.

The pain in his eyes couldn't be forced or fake. She knew it instinctively. And she knew, instinctively, she had caused it. He withdrew his hand from the tabletop to press his palms together, his index fingers against his lips as if in prayer. He leaned back, lowering his hands, eliminating the possibility of casual contact between them.

Her heart clenched and another painful shudder assaulted her. Kipling sucked in each breath, trying to will back the choking emotion. She couldn't take a deep breath. Kipling closed her eyes and lowered her head again, fighting for control.

You're so weak, Kip. You were never like this. Did he do this to you? Geez, Kip. You told me he was controlling, but he's destroying you! I don't want to imagine how bad it could have gotten if we hadn't rescued you.

She heard the drag of chair legs across the low pile carpet and held her breath. Kipling swayed in her chair, feeling suddenly lightheaded. Without opening her eyes, she sensed Grayson beside her and swallowed hard.

"Kipling."

His voice startled her because it wasn't above her, but below her, and she fluttered open her eyes. Grayson knelt on one knee on the floor beside her, one hand on the table edge and the other on his raised knee.

"As much as I wish I had the power and the ability to never speak of what happened and somehow heal what has been done, I'm sorry, but…I *need* you to tell me what happened to you. *Who* is responsible." He took in a quick breath through his nose that sounded more like a sniffle, and his hand on the table curled into a loose fist. "Darling, I need to know what they have done to make you fear me."

She couldn't catch her breath, couldn't steady it, and her heart wanted to pound free of her chest.

"Take a deep breath," he said. "Count to four. Release it. Count to four."

"Take a deep breath," he said, his eloquent accent a challenge -- British, but city or region she couldn't say other than it was a common accent -- until she focused on his lips for a few words. She'd noted the accent before, but the hall had been quiet and the only interference the damn clicking in her ears. His voice was a deep baritone, almost disproportionate to his tall, lean frame. Reading the words on his lips was different than anyone she'd encountered; he spoke with his lower lip, his defined upper lip not moving much to enunciate the words. "Count to four. Release it. Count to four," he instructed, stepping in front of her but back enough she didn't need to crane her neck to see him. "It will help with the adrenaline release."

His gaze held her captive, and he mimicked the action for her. Taking a breath, counting, releasing it, counting. After a few tries, her heartbeat slowed and her vision cleared. Without thought to reach out, her fingers hovered near his unshaven jaw. "Those are the first words you ever said to me. Well, not the *first*, but close."

Grayson smiled, but it was sad, and covered the back of her hand with his to draw it to him, kissing her palm. But he didn't hold it, releasing it right away, and she felt the loss. *Back and forth. Left and right. Tug and pull. Forward and back. Drowning and flying. Breathing and suffocating. Living and Dying.*

"Had I but known you would become my reason to breathe, I would have been more witty." Grayson studied her, but the shame or anxiety she expected didn't come. "Let us begin with a more precise question. I know what I can see; you have lost far too much weight, especially for the period of time you were away from me, and you were at the brink of exhaustion when you found us. I can give you food and allow you to rest, but I need to know if you have been harmed in *any way* that demands a physician immediately."

His words were heavy, pulling at her like a rope wrapped around her shoulders. A velvet rope drawing her to him. "I-I don't think so."

"I am going to request the help of Agent Flannery to at the minimum assist with some basic laboratory results. We may be dealing with deficiencies, but I need to know if there is more. Will you allow that?"

Warring thoughts clashed in her mind with such chaos she couldn't separate them, couldn't make them make sense.

"You were unaware of how long you have been missing—"

"Missing?"

He stopped, the corners of his eyes pinching. "Yes, missing. Kipling, I have had no idea where you've been, who forced you to go, and what has happened to you. It's why Greg is here. He came from London with nearly as much fear in his heart as myself. We have been doing all we can with Agent Flannery to find you. To bring you home."

Home. She wanted so much to go home.

Butter yellow walls with bright white trim and sheer curtains caught in a breeze, fluttering over an antique metal bed with rumpled blankets still askew from sleep.

She scowled and turned away from him, staring at the blueberry pancakes on her plate without really seeing them. She had been asleep, her body heavy but peaceful. Then someone shook her awake. She had barely opened her eyes when her hearing aids were shoved into her hands. Her eyes hadn't even adjusted to the dim light in the room before she set them in her ears and a frantic voice synced with the hands shaking her.

"Kip, wake up. Wake up! We have to hurry before he comes back. Come on. This is your chance to get away. Kip, wake up!"

"She woke me up," she recounted, a slow ache forming behind her eyes as she tried to piece together the broken movie in her head. "You were gone, and she said we had to hurry. Had to go. It was my only chance to get away." Kipling looked at him again. "To get away from you."

A muscle tensed along his sharp jaw, his expression dark.

"Who?" he asked. "Who woke you? Who took you from the apartment?"

Kipling blinked several times, the headache blooming angry until her eyes hurt. "M-Mina."

Grayson's eyes widened and he shifted back, practically sitting on his own ankle. "Mina…Russo? Your friend Mina Russo?"

Kipling nodded.

"Were you at Mina's home this whole time?"

She shook her head. "I don't know where we were. I was-we were hiding…until…"

The thoughts — and words connected to them — grew foggy, like her breath on a January day in Boston. Kipling groaned and pushed her fingertips to the center of her forehead.

"Until when, Kipling?"

"Until the trial was over. Until you gave up trying to find me. Until you went back to London. Without me."

"I would never go without you."

She blinked, feeling suddenly so tired she didn't know if she could sit at the table any longer. "I know," she managed to say. "It's why I ran…" Her head was heavy, and her tongue didn't want to work. "I wanted to go home."

Kipling couldn't keep her eyes open any longer. Everything was heavy. So heavy. Her chair moved, and then she was floating, carried in her husband's arms.

Husband. Husband. Remember your husband.

He laid her on the unmade bed and Kipling let herself sink into the soft mattress and blankets like clouds. Warm lips pressed to her forehead and Kipling hummed.

"Rest, my darling," Grayson's voice floated over her. "We will figure all this out together. I promise on my life."

She barely felt the touch at her ears, but then the world fell silent.

Chapter Fifteen

"Mina?"

"That is the one definitive thing she has said since she woke. Mina — though I believe Mina was not alone based on the evidence I noted at the time I found Kipling gone — woke her after I left the flat on the fool's errand to meet Patrick Flannery, which now we know to have been a ploy to separate us."

"But Mina?" Greg repeated.

"The logic escapes me as well. By what little Kipling was able to express, Mina somehow convinced her it was necessary to escape *me* and hide until such a time as I would return to London. Without her."

"Ollie, I spent enough time with Mina to know she held a pretty hefty grudge against you. She didn't trust you or the relationship, and she didn't hide it. But this…this is another level."

"You never saw anything in her behavior to imply this level of what I can only define at this moment to be jealousy."

"None. She didn't trust you, bloody well didn't like you, but I believe it was from a place of love for Kip. So how the hell is Doctor

Mina Russo — a lifelong resident of Massachusetts and friend to Kipling — connected to Langdon Howell?"

"I've not nearly enough clay from which to form those bricks."

Greg let free a diatribe of language that would have gotten his mouth washed with soap had Aunt Hazel heard him and ended on a deep sigh. "Could Mina be an attempted distraction away from Howell? Cast doubt he's involved?"

"If so, like many of his ventures, he failed. While it would seem our movement here to Lexington went undetected, I would prefer to find another place for her recovery. I need a favor—"

"Ollie, come on. Don't say it like you need to ask."

Grayson paused to acknowledge his cousin. "I need to coordinate with Patrick Flannery to complete a spectrum of laboratory tests. I can draw the necessary blood if you can bring me the supplies."

"What are you worried about? Anything in particular?"

"A starting point to guide her back to health. Her weight loss in such a relatively short period of time and level of exhaustion concerns me, but I noted injection marks. She has been jabbed and frequently. I need to know with what, and soon, before whatever may remain is no longer detectable."

"I'll contact Patrick and head back your way as soon as possible. Do you plan on reaching out to Sandi?"

"Yes." Grayson glanced toward the bed where Kipling slept once again. "I'm curious if Sandra has made any further connections and if Lynne has made any progress. I want to speak to Mac as well. The new aids are far superior, by her word, to those she had previously."

"Oh, you need to hear what Sandi found out. I mean, I can tell you what she told me, Ollie, but I think you need to see it for yourself."

"That sounds ominous at best."

"Not so much ominous as confirming."

"I will contact her immediately."

He ended the call with his cousin and accessed Sandra Sookoo's information. Thanks once again to the brilliance that was Mac

Hennessey, Grayson's mobile was not only in a constant scramble cycle and encryption coded, but he had initiated a program Mac created to effectively change his electronic signature and any other trackable data. After having had his phone confiscated by Howell in London, they had taken additional steps to secure information.

"Is Kip okay?" were the first words he heard when the line opened. "Greg gave me nothing except you have her back. Is she okay?"

"Perhaps I would answer if you allowed me…"

Sandra cleared her throat. "Sorry, Boss."

"Kipling is not anything I would define as 'okay,' but she is safe again and I intend to do everything in my power to assure her well-being."

"Greg said she found you, and she looked terrible."

"I don't know what power in the universe saw fit to put us where we needed to be, nor will I ever question it. She has been through an ordeal I have yet to fully understand. Greg said you had something to share with me."

"That's putting it in very simple terms. Yesterday, Langdon Howell had an absolute wobbler in his cell. Before yesterday, he was the model prisoner. Yesterday he was *roarin'*!"

"What time was this?"

"About one o'clock Eastern Standard Time…"

Grayson sank onto the couch and took his laptop from the satchel Greg had delivered that morning. Just like his phone, his laptop was untraceable and fully encrypted at a level above standard for the Intelligence Community. Thanks again to Mac Hennessey.

"Send it to me."

"Already did, Boss. Just waiting for you to take a look."

True to her word, Sandra had uploaded a four-minute CCTV video to their shared server. After the suspicion of Howell somehow having communication with associates outside Belmarsh, he was moved to a less posh, more visible cell with far more observation, far fewer privileges, and far less privacy. Belmarsh was the highest security prison in London, and even then it didn't feel like enough. Rather than a steel door and solid walls, Langdon Howell was now in a cell with bars, a single bunk, and the only illusion of privacy was the half wall on the landing side of the toilet.

Knowing the man as much as he did, Grayson knew the humiliation of the change in accommodations alone would be extensive. He watched while Sandra remained on the line, now on speaker. Grayson slid the volume control, not wanting to miss even the slightest bit of information.

He made note of the date and time stamp of the recording. It was, indeed, the previous date and the time showed 18:10.

Howell sat on the narrow bunk extending as a slab from the wall, staring across the cell to the blank wall on the other side, but the camera angle faced him so Grayson could watch his expression. About twenty seconds into the recording, he turned his head slightly to a spot beyond the range of the camera. Seconds later, he stood abruptly with hands clenched at his side but didn't move from the side of the cot. Grayson paused the image long enough to magnify the man's face, and his eyes were wide, his jaw clenched. He resumed play.

Another few seconds passed and the man didn't move.

Then he flew into a frenzy of rage.

The cell had little that could be qualified as personal, but in minutes every bit of it was thrown across the room. He tore the blanket from the bed and threw it. Books slammed against the wall to land, spine bent, on the floor. With little in the cell, he had little to act out his anger upon. He threw back his head, and Grayson didn't need sound to know he screamed. Moments later, the cell door opened and three uniformed guards entered to subdue him and restrain him before removing him from the cell. The recording ended shortly after he was removed.

"Who—"

"I'm working on it, Boss," Sandra said. "CCTV for the whole wing. I should have it by end of day tomorrow. They apparently don't have audio recording in most common areas, but I'm hoping to come up lucky with something."

"Time is not on our side. I hold no confidence Kipling is out of danger despite being removed from Boston."

"I'll press them. I'll get Lynne to help, too."

"Thank you. I have a new connection to be correlated from here in Boston. Doctor Mina Russo. I do not have a full name or other identifying information, but if necessary I can ask Kipling."

"The fact she's a doctor should narrow the search, but I'll let you know if I need more." Sandra paused before asking, "Wait, as in Kip's lifelong-but-recently-not-best-friend who refused to come to the wedding?"

"The same."

"Wow. Is this confirmed?"

"Kipling told me herself she has been in the company of Doctor Russo for the last three weeks. And Doctor Russo was present at her abduction."

"That must be tearing Kip apart."

Grayson let out a long breath, saying "I fear more has been done to Kipling than simply keeping her away from me. Her perspective is not skewed as much as conflicted."

"Bloody hell."

Chapter Sixteen

"Name's Kelly McCann. I'm sendin' her photo so you can be sure she's our girl. Gonna take everything right there to Lahey and we've got a rush going on it. Should be back to you wicked quick. If anything special is needed for the missus, it'll come out of Lahey, too. Top-notch care."

"I appreciate your assistance more than I can say," Grayson said to Agent Flannery as he wrote the information on the small notepad provided by the hotel.

"Nah, it's all good, chief. Whatever you need, I got your back. I'm just stoked she's back with ya."

"As am I."

The sound of movement from the bed drew Grayson's attention, and he looked over his shoulder to assure Kipling wasn't in distress. She sat up, facing the window away from him, and looked around with an expression of confusion.

"I must go. Thank you again."

Grayson ended the call with a tap on the screen and rose from the table to approach the bed. When he reached the foot of the bed nearest her and stepped into her peripheral line of sight, she startled and gasped and stared at him with wide eyes. For a split moment —

the briefest of fleeting moments — her lips curled into a quick smile that just as quickly disappeared when her expression pinched and she looked away.

He pushed his hands into his pockets as much to assure her he wouldn't touch her unnecessarily as it was to keep himself from instinctively touching her. A year before he would have had no difficulty refraining from physical contact.

But Kipling had changed him.

And now unintentionally tortured him.

Grayson moved into the space between her and the window and crouched beside the bed. He waited until she looked at him again before offering what he hoped was a reassuring smile. "She wrote love with her smile and magic with her eyes," he said. "It's good to see you smile, my darling, even if for a moment.

Kipling flinched, her expression twisting in visible pain.

Which only strengthened his resolve for answers.

"Agent Flannery has sent a nurse affiliated with the Bureau and working from a local hospital. She will be here within the hour. Due to the urgency of the situation, they likely will be able to advise us on the results later today. Tomorrow morning at the latest."

Kipling nodded and shifted beneath the down-filled duvet to put her back to the headboard. He stayed beside the bed, crouched to be slightly below her line of sight.

"What time is it?" she asked.

He flipped his wrist to look at his watch and back to her. "Quarter to three."

Kipling groaned and drew up her knees, resting her folded arms on them on top of the blanket so she could rest her head and see him. "I slept most of the day."

"If rest is what you need, rest is what you'll have. Whatever is in my power to give you."

Her gaze shifted to his mouth, as it always did when he spoke, but her focus lingered a few seconds more before she looked him in the eyes. "What do you think is wrong with me? Will they be able to figure out what's wrong with me? I feel wrong."

Grayson shook his head before she could finish and set a hand on the mattress, close to her but not touching her. "You have been harmed, and we need to know to what extent. That isn't something wrong with you, darling." Grayson tapped his cheek in front of his right ear. "I fear my manual language skills are yet still inadequate for a detailed conversation, and I don't want to exhaust you further by asking you to read my lips."

Grayson stood from his crouch, picked up the small case on the bedside table, and sat on the edge of the bed while opening it for her.

She raised her head from her arms and reached for the case, her hand visibly trembling. Grayson cupped his free hand beneath hers to steady it and placed the open case in her palm. Kipling managed to take the small devices from the case despite her unsteady hands, turn them on, and slide each into her ear canal. She put the case on the bed beside her with unnecessary caution before she raised her chin and made eye contact with Grayson. The hesitation, the uncertainty, the fear in her eyes pained his soul but he did his best to school his expression so as to not add to whatever emotions battled in her.

"Kipling," he said, keeping his voice calm and level. "I need you to tell me about what happened. I wish there were another way, but you are the only person who can tell me. We are working to assemble a puzzle and need as many pieces as possible."

She nodded, pushing her hair back from her pale cheeks. "I'll try."

"Mina is the one who woke you in the apartment."

She nodded and focused on him.

"Who was with her? I suspect at least one other, if not more."

Kipling blinked and scowled. "It was dark in the apartment. I couldn't see and couldn't hear until she pulled me from the bed and handed my aids to me."

She rested an elbow on her raised knee and rubbed her forehead between her eyes. Were it not for the fact the nurse would be there soon, he would have retrieved some basic analgesics for her headache but didn't want to potentially affect laboratory results.

"I can't remember getting dressed or getting from the apartment to a car, but then I was in the backseat with Mina and another woman." She blinked several times, her eyes shifting in tiny degrees implying she worked through some of the memories. "Patty. That was Patty. I told you about her."

Grayson nodded. "I remember. You were upset Mina had shared details about us, my profession specifically, with her especially considering we knew nothing about her. Did they say her last name at any time?"

Kipling shook her head, her eyes pinching at the corners. "I don't know. I can't remember right now."

"If you should recall, tell me. Who else was in the car?"

"Only the driver. A man, and I don't remember seeing him again after that. He smelled of menthol cigarettes and cheap cologne."

Grayson allowed a small smile. She had made note of the same specifics he had when he found the flat empty.

"How long were you in the car before reaching a destination?"

Kipling shook her head again. "I don't know. I think I kept falling asleep."

The only conceivable way he could imagine Kipling would have left the apartment without a fight would be if she were pharmaceutically incapacitated. While he'd entertained the idea Kipling being knocked down at the airport had been intentional, with the level of devices coming clear it seemed that had been the first step in orchestrating her abduction.

"What about yesterday? Do you know how long it took to reach the courthouse? Or where you came from?"

She blanched and shuddered, and Grayson fought the intense urge once again to touch her. He wanted so desperately to touch her and assure her of her safety, but every few moments he was reminded with hard impact that he himself caused her fear.

"They covered my eyes before we left the house," she said in a small voice, her blank stare unfocused across the room. "I was in a room in the cellar with a tiny bathroom. I'm not sure if I was ever anywhere else in the house. I never saw anything outside the little window I had except the backyard. There were tall fences and I only saw treetops and some other house rooflines beyond. I sometimes heard things like sirens or loud cars or music. I couldn't go outside."

"Kipling."

She didn't acknowledge he spoke. He leaned closer and said her name again. "Kipling."

She startled and looked at him, her eyes wide, and color replaced the sallow tint of her cheeks. Tears shined bright before sliding down her cheeks. Kipling didn't blink and another shudder went through her body.

"I told her I wanted to go home," she said barely above a whisper.

Grayson's heart broke more than he ever thought it would and he bowed his head, closing his eyes for a moment to somehow pull in all the raw anguish.

"Can we go home?"

He swallowed, the grip of heartache so thick he could barely breathe and he raised his head to meet his wife's eyes. "I swear to you, my darling, I will take you home as soon as I possibly can. I need to know first you will be safe, and I need to know the intended result from all of these schemes, and then I will take you home. I promise, my love. I promise."

She pressed her lips together and more tears trailed her cheeks. Hoping, praying he wouldn't regret it and wouldn't frighten her, Grayson raised his hand and smoothed his thumb across her slick skin.

"To Baker Street," she whispered.

"To Baker Street."

"What would you like for dinner?" Grayson asked, coming back to the couch after seeing the Bureau's nurse out of the room.

Kipling studied the folded bit of gauze Nurse Kelly had applied inside her left elbow after drawing several vials of blood. Her arm had looked foreign as the nurse had wrapped the rubber tourniquet and swabbed the area with alcohol. The inside of her forearm showed a row of marks in various stages of healing, including a spot on her opposite arm that looked fresh.

She stared, trying to dig through the fog of the last few weeks to remember when the marks would have happened. How could she not remember? Were they injections or blood draws like today?

Why couldn't she remember?

"Kipling…"

She took in a sharp breath, fighting to focus. Grayson was crouched beside the couch, elbows resting on his thighs, watching her with deep concern lines across his brow.

"I'm sorry. What did you ask me?"

"I asked what you would like for dinner, but perhaps I should ask first if you would like to go to the dining room to eat or would you prefer to eat here in the room."

"In the room," she answered quickly, the idea of going to the dining room sending a rush of cold panic over her skin.

"Room service then," he said, not missing a beat.

He picked up a folded paper from the floor, opening it and she noted the name of the restaurant on the front. The name of the hotel and restaurant felt familiar. She'd heard of it, but living in Chelsea or South Boston she never had a need to stay in Lexington. What she did remember was the fact it was a historical location.

Why could she remember that, but not what happened to her for three weeks without being drowned in smothering panic and fear?

"Where are we on the hungry spectrum? Famished or just a bit peckish?"

She let a smile tug at her lips. It felt good, familiar, and yet foreign at the same time. "Definitely closer to famished, but every time I think of eating I feel sick."

"Hmmm. Then perhaps we avoid the braised pork shank."

Kipling groaned. Grayson winked.

"How does a mushroom risotto sound? Their menu isn't exactly simple, but that may be the best option."

Her stomach rumbled in agreement. "It does sound good."

He stood from his crouch in a fluid, easy motion she almost

envied. Deep body aches had settled in her joints through the day, adding to the tenderness of the blisters on her feet. She couldn't remember the last time she felt good.

"I jumped on. Riley ran. Riley jumped the fence. I didn't quite make it. The fence broke. And so did my leg. The spot is where they had to perform surgery to return my femur to its proper place."

Kipling hissed. "How old were you?"

"Eleven. My point is, darling, that not every mark was a brush with death."

She thought about telling him she knew, but if she'd known he wouldn't have told her. She thought about providing some argument but had none. Instead, Kipling tossed the blankets out of her way and slid over him, kissing him before either said anything else.

"I would like dinner brought to our room, thank you," Grayson said to whoever had answered his call for service. "Your mushroom risotto, two dinners. Yes, thank you. Yes, the ginger molasses cake would be great."

Kipling wrinkled her nose, trying to ignore the way his American accent raked over her nerves. She felt like she watched a badly dubbed foreign film trying to reconcile his mismatched voice to the man she knew.

You don't know him, Kip. He's been lying to you — to everyone — since day one. You can't trust anything he says. You're the one who told me that. You're the one who begged me for help. What has he done to you to make you forget?

Chapter Seventeen

"Her B12, vitamin D, and iron levels are very low which would account for the exhaustion you described and apparent weakness," Doctor Nulton from the nearby Lahey Hospital relayed to Grayson. "Based on the limited information provided to us by the Bureau, may I assume Mrs. Williams has been under extreme stress in recent history?"

Grayson glanced toward the bedroom where Kipling sat on the bed against the headboard. The television was on, but her eyes were closed. She had eaten more than half the risotto at dinner and promised to try the cake he'd ordered after it had settled. Logically, he knew it had been not thirty-six hours since she escaped her captors, but his soul felt she'd been in this condition for days. Perhaps she had been, but he'd only stood witness a short time in comparison.

He saw the struggle in her eyes and expression. In calm or in the first moments she looked at him, he recognized the spark in his wife's eyes, and just as quickly the spark would be gone, snuffed out behind a pinch of her expression as if in pain. No bloodwork could tell him what created that response to him.

"Yes, extreme stress."

"Her cortisol levels are elevated, which concerns me because the blood was drawn in the afternoon. Cortisol levels this high so late in the day would indicate it's much higher. While there are some medications to reduce cortisol levels, they contradict her other medical indicators. I think to focus on improving her B12, vitamin D, and iron levels with therapeutic supplements. If it is possible to remove her from the stress, that would be helpful as well. Obviously, an improved diet and activity would be helpful."

"I'm already working on that stress reduction, Doctor. Would I buy these supplements or are they something you prescribe?"

The doctor sighed, answering on the release. "There are supplements you can buy somewhere like CVS or Walgreens, but I recommend prescription-level dosing. If you have a local pharmacy, I can have them delivered." The doctor paused, then added, "Or should I have the hospital pharmacy deliver?"

"That may be best, Doctor."

"Fine. I'll request that be taken care of for you. Now, at the Bureau's request, we did run screening for a variety of…pharmaceuticals. If she has been without her prescriptions she may experience insomnia, anxiety, headaches, dizziness, nausea, and even pain similar to electrical shocks in her nervous system. Do you know the dosage levels?"

Grayson shook his head, glancing back to her again. She hadn't stirred. His nerves prickled. "She doesn't take any prescription medication. What did you find?"

The doctor cleared his throat and huffed. "In normal circumstances, this isn't a conversation I would have without the patient's absolute consent. This isn't a normal circumstance."

"No, it's not."

"The test found traces of at least three prescription medications used commonly as antidepressants and antipsychotics. It's not a medically recommended combination and might likely have a variety of psychological effects. Stopping them abruptly will not be pleasant for her."

Nothing at this moment is pleasant for Kipling. "What are the medications?" He sat at the small table and pushed aside one of the dinner plates to set the hotel-provided scratchpad in front of him.

The doctor provided names, and spelling, and repeated the possible withdrawal symptoms she might experience. By the end, Grayson clenched his jaw with such force pain shot down his neck and into his ears.

"Could any of these medications be given by injection?"

"It's not a common delivery, but yes. Hospitals keep liquid forms in case they need administering when the patient can't swallow pills."

"Most doctors would have access to these."

It wasn't a question. He knew the answer. But Doctor Nulton confirmed it.

"Yes, these are commonly prescribed in mental health settings. But like I said, not typically combined."

Anger filled his chest and made his skin hot and he had to focus to maintain the American accent as his expanding desire to hunt down Doctor Mina Russo nearly overwhelmed him. "Doctor Nulton, I'm sure you've assumed things based on who asked for your help and what you found. I am going to be blunt with my questions, and I need blunt answers."

"I can do that."

"Would the combination of these medications, considering their usual purpose, possibly make a person more susceptible to manipulation?"

The doctor didn't answer immediately and Grayson clenched his teeth again, waiting.

"In my experience, yes, it might, especially when that is the intent. If that were the goal, I would say I'm surprised other illicit drugs weren't present in the results. Certain illegal drugs would make a person even easier to influence and, well, to put it bluntly, brainwash for lack of a better non-conspiracy theory word."

"There were not?"

"No, the only drugs the test found were ones that would be medically prescribed. While they, like any drug, could be abused these are medications any doctor, hospital, or pharmacy would have access to."

At least there was that one small grace.

The tableau of her abuse over the last three weeks, because what had been done to her was nothing short of abuse, became more clear as more puzzle pieces fell into place. With each piece, his anger expanded. And his hatred.

"When I send the supplements, I will assure the pharmacy includes some literature that might be helpful. They're a bit heavy on medical terminology, but—"

"I appreciate that," Grayson said, hearing the clip in his own voice.

Perhaps his university degrees in chemistry and biology would be of use finally. He ended the call, checking the time to calculate when the messenger might arrive, and scrubbed his palms over his face. His patience and rationale were stretched thin with each new revelation coupled with his own lack of sleep. He'd sat vigil over her most of the previous night, and what sleep he'd managed was shallow and non-beneficial. He wanted to rush forward to a point in time when all this was in the past, but knew the timeline wasn't in his control.

Kipling had dozed off *again* sitting on the bed. She'd slept so much she was pretty confident the aches in her joints were from being prone for so many hours. She groaned, tipping ear to shoulder on each side to try to work out the stiffness. Her muscles were so tight, she couldn't move far. It didn't take a medical degree to diagnose her with tension and stress.

"I'm sorry I keep falling asleep," she mumbled as she lowered her legs off the side of the bed and tossed back the duvet.

She'd fallen asleep wearing the aids, which would typically be so uncomfortable she would wake up and take them out, but these were so small she hadn't noticed. Of course, she wasn't actually lying on a pillow. Behind her, she heard the muffled scrape of the chair legs across the carpet.

"You have been through a great deal, some of which we're only beginning to understand."

The weight of his voice made her nerves prickly and Kipling raised her chin as he walked around the bed to her. His hands were in his pockets, his mouth turned down in not quite a frown but far from anything resembling a smile.

He lashes out at you. Over nothing. You've been walking on eggshells, Kip. What has he done?

She pressed her lips together. Grayson went to the bedside chair he'd slept in during the night and where he'd been when she first woke this morning — was that really only this morning? — and sat on the edge of the seat cushion, facing her.

"You're not happy."

Grayson made a sound in his throat, a cross between a chuckle and a groan, and shook his head. "That is an absolutely true statement, darling, but *not happy* is not nearly colorful enough. The more I learn, the angrier I become."

Kipling pulled in a sharp breath, and his gaze snapped to her face. He shook his head, not looking away. "Not angry with you, not ever angry with you. There is nothing in this entire course of events that can lay blame at your feet; not now, not yesterday, not three weeks ago. If anything, I am angry with myself for bringing you into this life."

"I don't remember you forcing me."

As soon as the instinctive words passed her lips, she mentally braced herself for some turn of her stomach or painful crackle of her nerves to remind her she needed to guard her words. None came, instead a pleasant, familiar, welcome warmth.

"I appreciate your attempt at assuaging my guilt," he said with a small, unconvincing smile. He pulled in a breath and released it with a sigh, leaning forward to set his elbows on his thighs, closing the space between them as much as the two pieces of furniture would allow. "I spoke to a doctor from the hospital here. He provided the results of your laboratory tests and is sending a messenger here with some supplements that may help. All supplements you could purchase most anywhere, but these are of a therapeutic grade."

"What did he say is wrong with me?"

"Not wrong, just temporary. Likely, your exhaustion and difficulty staying awake is because you are very low on B-12, magnesium, vitamin D, and iron as a start. You also have elevated cortisol, which is a clear sign of extensive and prolonged stress. None of which is a surprise to me. Combining that with your visible and drastic weight loss, your body hasn't been getting what you need."

"What else? There's more than that."

The lines around his eyes and bracketing his mouth softened and his forced smile slipped into something more genuine, though sad. "Your perception, as always, is sharp. Your lab results indicate traces of several drugs usually administered as antidepressants and antipsychotics."

"What? I don't—"

"I know, my darling. I informed the doctor as much."

Her blood went cold. Kipling looked down at the arm where the nurse had drawn her blood and stared at the marks she'd acknowledged earlier in the evening. With a jolt up her spine, she couldn't breathe or see and her heart wanted to pound free of her chest. She tried to say something, anything, and tried to look away from the marks, but couldn't move.

Then Grayson was kneeling in front of her, his hands holding her face, calling her name and asking her to look at him. Kipling trembled so hard she thought her muscles would splinter, but she couldn't stop, couldn't breathe.

"Kipling. Look at me, focus on me. Darling, please."

She forced her focus from the marks on her arm to Grayson's face, blurred from sudden and burning tears. He smoothed his thumbs across her cheeks and breathed in with purpose, releasing it slowly. After a breath or two, she tried to match him. A few moments more and the chaotic panic in her chest released its grip on her lungs.

"I swear to you with all that I am, because all that I am loves you beyond existence, I am here and we will figure this out together, we will get through this together."

Chapter Eighteen

Lavender-scented steam hung heavy in the bathroom air and the heat of the bath left her feeling languid, heavy, and sleepy. Once or twice in her life, Kipling had enjoyed the luxury of a long, relaxing soak in a deep tub usually while on vacation. Her apartment was designed for the conservation of space and didn't have even a small tub. The deep, antique clawfoot tub in Baker Street was an absolute dream and the realization of a fantasy she never knew she'd harbored.

The air skimmed her face and cooled her damp skin. She smiled a second before gentle fingers touched her cheek. Kipling opened her eyes, focusing her sleepy eyes on her soon-to-be-husband's face. He was beside the tub, one arm resting on the side while the other smoothed away the wisps of hair clinging to her forehead.

"I came to assure you'd not slipped away like Evienne," she read on his lips.

"Not yet," she said, "but the lavender has definitely relaxed me. I don't know if I'm going to be able to get out by myself."

Grayson smiled, the slow and sexy tip of one corner of his mouth followed a moment later by the other, and her blood warmed from the inside to match the heat of her skin.

"I am happy to assist."

Kipling licked her lips, the steam leaving them slick. "I have a better idea. Why don't you join me, Mr. Holmes?"

"I am equally happy to accept."

Kipling tipped her head to keep her attention on him as he stood and unbuttoned the front of his linen shirt, holding her gaze as he unbuckled his leather belt.

Kipling woke with a start when her chin dipped into the warm bath water and she gripped the tub edge to bring herself to a sitting position, splashing water onto the tile floor. For a second she expected to see the cream walls and white fixtures of her Baker Street bath and was reminded in the next breath she was thousands of miles from home.

The water was still warm so she hadn't been in the bath long, but she suddenly lost the desire to stay in the tub. It wasn't the same.

Nothing was the same.

She wasn't the same, and she desperately wanted to be.

Kipling left the tub and pulled the drain, drying off with the big, fluffy towels the hotel provided.

If he gets his hands on you again, Kip, he'll take you away and I'll never see you again. You can't let him do this.

Mina's voice rolling through her mind made her skin prickle and her jaw clench. She knew — she *knew* — Mina's words weren't truth, but something she couldn't clearly define like a shadow in the corner of a room kept trying to convince her it was.

Why would Mina say such things?

Why would she think Kipling would believe them?

Why did some part of Kipling *actually* believe them?

She dressed in the soft cotton pajamas that had been amongst the clothes Greg had brought her and brushed her hair. The number of strands left on the brush probably should have concerned her, but all she could do was acknowledge they were there. Darkness had fallen when she opened the bathroom door to the bedroom beyond, leaving the room dim except for a bedside lamp. Grayson was stretched out on the far-too-short-for-his-height sofa across from the foot of the bed. One leg was bent enough his knee rested against the back, but his other bare foot rested on the floor and his arm draped over his eyes. He'd changed into lounge pants and a novelty tee shirt that had also been amongst Greg's shopping, and Kipling smiled at the memory of when he'd found them.

The lounge pants were absolutely ridiculous, and the price tag showed Greg had bought them on clearance for all of three dollars. Bubblegum pink pajamas with cartoon unicorns, rainbows, clouds, and stars fell three inches short of his ankles. Mom would call them clamdiggers. Grayson grumbled when he held them up for inspection, saying his cousin probably took great pleasure in buying them because he knew Grayson would find them ridiculous.

Despite his grumblings, his eyes had smiled and he'd winked at her before tearing off the mangled price tag.

Kipling stepped into the space between the foot of the bed and the couch, glancing first at the rumpled bedding from her off-and-on-all-day sleeping and the couch where her husband tried to rest.

Every thought came at her from two sides, like the devil on one shoulder and the angel on the other. Except each tried to convince her they were the angel and the other was the devil to be feared. A thought. A counterargument. A rebuttal. Back and forth.

Why would her husband not want to sleep on the bed?

Why would you want him to? He belittled you all the time. He used you and mocked you.

No, he didn't. He wouldn't. He never would.

Then why did you tell me he did, Kip? Who's lying here? You? Him? I'm only reminding you of what you've said.

Kipling swayed and managed to sit on the foot of the bed before her knees gave way completely with the realization it was an actual conversation she remembered. Not just random declarations from her lifetime friend. Kipling had been arguing, denying her husband could be any of the things Mina said. Denied she would have ever made those accusations. And Mina had argued as adamantly it was all true. Then the memory went black and a visceral spark of pain shot up her spine.

She sat on the bed feeling lightheaded, her eyes blurring.

Walking toward the courthouse with Mina, Kipling experienced a moment of absolute clarity and made the decision to run. Later, she couldn't pinpoint the moment or the reason, but it had been perfectly clear. In the parking garage where she found momentary refuge, she'd known with another spark of clarity she had to destroy her hearing aids. She didn't know why, only knew she had to.

In this moment, that crystal clear moment of clarity cleared the fog. Her mind was muddled, but her heart — her soul — knew the truth.

Grayson was her home. Grayson was her safety. Grayson was her truth. Grayson was her strength.

Kipling pulled in a deep breath and turned her head to look at her husband again. She had slept through the previous night, and most of the day, and he had sat vigil. He had watched over her.

Kipling moved from the bed to kneel beside the couch by his shoulders, her heart losing its rhythm to flutter behind her ribs. Two days of stubble roughened his jaw. He'd taken a quick shower, saying he wanted to give her a chance to soak in the tub before bed to help her rest, and his hair and finally grown enough that the untamed waves tempted her. A temptation she gave in to, and the moment her fingers slid through his still slightly damp curls, a calm settled over her. She rested her other hand over his heart and laid her cheek in her hand.

Grayson pulled in a deep breath, his chest rising beneath her cheek and he lifted the arm covering his eyes. He looked down at her and smiled, smoothing his hand over her hair.

"Did you enjoy your bath?" she read on his lips.

"I did. Until I realized how much I missed our Baker Street tub." She combed through his hair and smiled when she felt the rumble through his chest. "It's big enough for two."

"We will be home again," he promised.

"When?"

"When I know it is safe. When I know you will be safe." Grayson laid his palm against her jaw and ran his thumb along her cheek. "When I know you'll feel safe again."

He didn't say "with me," but she knew.

Anger threatened to destroy her moment of calm.

She refused to let it.

Kipling closed her eyes, knowing it would end the conversation for the moment, but she needed a moment to silence the voice. To quell the wave of dread. Grayson gave her the silence she needed but grounded her with his touch. When she opened her eyes, she shifted back and used the edge of the couch to stand. On her feet again, she held out her hand to him and he took it.

"Come to bed, Grayson. We'll both sleep better."

On his feet, he closed the space between them and took her face in his hands, leaning in to press a long kiss to her forehead, and Kipling let the warmth of peace wrap her. The logical part of her brain warned her this peace wouldn't last. Too much had happened, and they had too far to go before this would be over even though she had no clear definition of what she faced to overcome. For now and tonight she'd sleep in peace.

Kipling was asleep within minutes, wrapped in his arms with her back to his chest, but despite his own exhaustion sleep evaded him. Tonight had been the first time since fate gave her back him that she had looked at him without apprehension or hesitation or fear.

When her touch woke him and he opened his eyes, a rush of joy hit his chest, expanded from where her hand rested.

He loathed the moments in the last three weeks when he'd allowed himself to fear the worst; that she was gone. The moments had been fleeting, and he had silenced those dark thoughts, but holding her as she slept the dread and darkness he'd felt in those moments reminded him with sharp clarity of the gift he had been given.

A gift he would treasure.

A gift he would fight to keep.

Whatever it took.

He hovered on the edge of rest, but the shrill ring of his mobile yanked him back. Grayson rolled to his back, keeping one arm beneath Kipling's head as he retrieved the phone from the bedside table. Fully awake, his gut clenched because he knew that ring. No name showed on the screen, nor would it. His mobile was equipped with a special bypass for urgent, immediate, and desperate contact and only one person knew the code.

Greg.

He didn't have a chance to say anything after answering before Greg ordered, "You need to get up and get out. Now, Ollie."

Unable to extract himself without disturbing her, Grayson pulled away and stood, turning on the bedside lamp. "What has happened?"

"We don't have time for me to explain everything, but let's just say your suspicion of a mole — moles — is confirmed. We haven't figured out who, and we have no idea what they know."

Grayson went around the bed, putting Greg on speaker before setting down the phone. Kipling had already woken and sat up as he moved to her side, looking from him to the phone and back.

"What's wrong?"

"*We need to go*," he signed abruptly, fearing the dim light in the room wouldn't be enough for her to read his lips. "*Now*."

She scurried from the bed, heading for the closet where the clothing and items Greg had brought earlier in the day still sat with the suitcase.

"Is anyone hurt?" Grayson asked as he matched her urgency.

"No, but that's only because we got damn lucky. Ollie, just go. I'll explain later. I am sending an address. Flannery will be waiting. He'll tell you where you go next. And Ollie…" He paused. "Be safe."

Chapter Nineteen

It was still technically Tuesday when Grayson turned into the parking lot of a Cumberland Farms station in Nashua, New Hampshire, but Wednesday was less than half an hour away. Monday afternoon in the John Joseph Moakley courthouse felt like days in the past. Not just the day before based purely on the calendar. The drive from Lexington to Nashua had been not three-quarters of an hour, but the sense of impending danger made the unfamiliar drive feel considerably longer.

He pulled into one of the multiple pump lanes and in an attempt to be as inconspicuous as possible, Grayson stepped out of the car to fill the tank. While the pump worked, he stepped into the space left by the open car door and bent to speak to Kipling. She sat with her arms crossed over her body, hugging herself, and offered a weak smile.

"We'll have answers shortly," he promised, hoping he spoke the truth. Motion near the door into the store beyond caught his attention, and he recognized the back of the red-haired FBI agent dressed in khaki cargo shorts, a tee shirt, and sandals. A far cry from his usual office attire.

Behind Grayson, the pump clanked as it shut off and he returned the nozzle to the pump, completing the transaction. "I would prefer not to leave you alone," he said, bending again to speak to his wife, then with intent spoke with his practiced American accent. "You said you wanted snacks?"

Kipling nodded and opened her door. He went around the front of the car to meet her, taking her hand to approach the store. Her fingers trembled in his hold and she walked close to him, her shoulder against his arm and her other hand tucked into the inside of his elbow.

The fluorescent lights inside made the interior brighter than daylight and he squinted. The aroma of coffee, baked goods, and smoked sausages kept warm in rotating beds mostly masked the lesser scent of cleaning products. Grayson stopped at an endcap of packaged sweets beside which was a short hallway leading to restrooms. He made eye contact with Flannery, who stood in front of the bank of glass-door refrigerators full of a large variety of beverages from beer to water.

"You may want to use the facilities," Grayson said low to Kipling, angling his head toward the short hall. "It may be a bit. I'll remain here."

She nodded and took the few steps down the hall, glancing back at him before going through the door.

"Your wife is a beautiful woman," Flannery said low from the crisp aisle perpendicular to where Grayson stood. "Course, you don't need me to tell you that. And don't get me wrong but…she's been through some shit."

"Yes," was all Grayson could say in answer. He picked up a package holding a massive pastry filled with lemon and cream and tried not to pull a face. It was entirely unappealing.

"Leave here and head north. Third right will take you into a shopping mall parking lot. I'll be outside Walmart. I'll explain next moves there." He looked up from his scrutiny of the crisps, snagging one from the top rack. "You might want to get a coffee. You've got a wicked ride ahead of ya. Cumbie coffee is pretty good. Not Dunks, but it'll do."

He turned away and went to the cashier as Kipling rejoined him. She looked past Grayson to Flannery's departing form. "We're meeting him a short distance from here for more details. He's advised me we may be on the road for a bit and coffee may be warranted. Would you like anything to eat?"

"Not from here," she said with a shake of her head, holding her hand to her stomach. "I don't think my stomach is prepared for anything I'd get from a Cumberland Farm at midnight. Maybe some juice."

"Done," he said and she found what she wanted as he made a coffee from the massive array of carafes.

In the car again, Grayson pulled into the quiet midnight streets and easily found the shopping mall Flannery had spoken of. The parking lot of the 24-hour department store had no more than a dozen vehicles, and Grayson identified Flannery standing near a dark blue SUV smoking a cigarette. Grayson parked with a few empty spots between them and on the edge of a circle of light cast by one of the tall lot lights.

"I'll speak with him," he told Kipling. "I won't leave this area without you, should that need to happen."

"Okay," she said in a low voice, once again holding herself with her arms wrapped around her torso gripping her own sides.

Grayson reluctantly left her alone, Flannery reaching the car as he shut the door.

"I'm more a desk jockey. I ain't used to this cloak-and-dagger shit," Flannery said, dropping his half-burned cigarette to the asphalt to crush it out with his sandal. "Did your cousin tell you anything?"

"Only that you and he have confirmation there is someone within likely both your organization and mine working against us."

"Hell of a thing." Flannery coughed, and since Grayson had never suspected the man to be a smoker, he assumed the cigarette was an uncommon occurrence. "Long story short, someone took some potshots at Mr. McQueen while he was in the garage. We put a few more pieces together, and it's pretty damn clear someone knows something. Since we don't know how much, we're assuming they know a hell of a lot." He held out his hand, and in it a USB drive. "I put on there what we got, figured maybe you and your super brain might see something we don't. Clay and bricks and all that. Isn't that what you said?"

Grayson smiled and took the drive. "Something akin to that, yes. Greg implied you had instructions for us."

"Yeah, sure thing." He pulled from the front pocket of his shorts a piece of folded paper. "I already put the address where you're goin' in the nav system." He canted his head toward the SUV. "You're takin' that. I figure you got stuff to move over to it?"

"Some, yes. What's this?" he said, unfolding the paper.

Federal Marshal
Donovan Greer

"He's the guy meeting you at the end of your long-ass drive. He's got a place on a lake up in Maine, 'bout four or five hours from here. Gotta say I'm wicked jealous. Hell of a spot," he said, hooking his thumb over his shoulder toward the SUV. "Should the plate be run for any reason, shows registered to Allan Champion. Papers in the glove box. I figured you probably got another set handy, but they're there if you need 'em. Meanwhile, I'll be taking this rental you picked up in Boston and headin' north toward Vermont. Figure if anyone had a bead on this vehicle, it's headin' in the opposite direction."

"Seems you're better at this cloak-and-dagger stuff than you think."

Flannery scowled and shook his head. "I know you're doin' it to not draw attention, but hearin' whatever accent that is you're usin' comin' outta your mouth is just weird."

Grayson smiled. "My wife says the same."

"Yeah, well, let me help you move whatever you got. Like I said, it's gonna be a drive. I'm sending you the slightly scenic route on the 295. It's a little out of the way, but the less you're seen—"

"I understand completely."

Kipling stepped out of the rental car when Grayson went to the trunk to retrieve their single, newly purchased luggage. "I will explain on the way," Grayson told her.

"It's good to see you again, Doctor Branson-Holmes," Flannery said with a dip of his chin.

"Kipling is fine," she said, trying to smile but Grayson recognized the fatigue around her eyes. "Thank you, Agent Flannery."

"Patrick is just fine," he said, returning the familiarity. "Just not Pat. My mom don't believe in nicknames."

With the luggage and their limited supply of food and beverages moved, they exchanged keys. Before taking his place behind the wheel, Grayson extended his hand to the man he considered a friend. "I appreciate your help."

Flannery gripped his hand with a firm shake. "Sure thing. We'll figure this out one way or another." He took a step away, then pivoted back. "I got one question for you, chief."

"Of course."

"Whoever is messin' with you could be anyone in the Bureau." He made the statement without leading into his question.

"When we were in Boston last, I was confronted by more than one member of my team about my absolute faith in Kipling," Grayson said, assuming the unasked question. "I have unwavering faith in my judgment when it comes to her. And you. Few people have earned that distinction."

Flannery pressed his lips together and nodded, then tapped the side of his fist against the open driver's door. "Thanks for that. Take it easy heading north. Once you're past Portland you're gonna see a whole lotta trees and not much else. Don't let it get to ya. There are some decent visitor centers, in case you need 'em. Donovan will be waiting for you. He's a good guy. And, ah, should you find them necessary the little key on the chain there opens a safe under the cargo mat. All things considered, I thought I'd make sure you got what you need."

"Understood. Until we speak again," Grayson said, climbing into the taller vehicle.

Flannery waited outside the rental vehicle until Grayson backed out of the parking spot and followed the GPS system's instructions to navigate back to the highway. It would be another long, sleepless night.

152

Chapter Twenty

Grayson's deep voice and the stroke of his palm on her arm drew her from the incomplete sleep she'd slipped into at some point. Kipling blinked open her eyes and sat up straighter, groaning at the kink in her neck from the odd position she'd slumped into. It was still dark. The headlights of the high SUV illuminated a gravel and dirt road canopied but thick, dense trees. There was little else.

Her nerves prickled when she glanced at the dashboard screen to check the time. Nearly six. The last time she remembered checking the time it was shortly after three in the morning. "I'm sorry. I didn't intend to fall asleep."

He chuckled a low rumble that smoothed her sudden anxiety. "Darling, I have been on enough road trips with you as my lovely passenger to fully expect you to slip away for a kip."

"But—"

He reached across the cab of the SUV, taking her hand, effectively silencing her counterargument. "I believe we've arrived."

She glanced at his fingers, folded over hers, and turned her hand so their palms were together. *Push it aside, Kipling. It's not real. He is real.* "How could you know?" she said with a chuckle.

"If the navigation system is to be believed, our destination is ahead on the right. I suspect the drive will somehow spring forth from the greenery." He leaned forward in his seat to scan the trees.

The onboard navigation system announced, "You have arrived," and Grayson slowed to a near crawl. A battered mailbox on a lopsided wood beam protruding from a large farmer's milk jug leaned toward the road with the name "Greer" in white paint on the side. Grayson turned the wheel and like an enchanted pathway to some fantastical land, the trees and growth parted enough to reveal a driveway of a sort leading downhill into the woods. The driveway was no wider than a single vehicle with parallel tire tracks creating dips in the dirt and gravel.

"The post box gives me hope we haven't been led too far astray."

The SUV bounced and rocked, even at their slow speed, as he maneuvered the winding path. Ahead of them, the crystal glisten of moonlight on water broke through between the tall trees. The drive curved to the left, and just like the end of the driveway had seemed to appear from nothing, a two-story, A-frame house with deep red stained board-and-batten siding and a wraparound porch appeared amongst the trees. A porchlight cast light on the patio and a recent model red pickup was parked behind the house at a perpendicular angle from the drive. Grayson drove past it to stop along the side of the house.

"Well, I feel better than I did a minute ago," she said.

Grayson chuckled as he turned off the SUV. The interior light turned on when he opened his door. "I feel the same. For a bit, I worried whether we would have proper plumbing and electricity."

He came around the SUV to offer his hand as she opened her door to slide from the seat. The air was cooler, making goosebumps dance up her bare arms, and smelled of earth and what Kipling's tired mind could only describe as "green." If one needed a visual definition of the word verdant, this place would be it.

The door beside the porchlight opened, and a tall man stepped outside. Grayson hesitated with the SUV between them and the house and she sensed his momentary tension.

"Donovan Greer," the man said.

"Friends of Patrick Flannery."

He walked the length of the porch to a short flight of stairs, descending them as Grayson led her around the SUV. He still carried tension in his stance, and Kipling tried not to make more of it than it might be. This was an unknown situation, and logically she knew that fact, knew he would be on alert. They met in the middle and Mr. Greer extended his hand.

"Any friend of Padraig's is a friend of mine."

Kipling grinned at Mr. Greer's version of Patrick. It wasn't Pat, so his mother couldn't get too upset.

"That's good to hear."

Grayson was again using the awful, non-descriptive beyond "American" accent and she tried not to let her face show her dislike for it. It just sounded wrong coming from him.

Donovan Greer was taller than Grayson, but only by an inch or so, with short, dark hair flecked with silver. He had angular features, and his nose had probably been broken at some point based on the slight bump below the bridge. The sun had begun to come over the horizon in just the past few minutes since they'd turned off the road and the view of the lake changed from dark gray blue to streaks of orange and yellow. The rising sun made it easier to see their host, and what Kipling saw made her chest ache.

There was sadness in his eyes. She didn't know if she could ever explain what exactly expressed that to her, but she knew it without a doubt. Even the shape of his mouth, neither a smile nor a frown, spoke of sadness.

"Padraig didn't give many details, and I don't need them." He angled his head back to the house. "I stocked up on some basics but if you need more for a longer stay there's a grocery store about three or four miles in the direction you came. You probably drove right past them. I left names and addresses in the house. The WiFi password is there, too. You won't be able to make general calls with a cell phone, so connect to the WiFi before you try to use your phone. Cell service isn't great out here, and you probably figured."

"Your hospitality is appreciated," Grayson said.

"I may not be in the community anymore, but that doesn't mean I can't have your back. Even if you're not American." He made the statement with slow intent, never blinking and never looking away from Grayson.

Grayson canted his head and made a low sound in his throat. "Flannery told you enough, then." The horrid, fake accent was gone.

"Didn't have to," Donovan said, then drew a deep breath through his nose. "Keys are on the table. I left my phone number, too. If you need anything, text. Easier than a call."

Grayson extended his hand again, and Mr. Greer gripped it for one solid shake before he turned away and went to the parked truck. He didn't look at them again as he backed the vehicle out of the spot and drove up the hill they had descended. The way the drive curved the truck disappeared well before it reached the main road; likewise, it shielded the house unless you knew where you were headed and what you looked for.

"What did he mean by community?"

"Intelligence services," Grayson answered once the truck was out of view. "Flannery said Mr. Greer was a federal marshal. I suspect former marshal is more likely. Many federal marshals migrate to service from another branch of the intelligence community." He walked to the back of the SUV and lifted the back hatch to remove their luggage. "Agent Flannery likely informed him I was of the community."

"You think Patrick told him you're Six?"

"No," he said, closing and locking the back of the vehicle. "I would surmise Mr. Greer is a very intelligent, observant man. He made the observation himself."

"Has that ever happened to you before?" she asked, following him to the lake house. "Someone figuring you out?"

"Only once." He glanced back at her as he ascended the steps. "Nearly destroyed the investigation. I got better after that. Perhaps I'm slipping."

At the door, before Grayson opened it, she said with a smirk, "I think you should call him Padraig next time you see him."

Grayson laughed and opened the door.

The sun was just above the horizon and filled the entirety of the two-story main space with light from the east-facing peak of the house. The wall was more glass than wood, and the sun made the polished pine of the house glow in golden hues. Massive beams stretched across the open space and the wall of glass gave an almost completely unblocked view of the lake further down the hillside.

The primary space served as a living room with a large couch and deep cushioned recliners, mostly facing the windows. A black cast iron wood stove sat on the far wall and the pleasant aroma of years of burning wood mingled in the air. The inside of the house was much warmer than the chilled air outside.

Across from the windows was a staircase leading to an open loft, and beneath the loft on the back side of the open space was a functional but not overly modernized kitchen with a table and six chairs around it.

An entire section of wall to the left of the door they'd entered was a heavy-laden bookshelf spanning six feet across and at least eight feet tall. The books filled every possible space with some of the shelves stacked two rows deep with books set horizontally on top.

Other shelves were full of picture frames of different sizes with different people. At least three had Donovan with two other men. They looked so much alike that they could have been triplets. To the right of the door sat an antique console piano.

"Oh...wow," Kipling said, walking further into the room toward the bank of windows. "This is beautiful."

"A treasure disguised from the outside," Grayson said, leaving the luggage and his satchel by the stairs. "My initial concerns are again nullified."

Kipling turned her back to the windows to take in the house from that angle. Every wall, ceiling, railing, and cabinet was golden pine sealed and polished to glow. The sunlight spread across the floor toward the kitchen area, inching along as the sun moved higher in the sky, and the beam fell across her husband.

One of a few fleeting moments of clarity wrapped around her like the warm sun against her back, and she wondered how she could have ever, even if for a moment, allowed herself to question him in any way.

"You take me to all the best places, Mr. Holmes."

Chapter Twenty-One

"*You're not hurting her. You're helping her.*"

"*It just seems so extreme. This is practically torture.*"

"*It will work.*" *The voice…the voice was familiar. But it wasn't Mina. "Keep it up and you'll break her.*"

Kipling fought against the fog that weighed her down like a thirty-pound weighted blanket. Voices sounded muffled like someone had stuffed cotton in her ear before putting in her hearing aids. Or like they needed cleaning.

"*I don't want to break her! I want to help her realize how bad he is for her. I know it's for her own good, but—*"

"*But what? You're the doctor, Mina. You know what you're doing. We don't know what he's done to her to make her so confused. You're just trying to help her see the truth. He's probably done the same to her, but to control her. You're helping her break free.*"

"*I think she's coming around. You'd better step out before she sees you.*"

Kipling tried to work her tongue to moisten the pasty, dry roof of her mouth. "Mmmmina," she tried to say. "What's going on?"

"*You barely got away from that abusive asshole of a husband, Kip.*"

She knew it was Mina, knew the voice, but the way she said husband left Kipling confused. Who was she talking about?

"*I believe everything you said. About him abusing you. Assaulting you.*"

Kipling tried to shake her head, but it felt like a bowling ball. She forced open her eyes, blinking against the bright light over her head. She tried to move, but pain shot up her spine and neck, ricocheting down her arms, and she cried out.

"Don't try to move, Kip. He dislocated your shoulder and you're covered in bruises. I've given you some pain medication, and I'm giving you more now."

A sharp pinch at the bend of her elbow made her flinch. "Where's Grayson?"

"Not here," Mina said, finally shifting into view over Kipling. "Don't you remember? He beat you and left you in your apartment. You called me to help you get away."

"No…"

"Yes, Kip. Try to remember. Your throat is bruised because he choked you." Her throat tightened and her eyes watered. She fought to take a breath. "He almost broke your wrist." Pain pierced her hand and wrist and she called out. "Don't try to move, Kip. I'm so sorry it took me so long to get you free. I always knew he was a narcissistic sociopath. I always knew. You had to learn on your own."

Hot tears overflowed her eyes and ran to her temples. Mina didn't make sense. She was lying. Grayson never —

"He did, Kip. You're rambling on like he's so wonderful. He's not! You're in pain! You didn't do that to yourself!"

Her arm burned and blinding pain shot behind her eyes.

Kipling wanted to crawl free of her own skin. Every nerve and cell sparked, itched, and ached at the same time. Her head was in a vice, and the world kept tipping, threatening to toss her down to the patio floor. Her heart wanted to break every rib on its way out of her body, and she couldn't take a deep breath. The world was a blur, her eyes burning. She wanted to scream but couldn't find her voice.

She dropped hard to her knees, pain shooting up her legs, and leaned forward to brace her hands on the wood planks.

She wanted to run to the water. Run down the dock and jump in, let the water overtake her. Maybe it would drown the panic.

Drown the chaos in her head. Drown the battling thoughts. Drown it all.

She wanted to push herself to her feet again and run inside. To call Grayson's name. To scream at him to help her.

In the same flash of panic, the pain told her to run away.

Kipling screamed.

Grayson was on his feet before he was fully awake, and halfway across the living space of the lake house when he registered the sound that had yanked him from his unplanned nap. His chest constricted around his lungs as he ran for the double doors leading to the wraparound patio facing the lake…where Kipling was on her knees, curled over herself, screaming.

Not screams of pain.

Not screams of fear.

Screams of despair.

"Kipling," he called, dropping to his knees in front of her, urging her to sit up and look at him. "Kipling!"

When he laid his hands on her arms, she recoiled, falling backward away from him. Grayson pulled back his hands, holding them up, fighting the twisting panic in his own chest. She fell back, holding herself up with her hands on the patio, staring at him wide eyes with tears streaking her cheeks. She fought to breathe, gasping through her tears.

She was pale, ghostly white, trembling.

It took all he had, but Grayson closed his eyes and pulled in a slow breath to appear as calm as possible. He sat back on his calves and opened his eyes again, meeting her wide-eyed stare.

"Darling, tell me what is wrong. Tell me…tell me what you need."

She sucked in a hard breath and twisted away but didn't try to stand. Her thin shoulders shook and her hair fell forward, baring the back of her neck and shoulders to him. Anger flared, slamming viciously with the need to comfort her. Round bruises dotted the back of her neck and down her spine, some slightly faded and some still red and as recent as a few days prior. He'd been hesitant to ask her to allow him to look for injuries, afraid it would be too difficult. Now, he berated himself for not asking.

What did he not see?

"Kipling, please," he begged, sniffing in a short breath against the thick emotion tightening his throat and filling his eyes. "My darling, please tell me. I won't touch you if you don't want me to."

She twisted back as violently as she had turned away, her features twisted in anguish. "Sh-she was—" She couldn't form the words, her overwhelming panic stealing her ability to speak. She extended her arms to him, wrists up, exposing the marks he had already seen and she had previously acknowledged. Her arms shook with the effort. "Sh-she—"

"Mina," he said with as much calm as he could manage.

Her chin came up and her shoulder jerked, tensing her entire body. He feared she would fly apart soon. "What did she do to me? Why? Why!" she demanded.

Grayson swallowed hard and took the risk of inching closer to her, never breaking eye contact. She didn't flinch away, watching him, tears falling freely. Grayson shook his head. "I don't know why. I *will* find out. I swear to you. But I don't know yet why she would do any of this. Darling…do you remember?'

She was nodding before he finished the question. "She kept saying — kept insisting — kept telling me y-you hurt me." Every word was an obvious struggle for her to speak. She finally lowered her shaking arms to rest them on her lap, staring down at them. "She said I had told her." She looked up and shook her head with such vehemence her hair fell again around her face. "I didn't. I didn't—"

"I know," he assured. "I know."

"She said I asked her to help me get away. She said you h-hurt me. It hurt." Kipling sucked in a sharp breath. "It hurt every time she reminded me what you'd done, it hurt."

With every piece of the puzzle, the picture became more clear. And his rage grew. He didn't yet know the threads to pull everything together, but what he knew was disgusting.

"What did she do to me? Grayson, please. Tell me. What did she do to me?"

He leaned forward on his hands to crawl the last feet to reach her and held hope when she didn't flinch or shift away. She watched him but didn't withdraw from him. "I don't know her reasons, but I do believe I know what she attempted to do. It isn't something I would imagine her doing, but I have seen it before in my… profession."

Her tears had slowed but hadn't stopped, and she still trembled but not with the same violence. Hoping he didn't act prematurely, Grayson reached for her and took her hand, enveloping it between both of his. It was her left hand, devoid of the band he'd placed on it less than two months before; a travesty he would repair as soon as he was confident she would accept. Grayson held her hand, palm to his, and smoothed his other over her knuckles to her wrist.

"She used…" He had no vocabulary to soften the answer without insulting her with the simplification and doubted she wanted anything less than the untethered truth. "…tactics of torture, both physical and using drugs for purposes in which they were never intended, to in the most crude and basic terms brainwash you and turn you against me. I can only assume her motivation, and the knowledge of the practice, came from elsewhere and that source logically would seem to be Langdon Howell." He bowed his head and brought her hand to his lips, kissing her cool skin. "You have once again been used as a weapon against me."

"How could I have let her do that?"

Grayson raised his head again to study her face. "No, darling. You didn't. Once again I am left in awe of your strength."

Kipling sucked in a hard breath and pulled her hand from his, clenching her fists. "Strength? I let them convince me to be *afraid* of you. Of *you*! They told me and I somehow believed them."

"No. No. No," he said over her argument and acted with instinct, taking her face in his hands so she would look at him. And see the honesty in his eyes. "Don't you understand, darling? They didn't convince you of anything."

"But I—"

"But you *ran*," he insisted. "The second you had the opportunity, you ran. You ran…to me. When your thoughts and body betrayed you, your heart didn't."

Kipling shook her head in his hold, her voice so small. "Finding you and Greg was—"

"The universe saving us." He had to take a breath, had to calm the chaos in his chest. Watching her face calmed him. "Kipling, where were you going on Monday? When you ran from the court-house, where were you going?"

She blinked, final tears sliding down her cheek to fill the crease where their skin met. "I was trying to get home."

"Home to your apartment?"

Kipling's lips parted to answer, but she paused, blinking. "No. I wanted to go *home*."

"Where is home?"

"B-Baker Street."

"How would you get there by walking through Boston?"

She pressed her lips together, her chin trembling, before she answered, "By finding you."

Chapter Twenty-Two

The old console piano was slightly out of tune, but not so far off Grayson couldn't work through a few warmup notes. The act of playing pieces by rote allowed his mind to drift in the notes and churn ideas and theories without the distraction of attention. He eased into Debussy, smiling with the memory of his mum sitting beside him on the piano bench, her eyes closed and her head back, a smile on her lips as she listened to him play "Clair de Lune." When he felt sufficiently warmed up, he paused his fingers over the keys and took a deep, centering breath before beginning Yiruma's "River Flows in You," a piece he always personally found soothing.

Both he and Kipling needed soothing now, and even though she was outside on the deck, he held hope the music might offer her some calm. He would play all night and until his fingers cramped if it brought her calm.

With the piece finished, he took a moment to work through his mind the bit of music he'd composed in the wee hours of the night before their wedding. Grayson hadn't gone down to the piano that night with the thought to make a rudimentary attempt at composition, but as he sat in the quiet solitude of the study thinking of the woman who had changed him forever, the music played through his thoughts. It was her ballad, his benediction.

He played it twice before taking his fingers from the keys, resting his hands in his lap until the rich sound of the final notes faded within the antique console. When still silence settled again, he slid from the bench to go to the kitchen.

After taking inventory of the food they had on hand. Grayson set on the counter a can of tomato soup, a loaf of bread, cheese, and butter to soften. Donovan Greer had done a decent job of stocking the house with provisions considering he knew little to nothing about the people utilizing his generosity. For tonight, they'd have a hearty comfort meal of soup and sandwiches. If here longer than three or four days, he would need to make the drive to the grocery Mr. Greer had mentioned.

Knowing he had time, he walked to the long couch facing the bank of windows and retrieved a crocheted blanket. Kipling was outside, calmer and more at ease now in the two hours since he'd woken to her screams, but despite that Grayson's senses were in hyper-awareness.

He wasn't sure whether he wanted — or didn't want — her to remember what had been done to her in the last three weeks. Knowing would help in her healing, but it would destroy parts of her life he knew she'd once depended on.

Such as a lifelong friend.

Until this, Mina had been an estranged friend at worst. Now, she was a criminal kidnapper at best.

He stepped outside and closed the multi-paned door behind him, crossing to where she stood looking out through the trees to the lake beyond. It was early evening, and the air had taken on a chill. He anticipated when the sun set they would appreciate the wood-burning stove in the house. A cool wind, heavy with the summer evening humidity, came off the lake carrying the aromas of wet earth and the not unpleasant scent of decaying foliage. Somewhere, possibly miles away since the cabin had no near neighbors, someone had a bonfire burning. Ten meters down the slope from the cabin balcony, water rippled against the rocky lake edge and the breeze rustled the trees all around the cabin.

Grayson stepped behind his wife and draped the yarn blanket over her shoulders to wrap it, and his arms, around her. The ember of hope he'd been fanning since she found him in Boston had ebbed and flowed from glowing bright to nearly extinguished in the last two days, but tonight when she settled back against him rather than tensing or moving away the ember flared to life.

The time for retribution would come, but not tonight, not here.

A boom of thunder had rolled through the hills ten minutes earlier, and cumulonimbus clouds shifted across the sky, sporadically revealing and hiding the moon.

Despite the thunderheads, the lake was serene, and the halcyon evening was a violent juxtaposition to the chaos battling in his chest.

"Your playing was a perfect soundtrack for this view," Kipling said, mirroring his thoughts. "Especially the piece you wrote. Have you thought of a title yet?"

"Not as of yet. Perhaps I will simply call it Kipling."

She didn't say anything but chuckled softly.

"I will begin dinner soon. Soup and sandwiches for tonight." He rested his cheek against the side of her head, the aroma of the lavender from her bath the night before still clinging to it. "Mr. Greer has left us formidably stocked for at least a few days. I even noted ice cream in the freezer."

She hummed but didn't say anything.

So, he held her as the wind shifted and the lake grew darker.

"I realized something," she finally said.

"What's that, darling?"

"Every time I remember the things Mina said, when she was trying to make me remember all the things that never happened, I remember her words and her insistence and the pain, but I don't remember anything else. She would say you hit me, and I would feel the sting."

Grayson was thankful she couldn't see his face because he doubted his eyes hid the anger slicing through him. He closed his eyes but let her continue.

"I told her you were violent when you were angry, and you could be angry at nothing at all. I told her you—" She choked on the words and stopped, taking in a deep breath. "She *told* me I said these things. When I said no, she accused *you* of being the one gaslighting me."

"I understand," he assured her so she would continue. He didn't want to hear but knew he needed to as much as she needed to say them.

"She said I told her you forced…I can't even say it," she whispered.

"I don't think I could bear hearing it." Grayson dipped his chin to rest his lips on her shoulder and tightened his hold.

"She said I was afraid of you, and that's why I lied. I lied about bruises and scars. I lied about so many things. They don't make sense now. There's no logic behind any of it. I don't know why I believed her."

Grayson lifted his head to kiss her cheek just in front of her ear, careful not to press to close. "You didn't. Perhaps in moments, but you didn't accept her lies. We established that. But tell me what it is you realized."

"I don't see what she told me. I can't picture it. I can't remember it beyond words — her words — and pain."

"Then you need to focus on everything else." He raised his head but kept his cheek against her hair. "Understand that when I say this, it isn't to compare any of this to an interrogation, but a way to help witnesses remember important details they may not even realize they know is to ask them to focus on each sense. Go beyond what pain you felt with her words, and beyond her words, to focus on memories you remember with touch and smell, what you saw, even what you tasted."

"I have been trying to, but sometimes the memory crumbles or changes like I'm having a dream instead of reliving a memory."

"Are they memories with me?"

She nodded, tipping her head to look back at him.

"Then let me help you."

"How?"

Grayson released his embrace and urged her to turn and face him, putting her between him and the railing behind her. "Tell me what you think you remember. Or, better yet, we can talk about what you believe is a memory. I will tell you details, that way you can determine on your own if what you remember is real or an aberration. If what I say matches your memories."

Kipling nodded, then lowered her chin, seeming to focus on the buttons of his camp shirt.

"You were shot," she said after a few moments of quiet, then shook her head. "I wasn't with you. I was in Boston. I was in a pizza place with Mina and...Greg. But, he was John then." Her voice tripped over the name, hesitant. "I remember the oregano smell and how warm it was inside. You called me. You'd been shot."

"Yes."

"I know you can't confirm this part, but Mina kept trying to turn everything back on you. It's when she told Greg what you do and I was so angry because it wasn't her place. It didn't matter ultimately." She tipped back her head to look at him. "John was Greg."

"I can't confirm, no, but I remember calling you. I was in pain and medicated but I needed to hear your voice."

She smiled, a slow bow of her lips, and she nodded. Then her expression shifted as she slipped into thought again. "In Sussex, after I surprised you. Was I a surprise?" she asked, diverting the thought.

"The most wonderful of surprises," he said with a smile, raising his hand to touch her cheek, brushing back a bit of hair caught by the breeze. In the distance, thunder rolled again.

"At your parents' cottage I asked to see the scar."

"Yes."

"There was a breeze blowing. I remember watching the tall grass and wildflowers swaying. I can smell the flowers. It was beautiful. Calm."

"Mum called us in for dinner."

"She called you Grayson Oliver," she added with a grin.

The twinkle in her brown eyes spread warmth through his chest, and he smiled with a low chuckle. "Yes, and I was relieved it wasn't my full name."

"Will you show me now?"

"*Grayson, I'm not in any way asking this to be fresh. Will you take off your shirt for me? It's obvious you're just fine. I'm being silly.*" Her voice whispered through his mind from what felt like both yesterday and years past.

"Yes but come back inside. It's growing cold and will rain soon."

He opened the double door and moved aside so she could follow him before he shut the door again. She followed him as he walked to the nearest lamp since the interior of the cabin had begun to get dark, unbuttoning his shirt as he went. He suspected the oncoming storm would move in fast and the house would be in darkness without the lamps.

When well into the circle of light, he angled back his shoulders and let the cotton shirt slide down his arms, catching it at his wrists to drape on the couch arm. The ring around his neck slid sideways before settling against his chest again. He raised his left arm to bend his elbow and let his hand fall behind his head, giving a full view of the fading scar. Months had passed since the injury, and his surgeon had done her usual exceptional job of overseeing the healing process, but as with the many marks on his body, a scar would always remain. The line was no more than ten centimeters and being positioned below his ribs he had a difficult time seeing any of it without a mirror, but he'd seen it enough to know what it looked like.

Kipling looked up at him first, holding his gaze for two thunderous beats of his heart before shifting hers to the scar. He studied her expression, and watched her eyes shift as she accepted her memory did match reality. She blinked rapidly several times before shifting her study upward to the scar that began behind his back below his scapula, then beneath his arm and along his ribs. Kipling's forehead drew down, wrinkling over her eyes as she stared.

"What would you prefer?" he asked. Her gaze darted to his face. He backtracked just enough to give her the context she needed to understand his question. "We were in Madrid, and you asked me where I received my scars."

The flush of coloring that spread from her throat to her cheeks was all the sign he needed to know she remembered the afternoon they'd spent in bed, enjoying the end of their honeymoon while just like in that moment, thunder rolled outside.

"Would you like to tell me what I said and I will confirm? Or would you prefer I tell you again, and you can decide if it matches your memory?"

"Tell me again," she said so softly he almost didn't hear her.

"Istanbul," he repeated from weeks before. "Hand-to-hand with a Syrian band of weapons runners."

Kipling began nodding as soon as he said Istanbul. "Serrated knife," she added.

With a slight tremble in her fingers, Kipling urged him to lower his arm again. As he let his elbow straighten, her delicate fingertips brushed along the inside of his forearm to his upper arm. The marks there were much newer, and the most recent of all his scars, but ultimately would likely be the least visible in years to come. Nurse Juds Oswald — Esther Mitchell's best mate — had done a wonderful job triaging the injuries left behind by his exploding Bentley, especially after the poor care from Howell's incompetent nursemaid.

His arm had been burned from clavicle to nearly his elbow, though not severely, and a jagged laceration had sliced his upper arm. The healing process was slow but would be complete. The skin was slightly discolored and rough, pink and red in some areas and white in others at the edge of healing. The surface of his skin was highly sensitive depending on the stimuli.

And his wife's gentle touch was brutal.

He watched the battle of thought shift over her features, her gaze shifting over the rough surface to settle on the much older scar hidden by the healing burn. It was the scar that had begun her questioning that afternoon. The scar was old and whether she had noticed it before that day he wasn't sure, but the new damage around it had made it more visible. This day she seemed more studious of that scar than the evidence of the burn around it.

"One of my first injuries in the field," he said, drawing her momentary attention as he retold the story. "Afghanistan while investigating a small Al-Qaeda cell, we infiltrated their safehouse and took seven into custody after a brief fight. The bullet would have likely gone straight through my deltoid were it not for the age and poor condition of the firing weapon. Greg had to cut the bullet free before we reached our people for treatment. The scar is more from his lack of skill as a field medic than the bullet itself."

He pointed to the shallow, ten-centimeter scar just visible above the waistband of his slacks, and she glanced down. "Appendix when I was fourteen."

Kipling skimmed his skin with her fingertips, and he could no more control his body's instinctive response to his wife's touch than he could stop his own heart. His blood rushed, demanding more. She raised her hand and touched the ring on the chain, a tremor shifting through her. Grayson laid his hands at her hips, steadying her as she lifted the ring from his skin to rest it in her own palm.

She took in a sharp breath. "I thought she'd taken it," she whispered so low he barely heard the words. "When I realized it was gone, I thought she'd taken it from me."

"I believe the intent was to send me a message." Grayson reached behind his neck and lifted the chain, slipping it over his head to unhook the clasp and free the ring. "It was left on your pillow, likely trying to say you'd left me rather than the truth." He put the chain in his pocket and took her left hand. It trembled in his hold, and he prayed the day would come soon when she no longer had to fight the physical effects of what had happened to her.

"I gave you this ring as a sign of our marriage. I gave you all that I am well before that day, but this ring declared it for the world." He slipped it onto her left ring finger again. It was loose, but not dangerously so, and as she regained her health it would fit again. Grayson brought her hand to his lips and kissed her finger, then turned her wrist to press a long kiss to her palm. "I love you with all I am and all I could ever be," he said against her cool skin.

She took in a sharp, shuddered breath and tears slipped again down her cheeks. If he never saw her cry again, it would be too soon in eternity. Grayson laid his free hand against her jaw, smoothing away the tears, and kissed her cheek. A year prior he would have scoffed at the idea of struggling to restrain his wish — his *need* — for physical touch, but now he ached with the struggle to hold himself back. Two days prior she'd been afraid of his touch, and just hours before she had instinctively recoiled from him. He wouldn't be the reason she was afraid.

Blinking at his own threatening tears, Grayson took a step back and turned to retrieve his shirt. Darkness had overtaken the house in the few minutes since they came in and thunder rolled closer to them. Through the window he caught the flash of a lightning bolt on the far side of the lake, and before he could put his arm into a sleeve the thunder cracked over them. The air vibrated with it.

"I'll start dinner. The cooker is propane, so even if we lose power I can finish the meal. We'll just eat by candlelight," he said as lightly as possible.

He pulled on the shirt but didn't button it and reached for a cast-iron skillet hanging on the wall.

"Grayson."

"Hmmm?" he hummed, setting the skillet on the stove.

"Grayson," she said again, touching his back.

He turned to her as she raised her arms and pressed her fingers into his hair, drawing him down to her. The thought to hold back burned away as a flash of flame, and Grayson embraced her, pulling her against him to fall hard and deep into the kiss. It ignited him, fiercer and faster than their very first kiss. She made a small, deep sound in her throat and parted her lips for him. Their tongues slid against each other, completing the conduit and he fought to breathe. He had to break the kiss with a hiss of breath through his teeth, only to bring his mouth to her neck.

Kipling cried out, tipping back her head to expose her throat. He turned them, her hips bumping the counter as he pushed his fingers into her hair, holding her head in his hands, and kissed her again.

Gasping for breath, Grayson forced his hands from her and curled them on the edge of the counter on each side of her. He lowered his head, touching his brow to hers, her breath warm on his shoulder.

"I'm sorry," he whispered.

"No, no," she said and laid her palms on his jaw. He didn't resist when she guided him to raise his head but kept his focus from her eyes. "Grayson, look at me. Please."

He swallowed and did as she asked. Her cheeks were flushed and her lips glistened from their kiss. Kipling ran her thumb over his mouth, he own lips parting as she focused on the point of contact.

"Make love with me," she said, meeting his gaze. "I need us."

Prepared for the onslaught, he covered her mouth with his, this time kissing slower, deeper, and with more intent. Her hands slid over his shoulders, leaving the once-again cast-off shirt on the floor. With her arms around his neck, Grayson bent enough to pick her up in his arms and carried her to the open staircase to the bedroom above.

Chapter Twenty-Three

Kipling eased from sleep with the warmth of her husband's breath on her shoulder and the arousing tumble of her stomach as his fingers traced down her spine. She smiled and opened her eyes, blinking against the sunlight coming through the skylight windows over the bed. He brushed aside her hair and laid his arm over her side, his palm against her stomach as he shifted behind her, his chest against her back.

Her skin flushed and her blood warmed.

Grayson's warm mouth pressed to her shoulder and she hummed. She turned into the contact, rolling onto her back and he set his bent elbow on the mattress beside her to angle himself over her.

"Good morning," she read on his lips. With his other hand, he traced a continuous track over her skin between her breasts up her throat to her mouth. "I have not slept so well in weeks."

Kipling smiled and touched the tip of her tongue to his finger, watching his dual-colored eyes darken as he watched. "It's been a tiring few days."

His lip ticked up in a one-sided grin. "True, however, exhaustion was not the reason I slept so well." His smile relaxed and he drew his thumb down her lip to part them. "I have missed you. So completely. My soul has come back to me."

Kipling raised her head from the pillow, and he met her invitation, covering her open mouth with his own. The need was instant, his kiss a lit match to gasoline and she was engulfed. He moved over her, covered her, and elicited a deep moan in her throat when he joined her. The evening before had been a desperate need to feel real again, to feel whole again, to feel right and without fear, dark shadows of memories, or uncertainty. Affirmation that all the beautiful memories were real, and neither Mina nor anyone else could take that truth from them.

This was healing.

She wrapped her arms around him and closed her eyes, focusing on the flexing and stretch of his back muscles beneath her hands and every point of contact — skin to skin — between them. The heat of his breath and his mouth on her throat, her shoulder, her breasts, and her mouth. The fluttering build that hitched her breath and made her hold tighter to him until everything released. Grayson braced himself over her, his bent arms on each side of her shoulders, and rested his forehead on her shoulder, his breath heavy and hot on her skin.

When her breathing leveled, he lifted his head to look down at her. "Good morning," he said again with a wide grin.

Kipling laughed, and it felt amazing.

An hour later, after a shared shower in the slate-tiled shower designed easily to accommodate two, Kipling joined him in the kitchen after dressing in another of the simple summer dresses Greg had provided and braiding her hair. Grayson stood barefoot at the stove wearing only a pair of khakis. He looked at her over his shoulder and winked.

"Breakfast will be ready shortly."

"You spoil me."

"Hardly." He moved the skillet and turned off the flame. "I am simply taking care, as is my honor to do. Sit and I'll bring your plate."

She did and picked up the steaming mug of coffee he'd already left for her. Kipling inhaled deeply and took a sip. It might not be the best coffee she'd ever had, but it was better than most and after the last few days — weeks — it was delicious.

Grayson came to the table and set her plate in front of her before he sat in the chair adjacent to her. Fried eggs, bacon, and two slices of well-buttered toast. For the first time since she could remember, with the last three-plus weeks being little more than a blur, she felt genuinely hungry. She used the point of her toast to break the yoke and took a bite.

It was delicious.

She felt like she'd really woken up for the first time.

"I have an idea," she said after taking a bite of bacon.

"Do tell."

"Let's pretend we are still on our honeymoon," she said, looking to him as he used the side of his fork to cut his eggs to bite sizes. "This is a beautiful, wonderfully secluded lake house you have rented for us until we decide to go back to the real world."

Grayson smile. "For the most part, I can completely agree with that plan. I will, however, need to step outside the fantasy on occa-sion." He set down his fork to reach for her hand, bringing it to his lips for a kiss. "Whether we like it, or not, there are pieces of a very large and dangerous puzzle I must work to put together. The danger is still real, and I won't allow it to continue."

"I know. Deep down, I know. I just want it behind me. Behind us."

"As do I, my darling."

She didn't manage to eat the whole plate, but ate enough Grayson was willing to accept some level of victory and promised lunch would be the soup and sandwiches he'd planned the previous night. When his phone chimed, a sudden clenching of dread hit her stomach and she hoped she didn't lose all she'd just eaten. Grayson squeezed her hand and stood to retrieve his phone from the low table in front of the couch.

"It's Greg," he said, before coming back to the table. "I'm placing you on speaker," he said as he opened the call and set the phone between them."

"I hope that means good things. Good morning, Kip."

"Good morning," she said.

"That's a voice I'm ecstatic to hear. I can hear the smile."

"The lake air is doing me good."

"Do you have any information?" Grayson asked.

Greg's heavy sigh came through the open line. "Some, but not much. Not enough yet. Sandi is digging deep, and I mean *deep*, and hasn't found any connections yet. Not even from that video from Monday. Whomever it is inside the prison knew how to avoid being ID-ed on CCTV."

"Video from Monday?"

"I will show you once we are off the call," Grayson answered in a voice loud enough Greg would hear but directed to her. She nodded and Grayson continued. "I suspect we must look beyond the obvious to the twisted machinations of Howell's particular psychosis. He has taken exceptional glee in reminding me of our family connections. He would go to Machiavellian lengths to create what he interprets as an ironic tableau of events."

"His failed plans put him in Belmarsh," Greg said.

"While I'm convinced Langdon Howell is mentally unstable, I also believe him to be of high intelligence and he has continued to seek revenge." Grayson shifted his attention solely to Kipling, speaking as much to her directly as to Greg. "He found a way to manipulate Mina Russo, and that did not happen quickly. He is playing the long game."

At the mention of Mina, Kipling was immediately and intensely cold, and a sparking wave of pain shut up her neck to the base of her skull. She instinctively laid her hand across the back of her neck beneath her braid, a shudder moving through her.

Grayson took the hand she rested on the table. "This is a matter we must resolve," he said. "Greg, I am limited but I will do all I can. Whatever you or Sandi find, forward it to me. In fact, send everything compiled thus far by any agency. I have full access here. While this is quite possibly the absolute best safe house any of us has experienced in our years of service, I am restless to be home."

When he said home, he squeezed her hand and Kipling tried to smile. She wasn't lost in the anger and physical pain she had been just the day before, but the shine of fantasy — pretending nothing could touch them here — had instantly faded.

"You got it, Ollie. We all want this done. We want Kip safe."

"What was the video about that Greg mentioned?" Kipling asked as she came around the couch to hand Grayson a drink.

He had his laptop open on the coffee table with several overlapping windows, the one in the forefront a video player.

"Thank you," he said, taking the glass. "While Mr. Greer has made it easier to access what I need with the wireless network here, it certainly isn't fast. I've been attempting to download files for half an hour. Had I been aware of our destination, I would have fully downloaded this prior to leaving Massachusetts."

Kipling sat beside him, leaning just enough to make contact, and he set his hand on her bare knee. She no longer felt the overwhelming urge to pull away from his touch, and she was thankful to no longer have the battle between her heart and body and the damage they had done to her mind.

"Where is the video from?"

"His Majesty's Prison Belmarsh. The prison in London where Howell is in custody," he explained. "This CCTV footage was recorded within a few minutes of your successful escape from your escorts. I think we can assume he was informed and it ruined his day.'

Kipling rested her cheek against his shoulder and he hit play. The video wasn't very long, but she couldn't help her chuckle when Langdon Howell had a meltdown of "toddler without a cookie" proportions.

"I definitely think I ruined his day."

"That you did, darling. It has also unequivocally confirmed he was not only aware of the situation in Boston, but he orchestrated it. Now the struggle is to link the dots."

"What do you suspect?"

"I have no proof yet—" he started to say, turning his head to look at her.

Kipling made a dismissive "psht" sound, waving off his words. "Your suspicions are as good as proof."

"Your faith in me is appreciated." He kissed her forehead before sitting back into the cushions of the couch. "My suspicion is Howell has people who either willingly work for him, or are otherwise persuaded to work for him, within both the Federal Bureau of Investigation in Boston and Six. And those individuals have access to Mina Russo."

He said her former friend's name in a softened tone, but it did nothing to cushion the slam of anger in her chest. Kipling shook her head, focusing on her own hands in her lap. "Why do you think she did this?" She looked over her shoulder to him. "Be honest with me."

"I would be nothing less than honest, darling." He sat forward again, rubbing up her spine with the palm of his hand. "My honest answer is I do not know. Greg shared his observations from when he spent time with the two of you, and while he says Mina expressed a dislike for me he never thought it to be anything more than a friend's concern."

Kipling sighed and shook her head. "He's right, but he didn't see all the times we argued about you. It got so I couldn't mention you at all. I couldn't say I missed you. I couldn't say I was worried for you. I couldn't talk about my insecurities and—"

"Insecurities…"

Her cheeks warmed and she looked down at her hands again, toying with her wedding band. "Seems silly now."

Grayson's fingertips beneath her chin gently urged her to look at him and met her with a long press of his lips to hers. He shifted back just enough to rub the side of his nose along hers and touched their brows. "I won't argue any part of that statement. My complete adoration is well established."

She smiled and nodded, their noses brushing again. "Well established."

"But due to circumstances, tell me what you can. It may be significant, not for confirmation of your mindset but clarification on hers."

Kipling snarled and groaned low in her throat. Before she could say more, his laptop beeped and she glanced toward the screen. A new video window had opened, showing an image of her seated at a table, looking at the camera. She didn't recognize the room or anything else about the video.

"What's that?"

Grayson looked to the screen, his smile leveling. "Copy of a video received by the prosecuting attorney's team and the Bureau presented a request to waive your requirement to appear in court. It was dismissed immediately."

"I don't remember—"

"Because you didn't," he said quickly, shaking his head. "It was dismissed out of hand because very quickly into the recording I told Director Stanton and Agent Flannery it wasn't you, and this was a fake."

"Wasn't me?"

"It's highly convincing, and might very well fool a great many people, but it didn't fool me."

A heavy dread landed in her stomach. "Play it."

"I haven't yet viewed the video in its entirety."

"Why does that matter?" she said, looking from the screen to him.

His eyes shifted from her to the screen, and back again. "It only matters because I know what I've seen will be upsetting, and I wish I could spare you from it."

"But we have to figure this out, right? Find all the pieces?"

"Yes," he affirmed and reached for the play button.

Chapter Twenty-Four

"*C*ould *you please state your name for the recording?*"

"*Kipling Marie Branson.*"

Grayson listened to the video but watched his wife. A deep V of concentration dug into her brow and she leaned forward to watch.

"*You hold a doctorate in literature, correct?*" A pause, and Grayson visualized the video he'd watched. She'd nodded. "*Be sure to verbally answer for us, Ms. Branson.*"

"*Yes, I hold a doctorate. I'm sorry.*"

"*No problem, Ms. Branson. We want to ensure the information presented is as complete and understandable as possible. Are you married?*"

"*Yes, I am.*"

"*What is the name of the man you married?*"

"*Grayson Holmes.*"

"*He is a British citizen, correct?*"

"*Yes. Um, he has dual citizenship. British and American.*"

"*He is an officer for MI6, correct?*"

"*Yes.*"

"*Does he frighten you, Ms. Branson?*"

"Yes."

Kipling gasped and sat back, looking to Grayson with wide eyes and parted lips. Grayson shook his head. "I know."

"Before I ask for clarification on your answer so we can accomplish the intent of this recording, can you confirm you have no desire to avoid testifying in the federal case against Isaac Sheldon regarding the events that occurred this past March?"

"That is correct. Isaac Sheldon did abduct me and attempt to kill me."

"That is testimony for the trial. Let's return to your husband. Why are you afraid of your husband?"

"How is this possible?" Kipling demanded, her cheeks flushed and her eyes already shining.

Grayson tapped the space bar on his laptop, pausing the video. From that point on he would be viewing new footage with her and needed the moment before they both moved forward to compose himself as much as his wife. "It's generally called a DeepFake, which is a digital image or in this case video created by AI technology with deep learning capabilities. The program takes data and samples and can be manipulated to appear to be an actual person speaking. Depending on the goal or resources of the creator, they may overlay the face and actions of a person over another, which is what I suspect was done here." He focused on his wife, wishing he could explain away the anxiety he already felt emanating from her. "Perhaps that was their downfall. This very spot is where I stopped watching and informed Agent Flannery it was a fake."

"This is a minute. Maybe. How did you know so quickly?"

Grayson smiled. "I have had the utmost and intimate pleasure of many conversations with you, darling. You may not even see in yourself what I see." He tipped his head back and forth and sucked air through his teeth. "They also made a rather sloppy and foolish error in that they failed to assure your doppelgänger wore hearing aids."

She looked to the screen and leaned forward, squinting. "Wow. You're right. That was a stupid mistake."

Grayson chuckled. "Indeed. Considering all things, the video request was analyzed by Sandra and Mac, and they fairly easily dismantled it."

"Then let's listen. See what CopyKip has to say. "

Grayson chuckled at the moniker and took her hand, lifting it to his lips for a kiss before restarting the video. He anticipated whatever they heard would be unpleasant, but his wife — despite the trauma and essentially torture she'd fought through — faced it with determination. As she had done since the first time they spoke at length.

He wondered how he had been blessed with her love.

Grayson backed up the video for a couple of seconds and played it again. "*That is testimony for the trial. Let's return to your husband. Why are you afraid of your husband?*

CopyKip's expression darkened and she looked away, her mouth twisting down in a dramatic frown. "*He's violent. He can snap from calm to enraged in a second, especially when there's no one to see it.*"

"*When did the abuse begin, Ms. Branson?*"

"*Not until I went to England in May. It was a surprise. In front of his family, he was happy, so I thought everything was okay. But, as soon as we were back in London…*" She trailed off, her voice shaking, and looked down at her hands. "*He wasn't happy with me.*"

"And yet, you married him."

CopyKip nodded, speaking down at her hands. "*He told me things he'd done. Terrible things. Terrifying things. I believe he thought I would tell someone.*"

"*Marriage privilege,*" the man off-screen said.

She nodded, raising her head again. "*He wouldn't let me out of his sight in London. I couldn't go anywhere or talk to anyone. He monitored my phone and my email because he knew I had friends and family. He didn't want me to confide in them and reminded me often with his fist that I needed to stay quiet.*"

"*You decided to leave him.*"

CopyKip nodded. "*Yes. When the FBI informed me I had to return to Boston for the trial, I thought I might have a chance. I have people here to help me. I didn't in London.*"

Kipling's grip on his hand tightened and a shudder moved through her. "Not your words," he said, watching her profile. "Not you. Not your words."

"I know," she whispered. "But it's hard to watch."

"Ms. Branson, are you willing to share what he confessed to you? What doesn't he want you to speak of?"

"He murdered Nelson Howell for starters," CopyKip said. *"He told me he convinced his director it was an act of self-preservation or whatever and MI6 covered it up for him. But he willfully and with intent murdered Nelson Howell. And took pleasure in it. Nelson Howell wasn't his first and wasn't his last. He made sure I knew it."*

"When did he confess this?"

CopyKip brought a tissue to her nose, sniffing as she patted her face. *"In London, after he beat me for the first time for surprising him at his parents' house. He told me it meant nothing to him to take a life, and he'd do it again. He said he could do anything he wanted. Anything. Then he raped—"*

"Stop it, please," Kipling whispered.

Grayson tapped the space bar and the video froze, already reaching for it before her plea. His blood went cold and his stomach roiled.

"Darling—"

"I'm going to be sick," she mumbled before stumbling from the couch and back through the lake house to the single bathroom.

Grayson closed his eyes, pressing his hands together in supplication with his head bowed. When would the assault end? When would they finally suffer through the last attack? When would his wife no longer be forced to justify the life she'd chosen to take on, even if the justification was to herself alone? To her family?

No answer came. Grayson slapped shut the laptop and stood to retrieve his wife a cold drink, putting on the kettle for tea when she was ready. He couldn't take back the reality of his life, but each day of it set firm his resolve to change his existence.

Kipling kept her eyes closed, the afternoon sun warming her face and arms. A humid breeze carried the aromas of foliage and lake water and someone somewhere cooked on a charcoal grill. Along the road the lake house sat on another neighbor was almost a mile away, but even if the houses were miles away, they were closer as the crow flies across the water. The soothing sound of water lapping against the rock and gravel shoreline and the slow sway of the hammock on the patio lulled her into a peaceful, gentle existence.

She wished this was the only existence she had to live through right now. Peace and calm and Grayson. It's all she wanted.

The hinges of the double door squeaked, then the latch clicked closed. Grayson was nearly silent crossing the deck to her, and she smiled.

"I'm not asleep. I'm just enjoying."

"I've begun to wonder if Mr. Greer would be opposed to renting out this place," Grayson said beside the hammock. "I could take a long holiday here with ease."

She opened her eyes and had to use her hand to shield the sun. "I was just thinking something very similar."

Grayson had his hands pushed into his pockets and he squinted to look through the trees between the house and the shoreline. They were sparse but enough to provide the house privacy. She wondered if much of the house would be seen at all from out on the water.

"When the mind is silent like the lake the lotus blossoms."

She smiled and hummed. "I see your Amit Ray and raise you a Lao Tzu. Make your heart like a lake with a calm, still surface and a great depth of kindness."

"Would you like company?"

"I would, but not in the hammock. Let's walk down to the water. We haven't yet."

He nodded once and held out his hand, steadying her as she sat up and shifted her legs over the hammock edge. She was better at getting in hammocks than getting out. She slipped on her canvas shoes, and hand-in-hand they went to the staircase leading to the ground, every few descended steps led to a landing before turning again to reach the ground. The steps and landings had been built to maintain the natural tree growth, and Kipling silently thanked whoever had been the architect who protected nature.

Twigs and pine needles crunched beneath their feet, and they stepped free of the tree shade a few feet from the end of the wide dock that extended out into the lake. Where the dock met the shore, they slipped off their shoes and walked the twenty-or-so feet to the end of the dock. Sitting on the end, Kipling dared lower her bare feet fully expecting the water to be frigid, but it was pleasant. Not warm, but not cold. Grayson did the same and they sat there in silence for a few minutes, only the sound of the water hitting the dock and the melodic call of a loon. Clouds rolled over the lake, darkening the water and the ambient temperature dropped several degrees with the lack of direct sunshine.

"Are you cold?" Grayson asked.

"Not enough to go back to the house," she said, smiling at him. "It feels good." Kipling pulled in a long breath through her nose, and let it go as she studied her husband's expression. He tried to minimize his tension and anxiety, she knew that, but she saw it. She felt it in the air around him. It lived in the lines bracketing his mouth and the subtle fidget of his fingers when he wasn't actively doing something with them.

"I want to pretend nothing matters," she said, keeping her voice and tone soft, "but I know it does. It all does. I know we need to talk about it. All of it. Because you can't fix it if we don't."

His lips tipped up in a momentary, tense smile but it slipped away almost immediately as he stared out over the lake. "I am perpetually torn between the need to protect you from reality and the understanding that in order to protect you, I need us to face reality."

"You don't have to protect me all the time—"

"Kipling," he said with a deep drop in his voice. He pressed his lips together and lowered his chin before looking directly at her. "Protecting you is as necessary for me as breathing."

Kipling covered his hand where it rested between them on the dock. "Okay then. Where do we start?"

Chapter Twenty-Five

Grayson stared at the array of papers, index cards, and sticky notes with information written in a variety of colors and mediums and taped in a pattern on the wall that likely only made sense to him, waiting for the solution to leap forward.

It hadn't yet.

Frustration sat heavy on his chest.

For five days he had been churning through all the information and videos provided to him by Patrick Flannery and every file, document, analysis, and data scrub worked out by Sandi and Mac. He and Kipling had made a trip to the nearby town to restock their pantry and he'd purchased every bit of stationery and office stock the small grocery carried. The large-scale mind mapping had begun.

And yet…no answer revealed itself.

He needed one puzzle piece to complete the 10,000-piece puzzle and the true image would be revealed like a pattern of falling dominoes. But the one all-binding piece still evaded him.

With a sigh, he discarded the notepad he held on the back of the piano where it sat beneath the mind map. Perhaps he'd stared too long. As he turned toward the kitchen to finish dinner preparations, he caught movement outside and saw Kipling reach the top of the stairs that led to the lake, walking around to the side of the house with the door. The temperature had dropped considerably in the days since they arrived and she wore an oversized sweatshirt in hunter green with the lake's name and the silhouette of pine trees and a moose across the front.

"Dinner will be ready shortly," he said as she came through the door. "Today felt like Mum's chicken stew."

"Grayson, I think I remember something that might be important."

He looked up and set down the spoon he'd been using to stir the stew with an audible thunk. "Tell me."

"It might not help. Might not mean anything—"

"And yet it might. Everything has the potential to be significant."

She joined him in the kitchen area, leaning her hip against the sideboard of the sink, her arms crossed. "I don't know if I'm remembering right," she said on a sigh. "When I ran from the courthouse, I broke my hearing aids. Crushed them. You asked me why, and I said I didn't know. I just knew I had to."

"You recall why you destroyed them?"

Kipling nodded. "Because they'd altered them."

"Did you witness them altering the aides?"

"No, but they'd taken the aides from me for a bit. They left me in a dark room. I couldn't see or hear or move. I think I fell asleep or was knocked out, but I started to wake up when they were putting the aids back in my ears. Mostly because they were very bad at it. I wasn't really awake." Her face paled and her eyes widened before she shifted her gaze up to him. "One of them said 'Hennessey can do it, so can we.' Grayson, how could they know what Mac did..."

A greasy unease slid through Grayson and he scowled. "How indeed. Very few people are aware of Mac's adaptations. Very few."

"That isn't good, is it..." There was no lilt of inquiry in her voice.

"I believe this to be a long Tube ride, two buses, and a lengthy walk away from good. But, it is another piece of the puzzle."

"You already thought Howell has someone in Six."

Grayson picked up the spoon and returned to stirring the stew. "Yes, and I've long suspected there are connections here as well. Howell knows far too much and far too quickly to believe otherwise. But despite my best efforts, the threads are not presenting themselves."

She looked back over her shoulder at the mind map, then walked to it as he opened the cooker to bake the canned biscuits they'd gotten at the market. Lord help him if his mother ever found out he'd made biscuits from a can, but the current situation dictated ease versus standards.

"Could you discern whether the person who mentioned Mac was a man or a woman?" he said while she examined the map.

"I'm pretty sure it was a woman."

"But not Mina or Patty."

"No," she more mumbled than spoke, her head tilted while she scanned the notes and cards. "The voice has come back in some of my other memories. Never where I could see them, and sometimes I feel like I should recognize the voice. But it's not quite right. It's off. Kind of like when you use the American accent. It's your voice, but not right."

"Which begs the question of whether the voice and accent you recall now is true and what you knew previously was deception, or whether the reverse is true."

"Hmmm."

Grayson smiled and proceeded with setting the table and the final preparations for the simple meal while his wife studied the chaos resulting from his fragmented thoughts. Minutes passed, and she didn't stray from the study of the wall. When his phone chimed the biscuits were ready, he took them out to cool and crossed the open space. The sun had dipped behind the trees enough to leave the horizon sky a gorgeous palette of pinks, oranges, and reds serving as a stunning backdrop for his wife's silhouette.

"Something speaks to you," he said as he stepped behind her to bring his chest to her back, studying the same portion of the map she did.

"Mmmm," she hummed, tilting her head to the left. "But it's whispering."

"Come eat," he said and kissed her temple.

"Stop questioning your decision, Doctor Russo. You are the only person in a position to take these actions to save your friend."

That voice…who is that voice? Kipling tried to turn her head toward the conversation, but her body was heavy — so heavy — and the darkness of the room weighed her down. She managed to move, but her ear pressed against whatever she was on and her aid whined. The words were lost beyond the sound until she rolled her head again.

Mina's voice snapped past the silence. " — don't understand how Kip has let herself be so fooled. I've never known her to be so gullible and I've known her for over twenty years. I would have never thought she'd be so tricked by a man—"

"She wasn't tricked by just any man. I barely know Ms. Branson beyond the few times our paths crossed, but I do know Grayson Holmes. He's a liar, a deceiver, and a violent killer. He believes in vengeance over justice."

No. No. Not Grayson.

"Shouldn't your — his — superiors stop him? If you know he murdered that man, don't others?"

"How do you think he got away with it? They know. They don't care. He does their dirty work for them, and they clean up the mess. I told you about him murdering Nelson Howell, but that man is just one of so many. If he can't kill, he manipulates. I've seen the women he destroyed. If you don't do this, he'll hurt her far worse than you can imagine. Your actions are to undo the harm he did, the lies he told her and convinced her of, and to make her see the truth. She's close. You see that."

Lies. They lie. Grayson doesn't lie.

"But I don't see it. When we first brought her here, I honestly believed she would be happy. She could think away from him. But she isn't. I don't know what else to do."

"He used cruelty to trap her, Doctor Russo. Mastering psychological warfare is an unfortunate requirement of our job, and Grayson Holmes relishes in power. We may need to counteract in much the same way."

"I won't hurt her."

Panic squeezed her chest and rose in her throat as bitter acid and she tried to call out. No, Mina! No!

"You're going to save her. Do you really think I would risk my career to be here if I didn't believe this is what needs to be done?"

"What you're suggesting is torture."

"It's deprogramming."

"I want to wait. I want to see——"

"We're running out of bloody time! Take the syringe, take the electrodes, and do what must be done, Doctor Russo. Unless you can live with the consequences if you don't."

The door opened and Kipling winced, the light from beyond cutting through her head like needles in her eyes. She squinted at the shadowed outlines, immediately recognizing Mina. Her head hurt so badly, and her throat was so dry it hurt.

"I didn't realize she'd woken up..." Mina said.

"Caralho," the other person mumbled, and Kipling tried to shuffle through memories for the meaning. It felt familiar. She felt familiar. Why? "Did you leave her with her hearing aids?"

"Yes."

"Bloody hell! You're about to see how Grayson Holmes deals with problems because you've turned his wife into a liability because of your stupidity."

"Sandra, I've attempted some rudimentary searches from here, but of course, public databases can take me only so far and while our host has provided the means to access the internet, things still tend to choke a bit on large sums of data."

"What, no good WiFi in the boonies?" Sandra joked.

Grayson chuckled. "Barely. Please compile for me an extended lineage on the Howell line beginning instead with Charles Augustus Howell's mother. Focus on her generation going forward."

Grayson hadn't had the opportunity to speak with the entirety of the team since Kipling's abduction and had been forced to rise painfully early to have the chance now. He had been passing messages, emails, and group texts and it was good to finally have a roundtable. If nothing else, the hive mind they created together was one thing he missed after having stepped back from Six. It was a near comparison to the time before Greg's supposed death.

The sound of keystrokes carried through the phone speaker. "Right, that's Henriqueta Amelia de Sousa da Rosa Coelho. Wow, bit of a mouthful. I'll get a crack on and send it your way, Boss."

"What you need that for," Lynne asked. "A séance?"

"Working on a hunch. Not even that, I suppose. A thought."

"Seems like a blind alley."

"We won't know until we step down it. As things stand, I'm willing to explore all avenues, alleys, and country roads." Grayson leaned forward on the couch, resting his elbows on his knees with his hands — palm to palm — together in front of him. "I must ask a difficult question, and before I do I need it clear I am not asking in anticipation of the problem stemming from this team."

"Well, that doesn't sound cryptic at all, Boss," Sandra said.

"Not my intention. Mac, the five of us, Kipling makes six, are aware of the manipulations you made to Kipling's aids to allow for two-way communication in London. Who, beyond us, would have knowledge of what you did?"

Mac made a "pshaw" sound before saying, "Canna think o anybidy in particular. I thought it best tae keep it tight."

"And you didn't discuss it with anyone." He made it a statement, not a question because his gut knew the answer. Mac wouldn't and didn't.

"Nah, Boss, nae even Cooper. It's a need-to-know basis, and he doesna need to know."

"Greg, I know the answer but I feel the need to ask."

"Nope," his cousin said, his voice slightly clearer for being closer than the few thousands of miles between Grayson and the

London team. "Never said a word. I'm not exactly on the payroll."

"Since when are we on the suspect list? What's going on?" Lynne asked.

"Communication amongst us is not my concern, but beyond our circle." Grayson picked up the phone to hold it in his palm. "Kipling has recalled a comment made by her captors specifically about Mac's modificat—"

"Grayson!" came Kipling's voice, shouting his name from the bedroom area on the second level.

He shot to his feet, turning as she ran down the stairs. "What's wrong?"

"I remembered…I know who—"

"Goodness," Sandra said, her voice coming from the phone in his hand. "Nearly gave me a heart attack."

Kipling stopped short of reaching him, eyes wide, staring at the phone. "Who are you talking to?" she asked on a ragged whisper.

"The team. Greg, Sandra, Mac, and Lynne."

Her gaze snapped from him to the phone in his hand. She raised shaking hands and signed, *"Hang up. Please."*

"I'll reach out soon," Grayson said. "Sandra, please send that information when you can." He tapped the screen with his thumb to end the multi-line call and dropped the phone on the couch. "What's wrong?" he asked his wife as he walked around the couch to meet her.

By the time he closed the space, she crossed her arms over her body in defense against the shaking that had already taken hold.

"Darling, tell me…"

"I know who it was. The voice I felt I should know, but it didn't sound quite right." She shook her head. "I can't-I don't want to believe it. I have to be wrong. I *have* to be wrong."

Grayson laid his hands on her upper arms. "We will determine that together." A cold chill of apprehension crawled up his spine to the base of his neck. "Who was it, Kipling."

"Lynne…" she whispered, a tear falling free down her cheek. "It was Lynne Connolly."

Chapter Twenty-Six

"I think it was when she spoke about risking her career, and when Mina said *your* superiors — yours and hers — that the pieces started to come together. Maybe not when I was in the moment. I was confused. Everything was…blurry," she said, hoping it made sense. So much of that time away from Grayson was blurry. "I'm confident they didn't know I was awake." Kipling relayed, sitting on the couch with her knees hugged to her chest, bundled in the granny square crocheted blanket from the back of the couch.

Grayson sat on the coffee table in front of her, hunched forward with his elbows on his knees and his hands pressed together in front of his lips, eyes closed. She felt like she hadn't taken a deep breath since shooting up from sleep half an hour earlier, and part of her hoped she was still asleep.

That this was a bad dream.

That Grayson hadn't been betrayed.

"You saw her," he stated, no question in his tone.

"Only for a moment when Mina pushed open the door to my room. They had been in the hallway outside, and for just a moment I saw her face but in shadow." Her chest hurt with the visceral awareness of the vivid memory slamming into her all over again.

"But it's like all these other blurry memories are coming into focus, and I think she was there a few times. She was pushing Mina."

"Do you know what she wanted Mina to do?"

The right words were lost in a jumble of confused thought, and Kipling tried to shuffle through them. "I think…I think she wanted Mina to do more. More than she had at that point to…convince… me. To…" She pulled a face and shook her head. Then her blood went cold when the last words she remembered snapped into clarity. "They realized I was awake and Mina hadn't taken my aids. She was angry and said I had become a liability. She said Mina had no choice but to—"

Then her stomach twisted and she flinched, the memory of pain slapping into the base of her skull. Kipling swallowed hard to push down the acid at the back of her throat and clenched her jaw against the instinctual and programmed physical reaction to the memories. She now understood all the emotions, sensations, and foreign thoughts she'd mired in during the first few days after finding Grayson. They had been trying to make her believe her memory of pain and fear came from Grayson, not them. They had tried to force her heart — her *soul* — to believe the worst of him.

All with the intent of hurting him. Of ruining him.

"I'm sorry, Grayson. I'm so sorry," she whispered, her throat so tight she could barely speak.

His hand came out before she finished, and his eyes opened when he touched her. "No," he said, shaking his head. He shifted to the edge of the coffee table so his knees pressed the couch cushion and drew her hands from beneath the blanket to bring them to his lips. "No, there is absolutely no part of this situation you should apologize for."

"But I know this hurts you…"

"It does, but it is not pain you have inflicted and is nothing compared to the devastation I felt when you were taken. My pain is great because they used you, hurt you, in an attempt to destroy me." He pressed his lips together, his gaze shifting away from her when he said, "This will not go unanswered."

"Grayson—"

His attention snapped back to her. "Forgive me. My anger is raw." His voice scraped in his throat, his lips jaw clenched, and his eyes rimmed in red. "She was at our wedding. She looked into my eyes and wished us well. She embraced you, all the while planning —" His words snapped off, and he covered his face with his hands.

Kipling reached for him, unfolding her legs so she could close the space. He met her and she combed her fingers into his hair. Grayson shifted off the coffee table to kneel beside the couch, resting his head on his folded arms in her lap. She wrapped herself around him as best she could, hoping she offered comfort but knowing she couldn't do anything to take the burden. Kipling kissed his hair and rested her cheek against the soft curls that had gained new life in the autumn, Maine air.

"I want to be wrong," she whispered. "I so desperately want to be wrong. Please tell me I'm wrong." He raised his head but stayed on his knees, looking up at her, and Kipling smoothed her thumbs along his cheeks. "You haven't once asked me if I'm sure."

"The thought to question your words never came to mind." His voice was stronger than moments before, but still rough and strained. "The weight of facts is such that I don't believe you would have told me with such conviction if you had any doubt."

"I was so sure when I woke up. Now I'm questioning everything. I just can't — I don't *want* to believe Lynne would…" She didn't even know how to qualify or define all the things Lynne would be responsible for and guilty of if Kipling was right.

Grayson moved from his knees on the floor to sit on the edge of the couch cushion beside her, holding her hands between his larger ones.

"We will work this out together and determine our next course of action." When he met her eyes, the shadows behind him made her heart ache. "I despise asking you to provide more details. I must take steps and must be clear with the information I relay."

Kipling nodded and took a deep breath through her nose, puffing her cheeks as she released it. "Okay."

"I will make you something to eat, first. Some coffee—"

"No, Grayson," she said, gripping his hand to keep him from

standing. "Let me get this out before I convince myself everything I remember is wrong."

He studied her face before dipping his chin in a single nod and settling fully on the couch beside her. "Of course."

Grayson sat silent as she relayed more of her memories.

Grayson stood on the deck of the lake house, leaning with his elbows resting on the rail, phone in his hand, looking down the path to the dock. Kipling sat in a deep wooden chair she'd told him was called an Adirondack, bundled in a hoodie and covered with the blanket from the couch. The temperature had shifted since they'd arrived at the lake. It had only been days, but so much had happened that their idyllic-yet-forced holiday felt deceptively longer. A breeze came through the trees and a curtain of crimson, yellow, and amber leaves drifted to the ground.

In barely six months, every assumption he'd made of his future had been swiped aside and replaced with the greatest gift he never could have imagined.

In less than four months, the wound in the Holmes and McQueen family had been healed but Grayson's faith in Six had been all but destroyed.

In less than two months, his life and existence joined without delineation with Kipling's.

In less than a month, his very soul had been torn from his body when Kipling disappeared.

In less than a week…so much had changed in less than a week.

In less than a few hours, the foundation of trust he'd stood on for years had crumbled, and what he had imagined as a fortress had become a house of cards destroyed by the wind.

It was time to build on a new foundation.

He unlocked the phone and opened his encrypted text program.

We need to speak.

The response was nearly immediate. The moment the message indicated it had been delivered, the undulating dots indicating a response appeared.

God damn it, Ollie. I've been sitting here with the phone in my hand for two hours.

The message screen disappeared, shifting to an incoming call notification. Grayson tapped to answer and brought the phone to his ear. He acknowledged that he should speak and say something, but not a single word formed.

"Ollie," Greg snapped when the silence stretched too long.

"I am here," he managed to say. "At least in body."

"What the hell is going on?"

A crawl of apprehension clawed up his spine to settle at the base of his skull. "What was said after I disconnected?"

"Everyone is worried. Ollie, the last few weeks have been hell and everyone needs to know Kip is okay."

Grayson glanced toward his wife sitting down the hill, bundled in the blanket with her gaze across the water. "Each day brings her closer to what might be defined as okay, though I fear and acknowledge neither she nor I will come through this without being irreparably changed."

"So what happened this morning?"

He pulled in a slow, deep breath through his nose and turned to go into the house. While his wife was painfully aware of everything he would speak of, he didn't wish to expose her to reliving memories needlessly. Once inside, he left the door open so he could hear if she called for him and stood at the large window to see her.

"Kipling told me yesterday she had regained memory of an individual who participated in her...torture." He choked on the last word, closing his eyes. He cleared his throat. "She spoke of feeling she should know this person. They were neither Mina nor the woman she has identified as Patty, on whom we have no other information. This was a third person, another woman."

"That isn't much to go on."

"This morning she told me who it was."

"I'm just going to assume I won't like this."

"This must remain between us—"

"Of course, Ollie."

He had wrestled with and pushed down the hot rage that had overtaken him in the second he knew Kipling's words were reality, but as he struggled to force himself to say the words the rage flared hot and vicious once again. Grayson clenched his jaw, a sharp tinge needling down the side of his neck. He closed his fist not holding the phone and thumped the glass with the side. "Lynne Connelly."

He let the silence draw out while his cousin processed the revelation. There would be questions. There would be arguments against the possibility. There would be anger. He knew because he had mentally processed every emotion and response. When he told Kipling he never doubted her word, that was absolute truth; but believing the truth and accepting the reality of the truth were two distinct events.

"Shit. Is she sure?"

"She doubts herself now that she has named Lynne, but in the moments following the realization she was absolutely positive and it is that intuition I trust."

"This is…I'm not doubting her, but it's a damn hard pill to swallow. And I'm not asking because I'm questioning Kip, but what makes her — and you — so sure?"

"She provided more details of what she remembers being said and being done, and in truth, the revelation of Lynne Connelly's involvement makes absolute sense. The techniques—" He choked on the word. "utilized are those known to the intelligence community, though not *recognized* in deference to civility. It is a connecting piece to the puzzle. The connections between her memories and reality are connections she would not be aware of, which is why I have no doubts."

"You're calm about this, Ollie."

"I assure you, I am far from calm."

"I get that. Damn." After a heavy sigh, Greg asked, "Now what?"

"I am at a difficult crossroads. Until a few hours ago I would have willingly placed my life and wellbeing in the hands of any member of my team, and I hate now that I must question anyone. But I need access to information."

"So, we limit this to Sandi?"

"Regrettably, yes. I don't instinctively question Mac's loyalties, but with this knowledge, I suspect Ms. Connelly has been manipulating his emotions since she joined the team."

"Bit of a *coincidence* she joined the team just months before what happened, happened."

"I've considered that, yes. With more and more threads becoming clear, confirming the likelihood she has been associated with Howell since before joining Six, it seems logical she worked to join our team specifically."

"Let's limit contact, just in case. Tell me everything Kip told you, and whatever else you might have, and I'll connect with Sandi." After a pause, Greg added, "I'm not sure how far under the radar this will be. When you hung up so abruptly, Lynne was asking a lot of questions about where you are, what's going on, etc."

"She now knows where we are," Grayson said, not asking a question. "She didn't previously?"

"Yeah, she does *now*. She didn't outright ask where you were, but I would guess the course of the call after you hung up probably gave her enough information to figure it out. I was about to say something like only our team has that information, but that's a dead point. I think we should get you out of there. It's not safe anymore."

Grayson looked out the window, confirming Kipling still rested in the chair near the water. "More's the pity. I've never seen a place that represented the term idyllic quite like this. Mr. Greer is a blessed man for having it at his disposal."

"Okay, so fill me in."

Grayson spent the next twenty minutes relaying to his cousin the details of Kipling's dreams and memories, as well as statements she'd made in the last few days as things came to mind. Greg confirmed many of Grayson's thoughts simply through his audible reactions to some of the information. As Grayson had explained, when seen as a whole the picture wasn't complete, but approaching clarity.

"It's a damn ugly narrative," Greg said, the echo of his pen hitting a hard surface coming through the phone. "But you're absolutely right. Kip couldn't have imagined some of these things, let alone understand how they would link up to show us the obvious."

"I wouldn't be surprised if she couldn't see the connections now that she has the final piece. Her mind works in ways I'm quite sure the intelligence community would love to manipulate."

"Well, that isn't happening. I'm go — put together…hang on." Greg's words had cut out mid-sentence, likely as a notification came through on his phone. "Sandi is trying to reach me. Let me touch base with her."

"Fine. Please let me know as soon as possible our next move. I feel a bit at wit's end here without resources to act on my own."

"You got it, Ollie. I'll be in touch."

The call ended, and Grayson slid his mobile into his pocket as he went back outside. Kipling looked back at him when his shoes crunched on the ground cover, a mix of leaves, pine needs, twigs, and soil. Her slow smile worked away some of the cold dread in his chest. She would forever have the means to soothe his soul. When he reached her chair he crouched beside it, one hand on the wide armrest to help him balance.

"How did he take it?" Kipling asked.

Grayson sighed before looking across the lake, squinting at the sun's reflection on the slightly rippled surface, making it sparkle like a field of diamonds. "As well as I would expect. Like us, he was first shocked and then angered. We all have had our trust destroyed."

"Did he ask if you were sure?"

"Not as such, no." He looked to his wife, making sure she would see the sincerity in his words. "He didn't doubt your word any more than I, and as I relayed details, he reiterated my interpretation of facts. All the dots are there, and your memory linked them. There is no question. Lynne Connolly — or whatever her name may be because I truly doubt that is her true name — has successfully fooled all of us for a very long time. Likely in pursuit of Howell's end game."

Kipling shook her head and looked away. In the silence, the gentle lap of water against the gravel and stone shore and the lyrical call of loons communicating across the water carried to them.

"I hate her," Kipling finally said, her tone flat.

"Kipling—"

"No," she said, turning her attention on him. "I hate her. I hate what she, and Howell, and every other monster in this disgusting chess game are trying to do. It's pointless. It's cruel. And they're destroying lives for no damn reason."

"They believe they have cause."

Kipling huffed a derisive sound. "They may believe it, but they're evil for it. Every villain is the hero of their own story, right? No heroes here. None of them. I hate them all."

He wanted to say something to calm her anger, but ultimately she was justified and he wasn't so bold as to think he had the right to tell her anything else. Because he felt the same.

His mobile vibrated and chimed, and he shifted enough to retrieve it from his pocket, seeing Greg's name on the screen. Grayson tapped the phone and brought it to his ear. "I'm here."

"Get out," Greg snapped, and the urgency in his voice pushed Grayson to stand. "Get out of there. Now!"

Chapter Twenty-Seven

"Get in."

Kipling didn't need Grayson's encouragement to propel her forward. She ran across the front of the SUV to the passenger side as Grayson tossed what they grabbed into the back: his laptop, her medication and supplements, and little else. She got in and slammed shut the door.

The SUV faced the direction of the lake, and Kipling's throat tightened as she stared through the trees to the glistening water beyond. As terrible as things had been the last few weeks, the cabin and the lake had provided a level of peace and calm comparable to nothing else in her life. The only place that came close was Baker Street or the Holmes cottage. Not Boston. Not her apartment. Not even her parents' home felt so right as Baker Street.

The common factor was Grayson.

The back of the SUV slammed shut and he climbed in behind the steering wheel, starting the vehicle before his door shut. She caught a glimpse of a handgun before he put it in the low pocket of the driver's door. He put the vehicle in reverse and backed quickly into the space between the outbuilding and the porch steps, turning the vehicle so they drove straight up the driveway to leave. Kipling braced one hand on the center console and the other on the dash, and as soon as he shifted to drive, she pulled the seatbelt across her body and buckled in. Grayson tapped the large display screen in the center dash, connecting his phone to the Bluetooth system.

"We are leaving the cabin now," Grayson said as soon as the open line connected. He'd never hung up with Greg even when shouting to her to come inside.

"Good. We don't have any kind of timeline other than knowing she flew back to the States within the last couple of days. She's not in England, or anywhere near. We have no idea where she is."

Kipling stared, wide-eyed, at Grayson's profile as he clenched his jaw while maneuvering the SUV up the steep, gravel and dirt path that barely counted as a driveway, the SUV jolting her as the tires gripped the ruts left by the rain. She felt flushed and cold at the same time and couldn't seem to force herself to blink. Fear simmered in her stomach and burned the back of her throat.

"I am getting away from the lake house, and once I'm in the vicinity of civilization to make a decision on direction, I will…"

He trailed off and the SUV slowed. Kipling had to force herself to turn her head and look out the windshield. At the top of the hill, barely down the drive enough to be off the road, sat a dark green SUV. Through the other vehicle's windshield, she saw the silhouette of at least three people.

"Ollie?"

"We have company," Grayson said, keeping his voice low. He barely moved his lips when he spoke.

"Shit."

Without moving any part of his body visible from outside the vehicle, Grayson took the handgun from the door storage, setting it on his thigh. The passenger door of the other vehicle opened and Lynne Connolly stepped out, a wide, disgustingly fake smile on her arrogant face. Grayson angled the phone toward her, and she instinctively took it staring at the screen that said Greg's name.

"Sync," was his simple demand. "Hide."

As he withdrew his hand, he tapped the console screen to disconnect the phone from the vehicle.

She didn't even dare nod, but stroked her finger across the screen to access controls and tapped the coinciding area to connect her new hearing aids to the phone. The aids were already set up to be recognized, which meant at some point Grayson had already linked them. The tiny devices in her ears chimed and a soothing voice said "Connect check. Devices connected."

"Grayson," Lynne called out, raising her hand as she approached their vehicle. The driver stayed in the vehicle, as well as whoever was in the backseat.

"Greg," she said softly, keeping her chin dipped.

"Is it Lynne?" he asked.

"Plus two."

Lynne's expression shifted, and while the smile was still there, it was instantly sinister. And Kipling's blood ran cold. "Neither of us need to play the game anymore," she said, reaching behind her back. "There's nowhere to go."

"Hang on." Grayson shifted the SUV into reverse with his foot already on the accelerator.

Kipling curled forward, her thought being to do nothing to block his visibility, and tried to keep herself from bouncing off the dash or door as he sped backward down the driveway. The path was rough, steep, and crooked but he'd driven it before. Hunched forward, she locked the screen of the cell phone and tugged up the hem of her jeans around her ankles and tucked the phone up her pant leg with the screen facing away from her skin. She had no idea if it would work, but it was all she could think to do. She heard Lynne shout and screamed when the front windshield shattered.

"Kipling!" Grayson shouted, still flying backward down the hill.

"I'm fine!" she shouted back and pinch-rolled the hem of her jeans making them fit snug to her ankle.

"Was that a shot?" Greg asked in her ear. She managed a sound she hoped sounded enough like an affirmative for him to understand.

"Unbuckle and be ready to run!" Grayson ordered.

She blinked against the tears burning her eyes, demanding herself to focus. Breakdowns could come later. Her hand shook when she pressed the buckle release just as Grayson jerked the wheel hard and they skidded to a stop in the same spot where he'd turned around just minutes before, second before, she wasn't sure anymore.

"Go!"

Kipling shoved open the door, the edge slamming into the side of the outbuilding because Grayson had cut in so close. She ran toward the back of the vehicle, stumbling before gaining her feet. Grayson met her at the back and gripped her hand, running into the thick brush and foliage behind the outbuilding where it hugged the forest. Behind her. She heard the ping and crunch of gravel as the other vehicle braked hard to box in their SUV. Grayson ran with one arm in front of them, deflecting as many branches as possible from hitting them.

Where they would go, she didn't know. They were in the middle of the woods on the shore of a lake with the nearest neighbor miles away. But she ran.

"Grayson, don't be an idiot!" Lynne shouted from somewhere behind them, her put-on British accent gone for the voice that now haunted Kipling's nightmares. "Run and you won't leave here alive. Neither will Kippie!"

He didn't slow and she pushed to keep up with his pace. They angled left, heading back up the hill. If they made it to the road, could they flag down someone? How much traffic would there be on the old, nameless road they'd taken to the lake? Where could they go?

"Kip!" Greg shouted in her ear and she winced. She made another sound that had to be enough for him to know she was still on the open line. "I've got Greer on the line. I've filled him in on everything. He's on his way with backup. But it's going to be at least twenty minutes."

"We have nowhere to go," she gasped on ragged breath, her weakened body and burning lungs making it hard to talk.

Grayson glanced to her but kept moving. Several shots echoed through the trees and she swallowed the scream. They reached an outcropping of massive boulders and Grayson pulled them around it. By some amazing, saving grace there was a natural ditch of sorts behind it and they tumbled into it but were now hidden from their pursuers. With his back to the slope of the ditch, Grayson leaned up and tilted his head to look the way they came, then shifted down out of sight.

"*Do you still have Greg?*" he asked.

She nodded. "*He said Greer will be here but it will be twenty minutes.*"

Grayson closed his eyes, his jaw clenched.

"Can you hear me, Mrs. Holmes?" came Donovan Greer's familiar voice.

"Yes," she said in a whisper.

"Okay, I won't ask for answers from here on." The sound of whatever vehicle he drove caused a low rumble around his voice, but not so bad she couldn't hear. "I'm on my way. I've got backup. If you can get back to the house, I've got a bolt hole I'll guide you to."

She signed the information to Grayson, having to spell out bolt hole because she had absolutely no idea what the sign would be for such a thing, especially since the actual definition of bolt hole was fuzzy. She risked one final "Okay," to him to let him know she understood, and that Grayson had confirmed with a nod they would find a way back to the house. It was midday, but the heavy tree coverage made the forest dim. She didn't think it would be enough to hide them, but whatever Grayson did she would follow.

"Under the deck on the north side of the house, there's a large boulder against the foundation. On the backside of that boulder is a latch release. The opening is small, but big enough for Grayson to get through. You'll be fine. That empties into the cellar. There is *no* access to the cellar inside the house, only from the cellar out. If you can get there, *stay* there. Once that hatch closed behind you, the only one who will know how to get to you is me. You'll lose any means of communication. There's no way the call or text or anything else will stay connected. But if you get there, we'll get you out."

Kipling relayed the information. She couldn't read his expression. It was most definitely not pleased. He wouldn't like being shut away. She knew it and didn't have to ask. The sound of people moving through the undergrowth without regard for the noise they made carried to them and her chest ached with the painful pounding of her heart.

"I knew you wouldn't come easy," came Lynne's taunting voice again. "But I didn't think you'd be so quick to risk Kip. Guess we were right, huh, Kippie? You're nothing to him. And right now, you're a liability."

A visceral response to her words jolted up Kipling's spine and she clenched her fists. It felt like terror and rage, but it also felt wrong. She understood now what they'd done. They'd conditioned her — or so they thought — to have a fear response to the mention of Grayson and how dangerous he could be. It was nothing more than the imaginary monster in her closet as a child; powerless to do anything but make her afraid.

And she wasn't afraid of Grayson.

Never was. Never would be.

She wanted to tell Lynne to go to hell. And sincerely hoped she'd have the ability to one day.

"I'm gonna kill that little fuckin' bitch myself when we catch her," came a male voice Kipling didn't recognize, not even in her nightmares. "I don't give a damn if he'll be pissed. I still have the damn scar from when she bit me."

Maybe she should remember him…

"Shut up," Lynne snapped. "Watch who you're talking to."

A third voice carried from somewhere back near the cabin. Another male voice, but she couldn't make out his words. It was enough, though, to let them know where the players were in the game.

"I'm in the fuckin' backwoods of this fuckin' hellhole of a state, getting eaten alive by goddamn bugs, chasing after his damn pet project. I don't give a damn who you're related to, or if he don't like it, but if I catch her I'm gonna kill her."

"Christ," Lynne cursed, and her voice was too close.

Kipling tried to make herself small behind the boulder, not daring to raise her head to look. Their shoes crunched on the leaves and twigs and pinecones that carpeted the forest floor, making it impossible for them to move silently. But that meant she and

Grayson would also likely be heard. How could they possibly get back to the house without getting killed?

Grayson's fingers touched her chin and she jumped, raising her head enough to meet his gaze.

"Focus on me," he signed.

She nodded, glad she didn't have to speak.

He pointed past her in the direction of the rutted driveway they'd raced back down. They were a hundred feet from the break in the tree line, and that hundred feet felt like a mile. She looked back to him.

"To the drive and down to the house. Once we get close, we can use the outbuilding and vehicles as cover to get around the house. We just need to make it to the drive."

Fear burned in her throat, but she ignored it. There would be time later to throw up. She just had to live until later.

Moving with painfully slow integrals, she and Grayson moved away from the boulder that shielded the ditch. After what felt like an hour of practically crawling along the forest floor, they reached the driveway and broke free of the foliage and bushes lining the edge. She silently hoped they hadn't inadvertently stumbled on poison ivy or poison oak. That would just be an insult. Once on the dirt and gravel, Grayson crouched, balanced on the balls of his feet, and scanned the woods. They could still hear the two moving, and the third had to be closer to the house. He would probably be their biggest problem now.

Grayson pointed to her sneakers. *"Take them off. Bare feet will make less sound."*

She nodded and sat on her bottom to take off the shoes. He did the same, his attention never leaving the forest. His handgun was tucked into the waistband of his pants, and the cold realization hit Kipling that if it weren't for her he likely would have already been done with this cat-and-mouse game. He would have likely dispatched them with extreme prejudice and moved on.

With the shoes off, Grayson moved into a low crouch, shoes in one hand and her hand in his other. He jerked his chin and that was the only communication needed to move them forward. The tiny stones dug into her bare feet, but it was nothing compared to what she knew could be.

She realized that somewhere between the ditch and the driveway the call with Greg and Donovan Greer had dropped. Donovan Greer had warned the signal was bad and she felt blessed they'd had it as long as they had. The phone flopped at the bottom of her pant leg, still held there by the pinch-roll she'd mastered in elementary school. They followed the curve of the path that had at one time been dictated by the easiest path to the lake, she was sure. The curve helped because they weren't visible from the house for much of the descent. When the house came into view, along with the two vehicles, the clash of panic and relief collided in Kipling's chest. Standing between their SUV and the green one stood the third person. He was broad through the shoulders, wearing a newsboy hat.

She might never like newsboys again.

Grayson raised his hand, palm to her, signaling for her to stay put. She nodded, holding her breath as long as possible as he edged forward. Using the building as his cover, he edged his way closer and closer to the other man. Then she saw the gun in his hand and sucked air into her burning lungs. A shot would alert them!

Instead he lunged and brought the butt of the gun grip down on the man's head, dropping him like a bag of flour. And without a sound. Grayson looked back to her and motioned for her to come to him. She followed the same path, but just as she reached him the rustle and crunch of the other two in the woods got louder.

"Get back to the house. They've doubled back. Duarte!"

Grayson grabbed her hand and they ran for the north side of the house. If they could get beneath the deck before Lynne and the other man reached the vehicles, they would make it to the boulder and the hatch. The ground cover stabbed her feet, barely healed from the blisters she'd given herself, but she didn't slow and didn't cry out. The boulder was exactly where Donovan said.

"Hurry," she dared speak.

They had to keep bent over to move under the deck. When they reached the boulder, Grayson reached behind the edge searching for the latch. Then she heard a click and he smiled. Relief hit her chest. A hatch appeared in the wood plants extended below the deck to the foundation, and beyond was blackness.

"Go," he said. "I'm right behind you."

Kipling crawled through the hole, darkness engulfing her. Chaos had descended on them. There was shouting and gunfire, but the moment Grayson followed her into the darkness and the hatch closed, everything went silent.

Chapter Twenty-Eight

Darkness engulfed them when the hatch closed and locked with a solid thud and click. Before Grayson could speak or step further into the space, Kipling's face was illuminated by the light of his mobile. She was crouched, the phone held low near where she'd removed it from her trouser leg.

"Brilliant hiding spot," he said as she stood and walked to him.

"Good thing I mastered the pinch-roll fashion in fifth grade." Her voice wavered, but she stood and walked toward him.

Grayson glanced behind him to where he knew the hatch edges to be and saw no sign of light. With daylight on the other side, the light from the mobile torch wouldn't be seen. Her hands trembled as she held out the mobile, and as he took it he pulled her to him, wrapping her in his arms. He needed to hold her as much as he knew she needed to be held. Today was another layer of panic he would never forget. Once again, he could have lost her in a second.

Kipling leaned into him, her cheek against his chest and her arms around him. She pulled in and released a shaky breath and he kissed her hair. The sounds were muffled by the thick foundation, but he would bet heavily on the arrival of Donovan Greer and whoever accompanied him. At least, Grayson prayed that to be the truth.

The small beam of light from the phone found a metal junction box on the wall, and he stepped away from her just long enough to flip the switch. Light from two bare bulbs on the ceiling flooded the space.

It was a complete bunker.

The walls were solid granite slabs only seamed at the corners. Impressive to say the least. The space wasn't quite the full footprint of the house, which left him curious about what he would find if he accessed the unattached portion. Now was not the time to investigate the details of airflow, heat, and an alternative exit but he assumed Greer — or whoever had created the space — had seen to every detail. Two cots sat against one wall, covered with large sheets to protect them. Boxes and shelves were stacked with canned goods and shelf-stable foods, and large bottles of water sat on the stone floor against the wall. There was a portable commode with a privacy curtain hanging from a semi-circle rod on the ceiling.

And against the final wall was what Grayson could only describe as an arsenal. Semi-automatic rifles and magazines, handguns with their own magazines, and a variety of other forms of weaponry should the need to defend-in-place arise. Were he alone, he would utilize some of them to assist the battle outside.

Were he alone, he would have dispatched the three offenders on sight. And one with extreme prejudice. But he hadn't been willing to place Kipling in any further danger, and a gunfight would have left her entirely too vulnerable.

"So romantic," Kipling said with acidic sarcasm.

Grayson chuckled. "Indeed. Had I known of this exclusive bungalow we would have utilized it during our stay." He rubbed her back, then moved her away from him so he could look into her eyes. "Are you alright?"

She nodded, her fingers curled into the front of his shirt. "You?"

"Other than tender toes, just fine."

He backed her up until they reached the first cot and urged her to sit. He hoped they would be liberated any moment, else he would have to begin the investigation into how to escape Greer's space. There had to be a way out; it was just a matter of finding it. She sank onto the sheet-covered cot and Grayson knelt on one knee. He wrapped his fingers around her ankle to lift her leg, allowing him to examine the soles of her feet. Dirty, but no damage. Same with the other. He retrieved their shoes from where he'd dropped them when entering and sat beside her so they could put them back on.

A loud crack of gunfire — four shots in quick succession — rebounded from beyond the stone walls. Kipling flinched, and Grayson reached for her hand.

"I cannot imagine Lynne and her cohorts would have any means or ability to find us here. If Donovan is successful, of which I hold no doubt, he will come for us soon. If not, Lynne will have to eventually admit defeat. She will either leave or we will have the benefit of surprise."

Kipling turned her head to look at him, her hair a bit wild from their adventure in the woods. "Do you honestly believe Lynne would just give up and leave? I know you don't know who she really is, but you know who she has pretended to be."

Grayson squeezed her hand. "No, I don't honestly believe she would concede and depart. But I realize now I know nothing of Lynne Connelly. I am absolutely truthful when I say I believe Donovan will persevere. He has the benefit of knowledge of this area, and he has clearly prepared it for unpleasant contingencies. I doubt this is the only secret this property holds."

Silence settled outside, and despite his words and his absolute belief, Grayson couldn't ignore the apprehension of anticipation clawing up his spine. A click implied the latch had been released, and Grayson stood, putting Kipling behind him and his weapon in his hand. Belief or not, he wouldn't face the unknown without at least making an attempt.

The hatch swung inward, a muted bit of light coming through the space from the limited sunlight beneath the deck. "Holmes," came Donovan Greer's now familiar voice.

Grayson engaged the safety and put the weapon in its makeshift spot at the small of his back. "Yes." He reached behind him for

Kipling, and her hand slid into his as she stood. Moving to the hatch, he grabbed the edge and pushed it toward the ceiling.

Unlike when they entered, likely because he hadn't pushed the hatch high enough, a magnet on the ceiling snapped the open hatch out of their way, giving him full view of Donovan Greer with at least two others standing behind him.

"Everyone good in here?"

"Better now. Come, my darling. Let's get you into the sunlight again."

Kipling stepped around him, and he lifted her to the open hatch with Greer assisting her from the outside.

"Quick question," Greer asked once Kipling was clear. He offered Grayson a hand, but Grayson jumped and leveraged his body on the edge of the opening, extricating himself from the bunker. "You sure the number of visitors was three?"

"Yes," Grayson said, gaining his feet on the other side. "The one woman known to us, and two men I cannot identify."

Donovan huffed, his hands at his waist. "Well, I guess that's a kind of good news. We've got the two men. Both were wounded, one of which I'm pretty sure you started. But the third — I'm guessing the woman you said you know — managed to get to their vehicle. She rammed my truck on her way out."

"She's escaped entirely?"

"Well, not yet. I didn't show up with just one vehicle. One of my guys is in pursuit."

Grayson extended his hand to the man, who took it in a firm hold. "Thank you. For offering your home, your protection, and your assistance."

"All good," Donovan said and motioned for them to follow from beneath the deck.

Holding Kipling's hand, Grayson followed and led her back into the sunlight. In the driveway sat their previously used vehicle, the front windscreen and back passenger windows shot through, and a flat front tyre. The green SUV Lynne Connolly and her men had arrived in was, indeed, gone and twenty feet up the ascending driveway sat Donovan's red pickup partially into the undergrowth with a large stretch of damage from cab to the end of the long bed. The rear bumper hung at a precarious angle to the ground and the shattered bits of a front headlamp and reverse lights covered the gravel.

He now understood the bitterness in Donovan's voice when he mentioned the damaged vehicle. It was, quite clearly, not a department standard-issue vehicle but a private-use truck.

On the ground where Grayson had dropped him was the man he'd heard Lynne refer to as Duarte. He was on his stomach, hands and feet cable-tied and a bleeding gash on the back of his head. His cap was a couple of feet away. He was still unconscious, which meant either he'd gained consciousness and Greer took him out again, or when he woke up he would be in for a bitter surprise. Walking around their now useless vehicle, they came on the man who had been in the forest with Lynne. He was on his knees in the gravel with his hands and feet cable-tied together so he could neither stand nor sit.

...but if I catch her I'm gonna kill her.

The man looked up, blood trailing from his nose and the corner of his lips. Regardless, he sneered at them and spit on the ground. Grayson released Kipling's hand and took the three long steps to the arsehole, drew back his fist, and punched down hard. Bound or not, the man slammed to the ground on his side, unable to do anything else. He yelled a stream of explicatives in what Grayson recognized as Portuguese. Grayson stood over him, pain throbbing from his fisted hands.

Greer stepped to his side, his hand purposeful on Grayson's bicep. "Now, Holmes," he said in a low and flat voice. "I can't be having you roughing up our witnesses. I'd have to stop you if you kicked him in the nuts."

Grayson slammed his foot into the man's groin, and he screamed, doubling in on himself.

"Okay, see, I said I'd have to stop you if you did that."

"Grayson," Kipling said from behind him, her soft tone breaking through his red haze sharper than anyone or anything else ever could.

He closed his eyes and pulled in a slow, metered breath before turning to face his wife. "As much as your home has been a pleasant reprieve, I fear it's time for us to find different accommodations," he said to Donovan, his attention on his wife.

She tried to smile, but her eyes were sad and her cheeks pale.

"You got anything in the house you want to get?"

"Yes," he answered. "Our initial departure was in haste, but if given the time I would like to retrieve our things. We have some in our vehicle as well."

"We'll move that. I've got another vehicle coming and we can take you out of here until you figure out your next move."

Donovan left them alone to go into the lake house that now somehow felt different. It was no longer welcoming, although nothing inside the home had changed. It had been tainted. Grayson told Kipling to rest on the couch while he gathered what few items they had since they had arrived with very little. She was pale and distracted, and he feared the weight and reality of today's events would crash into her. After the weeks she had survived, despite surviving, he knew how PTSD affected the soul.

While upstairs, he heard the chime of a text.

> Greer says you two are okay.

> As well as we can be, yes. We are unharmed physically. Do you have thoughts for our next destination?

> Actually, Flannery and I were talking. At this point, we figure the two of you should come on back to the city and we'll secure a location here. We know now where the leak happened and it wasn't even a leak. No one thought anything about giving Lynne information.

> This time we're keeping it closer to the chest.

> Understood. I will need a new vehicle.

He dropped the phone on the still-rumpled bedding while shoving clothing both clean and dirty into their suitcase. He read the next text as it appeared on the screen.

Grayson reached for the phone to answer when Kipling's voice carried to him from the bottom of the stairs, but the sound of it — distant and weak — immediately snapped his attention. Grayson bolted to the top of the open staircase leading to the living space. His wife stood at the bottom, gripping the banister, her face ashen.

"Grayson, I don't feel right…"

She hit the floor before he could reach her.

"I want to see my wife," Grayson forced through his painfully clenched jaw. "You've no right to—"

"I do have the right." The doctor with Sinclair embroidered on his white jacket attempted to intimidate Grayson by blocking his way toward the door leading to wherever they had taken Kipling. "Until that young woman can give me permission to allow you access, I don't intend to shirk my responsibility to protect her."

"Then protect her!" Grayson snapped, his barely maintained veneer cracking. "You are placing her in harm—"

"I don't doubt she has been placed in harm's way. The bruises and marks I found — both old and new — tell me what I need to know. What I *don't* know is who *you* are and who *she* is because nothing matches up."

Grayson twisted away, scrubbing his palms over his face before he laced his fingers behind his neck and looked to the ceiling. Years. He'd spent years moving through legends and scenarios and danger without a single waver in his calm, in his focus. Now…he couldn't even maintain a basic American accent, let alone be convincing enough to get past the doors to reach his wife.

"Please," was all he could form. He didn't realize the words had left his lips, and not just his soul until he heard his own strained voice. He lowered his arms and turned back to the doctor who was far closer to retirement than internship. "Please, just tell me. Is she going to be okay?"

He thought perhaps a shadow of compassion passed the man's expression, but his mouth was set firm. "Until I can confirm who—"

"I got you there, chief," came Patrick Flannery's sudden and familiar voice as he crossed the waiting area toward them.

Grayson hadn't seen him enter the room.

Greg followed immediately behind.

Agent Flannery led the doctor away from them, his hand drawing what Grayson assumed to be his badge from his jacket pocket, and Greg came to Grayson, his hand coming down firm on Grayson's shoulder. Grayson closed his eyes and pressed his lips together, swallowing hard.

"How is she?" Greg asked.

He shook his head. "I don't know," he managed to say, the words scraping his throat. "They won't tell me and I lack suffi-cient..." He couldn't find the words. "They won't tell me," he repeated.

"Flannery's got this. He'll work it out."

Grayson opened his eyes and looked to where Patrick spoke to the doctor. His focus was on the physician, but Dr. Sinclair slid a sidelong glance toward Grayson. This was a small, regional hospital in a relatively small town where they weren't in the habit of receiving FBI agents and MI6 officers in their ER. Even with proof, their story would be likely difficult to accept. He set his hands at his waist and looked down.

"I hate giving bad news, Ollie, but Greer reported she got away. She managed to get to town before Greer's guy caught up. She ditched her vehicle. He's checking with the local sheriff to see if anyone has reported a stolen vehicle."

He wanted to curse Lynne, curse them all, but his soul could only process one bundle of emotion at a time. "I don't know if I can continue to do this," he said as much to himself as to Greg.

Before his cousin to say anything more, Flannery and the doctor returned to them. "I'm sure you understand why—" Dr. Sinclair began.

Grayson raised a hand and shook his head. "I do. And on some level, I appreciate it. But please, how is my wife?" He didn't know what story Patrick Flannery had provided and didn't care, as long as it accomplished the end result of getting him to Kipling.

"She is still asleep, but that's not anything to worry about. She shows signs of extreme stress and several deficiencies in her labs. We are giving her some infusions now that should help until a medical plan can be worked out—"

"And for that, we'll be taking her back to Boston," Flannery interjected. "She can sleep the whole way if she wants."

Grayson looked to the FBI agent, and his friend, with relief.

"That a problem, Doc?" Flannery asked.

Doctor Sinclair drew in a deep breath through his nose, releasing it before he answered with a reluctant shrug. "Not my first recommendation, but as long as you commit to assuring she has future medical care, I'll sign off on her release once she's awake and feels up to it."

"May I see her?"

Dr. Sinclair nodded. "I'll take you to her."

Chapter Twenty-Nine

Kipling hovered on the edge of sleep, unwillingly inching toward being awake. Small things came through first. The air was cooler than it had been since coming to the lake house. It didn't smell right. Too clean, not enough nature. It was bright. So bright. She hadn't opened her eyes yet, and the light invaded her sleeping brain.

The back of her right hand ached.

Then the smooth, warm caress across her forehead overtook everything else, and she smiled when she felt Grayson's lips at her temple. She sighed, feeling the sound hum in her throat. Kipling turned to the touch before opening her eyes.

She immediately blinked against the harsh light behind her husband's silhouette and reality clashed together in a tumbling scramble to coalesce. Memories snapped clear. She remembered running and hiding, and the smell of dust and dampness. Donovan Greer had released them from the bunker. Grayson punched one of the men. They had to leave the lake. And she remembered feeling strange, stumbling to the bottom of the staircase, and calling for him before everything went black. This wasn't the lake house. It was yet another hospital room.

Grayson reached above her head behind the raised bed and turned off the offensive light. There was still enough light she saw his face and frowned at the strain around his eyes.

"Better?" he asked, the silent word on his lips.

"Yes," she says, but it felt like the word scraped her throat.

Grayson turned to a table beside the bed and came back with a plastic cup, a straw dangling over the top edge. He held it for her and she took a sip, the cold apple juice soothing her throat. When she finished, he took the cup away and leaned onto the edge of the raised head of the bed, returning to his gentle ministrations stroking her brow. He leaned close, but not so close she couldn't see his face.

"How do you feel?" he asked.

Kipling drew in a slow breath, releasing it. "I feel heavy," she tried to explain. "Tired. My head hurts."

"Badly?"

She shook her head. "Not too badly. Just a dull ache."

He tapped his cheek in front of his ear, and she nodded. Grayson turned away again and came back with her new, tiny aids in the palm of his hand. When she reached for them, she realized the ache in her right hand was from an IV taped to the back. Being careful not to jostle it too much, she took the aids and placed them in her ear canals. They chimed, connecting, and sound snapped into clarity. The room was quiet, but after being in silence, even the air vents in the ceiling were loud.

"Everything is fine," he explains, once again stroking her brow. "You are still recovering from your time away—"

She laughed softly. "Is that what we're calling it? My time away?"

He smiled, but it wasn't quite convincing. His eyes were strained, his brow pulled. "It is an illusion I require. While your health improved greatly while at the lake, you aren't fully recovered from the stress. Today was draining."

"How long have I been here? How far is this from the lake?"

"As far as distance, it took Donovan Greer twenty-five minutes to reach this hospital; however, I believe that may have been a land speed record." His lip ticked slightly, and the tension eased a tiny degree. "It would have taken considerably longer had we waited for medical assistance, and he had sufficient contacts to assure the path was clear. As far as time, it has been just past three and a half hours since we arrived."

"When can we leave?"

"After overcoming the first hurdle of trust between him and I, the doctor required only that you were awake and you felt ready to go."

"Hurdle of trust?"

"Not nearly as interesting a story as that might imply. In short, the doctor overseeing your care distrusted not only whether I was your husband, but whether I might be responsible for your current and recent health."

"How could he—"

She began to argue, but he paused her words by touching the pad of his thumb to her lips. His eyes remained downcast, focused on the point of contact, and he shook his head. "While it frustrated me to no end he denied access to you, in truth, I don't blame him. His concern was with a young, unknown woman brought to hospital with signs of abuse."

"Did you tell him?"

His gaze shifted up to her again, and he shook his head. One small, single motion. "Agent Flannery arrived and provided enough confirmation the doctor reluctantly conceded to allow me to you."

"I'm sorry…"

"For what, my darling?" he asked, his slightly mismatched eyes shifting as he seemed to study her face. "I am the one where the burden of apology lies, and I will spend my life doing so." The weight of his voice made her chest ache. He drew in a sharp breath through his nose and withdrew slightly, nodding toward the IV pole on the opposite side of the bed from where he sat. "They have been supplying hydration and a variety of other things to help you get back on your feet. Your blood pressure was also slightly elevated, and they provided medication that successfully brought it down. If you feel up to it, I can retrieve a nurse to remove it and we can prepare to leave."

"I'm ready," she said, nodding her head against her pillow. "Where are we going from here?"

"Boston. Greg and Agent Flannery arrived after us, as I mentioned, and they will take us back. Our approach to the situation has now shifted since we know who we are dealing with, at least in persona. Once in the city, we will follow up with your medical care."

"Will I be able to see my parents?"

"Yes," he said with a dip of his chin. "I promise. As soon as it can be arranged."

Kipling raised her hand to lay her palm against his cheek. He used his own hand to hold hers and turned into it to kiss her palm. "What is it you're not telling me, Grayson." He started to protest, but just as he'd done to her, she slid her thumb over his lip and he met her eyes. "Please."

He smiled, but it was a humorless curl of his lips. "I have always said you are exceptionally observant. But please know this, my darling, I am not…" He hesitated, visibly fighting to find words, which in and of itself was a strange thing to watch from Grayson Holmes. "I simply do not know what it is I need to say, or how I need to say it. I swear to you it is nothing of concern, nothing wrong, nothing…that needs resolution tonight." Grayson took her hand from his cheek and held it between both of his, smoothing his thumb over her knuckles and her wedding ring.

He kissed her finger and stood. "I will find a nurse and set about to escape," he said with a wink.

Before he managed two steps from the bed there was a knock at the door before it swung open and a man entered wearing a white coat and pale green scrubs beneath. The name *Dr. Sinclair* was embroidered over his heart and the bell and diaphragm of a stethoscope hung from his pocket. He carried a clipboard in one hand, and looked from Kipling to Grayson, and back to her.

"I'm glad to see you're awake. How are you feeling?"

Kipling raised her hand enough to touch Grayson's fingers and he wrapped them around hers, stepping back into place beside the bed. "Fine, other than tired. I'm ready to go."

"That's good to hear. Your husband and his…associates…have assured me you will continue your care when you reach your destination."

Whether he was intentionally being vague, or whether he legitimately didn't know their names or where they were going — which made sense even to her non-SIS mind — but she didn't intend to share anything more than she had to.

"Yes," was her simple answer.

The doctor pressed his lips together in a thin line and nodded, looking down at the clipboard he held. He pinched the top to raise the clip and removed some papers. "I've prepared a copy of the results of your labs from when you first arrived. I'm sure they'll be helpful to your treating physician."

"Thank you," Grayson said, his American accent again in place.

More pieces of the puzzle for her to pay attention to, at least until they could get out of the hospital and back home.

No, not home yet. She didn't know how long it would be until they were *home*, but it would be a step closer.

The doctor cleared his throat and focused on Kipling. "I've been informed that this man is your husband, but now that you're awake I would appreciate your verbal confirmation I'm free to share your medical information with him."

"He is my husband. You have my confirmation. Without hesitation," she added.

Dr. Sinclair shot a glance at Grayson again. "It's important you see an appropriate physician as soon as possible. I do not know what you have been through in recent weeks, but I know it has been harsh on your body." He cleared his throat. "It's important for the health of your baby."

Kipling gasped.

The sun was nearly gone beyond the horizon, and twilight left the highway in a monochromatic haze, the final red glow of the sun nearly gone as they crossed the green arch bridge from Maine into New Hampshire. It would still be over two hours before they reached Boston. Grayson and Kipling were in the back passenger seat of the black sedan Patrick Flannery now drove, with Greg in the front with him.

Patrick and Greg spoke occasionally, but the lack of conversation exceeded their idle talk, and music played on the radio, a mix of performers and bands spanning three decades. Kipling was beside him, curled against his side where she'd moved to shortly after they left the hospital. Even the small space between them in the backseat was too far, and he welcomed her against him with his arm around her and his far hand holding hers on top of his thigh. Thankfully, she'd slipped into sleep and had rested for much of the drive thus far.

It was purely her overwhelming exhaustion, he was sure, that allowed her to sleep because he had no doubt her mind would be as frenzied as his own with processing the abrupt announcement made by Doctor Sinclair before discharging Kipling. His words "your baby" had in the same tic, the same tiny instance, flooded Grayson's heart and soul with a crashing wave of incandescent euphoria and an equally overwhelming wave of cold dread.

She had been through so much. So much had been done to her. Things he still only suspected, some confirmed by her memories and words, and some confirmed by the results of laboratory tests. Deficiencies. Pharmaceuticals. Torture.

Grayson stared out the window at the passing landscape, the trees and signs blurring. He swallowed hard and closed his eyes against the burn but couldn't wipe away the moisture on his cheeks without releasing Kipling's hand. He needed her hand in his more than he needed to protect some façade of control.

"Ollie," Greg said, his voice just loud enough to draw Grayson's attention. He looked toward his cousin, who had turned enough in the front seat to make eye contact. "She's okay. It's going to be okay."

Grayson pressed his lips together and swallowed but couldn't force a word from his throat.

"No matter what, you're not alone. Neither of you are alone."

Grayson nodded, managing only a single sharp jerk, and looked out the window again. "Thank you," he whispered and his cousin shifted again to face forward.

A few miles into New Hampshire, Flannery left the highway for a brief reprieve stop. The exit had a variety of restaurants within the singular building, along with facilities, and a petrol station on the way out. Parked beneath a tall lamplight, Greg and Flannery left him and Kipling in the vehicle to go inside.

Before Greg and Flannery crossed the lot to the main door, Kipling stirred beside him and pulled in a long, deep breath through her nose before lifting her head from his chest. She raised her chin to look up at him, a dreamy, relaxed expression on her face.

"Where are we?" she asked.

"A bit into New Hampshire. Patrick believes it will be another two hours before we are back in the city."

She groaned and shifted, drawing her bare feet onto the seat to bring her knees to her chest and tilted her body toward him, cuddling closer. "I cannot wait for the day we are home, really *home*, and can just…"

She trailed off and even though the shift was small and restrained, he felt the slow pull of tension shift through her. Kipling dipped her chin and laid her cheek against his chest. The aids Mac had designed for her had the miraculous ability to allow her to do things like rest against him without the feedback she used to experience. Grayson stroked his hand over her hair and kissed her brow, closing his eyes.

"Neither can I, my darling," he said against her hair. "Do you want to go inside? Are you hungry? Or—"

"No," she said, stopping him. "I love Greg, and I really do like Patrick, but I want to be here with just you for a few minutes."

"How are you feeling?"

A low rumble moved through her chest that possibly resembled a wry chuckle, or perhaps another groan, and she tipped back her head again. The light outside the vehicle left shadows more than it illuminated her features. "I feel so many things right now, I don't know where to start."

"Let's start with the simple, then. Does your head still hurt?"

"No."

"Are you feeling stronger?"

"Yes."

"Any aches or pains?"

A small smile tipped her lips at his rapid questions. "A bit, but nothing a long soak in a tub and perhaps a massage from my husband won't cure."

Grayson moaned and allowed himself an earnest smile, leaning in to find her lips. It felt like it had been days since he kissed her the way he needed, and the simple, reserved contact soothed his ragged soul at least in some small degree. "I promise to deliver on that desire as soon as possible."

His wife rested her temple against the arm he now draped along the back of the bench seat, studying him. He waited patiently for whatever statement or question she formed in her mind; he recognized the look in her eyes. And today, he shared the pondering.

"Do you think we'll be okay?"

He wanted to adamantly promise her they would be, but it felt disingenuous, especially when he knew of anyone in the world Kipling could see the truth in his eyes. She always had. Even if she didn't know fact, she knew his soul. Like no other ever had or ever would.

"I hope," he said, and brought his hand to her face, brushing his fingertips along her cheek. "I hold hope. My sisters would joke I know a great deal about a great many things, but in this, I feel lost and ignorant. What I know is I will fight—" His voice strained, and he had to pause for control. "I will fight with everything and everyone at my disposal, I will call in every debt, every favor, every future promise I was ever granted to..." He had to stop again because he no longer knew what he could promise.

Her eyes glistened in the harsh parking lot lights and she

attempted a smile, nodding. "Okay," she whispered. "That's all I needed to hear."

"No." He shook his head. "There is more you need to hear because in the shock of the moment, I fear this fact wasn't made clear. I am…joyously happy. Yes, I am afraid. I am concerned. I am…angry for yet another harm inflicted on you, on us, in some arrogant pursuit of revenge. But from that moment when the meaning of his words formed, I am happy."

Kipling sniffed, tears spilling from her eyes that he stroked away with his thumb. "I love you, Grayson," she whispered, her voice rough.

Just as he'd said the night before their wedding, Grayson pressed another kiss to her forehead and said, "You are my world."

Chapter Thirty

"I've been provided some information about concerns you may have coming into today's appointment."

The middle-aged woman who had introduced herself as Dr. Andrea Kline looked over the top of her reading glasses to Grayson and Kipling. There was absolutely no judgment in her tone or expression, and Kipling was actually thankful to be speaking to a doctor who knew the whole truth. She was weary of dancing around questions and answers and dealing with men like Dr. Sinclair who had been cold and dismissive at best, condescending at worst. She and Grayson sat in separate chairs across from the doctor, but with hands held and resting on the chair arms between them. Kipling's stomach had been a fluttering mess since they woke up in the safehouse where they would live until things were "sufficiently resolved."

Another bed. Another house. Another step closer to home; or so she hoped. She'd been away too long.

"We'll talk more about that in a few minutes before we go for the ultrasound. I am likely not the obstetrician who will be with you through the pregnancy, but I want to make sure you're starting on solid footing and your eventual doctor has all the information you need."

"Thank you," Kipling said, swallowing against the queasiness in her throat.

"Yes, thank you, Doctor Kline," Grayson added.

Hearing his normal voice, not his false American accent, soothed her. Yet another layer of falsehoods had fallen away, making her believe they may return to their true reality soon.

She wanted to go home.

It would be better at home.

"Okay, I'm going to run through some standard history to get us started. Was this a planned or surprise pregnancy?

"Uh…we weren't trying not to get pregnant. Does that make sense?"

"Absolutely. Is this your first pregnancy, Kipling?"

"Yes."

"Do you know the first day of your last cycle?"

She huffed and cleared her throat. "I've been trying to remember, and honestly I'm not sure. Things have been…" She ended with a shrug of one shoulder and a shake of her head.

"I understand. No worries. We'll see what we can determine once we do the ultrasound. Do you have any kind of time frame?"

"Um…probably six to eight weeks?"

She made a note, nodding. She asked a list of questions, expanding on the simple questionnaire they had filled out in the waiting room about family histories. Questions about everything from diabetes and heart conditions in the family to asking if any immediate relatives were born with neural tube defects or diagnosed neurodivergence. Being the only child of only children, Kipling didn't have a long list of relatives to discuss. Grayson's wasn't much longer.

"I do have a couple of specific questions," Doctor Kline said, resting her arms on the desk with her hands linked. "Based on a couple observations. Kipling, do you know the cause or source of your hearing loss? Were you born with a hearing impairment?"

Kipling nodded. "My hearing loss was slight at birth, but it declined throughout my childhood. I had severe hearing loss by the age of twelve. My mother was sick while pregnant with a very high, prolonged fever. And I was born eight weeks premature."

"So, you've never been told it's genetic or hereditary in any way?"

"No," she confirmed. "Environmental."

Doctor Kline shifted her focus to Grayson. "Your heterochromia. Do you know the source?"

"Hereditary, traced back to my great-grandmother. Several but not all, of her descendants have varying degrees of it, most being mild. I am aware that in some instances, it can be linked to other and more severe defects or illnesses; however, no one in our family with the trait shows any signs of it."

"That's good. Heterochromia is sometimes linked to genetic hearing loss and other things. But if that's never been noted, I doubt you need to worry about it. Not that I think you would," she said with a smile. "There isn't anything in your histories I see as concerning. Your permanent OB will keep an eye on things, I'm sure." Her expression shifted to compassion to buffer the seriousness of her tone. "I've been provided extensive notes from Doctor Nulton at Lahey Hospital giving me lab results, observations, and his suggested treatment at the time. I did confirm by going through them, they did not do a pregnancy test."

"Would that have changed anything?" Kipling managed to ask and keep her voice firm. Grayson gave her hand a gentle squeeze.

"Actually, no. I would have recommended the same treatments, even if I had a confirmed positive pregnancy test. Supplements, recommendations of rest, all would have been the same. Perhaps some additional vitamins, but that's all. I do, however, need to ask some very important but likely hard-to-answer questions. The answers will tell me what I may or may not need to look for during the ultrasound and allow me to give you a better prediction for the next few months."

"We appreciate your candor," Grayson said.

Doctor Kline cleared her throat while looking down at the papers in front of her. "Agent Patrick Flannery provided some disturbing details when he contacted my office for help. It's not the first time I've worked with a government agency when my discretion is required. He explained that you, Kipling, were…" She shook her head, her eyebrows arching before she looked to both of them. "Abducted and subjected to what he defined as 'mind-altering techniques at a level defined as torture.'"

She had to swallow, her insides practically shaking, and gave a sharp nod. "I don't remember everything, but we've pieced together enough that yes, that's what I'd call it. What I remember is horrible."

"I'm very sorry," Doctor Kline said with sympathy. "And I am truly sorry if talking about it brings back traumatic memories."

"It's necessary. I know that."

"Okay. The lab results showed deficiencies in vitamin D, vitamin B-12, magnesium, and iron and elevated levels of cortisol. All of those indicate extreme stress both physically and mentally. I also see Doctor Nulton provided prescription-level supplements to help, and yesterday you also received IV infusions because Doctor Sinclair also noted low levels. I will point out, though, that while still low yesterday everything had definitely improved. So, that's good. If you are still in the city for a bit, I'll put in a standing lab order. I'd like you tested weekly until your levels normalize.

"Doctor Nulton indicated he found excessive levels of a variety of antipsychotic and antidepressant medications. He stated in his notes you do not take any of these medications under the care of a physician. Is that correct?"

Kipling was exceptionally grateful for the woman's demeanor. She was being direct, but with compassion.

"Yes, that's correct."

"His tests showed traces of lorazepam, haloperidol, and quetiapine. I have never known for these drugs to be used together, even under clinical circumstances. Did you stop them abruptly?"

She faltered in her answer and looked to Grayson. Those first few days were still very much a hazy, out-of-focus memory with large gaps of time. With her glance, Grayson stepped in.

"Yes, it was abrupt. At the time we honestly had no knowledge these drugs were forced on her, or in what dosage, or when the last administration would have been. By the point of Doctor Nulton's tests, Kipling had already begun to feel the effects of the sudden halt, which we were able to determine in retrospection."

"That must have been difficult," she said, offering Kipling a sympathetic smile. "I suspect you experienced everything from the inability to sleep all the way to the inability to stay awake. Weakness. Nausea. Lack of appetite. Anxiety. Dizziness. Paranoia."

"I'm pretty sure I went through all that. Plus…" She tried to find the best way to explain what she could only think to call brain-washing. "I had a hard time shaking off the—" She couldn't find the words, so she swirled her hand beside her head, struggling.

"The suspected goal of those responsible was to convince my wife of several untruths. They did so by associating their lies with pain."

The doctor shifted her glance between Grayson and Kipling, settling on meeting Kipling's eyes. She pressed her lips together, creating a straight line, before asking her next question. The fact Kipling knew the woman was preparing herself to ask the next question made Kipling's skin cold.

"Was there physical abuse as in beatings or assault?" She paused half a second too long for Kipling to find relief in the question. "Was there sexual assault?"

Kipling shook her head before the doctor finished the question. "No, no…I don't remember anything like…" Grayson once again made her feel his strong presence with a gentle squeeze. She steadied herself with a long breath. "No, I have no suspicions of that."

Doctor Kline shook her head, her mouth still a fine line, but she didn't look away, her attention only slightly more focused on Grayson. "Do you know or have suspicions about what else may have occurred?"

"Strong suspicions, yes. Likely sleep deprivation, electroshock, sensory and psychological manipulation."

"Completely non-medical opinion: I hope like hell you've got these bastards in custody."

"Not yet," Grayson answered, his hold on her hand firming and he turned his head to meet Kipling's eyes. "But I will."

Dr. Kline drew in a deep breath and let it out with a huff, ending with a smile. "Well, we will have a much more complete picture once we do the ultrasound, but I would like to offer some encouragement. While I would not, without extreme necessity, prescribe some of these medications to a pregnant patient and only under strict monitoring, no studies have shown significant instances of fetal complications during the first and even second trimester. Some would be ill-advised in the final trimester because it could result in early labor and the baby experiencing withdrawal symptoms after birth. There have been minimal findings of miscarriage in the first few weeks, but that is found to be rare and even if you are at the lower end of six weeks, you are nearly past that danger zone."

Relief — pure, powerful, and instant — poured over her. It felt like the balloon of stress and fear that had been lodged in her chest for the last twenty hours finally burst, and the haunting emotions flowed down her arms. She sucked in air, suddenly unable to breathe, the room blurring and tilting.

Grayson released her hand and she covered her face, overcome with the onslaught. He wrapped his hand around her head and drew her to him, pressing his lips to her temple. He didn't try to shush her, didn't try to tell her to be calm; he just held her as she fought to steady her breathing and quell the tears. When she lowered her hands, he slid a tissue into her palm and she laughed, a strange sensation bubbling up in her.

"I'm sorry, Doctor Kline," she managed to say. "I just…"

"No need to apologize. I've delivered a lot of news in this room, both good and bad, and every response is honest and justified. Do you need a drink of water before we go to the ultrasound room?"

Kipling shook her head. "No. I already feel like my bladder is going to burst. You told me to come full, and I'm full."

"You can take care of that soon."

"You'll have to forgive me. I'm a bit rusty doing these. Typically, my ultrasound technician does these, but given the circumstances, I thought it best to limit involvement. Don't worry, I know what I'm doing," she finish with a laugh as she worked at the computer connected to the ultrasound machine.

"I wouldn't know if you're doing it wrong or not," Kipling said.

Nervous, effervescent energy bubbled through Kipling's veins and made her lightheaded. While Dr. Kline prepared the machine, she looked to her husband.

He sat hunched forward in a chair aligned near her hip, elbows resting on his knees, and hands pressed together in a pose of supplication, fingers against his lips, his entire focus on the black and white monitor screen where the images would appear. Kipling reached out and stroked her fingertips through the waves of his hair. It had grown out even more since the wedding, and the soft curls had returned. Grayson drew in a breath and sat up, taking her hand to kiss her palm.

"I'm captivated," he said simply.

"The gel is warm," Doctor Kline said while moving Kipling's raised shirt a bit more out of the way, exposing her still relatively unchanged stomach. She squirted some of the pale blue gel onto Kipling's skin and began working the wand.

Almost immediately a sound, a steady thrumming beat, came from the machine. Kipling gasped.

"That's a good sign," Dr. Kline said, offering a smile. She held the tip of the wand in place, where the beat was loudest. "Definitely a good sign. Heartbeat is about 170 beats per minute. Solid."

The image warped and changed and in flashing moments Kipling thought she saw things that could possibly be their baby, and then it was gone again. She realized she held her breath and forced herself to release it slowly. Grayson held her hand between both his and against his lips, watching.

"Well, based on what I'm seeing I think your count was off a little bit, Kipling."

"What does that mean?"

"I'm seeing fingers and toes; they're tiny, but they're there." She pushed against Kipling's stomach and slid around the wand. On the screen, a round shape formed.

"Is that their face?"

Doctor Kline smiled and nodded. "Yes, it is. Good eye. I see the tiny nostrils there, and eyes, and ears. I'm guessing you're around ten or maybe eleven weeks, which is even better than we thought. I say possibly eleven because the baby may be a tiny bit on the small size right now. Still nothing to worry about."

"Ten weeks..." Kipling looked at Grayson, eyes wide, mentally counting backward. "That would be just a week or so before the wedding. Here I thought we had a honeymoon baby."

Grayson's smile was nothing short of beautiful, and the wonder in his expression made something warm and enveloping bloom in her chest. He closed his eyes, holding her hand to his lips.

She loved this man. Beyond definition. Beyond limit. She loved him.

Kipling realized the doctor had stopped moving the wand, and a flash of worry hit her. She turned her head to look, and found Doctor Kline watching them, silent, with a smile — though small — that made Kipling smile in return.

"I'm sorry," the doctor said. "I've seen a lot of parents, a lot of couples, but you two...I don't know. You're something special." She cleared her throat, blinked rapidly, and went back to the scan.

She would find an image she seemed to like and tapped a couple of keys to snap it in a still photo. When done, she printed a long strip of them for Kipling and Grayson to take with them, then wiped away the gel with a warm cloth.

"All things considered, you are doing amazingly well. The baby's development definitely says a gestation period of at least ten weeks, but they're a little small as I said. Nothing to be worried about, but you should focus on your nutrition. Now, this isn't often something I say to expectant mothers, Kipling, but if you can be sure to eat well. Both you and the baby can use those calories right now."

"I will see to it," Grayson promised, standing to offer Kipling his hand as she shifted off the inclined bed.

"I have no doubt you will, Grayson," Doctor Kline said, then pointed to a door behind them. "Facilities are there. I'll meet you back in my office to cover plans, and then you're done for today. Congratulations. I don't think I've ever been happier to say that."

Chapter Thirty-One

"I didn't realize the FBI kept your office available to you," Kipling commented as Grayson guided her through the open door.

The office was as nondescript and impersonal as it had been the first time she'd been here. Except months ago he'd added very slight personal touches like a family photo, giving her first glimpse at the special Holmes family dynamics. No photos this time, but the desk was the same, the generic art on the walls was the same, the old wood and upholstery chairs facing the desk were the same, and the leather couch across from the desk was the same.

"Not so much kept it available to me as didn't find another use for it," Grayson explained, motioning for her to sit on the couch. "After I left Boston in the winter, there was no agent to immediately occupy it. In the interim, they have not yet hired someone to fill Agent DiMatto's position. So when we came back, and when I was here, it remained available to me."

Kipling sank onto the leather couch and crossed her leg, her long, loose skirt draping over them. It had been easy and comfortable for the doctor's visit, and it was hard to know what weather to expect that time of year. Could be cool, could be hot, could be both in the same day.

"Perhaps Patrick and Director Stanton leave it unoccupied because they're still hoping you'll accept their offer."

She meant it as a tease, but his expression shifted, like a momentary thought, and disappeared again.

He crossed to the desk and picked up the phone, dialing an extension. It was only a couple of seconds before he said, "We are here," and followed up with a "thank you," a couple of seconds before he set down the handset.

"Are my parents here yet?" she asked.

"Not yet, but Greg is accompanying them here and he has already left Chelsea. It shouldn't be too long."

"Then come sit with me."

He looked almost out of place in the office. The last time she had been in this building to see him, it had been months ago and he had been dressed in one of the dark, well-tailored suits that accentuated his frame. All work. She hadn't seen him in a suit in weeks, not since the wedding, and that hadn't been a suit for work. As her mother would say, Grayson "cut a fine figure" in a suit. But casual slacks and a camp shirt hanging loose around his hips with the top buttons open to reveal the sexy hollow at the base of his throat beneath his Adam's Apple was highly appealing, too. There wasn't a version of Grayson she didn't find appealing.

Grayson didn't hesitate to cross back to her and sit, one leg tucked under him so he sat facing her. He stretched one arm across the back to be behind her head and with the other hand, laid his palm to her cheek to kiss her. Not deep, not inviting, not satisfying to the warm tumble low in her stomach, but enough to distract her for the moment. Her parents were coming to the FBI building to see her. The first time since the wedding, and the first time since she'd disappeared. Part of her desperately wanted to see them, but part of her dreaded it. She'd spoken to them on the phone earlier that morning, and the strain in her father's voice, especially, was obvious.

"How are you feeling?" he asked, settling beside her but still close enough she could kiss him again if she wanted to.

"Better now that we know everything seems to be okay with the baby." The words felt like giddy flutters in her throat and she smiled. All the fear she'd harbored for what felt like far longer than a day had been replaced with excitement.

One corner of his mouth ticked up in a lopsided grin and he looked down, resting his palm on her stomach. There were no outward signs yet, but knowing their baby existed pushed back every horrible moment in the last month. They still had much to deal with and the danger was far from behind them, but for the moment, for the hour, she felt light.

"You have so much going on behind your eyes," she said. "You have for days now. What are you mulling over, Grayson?"

He tilted his head and rested his brow against her temple and drew in a long, slow breath through his nose. "I have so many thoughts, so many emotions, so much I want to express, to assure you know, but the words of far wiser and more eloquent men than I have thoroughly escaped me, or I've dismissed because none of them knew the beauty that is you," he said low and soft as he exhaled. "I did not live until you loved me."

"There you go again," she said in a whisper between them. "Are you seducing me, Mr. Holmes?"

A low rumble stirred in his chest. Grayson brought his hand from her stomach to her jaw and tilted her head to kiss her again. He held her head in his hands, kissing her long and slow and deep. The actual passage of time since he'd made love to her last was only a couple of days, but so much had happened, so much had nearly been taken, and so much had been given.

The phone on the desk rang, and Grayson groaned as he pushed himself up from the couch. "Yes," he said when he snatched up the handset. "Thank you."

Again, he hung up and came back to the couch, offering his hand to help her to her feet. "Your parents are on their way up with Greg. I will stay for a few minutes, but I think it's important you spend time with your parents alone. They will want to speak with you in private."

Kipling tilted her head, shifting her focus from his pinched eyes to the slight down curve of his lips, to his eyes again. "Why do you think that?"

"Because you are their daughter, their only child, and they will need to know you are okay." His voice had weight, like sorrow, and it skimmed up her spine. "They will need to hear it from you."

"And they will, but that doesn't mean—"

"I won't be far, I promise." He pressed his lips to her cheek when he spoke, then kissed, and kissed again her forehead before taking a step back to release her hand and move toward the door.

Greg appeared as Grayson opened the door, with Mom and Dad immediately behind. When her mother saw her, she cried out and rushed forward with her arms open. Kipling didn't realize until she was enveloped by both her parents how very much she needed that moment.

"Where are you staying? Can you come home to Chelsea?"

Kipling shook her head, squeezing her mother's hand. She and Mom sat on the couch, side-by-side, and Grayson had brought over a chair from near the desk so her father sat across from them. Grayson stayed on his feet, but beside the couch closest to Kipling, hands pushed into his pockets. For the most part, he'd remained quiet, and Kipling didn't like the tense pressure in the air buffering between her husband and her parents. When they arrived, he had shaken Dad's hand and kissed Mom's cheek, but Kipling didn't need to be an agent or officer in the SIS to see the distance.

"We can't yet, Mom. We're back in Boston, but we have to stay somewhere safe until…" Kipling stopped, sighed, and shook her head. "There's just so much to tell, and I don't know where to start or how to start. There's so much unresolved."

"Don't they know who took you?"

"Yes, but it's not that easy. That's part of why we needed to bring you here, so Grayson can explain." She glanced up at him, and when she looked back to her parents she caught the split-second scowl on her father's face.

"Then perhaps Grayson should do that," her mother said, her voice cold enough to send prickles over Kipling's skin.

Grayson sat on the arm of the couch, one leg bent with the other still on the floor, his hands linked in what should have been a casual position but the air was too thick for it to be any kind of relaxed.

"Please understand while we have discovered a great deal of information, we don't have all the answers quite yet."

"That seems to be what we've heard since you showed up on our doorstep to tell us our daughter was gone." Mom's terse words caught Kipling off guard, and she stared at her mother for several seconds.

"Mom…"

"Your mother is absolutely correct. I have had very few answers for them in the last month. I have more than I did, but my answers are far from adequate." Grayson leveled his attention on her parents. "When I came to you, I told you who we believed to be responsible for Kipling's abduction. We still believe Langdon Howell is behind all of it and continue to link the dots. And we now know at least two individuals directly responsible for taking Kipling."

"This is going to be a shock, Mom, Dad. But we wouldn't tell you this if we weren't absolutely sure."

"Well, say it already."

She looked up to Grayson, and he reached for her hand.

"One of the people who took Kipling from the flat and was responsible for her imprisonment and all that occurred, was Doctor Mina Russo. You may also recall Lynne Connelly who attended our wedding." His tone leveled flat, an attempt at hiding his anger.

Mom gasped. "That's ridiculous! Mina would never—" she cried, completely passing over the information about Lynne.

"She did. Mom, she did," Kipling managed to say before her throat restricted, making it hard to keep going. As long as she didn't think about Mina's betrayal, she was okay, but when reminded of the truth her physical response was visceral and overpowering. "She was part of it from the beginning."

"She's your best friend! She's a part of this family!"

"She was, at one time, yes, but she's been different since last winter after Grayson went back to London."

"She's not the only one," her mother mumbled. Her venom was so uncharacteristic that Kipling had a difficult time processing it.

"Did Doctor Russo contact you at any time during those weeks after Kipling's disappearance?" Grayson asked.

"Yes, of course. But she didn't know Kipling was missing. She just said she hadn't heard from you and wanted to check with us. She didn't even know you were back in Massachusetts. Didn't you tell her you were coming home?

"Mina and I haven't been speaking. I had honestly hoped time would change her opinion. Especially after we were married. No, I didn't tell her I was coming back to Boston. That doesn't matter because she already knew. She knew when she contacted you because she'd already taken me. What did you tell her?"

"What *could* we tell her? Grayson had asked us not to say anything to anyone. I just, I can't believe Mina would hold you against your will."

"She did more than that, Mom. But, that's information we'll share another time. What matters is I'm home, I'm okay, I'm getting better, and I'm safe. Grayson is working with the Bureau here to—"

"None of this would be happening if he—"

"Don't," Kipling said firmly. "Daddy, please. Don't. Look, I can feel the tension between you. I feel the anger you're projecting at my husband." She picked the words carefully, emphasizing his role in her life. "I feel him trying to walk carefully. We can't do this. Please, don't do this."

"Darling, your parents are justified in their anger."

"That isn't fair to you."

"Princess, in the last few months you have had your life in danger again and again and *again*. We're not so old and senile to think you've told us everything. Either one of you," her father said, his glare on Grayson.

"Dad—"

"I don't give a damn if we're being fair to Grayson, or not. I don't know how much you can expect us to accept."

"I'm not asking you *just* to accept anything, Dad. But, this is…" She struggled with the words, a smothering wave of undefined emotion slamming into her. "This is our life. This is *my* life. I chose it. And I would choose it, choose Grayson, again and again.

Chapter Thirty-Two

"Lyana Amelia de Sousa da Fernandes da Guerreiro," Sandra said, reading from the notes in front of her. "That's her given name. She — or someone — put a lot of effort into hiding that fact."

"What is the relation?" Grayson asked, leaning forward toward the large computer monitor. Greg sat beside him in one of the rooms appointed as a conference room of sorts in the large safe-house utilized by the FBI for their protection.

"Great-great-niece of Charles Augustus Howell's mother Henriqueta Amelia de Sousa da Rosa, so Howell's mother's sister's son's son's daughter." With each familial designation, Sandi tapped the air with her pen as if ticking a list or linking dots. "One of two daughters, actually. The other is Patrícia Henriqueta followed by all the other names. Born ten months apart."

"Interesting…"

"What, Boss?" Sandi inquired.

"Mina frequently mentioned a Patty to Kipling, implying this Patty was a new acquaintance. Mina had made statements implying this Patty had opinions about me, about us, and cast doubt on the relationship. A doubt Mina seemed to readily accept."

"That's how Lynne got to Mina. She couldn't just go straight to Mina; there was too much risk Mina would tell Kip straight out and blow everything. Patty, or Patrícia, made contact first and set the stage for Lynne. Once Patrícia convinced Mina you were evil incarnate, Lynne stepped in. She may not have even revealed the connection. If Patrícia did her job, Lynne could reach out as someone concerned for Kipling's safety and go from there."

"In hindsight, it's both logical and obvious."

"Don't beat yourself up over this, Ollie. Even you can't see everything." When Grayson stayed silent, unable to agree, Greg huffed, his cheeks puffing out, and shook his head. "Talk about keeping it in the family. I mean, I couldn't tell you the name of most of my relatives on my father's side beyond maybe second cousins. This is next-level blood revenge."

"If I weren't so enraged by her lies and gutted by what she's done, I'd love to know how she built such an intricate and flawless legend, Boss. The family and background search done by Six found nothing, absolutely nothing, to send up even a pale yellow flag, let alone a red one. She has a full work history throughout the SIS in different places and areas. Either she somehow managed to forge actual records, or she's been in this for the long, long, *long* game. I had to know how and where to look, and only because you told me to dig into Howell's family tree."

"I suggested it because Kipling urged me to. I suspect my wife made more connections and had more perception before she realized it, thus culminating in the final realization."

"How is she doing?" Sandra asked, shifting the conversation.

"Improving daily," Grayson answered. "I hold no illusion her health will be miraculously repaired, but I'm relieved to see improvement. Both physically and mentally. She has aggressively pushed back against the conditioning they attempted; to the point I am in awe. I have seen agents with more training not fare so well."

"I'm glad to hear that, and I know David will be happy. We adore Kip, but you know that."

"Thank you."

Sandi smiled, but it wavered quickly, and she sighed. "Are you ready for what I've tracked?"

"Yes. It may not be information to assist going forward, but understanding the events might fill in gaps."

Sandi spent the next half hour providing details of dates and locations when 'Lynne Connelly' should have been in one place, but Sandra had found records to indicate she was likely in America. And participating in Kipling's abduction and torture. In retrospect, each alignment both made sense and enraged him. With the timelines and data, it also seemed likely Lynne was the one who entered the prison holding Howell and informed him of Kipling's escape. As intricate a web as she had spun, she had the common sense not to show her face anywhere in Boston that Grayson or Greg would see.

She had sufficient credentials and connection to the entirety of the case and investigation, no one at Belmarsh would question her presence or movement with and around Howell.

In the past weeks, she had traveled between Britain and America numerous times but managed to overlay her work expectations so her presence wasn't noted nor missed. Either recorded travel or unexplained absences, which was relatively common for a variety of reasons, coincided with their return to Boston, Kipling's abduction, and throughout her absence. In the last handful of days, she had been documented as being in Edinburgh, but she had clearly been in New England likely near Boston and searching for them.

"Agent Patrick Flannery is conducting an internal investigation to determine if anyone within the FBI shared our location since leaving Boston. The information was very limited, so the list of possibilities is short. Either way, if she was provided the information by someone who believed her to be a member of my team, the individual here is not at fault." He glanced at Greg, who met his eyes in silent agreement to an earlier discussion and focused again on Sandra. "Sandra, I must ask a difficult question."

"No," she answered with a soft but firm tone, shaking her head. "I don't think Mac is compromised. That's what you're going to ask, right?"

Grayson pressed his lips together in a tense attempt at a smile. "Yes."

"Mac has been an absolute fool at times over Lynne, and in consideration of all the things we've learned, I have no doubt she manipulated that fact to either cast doubt or in hopes of using him later, but as much as this will probably hurt him deep, he's loyal to you. You first, Six a far, far second."

"Have you spoken to him about any of this since the team call?"

"No." She shook her head and sighed, her shoulders dropping as she leaned back in her chair. "Mac and I have been doing a lot more desk work, which is fine because it's given us the freedom to help you on the quiet. He's not in Vauxhall. Cooper's got him working some useless project somewhere."

Grayson looked to Greg. "Dividing…" he said.

"Makes sense in retrospect."

"Cooper tightened the reins the last few weeks — the only one of us who has really been out and about has been…well, Lynne. The case files she's working on haven't come to me, and I'm not involved. Cooper keeps putting us off saying he's waiting for the full team to be back on board."

"Given Cooper's deception and compliance to the actions taken against Greg, he is hopeful without justification to be so."

"He keeps talking like he thinks it'll be soon."

A now familiar crawl of perception stomped up Grayson's spine. The offer had been made by Cooper to provide assistance with Kipling's disappearance, but Grayson had been personally unwilling to accept. He didn't require direct help from Cooper or Six since he had his team.

"What, if anything, did Director Cooper say to you or Mac about the events here in Boston?"

"He told us Kip had taken off. His words."

Grayson clenched his jaw and let his head fall forward, the action causing a pull in the tense muscles along his neck and shoulders. Again and again, he had been betrayed by the institution in which he placed his trust. His life. Betrayed by people who exceeded his skills of perception to meet his eyes with deception in their souls.

Lies. Machinations. Cruel games with no consideration for the destruction left in their wake.

Loyalty means nothing unless it has at its heart the absolute principal of self-sacrifice.

Had his loyalty been leveraged against him?

There will be no loyalty, except loyalty to the Party.

Woodrow Wilson spoke of the value and gift of loyalty; Orwell spoke of a dystopian world where loyalty was a demand and a requirement. How far a cry was Orwell's prediction from where Grayson stood now?

Greg placed his hand firm on Grayson's shoulder. "We'll talk tomorrow, Sandi."

"Sure," she said, her voice softened and echoed with sympathy.

The call ended, but Grayson remained still and silent.

Kipling sat alone in one of the white wicker chairs, wrapped in a crocheted afghan, looking out over the large backyard of the safe-house where they had been placed. The massive home was a far cry from the lake house, and she was surprised at how much she missed the slightly rustic, far-from-luxurious cabin on the shore of a Maine lake.

The house was close to 4,000 square feet with multiple bedrooms and wide open spaces sitting on two acres of land. From the outside, the home just looked like a sizable and well-monitored estate of a wealthy owner and not a well-armed, well-fortified safe-house for the Federal Bureau of Investigation. She supposed depending on who utilized the house, the Bureau wanted them to be as comfortable as possible.

She felt out of place and longed once again for a 150-year-old, multistory townhouse in the heart of London.

The french door behind her opened, and she looked over her

shoulder to see her husband step onto the closed porch, a steaming cup in his hand as he pulled the door shut behind him.

"Hey…"

"I made you some tea."

"Thank you."

Grayson set the cup on the table beside her and sank into the chair adjacent to hers, slumping slightly. His expression was dark but shielded, the lines at the corners of his unique eyes more prominent than usual and it left her chest heavy. So much…he had been forced to shoulder the weight of so much.

"How did the call go with Sandi?"

He inhaled deep through his nose, his mouth attempting a convincing smile when he looked at her. "With the new revelation in the last forty-eight hours, she has managed to link many of the dots previously floating without a pin, so to speak. She was able to determine the woman we know as Lynne Connelly is, in relation to a typical family tree, a far distant branch to Langdon Howell. Third cousin once removed, if I've followed the chart properly, but a relative nonetheless, and apparently blood loyalty is unbreakable."

Kipling shook her head and made a frustrated sound low in her throat. "I understand family loyalty. If I had a larger family, I might understand it better, but I cannot fathom that level of obsessive devotion to a grudge. A stupid grudge."

"Crime has been the Howell family business for generations. Charles Augustus Howell was far from the first, and Langdon Howell will probably not be the last."

"It's still a stupid grudge held against a man who has been gone a very long time. And there's no proof Sherlock had an actual hand in his *archnemesis'* downfall." She snarled out the word. She scowled and looked to Grayson. "Does Langdon Howell have children?"

"None he acknowledges," Grayson said with a slight smirk. "None who carry the Howell name. Nelson Howell, however, had multiple sons to carry on the family business."

"Well, hell."

Grayson chuckled softly and they settled into silence. Kipling slipped her arm from beneath the blanket to retrieve the tea, taking a sip. He'd added honey, and while it was delicious, it made her melancholy for Holmes Honey.

Everything reminded her of home.

She was lost in her thoughts until Grayson curled forward from his chair, setting his phone on the table as music began to play from his library. It wasn't the version from their wedding party in the garden, but it was the same song. As the singer crooned "I can't help falling in love with you," Grayson extended his hand to her.

"Dance with me."

Kipling smiled up at him and extended her arm to take his hand and stood, the blanket sliding from her shoulders to land in a rumpled clump on the chair. Grayson raised her hand over her head and with a small laugh, she let him twirl her before his arm came around her waist and he pulled her close. Kipling closed her eyes, her palm over his heart and his hand over hers, and they swayed to the music.

The song changed, moving into another from the reception and one that worked perfectly well for continuing their slow dance. They were well into a third song when the music was drowned out by a chime on Grayson's phone.

"Call?" Kipling asked when he released her.

Grayson snatched it up and tapped the screen to stop the sound. "Of a sort. It's a reminder to call my parents before it gets too late in Sussex."

"I didn't realize it was getting late. Do you want to call out here or should we go upstairs?"

He pocketed the phone, squinting as he looked out onto the large lawn. "Probably best to call inside. They will want to see you're well, and other than Greg, no one else needs to eavesdrop on our conversation. Even if unintentionally."

Grayson reached for her hand, but instead of leading them inside, he stepped to her and touched her chin with his other hand. Kipling looked up at him and her chest ached for the tense lines around his eyes. The pinch had lingered for days and she'd only seemed to lessen, never quite going away.

Except for earlier that day when they saw their baby on the

ultrasound monitor and heard the beat of the tiny heart. Then his eyes had been filled with wonder and she'd fallen in love all over again.

"We need not tell them today," he said, his gaze focused more on her lips and his thumb stroking across them. "I fully understand and support the choice not to tell your parents today. The news shouldn't be overshadowed by tense emotion as it would have been today. Perhaps we should—"

"No," she insisted, shaking her head and his eyes shifted to meet hers. "My parents will find out soon. Someone has to hear it first," she added with a grin. "I'm excited to see their faces."

Before he could offer any other argument or alternative, Kipling toed up and pressed a kiss to his lips. He released the hand he still held and wrapped his arm around her waist, pressing his palm to her back, and deepened the kiss. Just like she hoped. Kipling raised her arms to wrap his neck and slid her fingers into his hair. When she was sure he was sufficiently distracted, Kipling broke the kiss but touched her forehead to his, meeting his gaze nose-to-nose.

"In case you needed reminding," she said with a wink.

Annalise Holmes laughed again while dabbing her eyes with a handkerchief her husband had produced with one hand and gripping the hand of her husband with the other. Emerson Holmes hadn't said much, but his smile — so genuine and pure and full of glee — said more than any words could have.

Kipling was so glad they reached out with a video call with Grayson's laptop instead of just a voice call on the phone. It made her so happy to see them and to hear their voices. Especially when they learned of their first grandchild.

"I don't think my heart has ever been so full," Annalise said, taking in a deep breath with her hand pressed to the base of her throat. "We are beyond words."

Kipling smiled, fighting her own tears. She'd left the speaking of the words to Grayson, and was thankful now she had because the intense, immediate, and ecstatic reaction from her new in-laws had been so overwhelming she'd lost the ability to speak at all.

"You've been through a terrible ordeal, my dear girl, the details of which I accept we will probably never know. That comes with having a child who has committed his life to the SIS; we don't like it, but we accept it." Kipling stole a glance to her husband, who had diverted his gaze from the screen at his mother's words. "No matter, it had to be terrible. How are you? Everything is well?"

Kipling nodded, taking the moment to swallow hard against the emotional lump in her throat. "I'm good and getting better each day. Grayson is taking great care of me."

"As well my boy should," Annalise said with a watery smile. She took a quick breath and released it through pursed lips. "Do you know when you'll be able to come home?"

The word *home* tightened Kipling's throat again.

"Not yet, Mum. There are things we must settle here in Boston first, the greatest of which is assuring those responsible for Kipling's abduction have been apprehended. We certainly hope it is soon. Will you please pass on to Uncle Elton and Aunt Hazel that Greg sends his love?"

Early in the call, Grayson had instructed his parents to not speak to anyone about Kipling or himself, including "his team," leaving out the detail of Lynne Connolly's involvement. That would have been unnecessarily upsetting, and just as Annalise said, they understood reality.

"Of course," Emerson Holmes said, his first words since Grayson had told them of the baby. His voice was like rustling leaves on the wind.

"We'll have the family to the cottage when you are home. You can tell everyone then. We won't say a word. It's your news to share, but oh…we are so happy. So very happy."

"Thank you," Kipling managed to say without her voice cracking.

"Much love for you both. I do believe I will need some warm milk and honey to calm me if I have any hope of sleeping tonight. My happiness overflows."

"We will speak again soon," Grayson promised.

"Good night, my darlings," Annalise said, dabbing her eyes again as she kissed her fingertips and motioned the long-distance kiss their way.

Emerson raised his hand to disconnect the call, but paused, clearing his throat. He raised his chin so he looked directly into the camera, an approximation to looking Grayson in the eyes. "I'm proud of you," he said, simply. "I love you, son."

"I love you, as well, Dad. Thank you."

Emerson pressed his lips and gave a nod before the video call screen went black and the message "Call Ended" appeared.

Kipling turned in the chair to face her husband as he sat back in his own. "Okay, talk to me."

He turned his head to look at her, his expression carefully schooled. She knew it; she recognized it. She wasn't going to let him get away with it.

"What do you wish to talk about?"

Kipling shook her head. "Nope, don't play coy with me, Grayson Oliver Sherlock Holmes. Talk to me about what's been storming in your head the last two days. It's more than the stress of what's happened. You're thinking big thoughts. Share them with me."

Rather than speak, he studied her in silence. Grayson drew in a long, deep breath through his nose and as he released it he raised his hand to run his knuckles along her jaw. Kipling tilted her head into the touch and he flipped his hand so his fingertips brushed her cheek. His eyes shifted as his touch moved, his thumb stroking her lower lip.

"From a young age, I knew what I wanted," he finally said with his focus still on her lips. "I knew who I am. I knew my ancestry. I knew what I am capable of. And I knew I would accomplish my goals with Six."

Prickling cold hit the base of her skull and she forced herself to breathe.

"You're speaking in past tense," she managed to say.

Grayson nodded but still did not look away from the contact between his thumb and her mouth. "All I knew is I knew nothing."

"Socrates…"

Not taking his hand from her face, Grayson shifted in his chair to face her the same way she faced him and brought his other hand to her cheek to hold her face within his palms. Kipling's heart fluttered and her skin warmed, but the prickle at the base of her neck still tingled. Grayson leaned forward until he was within an inch or two of his brow touching hers, his eyes still down and focused on her mouth. She was tempted to close her eyes but was mesmerized by his slow study.

"What do you know now, Grayson?" she asked in a whisper.

"If I know what love is, it is because of you." She smiled, and even this close, she caught the small tick of his lips doing the same. "All, everything that I understand, I understand only because I love you."

"Is this what's been in your thoughts?" she asked, pursing her lips to kiss his thumb tip. "Remembering quotes by Herman Hesse and Tolstoy?"

"And Paolo Coelho." His voice was low, and rough, and skimmed over her skin like sparks on flint. "So, I love you because the entire universe conspired to help me find you."

"And think not you can direct the course of love, for love, if it finds you worthy, directs your course."

"Kahlil Gibran. You challenge me, Mrs. Holmes," he said, and her heart fluttered. "I counter with Ian McEwan. I've never had a moment's doubt. I love you. I believe in you completely. You are my dearest one. My reason for life."

"Then, Mr. Holmes, I'll finish with Sylvia Plath. Kiss me, and you will know how important I am."

He covered her mouth with his own, stealing her breath with the last word. Grayson leaned into her and she clung to his shoulders as he stood, bringing her with him without ever breaking the kiss. But when he did, it was to press his lips to her throat and sweep her into his arms, carrying her to the side of the bed.

By the time they laid down, naked and flushed, Kipling could barely catch her breath. But as her husband kissed and nuzzled his way up her body to her lips again, she stopped him with her hands on his afternoon-stubble roughened cheeks and looked into his eyes.

"Don't think I don't realize you changed the subject."

He smiled, his lips slick from the kisses, and leaned into her until his delicious weight pressed her to the bed and his tongue and teeth abraded her throat near her ear.

"You, my darling, are always the subject."

She gasped and held on as he endeavored to make her forget.

Chapter Thirty-Three

Rapid knocking at the bedroom door brought Grayson from the attached bathroom. He opened the bathroom door, pausing as he rubbed a towel over his hair to make sure he'd heard correctly.

Greg called through the door. "Ollie. We've got a problem!"

Grayson tossed the towel back into the bathroom, grabbed his loungers from a chair as he passed, and managed to step into them while going to the door without tripping himself. The sun wasn't up yet, with just enough light in the room to cast everything in shades of gray. He'd struggled to sleep and had finally gotten out of bed before his restlessness woke Kipling. Grayson glanced at the bed and confirmed both the fact his wife still slept and that she was unexposed.

"What's wrong?" he demanded, yanking open the bedroom door.

Greg looked as though he'd been abruptly roused from bed as well. His hair was haphazard and his t-shirt and shorts rumpled, and he held his mobile screen upward, the screen indicating an open call.

"Go ahead, Sandi."

"Howell is out of prison." She spoke fast and loud and frantic. "That bloody bitch strolled into Belmarsh like nothing, convinced the bloody knob of a guard the restriction warning on her ID was a computer glitch, and skipped her arse right out with Howell in hand."

Grayson's blood went immediately cold. "When?"

"Nearly five hours ago."

"How are we learning this just now?" he demanded.

"She did it in the small hours of the morning. The guard she tricked fell suddenly ill." Her voice dripped with sarcasm. "In the ensuing chaos, she and Howell left the facilities."

Grayson clenched his jaw and closed his eyes, shaking his head. Whether her skill or the prison guard's fate was to blame, didn't actually matter. It was enraging. "Has Heathrow been—"

"Yes," she interrupted. "All agencies and channels are on high alert." With reluctance heavy in her voice, she added, "I had to tell Cooper."

"Bloody hell," Grayson cursed, scrubbing his palms over his face. He couldn't shake the suspicions he held for the man.

"I'm sorry, Boss. I didn't have the authority…"

"I know." He looked over his shoulder into the bedroom. Kipling was still asleep. Sometimes he was thankful she wouldn't hear early morning revelations like this. He could protect her to some small degree. "I won't ask what measures you've taken and will take. I trust you to do all you can." He made eye contact with Greg then asked, "Have you spoken to Mac?"

Greg offered a slight nod, indicating he had.

"I did," Sandra answered, adding her confirmation, her voice heavy. "We had a face-to-face on neutral grounds. He's hurting, Boss. Hurting because of the betrayal and hurting because he's worried we didn't trust him."

"When this is done, I will do all I can to ensure him otherwise. For now, enlist his help as much as possible. I want him to know our trust isn't lost." He bowed his head and closed his eyes, sighing deeply. "What a bloody mess. Keep me—"

Before he could finish, his phone still on the bedside table chimed with the tone assigned to Agent Patrick Flannery. Behind Greg, Grayson spotted Elton Wachsberger, one of the agents assigned to the safe house, running up the staircase.

"I'll speak to Patrick. You deal with Elton," he said, jutting his chin past Greg. "I've no doubt it's the same subject. Sandra, keep me informed. No detail, even if seemingly unimportant, is to be ignored. I believe Howell is at worst insane, at best a sociopath, but he's also a genius and has been playing a long game."

"Yes, Boss."

Greg tapped off the call and turned to meet Wachsberger as Grayson shut the door and ran back to the bed, snatching up the phone. "I'm here," he said, opening the line. "I assume you've heard."

"How the hell — you know what — never mind. I could be callin' to tell you pumpkin is back at Dunkin."

"It would be preferable. Sandra Sookoo contacted us this morning. Steps are being taken as we speak in an attempt to locate Langdon Howell and Lynne Connelly. By this hour they could very well be in the air over the Atlantic."

"They could just be running. Get outta Dodge, or in this case, London."

"No, my assumption is he will be coming here. He has quite literally committed years to enact his misguided vengeance. He will not just simply hide. He's coming for me. His stratagems failed to deliver the effect he sought. His actions now may be out of impulse, which will make him more difficult to anticipate, but he will come here."

"Damn, chief. That doesn't sound ominous at all."

"My intent wasn't to be ominous, but truthful."

"Yeah, I know. We're coordinating with your people and the connections we've got in Britain. I'm heading out your way in a couple of hours and bringing some more people with me."

"At the least, we know we have a minimum of three hours before it's possible for him to be here, even if his departure was not delayed. Time to coordinate." Kipling stirred, and Grayson glanced toward her, waiting to see if she was awake or just shifting. She stilled again. "I have a favor to ask."

"Whatever you need."

"They will be reluctant but given the circumstances, I would prefer we change the plan for surveillance from a distance for the Bransons to full, custodial protection."

"Agreed. How you wanna to do this?"

"We have a brief period of time, and I wish to utilize it. We will leave here in one hour — myself, Greg, Kipling, and whichever of your men you prefer accompany us — and go directly to Chelsea."

"You got it, Chief. Director Stanton's already said what you need you get. In fact, I'll head your way now and take you myself."

"Thank you, Patrick."

Grayson ended the call and set the phone on the bedside table, walking around to the other side to crouch to his wife's eye level. She slept on her stomach, burrowed beneath the marshmallow-like duvet, with her face turned in his direction and her hands tucked under her pillow. Her hair fanned over her face, the pillow, and blanket and her expression was relaxed in sleep. He regretted disturbing her, and for a brief second, he recalled the evening what felt like months ago when he'd crouched beside her to let her know he was stepping out to supposedly meet with Patrick Flannery.

They'd lived through a kind of hell since then.

If only they could come out the other side and leave it behind them.

Grayson first stroked his fingers along her exposed arm, around the bend of her elbow, to her shoulder. He tugged back the duvet and smiled when she took in a deep breath, making a low sound in her throat as she released it. Grayson brushed her hair from her cheek and shoulders so he could lean in and kiss her temple. Until she opened her eyes, he would rely on touch, which was no hardship.

As he leaned back, she blinked open her eyes and smiled, humming low. "Good morning," she said, her voice rough.

He waited until her eyes opened again and she focused on him before he said, "Good morning."

"What's up?"

Grayson rubbed his lips together, churning in his mind the best way to explain without being too alarming. It was a morning of concern, but a full alarm wasn't yet called for. "We have news from London of substantial importance."

Her head popped up, and some hair fell over her face. Grayson tried not to chuckle when she struggled with the blankets to sit up and get her hair out of her eyes. "What? What happened?"

As she scrambled to sit on the edge of the bed, Grayson stayed where he was so when she was settled they would still be close to eye level. He waited until she stilled and looked at him. Grayson took a deep breath before explaining, keeping his speech steady so she could read his lips.

"Since we left Maine, Lynne has successfully returned to England and as of this morning escorted Langdon Howell from the prison. We do not currently know where they are, but all resources are being utilized."

His wife blanched, her eyes widened, and her lips parted. Grayson waited, letting her process the information. After a few moments, she blinked rapidly and closed her mouth before saying, "Howell is out of prison, and Lynne is the one who got him out."

Grayson nodded. "Yes. Their location is not currently known but I have no doubt they will be coming back to the United States by whatever means they can manage."

"I'd say that's *of substantial importance*," Kipling nodded, deep lines digging into her brow as she scowled. "What now?"

"In about an hour, Patrick Flannery will arrive here. He will then personally escort us and Greg to Chelsea where we will encourage your parents to return here with us. We have agreed considering Howell's temerity and obsession that it would be best to remove as many targets as possible."

She pressed her lips together, visibly swallowing, and nodded again. "Thank you for considering them."

"I hold no ill will toward them, Kipling. In fact, I firmly believe they are absolutely justified in their opinion; I would likely feel the same way were it my child in the same position. They are my family."

Tears filled her eyes and she nodded rapidly, not trying to say more.

Grayson took her hands in his, holding them on her duvet-covered lap. "It will take time for Patrick to arrive. Shower if you'd like. I will go confer with Greg on our next steps and make breakfast."

"Okay," she said, still nodding. "Okay," she repeated as if confirming for herself.

Grayson rose from his crouch and kissed her forehead as he righted himself. Once she tossed back the duvet and crossed the bedroom to the attached bath, and he heard the water of the shower running, he dressed and went downstairs to find Greg and make something for his wife for breakfast.

Kipling sat on the edge of the bed to put on her shoes and place her aids into her ears. As soon as they chimed, indicating they were on and engaged, she heard a ringtone she hadn't heard in weeks.

Mina.

Her phone sat on the bedside table, screen up, and the photo she'd assigned to Mina's contact information glowed on the screen. Deleting the information or blocking Mina's number had never occurred to her. Before all that happened and what Kipling realized, she had held hope they would make it back to being friends. Since finding Grayson in Boston, there had been so much else going on in her head she didn't think of it. Kipling had honestly assumed she'd never hear from her once-best friend ever again outside of a courtroom.

The realization left her cold.

She picked up the phone and stared at it as it continued to ring, vibrating in her palm. Then the ringing stopped and the phone went back to her wallpaper image — one of their candid wedding photos Grayson's niece Erika had taken and sent her. Erika had a tendency to capture the most beautiful photos of them. The first had been at Shirl's wedding a few months earlier, and this one had become Kipling's favorite. They were dancing, and the photo showed Kipling's back and Grayson's hand pressed to it to hold her close, holding her hand against his chest with the other. He was smiling, and so was she, and Kipling knew it had been as she teased him to sing to her. It was such a genuine moment.

A notification popped on the screen, hiding their faces.

Voicemail from Mina Russo

Kipling stared at the screen, her hand shaking. What could Mina possibly have to say to her? After all she'd done. After all the cruelty, lies, and pain...what could she say?

Before Kipling could make a decision to either listen or take the phone to Grayson, another notification came on screen. A text notification.

I'm sorry.

Kipling nearly laughed, but the sound curling in her chest was more akin to a strangled sob and her hands shook so violently she could barely focus on the screen. It buzzed again. And again. More messages came by text, but only those first words appeared in the notification.

I'm sorry...

Rather than unlock the phone and see what her former captor had to say, Kipling forced herself to stand on weak legs and crossed the bedroom to the closed door. The hallway was a balcony that looked over the two-story open space below that served as a sitting area with couches and a large television mounted on the wall. The kitchen was to the right, but she couldn't see it from the railing. She eyed the stairs, but her knees threatened to give out beneath her.

Stop being so weak!

She shook her head and went to the railing, gripping it to lean over, and called his name. Her voice cracked, and she tried again, managing to project it enough to echo in the open space. "Grayson?"

"Coming!" he called from the unseen kitchen, then stepped into her view to look up at her. "Breakfast is—"

He stopped and ran for the stairs, climbing them two at a time. She took a step backward from the railing, afraid she'd drop the phone or topple over. She extended her shaking hand, phone screen up, as he reached the landing. It buzzed in her hand again with another message and it was all she could do not to drop it like a hot coal.

Grayson studied her for a moment, his brow pulled, then looked down at her hand and his eyes widened.

"I can't open it. She left me a voicemail, too."

"Greg!" Grayson shouted, making her jump.

Kipling heard Greg answer from downstairs but didn't look away from Grayson or the phone. It buzzed again, and she flinched. Something about the haptic buzz sizzled on her nerves and made her neck crawl. Greg didn't ask what was needed, but seconds later she saw him behind Grayson ascending the stairs. Grayson took the phone from her, and she let her arm fall to her side, limp once freed from the weight. With her phone in one hand, Grayson stepped closer to her and reached his arm behind her, curling his hand around her far hip to support her. He showed Greg the phone once Greg reached them.

"Contact Mac," he instructed.

Greg nodded and produced his own phone. Two taps on his screen and he had it to his ear, stepping away to speak.

"What's Mac going to do?" she asked, finding it remarkably easier to think and speak with the phone out of her hand.

"Text signals can be traced just as well as call signals. My hope is we'll be able to gain an idea of where she is. The timing of Lynne's departure with Howell is too perfectly timed to be happenstance."

The phone buzzed and chimed, and Kipling flinched.

With only a brief glance at her, Grayson muted the phone so at least she wouldn't hear the chime.

"Should I have answered her call? Or opened the text?"

"I'm glad you didn't," he assured, pulling her closer to his side. "While Mac long ago worked his talent to block any reverse tracking Mina or others may attempt on either your phone or mine, it's likely best he is active in the process. But beyond that, this is not something to do on your own."

"A phone can be traced from listening to a voicemail? I thought calls could only be traced when the call is active."

"That makes for exciting television," Grayson said with a wink. "While it is completely possible to trace an active call, locations can be traced when not active as well. And I feel safe in saying not everyone has Angus Hennessey at their disposal."

Greg came back, holding up his phone so they saw Mac on the screen. Kipling couldn't help but smile at seeing him. Mac was the gentlest of giants.

"Halo," he said, his Scottish brogue as calming as his bushy hair and beard. "Just gies a meenit, I'll get masel locked in. "

Chapter Thirty-Four

"What should I do first?" Kipling asked when they settled into a room of the house that appeared more as a conference room or meeting hub than an additional room in the luxury home.

The phone was on the table in front of her, and she sat with her hands in her lap tucked beneath the table. She didn't want to touch it. Grayson had brought his laptop into the room and Greg had connected his phone so Mac was now full screen on the laptop. He squinted a couple of times, clearly looking at something else on the same monitor where they appeared as video.

"Go on with the message, love," Mac said with a nod.

Kipling looked to Grayson, who sat beside her close enough that his hand rested on her back. He nodded, confirming she should go ahead, and Kipling brought her hands from under the table. She'd already unlocked the screen, but before opening the voicemail she turned the sound back on, went to settings, and disconnected her hearing aids, otherwise, she would be the only one to hear the message. Once the disconnected message played in her ears, she tapped the thirty-nine-second voicemail notification and braced herself.

For the first couple of seconds of the recording, there was only ambient sound. A rustle. A breath. A cleared throat. "It's me, Kip. Um, I'm probably the last person you expected to get a voicemail from. A big part of me wishes you'd picked up, but…maybe it's better this way. Um…I…you know what? I'm going to text you. Maybe I can say what I need to say if I'm not actually saying it. But, if you don't want to read the texts…" She paused long enough Kipling thought the recording had ended, then spoke again. "I'm sorry. This wasn't the ending I wanted. I'm sorry."

The recording ended. And Kipling sucked in a breath. Grayson rubbed his palm up and down her spine in comfort. It might have been the only thing keeping her grounded.

"Open the text. Mac can likely do what he needs with the voice message, however, I admit I have what may be described as a morbid curiosity as to what she would feel justified in saying."

Kipling nodded, thankful she wasn't required to speak through the process. What she'd say she didn't know. Since hearing Mina's voice, a slow, stinging crawl had worked its way up her arms to her neck, like spiders with poison darts on their feet. An irrational urge to pull away from Grayson's calming touch made her hands twitch as she denied it, refused it, silenced it, and shoved it down.

Mina and Lynne and whoever else had done their hardest to permanently rewire her brain to flinch at his voice and shrink from his touch. She knew it. Her logical, undrugged, no longer tortured mind knew it but deep down, some part of her wanted to listen.

"Darling?"

Kipling startled at his voice and realized she had been staring, unseeing, at her hands on the table. She turned her head to look at Grayson. *My husband.*

"Will you do something for me, Grayson?"

His eyes shifted, pinching at the corners. "Of course. Whatever you need."

"Kiss me."

He didn't ask why, didn't hesitate, but leaned to her and pressed his lips to hers. The burn subsided, the anxiety dissipated, and her thoughts cleared. No matter what Mina had done, nothing was more powerful than Grayson's love. He drew back, but not far; enough to speak.

"Did that help?" he asked, and she wondered if he knew, or at the least, suspected why she needed him.

Kipling nodded and smiled. "Yes."

Greg, sitting further down the table, cleared his throat uncomfortably and Kipling smiled wider. Grayson winked and shifted back to the position he'd been in before; close enough to touch her and support her but far enough to facilitate the process.

She drew a slow breath through her nose and focused again on the phone in front of her. A swipe of her thumb and a tap on the chat icon, and Mina's text opened. Prior to the text that day, it had been weeks — months — since she and Mina had texted and even then, things had begun to disintegrate between them. Kipling didn't scroll back, focusing on the messages today.

I'm sorry.

I don't actually expect you to forgive me, but I still wanted to say it. When you took off at the courthouse, I realized it didn't matter what I said or what we did to help you, it wouldn't ever be enough.

I'm sorry Grayson Holmes cost us our friendship.

I'm sorry I couldn't do enough to help and break whatever hold he has on you.

When Lynne confided in me how horrible Grayson Holmes is, I didn't want to believe you'd be so gullible to fall for the lies of someone so horrible. I've never known you to be so easy to lead. Maybe I was wrong or maybe he's just that manipulative.

I'm not sorry I tried. I'm sorry for how it ended. I don't expect you to forgive and forget, but I hope you remember our years of friendship when the time comes.

Kipling's face flushed hot and she clenched her fists where they rested on each side of the phone. She tried to read the words again, some part of her brain not wanting to accept the Mina Russo she'd known nearly her entire life could be the same person in the text, but the words blurred.

"This is not the Mina I've always known," Kipling said in a low voice, staring at the phone. "We used to pretend we were sisters. We were inseparable through school. She calls my parents Mom and Dad. She took care of me after the…" She stuttered over the words, not wanting to remember in too much detail the bombing at the university that had hurt and killed so many but had brought Grayson to her. She cleared her throat. "I don't know when things changed."

"She was jealous as hell."

Kipling turned her head to look past Grayson to Greg, who had his hands linked together in front of him on the tabletop, rolling thumb over thumb in an act of nervous energy. Grayson shifted in his chair to focus on his cousin. After a moment, Greg raised his head and looked at them, strain lines around his mottled eyes. His last name wasn't Holmes, but he still carried the unique eye color combination.

"She told me how much it irritated her that you and Ollie had happened so quickly. She didn't believe your relationship could be legitimate." He held out his hands, palms up, and motioned toward them. "I honestly…wasn't. Not once I knew you, Kip, even if you thought I was John. I saw easily who Ollie fell in love with, and why."

Kipling glanced at Grayson, who held his focus on her, unwavering. His lips tipped up in a small smile and covered her hand with his.

"But that doesn't justify a damn thing she's done," Greg added.

"No, it does not," Grayson agreed.

Her cell phone vibrated, making her jump, and she glanced at the text still open on the screen.

I know you've read my message. Won't you talk to me at all, Kip?

"What should I do?"

Grayson leaned toward her to read the message, his expression deceptively flat. "Do you have what you need, Mac?" he asked before turning his head to focus on the laptop screen.

"Naw, Boss, yer aright. She canny be arsed blockin' the trace. I'll hae her pinned tae the wa' just the noo. Haud on…near got her."

"I'm out of practice," Kipling said in a low voice, leaning toward her husband.

He offered a wink and a smirk. "Mac can't find any evidence of a tracking block on Mina's phone. He can follow the trail back to her and figure out where she is."

Kipling nodded and smiled.

"Is the trace attempting a loopback?" Grayson asked.

Mac squinted, the expression making the whiskers of his beard fluff and his nose flare. Something about Mac always made Kipling smile. "Aye but can't get fu—" He stumbled over his phrase, his eyes shifting in the general direction Kipling thought she might appear on his screen and cleared his throat. "Sorry, love. There's an attempt, but they're nae getting anythin' but static. Seein's ah ken how the bitch's games play, I added a wee bit more of a twist."

Grayson focused on Kipling again, squeezing her hand. "Do nothing, darling. She certainly has not earned a timely response, and if she is irritated by the delay, then so be it. Her reckoning will come in time. For now, she gets nothing but silence. Patrick Flannery should be here shortly and we need to leave for Chelsea. And you need to eat some breakfast before we leave."

"I don't think I can eat right now." Kipling pressed her hand to her abdomen. "My nerves are doing somersaults in my stomach."

"We can take it with us." Grayson looked back to the monitor. "Keep either Greg or myself informed, Mac."

"Aye, Boss." The grizzly man nodded and raised his hand.

"Mac," Grayson said before the call ended.

"Aye, Boss."

"I appreciate your work." He paused, dipping his chin. "And your friendship."

"Ya always had it, Boss." Mac winked and the call closed.

Grayson opened the SUV door and slipped from the backseat, extending his hand to Kipling. She took it and he helped her from the vehicle.

"It's likely best if we speak to Kipling's parents alone first," Grayson said to Patrick Flannery standing outside the vehicle as well. "The information will be upsetting, and I don't wish to make the conversation any more difficult than necessary."

"Sure, chief, your call. Just stick your head out when you're ready. We'll wait here. Not that I'm rushin' you, but I'd sure feel better if we didn't fart around about gettin' back to the house."

"Understood." Grayson looked down at her and squeezed her hand. "Are you ready?"

Kipling gave a dismissive snort. "To go tell my parents the guy responsible for *everything* horrible that's happened since February has broken out of prison and is probably heading this way so we should probably skedaddle back to our FBI-fortified safehouse? Sure. Who isn't ready for that?"

He smiled, but it wasn't convincing, nor did she ever expect it to be. As they took the walkway to the front porch, Grayson lifted her hand and kissed the back, his fingers laced through hers.

"Though, I suppose not everything since February has been all bad," she said, attempting to sound droll.

"I appreciate the assurance."

When they reached the porch, Kipling took the lead and opened the door, not surprised it was unlocked. "Mom? Daddy?"

The house was quiet, which made her wonder if they were home. She hadn't thought to look if the car was in the side driveway. Kipling shut the door when Grayson stepped inside, and took a couple of steps toward the kitchen, glancing sideways to the front room where Dad would usually be seen watching television.

Then the stench slammed into her like a battering ram to her chest, and in a single moment her breath was gone and her stomach clenched painfully. She swayed and gripped the newel and handrail of the stairs.

"Kipling—" Grayson called, and his hands on her back and waist kept her on her feet.

She fought not to breathe as much as she fought not to vomit.

Grayson tensed, and she managed to look at his face.

He smelled it, too.

The cloying funk of clothing suffused with cigarette smoke and chemical cloaking. Menthol and cheap cologne.

"Come on into the kitchen, Kip. Mom just made tea."

She went cold at Mina's voice and looked at Grayson. His jaw was set and his full attention was on the kitchen doorway past the stairs. He withdrew his hand from her waist and reached behind his own back, his lips firming into a thin line.

He'd left his weapon in the vehicle, not wanting to make the conversation and situation any more difficult.

"Grayson..." she whispered, not sure if she was making a request or asking a question.

"Tell her, Mom." Mina's tone was light, but it crawled over Kipling's nerves like fingernails on a chalkboard.

"I've made tea, Kip," came Mom's voice, shaky and stuttered.

From the hidden corner of the living room came two solid footfalls, and the man she remembered in a broken flash of images as the man who had helped Mina pull her from the apartment and had driven them to her prison. Grayson took a shifted step to put himself between Kipling and her previous abductor.

"Fancy bumpin' into you again," the man said with a patronizing sneer. He motioned down the hall toward the kitchen. "After you."

Grayson kept himself between Kipling and the man, his arm around her to hold her firmly to his side. A muscle along his jaw twitched and he swallowed, then met her eyes. With an almost indiscernible nod, he moved them forward.

Her heart pounded viciously and she crossed her arms over her abdomen to hide the tremble in her hands. It was only half a dozen steps to the kitchen, but the walk felt endless. Mina's henchman stepped in behind them, blocking the path to the door. Mom and Dad sat at the table, mugs in front of them but no steam curled from whatever was inside. Mina stood behind Mom, her hand on Mom's shoulder in a stance that at any other time, Kipling wouldn't think twice about. In that moment, Kipling wanted to lash out and tell Mina to get her hands off her mother.

"I knew if I waited long enough, you'd come to Chelsea," Mina said with a proud smile as if she praised herself for being clever. "I didn't have to wait long. I've only been here a few minutes. See, Kip? I still know you. Maybe better than you know yourself."

Grayson's phone rang with a sharp trill. He didn't move.

"Take it out," the man behind them said, his demand followed by the distinctive click of a handgun safety being removed.

She hated she knew the sound.

Grayson took the phone from his pocket, and Mina took it, glancing at the screen before she put it on the table. "Mac can wait. You might as well give me your phone, too, Kip."

"I don't have it with me," she said. "I left it in the car."

"Don't lie to me. You never go anywhere without your phone."

"Look!" Kipling snapped, her fear jerking violently to anger. She raised her arms, then turned so Mina could see all the pockets of her jeans. "Who the hell would be calling me that I'd need the phone, Mina? Mom? Daddy? I'm here to see them. Grayson? You?" she shouted. "Is this how you get me to forgive you?"

"Kipling," Grayson said softly beside her.

"Shut up!" Mina's shout made Kipling jerk, and she thrust a finger in the air toward Grayson. "You're the whole damn reason we're here, you asshole. You're acting like you're protecting Kip from *me*, but I'm the one trying to protect her from *you*. This is such bullshit!" Mina shook her head and huffed a breath through her nose. "We're leaving. Come on, Mom."

Mom looked to Kipling, then Grayson and the fear in her eyes made it hard for Kipling to breathe; her eyes burned with tears. Her parents stood as ordered and Mina motioned toward the back porch. They couldn't leave through the front without being seen, but of course, Mina knew about the alley behind their back fence since the two of them had snuck in more than once in high school when they were past curfew.

The phone chimed again but with a different tone. This one Kipling recognized as Greg's. The phone shimmied on the table, ringing again.

"Move it," the man behind them ordered and waved his hand toward the back door. His pungent stench made Kipling nauseated again.

They all moved toward the door, with Mina in the lead making sure her parents followed next. Mom looked shaky on her feet, and Dad was so flushed red Kipling worried his blood pressure was dangerously high. Mom stumbled, and Grayson caught her, steadying her. She looked up at him, but he said nothing, his expression unreadable.

The phone rang again as they walked through the closed-in back porch and Mina opened the back screen door.

Then the ringing stopped.

A second later, a ping in Kipling's ear nearly made her gasp but she hid it by sidestepping as if she'd lost her balance. Grayson caught her elbow, his eyes shifting to her for only the briefest flash.

Connect Check. Device Connected.

"Ollie," Greg shouted so loudly through the connection Kipling couldn't imagine it went unheard. "Ollie, Mac tracked Mina to Chelsea before the ping went dead. She may be headed this way."

Kipling swallowed and kept her attention down as they walked away from the house. How long could she stay connected?

"Where are we going?" she asked, her voice nearly silenced by the dryness in her throat.

"To hopefully finish what we started," Mina said, marching across the grass to the back gate. "Lynne says she knows how to convince you of the monster you married."

"Shit," Greg said in her ear.

The connection can't last.

"I don't remember—" Kipling said, then feigned a stumble and landed on her hands and knees, grunting.

Grayson crouched beside her, taking her elbow in his hand. Kipling looked up and met his gaze. How could she tell him?

She didn't have to.

He knew.

"We're coming," Greg said. "Now! Go! Inside!"

Before Grayson could help her stand, Mina's henchman grabbed her other arm and hauled her to her feet, shoving her forward. Grayson lunged forward but immediately had a gun muzzle in his face.

"No!" Kipling screamed.

"Enough, Victor," Mina said. "We need to leave."

"Move it," the gunman growled with a shove. "Do that again, and you're done. Capiche?"

Behind them, over the fence enclosing the yard and around the house, the sounds of shouting and banging echoed in the quiet neighborhood. She was shoved through the gate and it closed behind them, invisible to anyone who didn't know it was there.

Greg would have no idea where they went.

The connection broke and the shouting in her ears went silent.

Chapter Thirty-Five

"Grayson, please wake up!"

His mother-in-law's distraught plea yanked Grayson from the darkness and he bolted up, his vision blurred in black shadows, and pain pierced his temples. He managed to brace himself with one hand to stay sitting upright, willing to control the intense nausea.

"Kipling," he managed to say and rolled to his feet, acknowledging Mum Branson kneeling near where he'd been prone. "Where is Kipling?"

He pushed to his feet but tipped forward, his shoulder slamming into the painted cinderblock wall.

She spoke, but the pounding ring in his ears muffled her words. Grayson managed to fully stand by setting his forehead on the wall. The room tilted, but before he hit the floor again two sets of hands gripped him and kept him upright. Grayson squinted despite the low light in the room.

"Come, my boy. Sit."

He couldn't offer any verbal response to his father-in-law and briefly wondered if he looked as bad as he felt. With a few shuffled and stumbled steps, Jack Branson helped Grayson to one of the two wooden chairs in the room. There was no other furniture. On a steady surface, the room stopped tilting but the nausea and pain remained just as intense. Grayson rested his elbows on his knees and held his head, eyes closed. His brow and temple were sticky and the slight, metallic tang of blood mingled with the musty, stale smell of the room.

"Where is Kipling?" he asked again.

"We don't know. We haven't seen her since they took her in one direction and brought us down here. Do you remember any of it?" Mum Branson asked, and the quiver in her voice was enough to twist his gut.

He focused on steadying his breathing in an attempt to quell the nausea and push past the throbbing pain in his temples. His jaw ached, too. Though it hurt, he nodded his head within the grip of his hands. Unfortunately, he did. They had arrived at the small, relatively nondescript home after over an hour of travel in the windowless van so cliché it should have alerted the police simply based on stereotypical implication. Mina had left it to Victor Barriero — the unwanted guest at his sister's wedding months before — to order them inside at gunpoint, but in the moment Mina attempted to separate Kipling from them Grayson had reacted. With painful clarity, he remembered the blinding impact of Victor's weapon against his head.

His irrationality and loss of control may have destroyed everything.

Anger with himself clashed hard and vicious with the pain and he turned his wrist to look at his watch. But his watch was gone. Since Lynne would know a watch is never just a watch, he didn't have to guess why it was gone. Grayson raised his head and looked to the egress window along the low ceiling line. They were in a basement, and in a cramped room made to serve as a bedroom of sorts. It was still light out, but he had no way of judging time without more information.

"How long have we been here?"

"It's so hard to know," Mum Branson answered, seated in the other wooden chair. Dad Branson still stood near him within arm's reach likely to catch him if he toppled. "I think maybe an hour? We've been trying to wake you since they put us down here."

"I'm sorry," he managed to say, then pressed his lips together to both combat the nausea and pain and his anger.

"What do we do now?" she asked.

Before Grayson was able to form an answer, a click at the door as the lock was disengaged had him on his feet. When the door opened, rage — raw and hot — slammed through him. The bitch formerly known as his team member Lynne Connelly stepped into the room with a callous sneer twisting her features. It took restraint of every nucleus of every cell in his body to keep from lunging forward. Were it not for the two elderly parents he'd come to love standing beside him and were it not for the lack of knowledge of his wife's whereabouts and physical state, he would have killed her with his bare hands. Then and there.

He moved to stand, Dad Branson's hand at his elbow giving him the stability he needed to not look the weak fool.

"Don't do anything stupid, Grayson," she said, without a single touch of the accent and articulation he'd known for years. "We all know you're not stupid. Violent, yes. Stupid, no."

"And yet you tempt my anger," he ground out through clenched teeth and dared a step forward.

Rage had all but destroyed the limitations of pain.

Rage cleared his vision and fired his thoughts.

Rage left a bitter burn at the back of his throat.

She crinkled her nose and clicked her tongue behind her teeth, taking another step into the bare room to allow more to enter. Behind her first came Victor into the room with weapon in hand. Then Langdon Howell. His complexion had dulled after his time in Belmarsh, leaving the pockmarks shadowed by the fluorescent overhead lights, but his smug, superior air had not diminished.

"Your hubris is as distasteful as ever, Holmes."

"And your existence is equally as distasteful."

Howell made a dismissive sound and looked past Grayson to the couple behind him. "It's agreeable to finally meet you, Jackson and

Jane Branson of Chelsea, Massachusetts. I know so much about you I feel as though I know you already."

"Who are you?" Jack demanded, his stance already having shifted to be between Howell and his wife. "Where is our daughter?"

"Perhaps in time we will expand the niceties, but today is not that day." He shifted his focus back to Grayson. "To be quite, quite honest, Holmes, I feel our journey is in shift. I've yet to decide where the road will lead, though I do feel things have become increasingly interesting. Don't you think so, Holmes?"

Grayson stayed silent, refusing to feed Howell's deadly form of psychosis.

Howell gave a disappointed sigh and shook his head. He took another step into the room, coming into Grayson's space. "You do know, Holmes, that this won't end until you are a broken man. Not until I have my retribution."

"You hardly have authority to speak about retribution considering the wreckage your name has left in its wake."

He saw the flash, the twist of Howell's expression, the pinch around his eyes and the downward slant of his mouth that implied the tip of Howell's calm. Howell drew in a slow breath, his nostrils flaring, and he took another step. Close enough he had to adjust his chin to hold Grayson's gaze.

Through tight, white-rimmed lips Howell hissed "You took my brother's life."

The rebuttal nearly slipped, but Grayson clenched his jaw. There was the core of it. Grayson, in his grief, had taken the life of Nelson Howell as his form of justice no matter how unjustified.

"And how much blood is on your hands? How many have died by your order?"

"Not enough," he hissed so sharply a drop of spittle hung on his lips and his cheeks flushed red. "Not until I see Sherlock Holmes weeping."

It wasn't the first time Langdon Howell had called Grayson by his ancestor's name, but each time only confirmed how deep in his delusion he was anchored. As if he either realized his error or his teetering control, Howell pressed his lips together, took a step backward, and tugged on his waistcoat. With a sniff and a small scrape in his throat, Howell turned his attention to the people behind him.

"Take him to his wife," he said. "And them to their daughter. Let them see what she has become because of Grayson Holmes."

Victor holstered his weapon and stepped around Grayson and Howell, his hand extended toward Mum Branson. Grayson snapped his stare on the man.

"Touch her and I swear to you I will kill you."

Something flickered in the man's eyes, then he squinted and snarled. "Let's go," he ordered.

Grayson reached behind him and Mum Branson's cold hand slipped into his. Dad moved to her other side, taking her other hand. Swallowing his shame, Grayson met the eyes of his father-in-law and hand-in-hand they left the basement room. The house was small, and the basement was cramped and damp. Little was visible except for another door at the furthest corner from where they had been, as far from the stairs leading downward as it could be. Grayson followed Victor, without acknowledging Howell again, to the far door. Behind them, the stairs creaked as Lynne and Howell ascended.

A flicker shifted through his mind that he could easily disarm Victor in that moment, but he tamped it down. Not until he knew where his wife was and her physical state. Victor turned the knob without unlocking it and shoved open the door. The room beyond was illuminated brighter than the rest of the basement.

Before Grayson stepped through the doorway, Victor shifted to block him, leaning in close enough that the stench of cheap cologne and cigarette smoke-saturated clothing assaulted Grayson's olfactory senses.

"Just let me know when you want to dance, pretty boy," Victor threatened.

Rather than participate in the pissing match, Grayson stared with his mouth set firm until Victor moved out of the way to let them enter.

He dropped his hold on Mum Branson's hand and crossed the

small space to Kipling where she sat, unmoving, on the edge of a twin bed. She didn't look up when they entered, didn't react to their voices, and didn't respond in any way when Grayson reached her and said her name. She sat on the edge of the bed, head tipped forward, eyes closed, and hands clenched in her lap.

Victor closed the door with a loud thud and the lock engaged with a click.

With full attention on his wife, Grayson crouched in front of her, watching for any change with his hands resting over hers, watching.

"Where are you, my darling," he asked softly in the space between them, touching her cheek.

She swayed, first away from his touch and then back into it. But that was her only reaction. Regardless, he took the movement as a positive step. With a gentle touch, he turned her hands until the wrists were upward and eased her sleeve up her arm to expose the skin inside her elbow. Her left arm was free of any new marks. A new, hot flash of fury gripped him when he examined her right arm. A single injection mark with a flake of dry blood confirmed the violation was fresh.

"Kip..." Her mother's voice wavered and she stepped beside Grayson to touch her daughter's shoulder. "Sweetheart."

He drew her sleeve back to her wrist, covering the mark hopefully before either Jack or Jane saw. The reality of her abuse was undeniable, and he knew it was necessary to elaborate, but he had no wish to upset them any more than absolutely possible.

Grayson took a few seconds to take in the space to know his surroundings. The room was only large enough for a small bed, small table, single chair, and bureau. A basic bath was attached to remove any need to take her from the cell until they wanted. The walls were all cinderblock, painted an ashy white. Being below grade, a single egress window provided light from outside. He assumed the view was as Kipling had said...a fenced yard with distant trees the only thing visible.

"Why won't she move? Why won't she answer?" Mum Branson demanded, her voice pitched high while she shook her head. She looked from Kipling to Grayson. "She's wearing the new aids you gave her. Could they be malfunctioning? But we shook her and she still didn't respond."

"She's in a state of catatonia," he explained, purposefully keeping his voice low, level, and calm. "She is forcing herself to fully disassociate from her surroundings. I assume this is the room where she was imprisoned for the weeks her location was unknown." The words burned his throat and the battle to remain calm was daunting. "This may very well be how she kept her sanity and fought their efforts, and why she doesn't have a clear recollection of all she went through."

"What haven't you told us," his father-in-law asked. "No bullshit."

Dad Branson's ragged, deep voice pulled Grayson from his focus to look up at the two of them. Jack Branson supported his wife, and while Jane Branson's expression of pain and fear was easily readable, his pain lived fully in his eyes. A pain so raw Grayson felt it. The pain of a father.

He steeled his resolve to answer. As much as he despised taking his hand from his wife, Grayson did and stood to face his father-in-law. He sincerely hoped that one day he would be able to regain the man's respect and trust, but today he would give the man as much truth as he could provide. Dark, and a reflection on him as a man — a human being — he owed the two of them nothing less.

"We purposefully withheld the most upsetting facts around Kipling's abduction because we believed while danger was still present, it was mitigated. Our plan together had been to share everything upon the return of all of us to the safehouse."

"I don't really care what the plan was. You'll tell us now."

Grayson confirmed with a tight nod. "Kipling has little memory of actual events while here previously; only enough for us to piece together the knowledge that Mina Russo and Lynne Connelly were involved, which is now absolutely confirmed." He paused, trying to find some way of sharing the truth without destroying them. "Tactics were used against her in an attempt to, for lack of a less cliché word, brainwash her. Quite specifically to convince her to turn against me." Grayson shook his head, clenching his jaw until pain shot along the side of his neck before he spoke again.

"Why?" Mum Branson asked, her eyes shining. Tears had already left trails down her cheeks. "Would preventing her testimony accomplish anything against you?"

"While her abduction initially seemed connected to the trial, it is my belief our return to Boston for her testimony was purely the opportunity Langdon Howell needed. He doesn't give a damn about Isaac Sheldon or Charles Malcolm. He'll let them burn." He looked between them. "Did you catch his error?"

"I didn't imagine it," Mum Branson said, her eyes widening. "I thought I heard him call you—"

"Sherlock," her husband finished.

Grayson pressed his lips together and nodded. "It isn't the first time he had addressed me as such. His grip on reality is faulty."

"What did they do to her?"

Grayson met his mother-in-law's frightened gaze. "They used physical and psychological torture coupled with a cocktail of various mind-affective drugs to try to manipulate her thoughts, perceptions, and memories. They quite literally attempted to rewrite her reality." Despite the acidic anger, Grayson allowed the smallest slant of his lips to a restrained, proud smile. "Despite their efforts, Kipling was stronger. It is why she ran away from them at the courthouse. They did not succeed. She was too strong."

"So they're trying again?" Jack asked.

"Yes. All Langdon Howell wants is to see Kipling turn on me. He sees it as the only way to break me." He had to stop, his throat tightening, and look down to his wife. "He had no idea how close I am. She should never be exposed to the stain of evil in my life."

Jane Branson's strangled sob crushed him.

But his confession wasn't yet complete.

"There is no force on this Earth that will stop me from seeing her and you safe again. There is more at stake than Howell or anyone else knows." Grayson forced himself to look at them again. "Kipling is pregnant."

Mum Branson's cry broke his heart.

Chapter Thirty-Six

"**P**lease distract me, Grayson. I desperately need a distraction or I'll never go to sleep again, and no one likes a haggard looking bride."

He laughed and lowered his hands, shifted to face the piano again. So she could watch him play, she pivoted around the end of the bench to face the keys as he first played a single note with his right hand, then a short series with his left. It sounded close to what he'd been playing when she found him, but not exactly.

"You never said why you were up in the middle of the night playing piano," she said, glancing quickly at him before returning to her study of his hands.

"Distraction," he answered simply.

Kipling chuckled and leaned her cheek on his arm, swaying with him a moment before righting herself to watch him play. After what seemed to be test or warm-up strokes of the keys, he slid with an apparent effortless ease into the same melody she'd heard from the top of the stairs. It was delicate, and soothing, and made her think of a gentle breeze or a ballet dancer. If watching him play didn't have her so entranced, she would have closed her eyes and swayed with it. He finished the piece, and the final notes eased away as he dropped his hands into his lap again.

"It's beautiful. What's it called?"

Grayson shrugged and cleared his throat, a thoroughly un-Grayson-like move. "I don't know."

"Who's the composer?" He didn't answer, giving her a sidelong look, his fingers laced in his lap with his thumbs rolling slowly over and around each other. He didn't answer but arched a single eyebrow. Kipling squinted, a niggling realization skimming up the back of her neck. "Grayson, did you compose this?"

"Yes," he said, then cleared his throat and shifted on the bench, tapping on a single key, the note resonating within the antique body of the piano. "It's rough, I suppose. Needs work."

"How long have you been working on it?"

He sighed and bobbed his head back and forth, wrinkling his nose as if considering some extensive timeline. "An hour and a half."

Kipling gasped, staring at him with her jaw hanging open. "An hour and a half? Grayson, that's amazing. When did you begin composing music?"

He chuckled; a deep, low rumble in his chest that seemed louder in the stillness of the cottage. "An hour and a half ago."

Kipling couldn't form a response, only able to stare at Grayson with her hand pressed to her chest. Just when she thought perhaps she had a good understanding of the complexities of this man he shocked her with another aspect of himself.

He plucked the note again, holding down the ivory key to stroke it from hinge to edge. The note slowly faded. "I came down seeking a way to distract myself from your absence, and even in your absence, you inspired me."

"Grayson," she managed to whisper, her throat tightening with a surge of intense emotion that threatened to leave her completely mute. She swallowed and grabbed his hand. "I love you."

He smiled slow and warm and leaned toward her to press a kiss to her brow. "You are my world."

"Would you open your eyes, darling?"

Grayson's voice, so soothing and gentle, slipped into the memory and the vision of the study and piano faded away when she opened her eyes. Kipling blinked, bringing his features into focus, trying to remember falling asleep. She was on her side, her own hand tucked beneath her cheek. Grayson smiled and tilted his head, studying her features as he smoothed his fingers over her hair.

"There you are," he said softly.

"Did I go somewhere?"

"By the tune you hummed in your sleep, I'd say you were back in Sussex. Or perhaps the lake house," he said with a whimsical smile that tipped one corner of his mouth. "Do you feel like sitting up?"

It wasn't until he shifted back from his crouch beside the bed that her surroundings registered. The bed. The cinderblock walls, painted a depressing gray. Dark. Cold. The mingled smell of dank air and charcoal. Everything crashed together. Her blood went cold and drained from her face and her vision blurred, the room tilting when she shot up from lying on her side.

"Kipling," came Grayson's calming voice and he knelt in front of her and steadied her, taking her face in his hands. "Look at me, my darling."

She blinked, hot tears masking her eyes until they slipped free. Kipling's chest tightened and she struggled to take a breath. With her focus on her husband, he drew in a breath and held it. She matched him, and when he released his breath so did she. Her chest still hurt and her heart felt like a panicked bird trapped in a cage but after a few repeats of the pattern, she wasn't calm but wasn't flying apart either.

"You know where we are," he said, and she nodded. "Do you remember coming here?" She nodded again. "Do you remember anything after we arrived?"

Goosebumps prickled over her arms and up her spine and she swallowed against the new flutter at the base of her throat. "Some, yes. Where are Mom and Daddy?"

His eyes shifted, looking past her, and back again. "They're here and very much want to hug you, I believe. But they know I need your answer first."

Kipling tipped her chin again. "Mina and Lynne pulled me away. I heard you shouting." She pushed down the memory of panic they'd kill him because he was there. He was in front of her.

He was okay. "There's a room upstairs. Their torture chamber." Her voice wavered.

"You once told me you didn't think you ever left this room. You remember now differently."

Kipling nodded. She flexed and clenched her fists in her lap, and Grayson laid his hands over hers.

"You aren't there. You're with me. Tell me."

She nodded, drawing in his calm for strength. "There's a chair, it looks like something from a dentist office. They used to strap me in and did again. Mina—" She stumbled over the word and pushed up her sweater sleeve. A small bruise had formed in the bend of her elbow. Grayson curled his hand around the area, covering it, and she shifted her focus again. "Lynne was angry. She demanded Mina *dose* me and get it over with. I tried talking to Mina, get her to listen to me, but Lynne kept shouting. She grabbed the bottle and needle Mina was filling and tried to draw more. Mina knocked it out of her hand and it broke."

She closed her eyes and pulled in a slow breath, trying to push down her visceral reactions to the memory. Grayson's fingers on her arm squeezed gently and she nodded, letting him know she was okay, before she opened her eyes again. "Mina reminded her who the doctor was," she had to force through clenched teeth. "I...I remember her injecting me, but I don't — I can't remember after that. I'm sorry."

"You've told me a great deal," he said and kissed her forehead before standing. "Now, I believe if I don't allow your mum to hug you I may be physically removed."

Grayson leaned against the painted cinderblock wall that separated the bedroom — if one could call it such, more a cell — from the utilitarian and cobbled together bathroom, arms crossed and head tilted forward, listening to his wife and mother-in-law where they sat on the bed. She had been silent in her deep dissociative state for what he estimated to be two hours, eventually closing her eyes and slipping into sleep. With the passing time, he worried whatever was done to her when they arrived would be too much. Regard for her health seemed the least of their concern.

Which infuriated him so much more since Mina, a physician sworn to cause no harm, had been a friend to Kipling, seemingly a best friend, until the past few months. Kipling had been hurt deeply when Mina first began to change, pushed her away, and warned Kipling against him. This betrayal was deeper.

Though not on such a personal level, Lynne Connelly had done the same. She had not been the woman he believed he knew and had wielded her deception masterfully. He had always prided himself on typically knowing more about people than they knew themselves, and yet both Jeffrey Cooper and Lynne Connelly had tricked him. Grayson had known Lynne to be exceptional at her job, which ultimately was that of deception, so in that he had not been wrong. He hadn't anticipated her deception would be so deep, so dark, and so evil.

Perhaps he no longer had, or wanted to have, the impersonal observational neutrality required to analyze and infer reality on the people around him.

"We've only known a few days."

His wife's words drew him from his thoughts and Grayson raised his head. Jane Branson's cheeks were ruddy and damp and she gripped Kipling's hands. "But you've been through so much! Grayson said they tortured you! They drugged you!"

"And everything is okay, Mom," Kipling assured, but Grayson recognized the false calm in her tone. "We've been to a doctor who knows what happened to the best we figure, and she confirmed everything is fine. Nothing rest, vitamins, and a hearty breakfast won't fix. We were going to tell you all this today after returning to the safehouse."

"Did you know yesterday?"

A hint of hesitation skimmed her features and she intended to answer, but stopped and pressed her lips together. Kipling looked to him before meeting her mother's eyes. "We did. I made the decision not to tell you when we saw you."

For the briefest of moments Grayson thought Mum Branson would ask why, but while she opened her mouth to speak, she stopped short and her eyes widened. She released a long breath that forced down her shoulders and she looked from Kipling to him, and back again. Jane Branson was eccentric, and Kipling had described her at times as whimsical, forgetful, and unconventional, but Kipling's intelligence was not a fluke nor a coincidence. Both Jack and Jane Branson were brilliant, and in that moment, Grayson saw the realization.

"Oh, sweetheart," she began.

The distinct click and scrape of a key in the door lock propelled Grayson from the wall and he moved between them and the door. Kipling and her mother stood from the bed, and Jack Branson took a stance beside Grayson. There may have been a time when Grayson could have successfully schooled his expression, but when Victor Barriero opened the door, weapon in hand, Grayson made no attempt to hide his contempt.

"Missed you, too, pretty boy" Barriero said and winked.

He stepped into the room and moved aside for Langdon Howell to enter. Heat crawled under Grayson's skin, pumping hot and vicious through his veins. The urge to squeeze the life from the man until his eyes bulged and his lips turned blue was a flash of lightning; striking the ground and burning everything it touched, and then gone. The scorched earth remained.

"What a precious moment," Howell said, making a show of attempting to look past Grayson and Jack to their wives, then focused on Grayson again. "It warms my heart knowing the part I played in creating this touching portrait."

"Perhaps you should not be so smug since what you see is your failure, not your success," Grayson forced through tight lips.

"Failure is the key to success, my dear Holmes. Ueshiba said every mistake teaches us something. And in my failure, I learned a great deal about you. Perhaps more than you know yourself."

"Highly unlikely."

Something shifted in Howell's eyes; the spark of superiority slipped to something dark, and the smile didn't leave his face but it did became a sneer. "Your hubris will be your downfall, Holmes. It already is your downfall and it will be your end. The decision now is whether I choose to destroy your world before I destroy you, or whether I embrace my solicitude." He took in a sharp breath, the psychotic glint returning again. "Come, Holmes. We've much to discuss."

He pivoted on his heels to leave the room, tilting his head to Barriero who took a step forward. Kipling gripped his arm, pressing to his back.

"Grayson…"

"Say goodbye, pretty boy," Barriero ordered, waving his handgun toward them and motioned toward the door left empty by Howell's departure.

Holding his stare on Barriero as long as possible, he turned enough to look his wife in the eyes. Grayson pressed a kiss to her forehead. "I love you," he whispered.

"Grayson, no!" She gripped his shirt, not letting him move away.

He swallowed hard and wrapped his hands around hers, pulling them free from their hold. "It will be fine, my darling. Please."

"Grayson—"

He took her face in his hands and pressed a kiss to the corner of her lips, whispering "You are my world," before stepping away. The sound of her tears followed him out the door.

Barriero closed the door when Grayson was clear, and the sliding click of the lock choked him. Howell had already ascended the rickety stairs leading back to the main level and waited for Grayson at the top. With Victor Barriero behind him, Grayson followed. He had only briefly taken in the first floor when they arrived, and before being knocked unconscious. He supposed the descent to the basement was the reason for several tender areas of his body he hadn't noticed at first, their ache overshadowed by the throbbing headache from the butt of Barriero's gun.

The basement door opened into a small, outdated kitchen. No one else was visible, but Grayson had no doubt they were nearby. Howell led the way down a narrow hall. The house was old, cramped, and at first glance looked as though it had not been updated in decades. A musty smell like old carpeting hung in the air and sheet paneling created cheap wainscoting in the hall.

"I realize the accommodations aren't what you and I are accustomed to as gentlemen, but it has served my purpose."

Grayson followed in silence. Partially because he knew Howell sought the engagement, and partially because he needed to know the game he played. The hallway opened into a lounge with a yellowed carpet that may have once been cream, and clean but worn furniture. A fireplace with white painted bricks smudged with decades of soot sat against the central wall, and Howell took a pipe from the mantel.

He struck a match on the brick and set to lighting the already packed pipe bowl. A few shallow puffs and the charring light glowed. He let the flame die, tamped the tobacco and lit again, this time allowing the flame to emit fragrant smoke. Grayson stood silent, hands hung at his side, with Barriero guarding the door. It was a show. Howell had all the time in the world and he wanted to be sure Grayson was aware of the fact.

He believed time was on his side. Time would prove him wrong.

"I would offer you a pipe as well, but I understand you never took up the habit again."

Grayson didn't offer any response, whether spoken or in his expression, preferring to stand silent.

"I miss your eloquence, Holmes. I always found you to be a nimble and adroit conversationalist."

"Not feeling much up for conversation," Grayson said, making sure he sounded bored.

Howell blew a fragrant cloud of smoke into the air. "So be it. Then I will carry the weight of the discourse until you find the topic of interest. I am driven to correct your misplaced assumption. My grip on reality, as you stated it, is not faulty."

A cold prickle crawled up the back of Grayson's neck, but he rigorously schooled his expression, holding his stare on Howell's face through the cloud of tobacco smoke obscuring his features. Howell sucked on the pipe bit until the tobacco in the bowl glowed and smoke curled from his mouth.

"You are Sherlock Holmes."

"No, I am not," Grayson ground out.

"Generations have passed, and not until now did the threads of time and existence weave together for us to face each other again. We have unfinished business."

"You are correct in that," Grayson said with a sneer. "We do have unfinished business."

"Oh, there it is." He grinned with a chilling psychosis, his eyelids slipping low over his eyes as if in some sick euphoria. "The thrill. The retribution. The tit-for-tat. Vengeance." Howell made a low, humming sound of pleasure deep in his throat. "It is what we were created for, Holmes."

"You're daft."

"No, I am enlightened. Soon, you'll understand. You'll accept it. We have been playing this game for millennia. Cain and Abel. Michael and Samael. Romulus and Remus, William of Normandy and Harold Goldwinson, Francis Bacon and Edward Coke—"

"I suppose you are the archangel and I am Lucifer in this delusion."

Howell slammed the pipe onto the mantle, and burning bits of tobacco erupted from the bowl, the glow of each bit extinguishing before reaching the shag carpet. "Enough of this game!"

"Finally a statement I can agree with."

Grayson kept his tone level, dismissive, but the tableau of insanity formed in the lounge of a rundown house somewhere in the Commonwealth of Massachusetts made every instinct he'd ever fostered bloom into a heightened awareness of mortality.

Howell's pasty complexion grew ruddy and his features twisted in rage, a spastic tremble shaking his hands. "I will have my victory."

"Then end it!" Grayson shouted back, his outburst startling Howell for at least a moment. "What will it take for this to end!"

"You. Crushed." Howell left the mantle and the pipe toppled to its side, spilling ashen tobacco on the painted brick. "I want to see you destroyed. I want to grind your heart beneath my heel and burn your soul and leave you nothing. No one." With every promise, Howell moved closer to him until he stood close enough the odor of stale smoke burned Grayson's nose. "If I can't turn your wife against you, I will take her from you. And the abomination of a child she—"

Grayson lunged, but the room went black before his hands found Howell's throat.

Chapter Thirty-Seven

Kipling hunched over the shallow sink in the cramped bathroom off the room that had been her cell for weeks, water dripping off her chin and the end of her nose from splashing her cheeks. She cupped her hands under the lukewarm stream and splashed her face again.

She hadn't been able to shake the heavy stupor that had dragged her senses and fogged her mind since she woke up. The prick mark on her arm told her why, and every time she thought about it too much the anger and resentment crashed into her chest, colliding with the terror choking her since they took Grayson. She knew when the haze cleared, the panic would be worse.

It was a ticking clock.

Kipling dried her face and tossed the towel on the Formica vanity. It was probably a good thing there was no mirror in the bathroom. She didn't want to see the ravages of the last few hours played out in her blotchy cheeks and red eyes.

It was bad enough sitting on her chest.

She had no clock, no watch, no way to know how long Grayson had been gone. The best she could surmise was that it was early evening since the daylight coming through the egress window had diminished enough they had to turn on the lights. It felt like hours. Days. Logically, she thought it had been perhaps an hour.

Every moment that passed without Grayson's return, she felt more ill, more dread, and more anger.

Why couldn't everyone just leave them alone?

Why couldn't they just be happy?

Why couldn't they just *go home*?

Kipling opened the bathroom door and stopped short, the hot crawl of anger overtaking her neck and cheeks. Mina stood in the open doorway, her hand on the knob, and her attention snapped to Kipling. Her mother and father sat on the bed, holding hands, silent.

"I was just about to offer Mom and Dad—"

"No," Kipling ground out, crossing the small room to put herself between her parents and her once friend now enemy. "Don't you dare. You have lost *every* right to call them Mom and Dad."

"Kip, don't be petty." Mina cut off whatever else she intended to say and crossed her arms over her body. "I want to talk to you."

"You decide *now* maybe we should *talk*?"

"Kip—"

"Kip*ling*," she snapped, stressing her full name as she took another step toward Mina.

Somewhere over the last few months, she had stopped being Kip Branson. She had changed. First from Kip to Kipling, and then from Branson to Holmes. She wasn't anything or anyone close to that woman, and nothing about her missed it. There hadn't been anything wrong with Kip Branson, but Kipling Holmes was who she had become.

Mina grabbed Kipling's arm above the elbow and yanked her closer. "This room is bugged," Mina whispered, her nose just inches from Kipling's. "We've heard everything. So shut up and come with me without a fight."

Kipling firmed her lips and stared at Mina, wanting for all the world to practice some of the "hurt them as much as possible," unconventional self-defense classes she'd taken months before. But she didn't know this woman and had no idea how far she'd go. Mom and Dad — and her baby — were too at risk.

"Why are you doing this, Mina?" Mom asked, her voice closer than Kipling expected. She came beside them and laid her hand over Mina's where it gripped Kipling. "Please, Mina. Do what's right. You know what's right," Mom said in her most level, most convincing tone that had worked every single time when they were young.

Mina shifted her stare from Kipling to Mom, and Kipling thought maybe there was a small degree of softening in her eyes. She swallowed and released a slow breath. "I'm trying. I've been trying to do the right thing for months." She turned her head to level her attention on Kipling again. "I need Kip to do the right thing, too."

"Fine," Kipling managed to force free of her tight throat. "I'll come with you."

"Princess—" Daddy began.

"It's okay, Daddy," she said, not looking away from Mina. "We'll all be okay. Grayson won't let anything happen." She made sure the unspoken emphasis on anything was clear in her tone.

Mina's eyes narrowed the tiniest of degrees before she turned toward the open door, breaking Mom's touch from Kipling's arm, and pulled Kipling into the basement space outside the room. Still gripping Kipling's arm — as if Kipling could possibly break away and run because where would she go? — she closed and locked the door with Mom and Dad inside.

Without speaking, Mina started up the rickety stairs leading to the main level, pulling Kipling along with her. Flashes of memories, like déjà vu, flashed through her mind like strobe lights. She remembered the stairs. The smell of the basement. She visualized the kitchen just seconds before Mina opened the door and the room came into view. Small, outdated, and grimy and the smell of greasy food made Kipling's stomach twist.

It had been hours since she ate anything and even then, she had only nibbled on the muffin Grayson had insisted they take from the safehouse on their way to Chelsea.

That felt like days ago.

Not hours.

"I'm not willing to give up on you just yet, Kip," Mina said as she pulled Kipling toward a sliding door opening onto a fenced in backyard.

Kipling realized the fence, and the tops of houses. Beyond, had been her only view from the egress window in her cell. The grass was patchy; overgrown in some spots and bare dirt in others. The entire house was oppressive with age and neglect, and it sat on her chest like an unpleasant memory.

Then a familiar scent, subtle and faint, brushed over her like stepping through a cloud. Grayson didn't wear cologne, but the smell of his soap and shampoo was familiar. She resisted Mina's pull.

"Where is Grayson?"

Mina huffed. "Grayson. Grayson. Grayson. Grayson. All I've heard for months is *Grayson*," she snapped, her voice tinged with distaste.

Mina unlocked the slider and yanked it open, pulling her outside. Despite the depressing neglect of the property, the air was heavy with the smells of Autumn and earth and leaves. It erased Grayson's olfactory presence, and Kipling resented it. They stepped out of the house directly to the grass. Cement footers marked out where a patio might have once been but was gone now. Once outside, Kipling saw a woman seated in an Adirondack chair, the paint chipped and the exposed wood now gray. She was probably near forty with medium-tone skin and black hair piled at her crown. She stood when they approached, her expression flat.

"Kip, this is Patty."

Kipling's nerves immediately singed and she pulled back from Mina, who released her arm. Where would she go anyway? The sliding door to the house was open, but she couldn't leave. She stepped away, putting distance between herself and the women.

"Do you remember—"

"Do I remember?" she snapped, glaring at Mina. "Remember

who I might have met while I was your prisoner? No. Remember what you did to me? How you tortured me? I'm starting to."

"We didn't torture you. We were trying to—"

"Help me? Damn it, Mina! Do you really believe the hell you put me through would actually change anything?"

"You need to hear her out. She's the one who convinced me I needed to help—"

"No," Kipling said, cutting her off. "Mina, there's absolutely nothing you or Patty" — she shot a glance and tossed a hand toward the woman—"or anyone else can say or do to make me change how I feel about *my husband*."

"But you don't know him—"

"No!" Kipling shouted, jabbing a finger in the air at Mina. "I don't know *you*! I thought I did. I thought—" Sudden, overwhelming, choking sadness slammed into her and stole her voice. She steeled herself and straightened her spine, sniffed, and crossed her arms over her body. "You said you heard everything we said downstairs."

"Yes."

"Then you know," she forced herself to say, her vision blurring. "I always believed we'd be the cool aunties to each other's—" She couldn't finish.

Mina took a step toward her, and Kipling matched with a step backward, keeping the distance between them. Mina stopped, and looked from Kipling to Patty and back again, her eyes shining bright.

"Nothing we tried would have hurt a baby," Mina justified. "It wouldn't hurt you. It was all safe. I-I made sure to be careful," she said fast and loud. "It was just to help you break free of him. To help you—"

"To *make* me," Kipling cut her off. "You tried to *make* me hate my husband. You drugged me. You tortured me." Mina opened her mouth to counter, but Kipling spoke louder. "You tortured me! You tried to break me! You weren't helping me!"

"Enough!" Patty yelled, speaking for the first time. "You want every goddamn *rego do cu* calling in a complaint?"

"Oh, you *do* speak," Kipling mocked. "Honestly, it's a relief to see you're real. I was beginning to think you were Mina's imaginary friend."

The woman smirked. "You've got a loud mouth now that you're not drugged and drooling."

She was about to snap back when something in her brain flipped and she squinted, staring at the woman. A piece of the overall puzzle slipped into place. "*Rego do cu.* Portuguese. Right?" Kipling took a step around to avoid Mina and move closer to Patty. "Interesting. If I tilt my head and squint, I see the family resemblance."

The woman's expression turned cold and she ticked her head slightly to the side. "Mina said you were smart, but to be honest, I never saw it. Not while you were here, anyway. Damn stupid if you put your trust in a killer like Holmes."

Kipling tossed back her head and barked a laugh, spinning to walk a few feet away, waving her hand in ridiculous dismissal. "Oh, that's...that's...wicked rich. Killer Holmes. Real rich coming from a damn Howell." She shouted the name, pivoting back to look at the women. "Maybe not a Howell in *name*, though, right? But then again, neither is Lynne."

Patty's straight mouth curled into a sneer.

"What are you saying, Kip?" Mina asked, looking between Kipling and the other woman. "Patty?"

"When did you make friends?" Kip asked, ignoring Mina's question directly. She closed the space between them to stand in front of Mina, hoping to keep Mina's attention on her. "When did you meet Patty and when did you tell her about Grayson?"

"Why does that matter?"

"Did you know Patty before I met Grayson?" she asked slowly.

Mina's gaze shifted away, and then back to Kipling. "No, it was some time after. But, Kip—"

"Did *you* introduce the topic of me and my boyfriend?"

Something shifted in Mina's expression. Not enough for Kipling to believe Mina realized all the levels of deception, but maybe enough that Mina would question. "I-I don't remember. But I told her…" She trailed off, scowling. "I told her how it seemed so fast and I didn't think he was for real."

"How did you start talking with Lynne Connelly?"

"She contacted me," Mina said quickly, visibly dismissing the row of dots Kipling laid out. "It was after you made that ridiculous trip to London and decided you weren't coming back. And you told me you were getting married!"

"Do you even see the ridiculousness of this, Mina? Your biggest bitch and complaint was that you didn't believe Grayson was an MI6 officer. You didn't believe him. Thought he was lying. Didn't believe me even when I said there was no doubt. But, when a woman who claims to *work with* him — at MI6 — the place you didn't *believe* he worked — contacts you randomly and out of the blue to express her concern over my wellbeing you just what…invite her for tea and a chat?"

"She knew so much about—"

"Do you know who that man is in the house right now?" Kipling pointed toward the open slider door and house beyond. "Do you *know* who that man is who came here today with Lynne Connelly?"

"Mr. Howell? He was just exonerated in a British court for crimes Grayson and MI6—"

"You mean MI6 that Grayson doesn't work for," Kipling interjected.

"Stop being petty, Kip."

"Stop being stupid, Mina!" Kipling stepped around Mina and shot her hand toward the silent Patty, who stood watching with her arms crossed and the damn smug smirk on her face. "He wasn't exonerated of anything! Lynne Connelly broke him out of Belmarsh Prison. That is Langdon Fairfax Howell, 21st century head of the Howell crime family. Descendant of Charles Augustus Howell. He's an insane criminal who has some twisted, broken, psychotic idea in his head that *he* is actually Charles Augustus Howell and that Grayson is *actually* Sherlock Holmes. He's crazy!"

"Grayson killed his brother and framed him!"

"No!" Kipling shouted, her voice echoing off the walls of the house and the worn wooden fence. Maybe if she shouted loud enough someone *would* call in a complaint. "His brother tried to kill Greg. John. Let's skip the righteous indignation," she added with a slice of her hand through the air to cut off any 'what about' argument from Mina. "Grayson thought he *had* killed Greg."

"Holmes killed Nelson in retribution," Patty added in a level voice.

"Damn straight he did," Kipling snapped. "Grayson has never hidden that and he won't deny it. But this has turned into some insane eye-for-eye, back and forth game that has to stop! Mina, that man is responsible for my kidnapping in Boston last winter. That man is the reason I could have died. That man is responsible for the car explosion that nearly killed Grayson. *That man* is criminally insane!"

"No," Mina mumbled, shaking her head. "No, Grayson convinced you of all this."

"No, Mina." Kipling closed her eyes and took in a deep breath. "Langdon Howell played you. Patty over here is one of his family members. I don't know how exactly, but I'd bet my doctorate on it. I'm already betting my life. Lynne Connelly, too. They've been orchestrating *this* moment, and *this* day for years all in an attempt to destroy Grayson just because his name is Holmes." She paused to scrub her palms over her face and groaned in frustration, then flung her arms wide. "I just want to go home!" she shouted to the sky.

Mina stared, silent. Then shook her head. "No, no. That can't be. I wouldn't — I wouldn't have — I did all this to save you!"

"From what?" Kipling demanded. "You're not saving me from anything! You delivered me right to the man who wants to hurt me. The man who wants to destroy my husband and I am just collateral damage. My baby will just be collateral damage. And you did this. You handed me to them."

Mina didn't blink, her eyes welling, a tremor shifting through her. When she finally blinked, fat tears sliding down her cheeks. She turned away from Kipling to face Patty, and when she shifted, Kipling saw the gun in Patty's raised hand.

"No!" she screamed a split second before the crack of the gun echoed in the backyard and hot splatter hit her face.

Chapter Thirty-Eight

Kipling's scream ripped Grayson from unconsciousness.

He pushed away from the surface he was on before his eyes opened, and he only processed a spit second to realize he was still in the house lounge before something hit him between the shoulder blades and slammed him back on the floor again. The impact stole his breath and blackened his vision, but he refused to slip back into unconsciousness.

Kipling screamed again from somewhere in the house. A heart wrenching sound that tore at his soul.

He tried to call out to her, but his voice disappeared when what he now realized was a boot slammed into his back again, and any breath he had gained was shoved from his lungs.

"Calm yourself, Holmes," Howell said from nearby and Grayson fought through the haze to focus on the man's shoes a few meters away. "Seems we've had some excitement, but your bride is not harmed."

"I will kill you," Grayson promised on the first breath he could manage. "I swear it."

Howell chuckled, a sardonic and taunting sound. "Let him

stand, Victor. It's either allow him to calm his wife's hysteria or let Lyana deal with her, and I think he'd much prefer the former."

Victor Barriero lifted his foot from Grayson's back and he pushed up to his hands and knees. He managed to gain his feet as Lynne — or Lyana — propelled Kipling into the lounge with a shove. Kipling stumbled forward, catching herself from falling with the back of the worn sofa blocking her path.

His heart stopped at the blood splatter on her clothes and face. Kipling raised her head, and when she caught sight of him, she gasped and cried out his name. Grayson managed to straighten and catch her in his arms without toppling when she came around the furniture. His head pounded viciously from the blow that had rendered him incapacitated again and for how long he didn't know, but his heart hurt infinity worse for the trauma his wife had been forced to live through.

"Patrícia dealt with the doctor," Lynne said, any pretense of the accent he'd known for years gone. "She wasn't useful anymore."

Grayson released his hold on his wife only enough to take her face in his hands and tip up her chin. His hands slid on the blood, and tears streaked the crimson she struggled to breathe, but one name was clear. *Mina.* He wrapped her in his arms again and held her against his chest.

"This complicates the situation," Howell said on an annoyed sigh. "Is the body at least out of sight?"

"She's taking care of it right now."

"We may find it necessary to adjust our timeline; however, this neighborhood was selected for a reason. The lower likelihood our neighbors may call in disturbances." Howell shifted his attention from Lyana to Grayson. "More's the pity. I rather enjoyed our journey this time, Holmes."

"I think I have earned an answer," Grayson said, keeping his voice level despite the war of emotions raging in his chest beneath where his wife's cheek rested. "What is the end, Howell? What possible outcome could you want?"

"You still have yet to accept the truth."

Howell released a long sigh and shook his head, taking steps toward them. Grayson firmed his hold on his wife and turned a few degrees, putting himself more between them than have Kipling any nearer to the man than he could help.

"That we are what? Two entities — dark and light, good and evil — who have fought across the millennia?"

"No!" Howell shouted and threw the smoldering pipe he'd been nursing across the room to hit the far wall, falling to the floor. "You are not so dull as this, Holmes! Good and evil means nothing to us. We are infinite! We are existence! We are the past and the future, locked in an eternal battle of wills! Accept it!"

"To what end?" Grayson shouted back. "If this is just one more life we have possessed, and you believe you've earned the upper hand, what does it matter if I accept? What does it matter if I concede? You have already sworn to destroy me. My concession will not change that."

"If all I required was your death, I could have had it," Howell forced through clenched teeth, spittle landing on his chin. "I will be declared victor from your lips and look into your eyes as I snuff out your life in this round."

"Only to begin again? When will it end?"

"When existence is no more." The anger in his ruddy face slipped away to a wide-eyed expression of wonder and Langdon Howell stared somewhere beyond them all. "Imagine it, Sherlock. Nothingness. Purity. Silence. Stillness."

Where there is no imagination, there is no horror.

What Grayson imagined was more horrific than his worst nightmares. Langdon Howell was insane. There was no way to play a game to win if the maker of the rules was a lunatic. Cluedo with the instructions written in Egyptian hieroglyphics.

The spark of hope he'd harbored and stoked…flickered and dimmed.

He wouldn't allow it to die.

"I am the only blood you need to shed," he forced himself to say. "So be it."

"Grayson, no!" Kipling cried, taking a step back from him. "No!"

"Your blood ends the game, but it is your destruction I want."

"Stop this!" Kipling screamed at Howell. "Stop this!"

"Kipling—"

"You have lied, deceived, manipulated, machinated, and still you *lost!*" she shouted, stepping free of Grayson's touch. "You've blown us up, *twice!* You've played games and *lost!*" She jabbed her finger in the air at him with each point. "You've stalked, terrorized, and kidnapped us. You've touched my *mother*! You took my best friend!" Her voice wavered, but her stance didn't. "You are pathetic!"

If anything, Howell's face held wonder rather than rage.

"Oh, Sherlock. She's glorious."

"I'm not done," his wife ground out. "You tortured me, drugged me, abused me, and tried to turn me against my husband. You failed! You are a failure! A pathetic failure!"

"Did I?" he said, the cold of his voice sending a chill over Grayson's skin.

Grayson moved toward her, but the engagement of weapons held him back. Both Lyana and Victor leveled weapons on him and he eased back onto his heels.

"Kipling, please," he said softly.

"Yes," she answered as a hiss through her teeth. "You failed. I did not and will not ever doubt him. I did not and will not ever fear him. I did not and will not ever leave him."

"I see that." His tone was cryptic, and the way he allowed his gaze to take in Kipling from head to feet made Grayson's skin crawl. "How did you manage that, my dear? Lyana and myself are no strangers to the more convincing means of altering one's thoughts and emotions. And yet, you eluded our tactics and took your leave. How is that?"

"Because nothing you do is stronger than us. I suppose that's one thing you did right, at least in part."

His smirk twisted into a sneer and he looked from Kipling to Grayson. "Did your husband tell you the details of SIS interrogation methods, my dear? How insidious and painful it can be?"

"He didn't have to. I remember."

"Do you?"

"I remember enough."

Howell shifted his attention from Kipling to Grayson. "Memory manipulation was our first approach, negative reinforcement, associating memories of your beloved husband with pain."

"Didn't work," she snapped.

"Sleep deprivation. Withholding food. Drugging."

"Didn't work," Kipling said again.

"Clearly." He never looked to Kipling again, focusing on Grayson. "Those were not our only tools. Do you know much about hypnosis, Kipling?"

Grayson's blood went cold.

"What, make me cluck like a chicken or bark like a dog?" she countered, the derision thick in her voice.

"Something like that." Howell's smirk grew. "There once was a famous hypnotist who resented one of his employees for quitting. Before their final hour, he hypnotized her. The next time she saw him, she would immediately be in a hypnotic trance and pliable to his commands. He didn't see her for fifteen years, but she walked by his table in a restaurant and immediately…she snapped into a trance. The effectiveness of hypnotism can be exceptionally powerful."

Grayson held Howell's stare, keeping his own expression flat and unemotional despite the tremor of dread clenching his insides. Anything could be a trigger. A word. A sound. Even a smell. Literally whatever the hypnotist desired. There was nothing he could do to predict it. Nothing he could do to break it.

Kipling turned her head, her eyes wide, and stared at him.

She understood.

She *thought* she understood. Hypnosis wasn't nearly as overpowering as most people assumed.

But she was afraid. And for that, more than anything else, Grayson hated Langdon Howell.

Grayson brought his closed hand to his chest rubbed it in a slow circle. *I'm sorry.* The anger in Kipling's eyes extinguished, overcome by silent panic. A tremor shook her.

"Oh, this is delicious," Howell said with disgusting glee. "I had contemplated keeping this little surprise in my pocket, but now I see how much more exhilarating the anticipation can be."

Kipling blinked, tears silently streaming her cheeks leaving streaks in the bloodstains still on her skin.

"Sherlock knows this already, but I doubt you are aware of the possibilities, my dear. I can make you say anything. Do anything. I could require you to spurn your husband, to denounce your love. But where is the victory when he would know the words weren't yours?"

Howell took a step closer to her, and Grayson fought the urge to lunge forward. Lyana and Victor wouldn't hesitate to shoot him. Or worse, Kipling.

"I could do it with a sound. A single word. A phrase."

She brought her hands up, reaching for her aids.

"Don't!" Howell threatened.

Kipling stopped, swallowed, and lowered her hands again.

"You have made this adventure far more interesting, Kipling." Howell's voice reeked with condescension and he took another step toward her, near enough he could touch her. "Lyana has her own technological skills not unlike your Angus Hennessey. She assured me she would have the ability to send you a silent message any time we wished through those tiny bits of hardware in your ears. It was quite distressing when we realized you had discarded them. Perhaps you knew more than we imagined. Did you?"

Kipling didn't answer, holding her gaze on Grayson.

"Did you!" Howell yelled.

She flinched.

Howell teetered on the edge. The game was to his advantage, but he didn't have the control he wanted. He was a dangerous unknown.

"I didn't know what you did," she said in a whisper, her voice rough and strangled as more tears streaked her cheeks. "I knew you'd done something."

"So you crushed them beneath your shoe. Is that right?"

"Yes," she answered.

"Well, nothing to be done about it now. I much rather enjoy this turn of events." He turned to Grayson. "Do you like this new game, Sherlock?"

"Hardly," Grayson answered flatly. "It shows an utter lack of effort and intelligence."

"And yet I am in control. You have nothing."

"Your control is a mirage. Even the most powerful hypnotist cannot make one act in contrast to their own morals. Cannot make them do something they would never do otherwise. Whatever power you think you wield is hollow at best."

"Or free her to act on doubts and desires she wouldn't acknowledge otherwise," Howell countered. "Do you believe you know her so well? She stands with you now, but are you without concern she may have accepted our truths? Are you confident she holds no resentment? You have brought nothing but pain and chaos to her world, Holmes. Her life had been threatened. Her family upended. Her friend…dead."

Kipling flinched at his words, closing her eyes for a moment. But when she opened them, her focus remained firm on Grayson.

"Interesting how you, the engineer of all that is negative, would think the blame should be mine. You will not get what you want."

"I want your humiliation!" Howell screamed, pounding the air with his clenched fists. "I want to see the light leave your eyes when you know I have won. I want your destruction! I want you to admit the truth! I. Win." He turned on his heels and faced Kipling, leaning toward her even though she refused to look away from Grayson.

"You remember some, but you do not remember all," he hissed near her cheek. "Do you remember confessing your hatred for the man who you now call husband? Do you remember confessing you wished you had never known him? And even now, I've no doubt you wish to be free of him. To return to your life."

"No," she answered, not averting her eyes to look at Howell.

Only at Grayson. "Never. I never would and I never will. He is my life. My life is with my husband."

"Tell the truth, Kipling. Your husband needs to hear it." Howell kept his face near hers but turned his head enough to watch Grayson. "After all, as your dear Sherlock once said, any truth is better than indefinite doubt."

Kipling's shoulders dropped and her chin ticked upward so she looked straight ahead, past Grayson, to nothing at all. His heart stopped and he couldn't breathe. He knew reality. He knew capability. He knew limitations. But he also knew the possibility of harm at her hands would destroy Kipling.

"Stop this," Grayson asked. "Please. I beg of you. She has done nothing to deserve this."

"Of course she has," Howell stated, shifting to stand so he could look between them. "Lyana, please give Kipling your weapon."

She didn't hesitate, closing the space between herself and Kipling, holding out the Beretta she'd moments before had trained on Grayson.

"Take the gun, Kipling," Howell ordered. Kipling turned her head and extended her arm, taking the weapon from Lyana, who smirked with an infuriating grin. "Are you still so confident, Holmes? Are you still convinced you haven't planted the seeds of hatred in the woman who you profess to love? This is going to be fun. Kipling, look at me," Howell ordered.

She pivoted her head to look at him, unblinking.

"Who have I been?"

"Cain. Samael. Romulus." Her voice was flat. Emotionless.

"Who am I now?"

"Charles Augustus Howell."

"Good, Kipling. Who is he?" Howell pointed at Grayson.

"Sherlock Holmes," she answered.

"Good. Kipling, you will do what I say."

"Yes."

"Put the gun to your head."

She bent her elbow like a snapped twig, bringing the muzzle of the gun to her temple.

"No!" Grayson screamed, reaching for her, the act of stopping his own instinctive action more painful than anything he'd ever done. "No, please. Kipling!"

"She doesn't hear you, Holmes," Howell said. "She only hears me."

"I concede," Grayson begged. "I concede to it all. You are right. Please, just release her."

"Mmmm." Howell pulled a face and shook his head. "A bit too little and far too late, Sherlock. I do not accept. Are you still so sure of her intentions? Of her feelings? Of her deepest wish? The one she wouldn't admit otherwise? Kipling, point the gun at Sherlock Holmes."

She took the muzzle from her temple and extended her arm, the gun inches from his chest, her eyes cast down so her focus was on the weapon and not him.

"Kipling, if I told you to pull the trigger, would you?"

"Yes," she said without pause, her voice the same flat, emotionless nothing.

"Here is the beauty of this little parlor trick, Holmes. The second she pulls that trigger, the second she follows my command, the trance will break. She will know she has killed you, and you will know who brought you to death. Not I. Not anyone else in this house." He paused and sneered. "But your wife. And it will be her because you have lost, and I have won once again. I have outwitted the *brilliant* Sherlock Holmes."

"I love you," Grayson forced from his throat.

"What agony it must be to know your words mean nothing now." Howell chuckled and turned away, putting several meters between them. When he turned again, watching from a distance, he had the gleeful gleam in his eyes of a child at Christmas. "Go ahead, Kipling. Pull the trigger."

Grayson sucked in a sharp breath.

She shifted the weapon in her hand like someone who had handled a Beretta her whole life. Then her eyes shifted and she met his.

Then in rapid succession, Kipling reangled her arm and fired twice. The first bullet went past Grayson to take down Victor Barriero with a grunt before he hit the floor. She pivoted again, and fired, shooting a shocked and unarmed Lyana. The traitor fell backward into the wall, leaving a bloody streak on the old wallpaper. Another pivot and Kipling shot the unarmed Langdon Fairfax Howell.

Chapter Thirty-Nine

The moment the third shot echoed in the confined space, the weight of reality slammed into Kipling and she stumbled, struggling to keep her legs under her. Grayson bolted forward, catching the gun before it slipped from her hand and hit the floor. He wrapped one arm around her waist, keeping her on her feet, and held the gun in the other with the muzzle pointed to the floor. Her shaking was immediate and intense. It stole her breath and made the room tilt.

"Oh, god…" she whispered. "Oh, god…"

"Shh Shh Shh Shh," he whispered, a staccato rhythm against the side of her head, holding her close. "I've got you."

Kipling blinked and stared at the motionless Langdon Howell on his back, arms spread like a bloody snow angel, and her stomach flipped. The room tilted and darkened. Grayson bent at the knees and got his arm around her body, and she turned into him, holding on with arms like overcooked linguini.

"Are they dead?" she asked. "God… Grayson, did I kill them?"

Holding her, he looked toward Howell, and then behind them where Lynne and the man were. Kipling couldn't look. Seeing the crimson stain of blood wicking across the old carpet from beneath Howell was more than she thought she could handle.

"I don't believe—"

Running footfalls echoed through the house, coming for them. Grayson pivoted them, shielding her, as the woman Lynne had called Patrícia ran into the room with her weapon drawn. Kipling gasped and screamed into Grayson's chest when he took aim and fired twice. The woman's head snapped backward and she dropped to the floor. Blood splattered on the wall behind her.

Kipling's insides felt like they were going to shake themselves free of her body. Violent tears blurred her vision. Beyond Grayson's embrace came the sound of movement, shuffling.

"Don't," Grayson ordered.

She tried to turn her head, needing now to see, and only caught the blur of movement from where she knew Lynne had fallen. Kipling realized in a half-second he'd ordered Lynne — or Lyana, the name Howell had used — to stop reaching for the weapon Patrícia had dropped.

"Lynne!" he shouted.

She lunged, retrieving the fallen weapon, and swung around. Before she had the gun raised, Grayson fired three times in rapid succession that sent echoing pain through her hearing aids. Kipling covered her ears, crying. When silence settled again, Grayson lowered his arm with the gun and turned them to bring her to the old couch.

"Sit," he instructed. "I need to insure—"

Kipling nodded, sinking onto the rough cushions before she collapsed completely. Grayson moved around behind her, out of her line of sight, and she heard the sounds of him picking up the dropped weapons and checking on the fallen people.

People she had shot.

Months before she had dealt with the lack of sleep, and nightmare-ridden dreams when she did sleep, in the weeks after Grayson first left Boston by taking self-defense classes to teach her how to never be grabbed off the street again. And she had taken gun safety training. The instructor had told them he sincerely hoped none of them were ever forced to draw a weapon in protection. But if they did, don't hesitate.

Because hesitation could be the difference between life and death.

Her stomach twisted. If she had eaten anything in the last several hours she was pretty sure she would lose it.

Grayson came back into her line of sight when he crossed the room to where Howell lay still. He hadn't moved, hadn't made a sound beyond haggard breathing.

"How many others have you seen in the house today?"

Kipling forced herself to blink, her eyes burning. She knew Grayson directed the question at her — who else could he be speaking to? — but her throat wouldn't cooperate to answer. The tremors twisting her insides were growing painful, like when she was little and stayed outside in the snow and cold too long. It took over every part of her.

"Kipling..."

She blinked and redirected her focus, realizing Grayson had come back to her from checking on Langdon Howell. "Is he dead?"

He crouched in front of her, placing his hands on her knees. *Where were the guns? What had he done with them?*

"No, but he will require medical intervention if he is to see justice. I need to assure it's safe to reach out. Did you hear my question?"

Kipling nodded. "I only saw Mina and Lynne and Patty."

He nodded. "Then I believe everyone is accounted for other than your parents. Were there others, I would have expected them to make themselves known when the shooting began."

Movement past Grayson caught her attention and she focused on the picture window facing the street. Vertical blinds blocked the view, but not the late afternoon sun. A shadow passed along the bottom edge.

"Grayson..." she said low.

He pivoted on the balls of his feet to follow her gaze, and when another shadow edged the window, rose to his feet and took the gun she'd used from the back of his waistband.

With a slide and click, he disengaged the safety and with a cold rush she realized she didn't know what kind of gun he held — that she had fired — and if asked with it pointing at her, she wouldn't know how to turn off the safety. If Lynne hadn't handed it to her with the safety off, which some part of Kipling's brain just assumed, what would have happened?

She had only moments to process the fact he thought she would act under his hypnotic suggestion, and in the second she realized she wasn't, and it was her opportunity. Kipling felt even more sick at how it all might have failed.

Grayson moved to the living room wall so his movement wouldn't cast any shadow on the blinds, and with gun pointed toward the ceiling, edged his way to the window. He motioned with one hand for her to get down on the floor, and she immediately did as he said. When he reached the window he was at the corner where the movement had originated and slowly shifted a single vertical strip, peering outside.

Then he swept away the strips with a flourish and shouted "Greg!"

The next thirty seconds were a flurry. Before Kipling could process what happened, the front door burst open and then Greg was there with Patrick Flannery and a handful of other people; some of which she vaguely recognized, and some not. Had they really only left the FBI safehouse that morning?

She just wanted to close her eyes.

She just wanted peace.

She just wanted sleep.

"Sit with her, Greg," Grayson's voice said somewhere near her, but she couldn't seem to look away from the soles of Langdon Howell's shoes. They were smooth, barely scuffed, as if they were brand new. "Please. Emergency services and police are on the way. Flannery will meet them outside. If I haven't come back up, please put her in priority."

"Of course, Ollie."

She was aware of Greg sitting beside her, and rubbing his hand across her shoulders, but everything was muffled and in slow motion. Kipling blinked, rolling a question through her head until she could finally focus on him.

"How did you get here so fast?" she asked.

Greg smiled. "With everything going on, Ollie had Mac add a tracking ping to your" — he tapped his own cheek in front of his ear—"but something is working quite right because the range is awful. I didn't know which way they took you." Greg stopped rubbing her back to take her hand, squeezing it gently. "We spread out. Sandy did some of her magic analysis stuff to give direction. And we finally got a ping."

Kipling nodded. "Mina is dead."

"I'm sorry we weren't here sooner, Kip."

Grayson ran down the unsteady basement stairs and to the locked door to the room that had been Kipling's cell, now holding his in-laws. He took in several breaths in an attempt to push down and calm the adrenaline thumping in his temples, leaving a bitter taste at the back of his throat.

With one final breath, he gripped the knob and tried to turn it with no luck. It was too easy to believe he could just open the door.

"Jane!" he called through the wood. "Jack!"

"Oh, my god, Grayson!" came Mum Branson's voice, growing louder as they approached the door on the other side. "What's happening? We thought we heard gunshots!"

As she spoke, he reached up and ran his fingers along the top of the door jamb, a fleeting hope a key may be there. No luck.

"Everything is fine now," he assured, leaning so he spoke close to the door. "I need you to step back from the door. Get into the corner. I'm going to force it open."

They confirmed they understood and he gave them a few moments to be out of the way. The door was not particularly hearty, and he didn't anticipate much resistance. He took a step back and kicked straight forward, the hollow veneer splitting apart. Another solid slam of his shoulder and the door was destroyed. Mum and Dad Branson stood together in the corner, holding each other, eyes wide.

"Are you okay?" he asked, crossing the small room with wide steps.

They both nodded. "What's happening, Grayson," Jack asked. "We heard Kip shouting outside and then a shot and screaming."

"Then more shouting and more shooting," Jane added. "I'm terrified. I don't think I've ever been so terrified. Not since Kip was a baby."

Grayson circled Mum Branson's shoulders with his arm, drawing her against his side. She gasped, her eyes wide, and with a twist in his chest Grayson realized it was the blood on his shirt.

"Not mine," he assured. "And not Kipling's. That is the most important fact."

Mum Branson covered her face with her hands, a trembling breath shifting through her. Grayson set his hand on Dad Branson's shoulder, squeezed gently, and did his best to be reassuring.

"The details aren't important right now except to say the FBI are here, police and medical are on their way, and Kipling is physically fine. She's shaken, as are we all, but her the most." He paused, knowing there was no way to be gentle and what he had to say needed to be said before they went upstairs. "Mina is dead."

Mum Branson gasped and shook her head, still covering her face.

"I'm sorry to be so blunt—"

"Was there a way you could have been anything less?" Dad Branson said, his voice heavy. "All of this has been a great deal for us to process, son. We're retired English professors. Such chaos is…"

"Exhausting," Mum Branson finished.

"I will never be able to adequately apologize for bringing such chaos into your lives—"

"No," his father-in-law interjected. "Grayson, that's not why I said it. There are conversations to be had, but in the end, our Kip loves you and we know you love her. That's the most important thing."

"Thank you," Grayson said, not ready yet to allow himself the grace of accepting their words. "Kipling is upstairs with Greg. Let's get you to her. Are you both physically all right?"

"Nothing a good meal can't fix," Dad Branson assured.

With a nod, Grayson stepped away from them to guide them upstairs. When Jane Branson slipped her hand into his, he glanced down only a moment before firming his grip. The door at the top of the stairs was still open and through it he heard sirens and the scramble of feet on the floor. Before they reached the top, Agent Patrick Flannery stepped into view with a uniformed officer behind him.

"This is Grayson Holmes," Flannery said in introduction, and the way the officer nodded, Grayson presumed Flannery had provided explanation. "And that would be Jack and Jane Branson, parents to the lady in the other room. We're gonna let you get back in there, Grayson. I've got this. Just wanted Officer Sickle here to know who you are."

Grayson nodded in gratitude and diverted around the two men. The lounge was crowded with uniformed officers and emergency medics with stretchers and equipment. The EMTs saw to the injured and the officers oversaw the care, likely assuring all considerations were taken for their custody. Lynne and Patrícia were no longer a concern.

He had seen to that.

As soon as they stepped into the room, Mum and Dad Branson saw Kipling and left him, rushing to her. She still sat on the couch where he had left her with Greg, except now a female EMT checking her over. As her parents reached her, skirting around the EMT taking her vitals, Greg stepped away and came to where Grayson stood watching.

"She's in shock," Greg said, keeping his voice low even though it was doubtful his words would carry through the cacophony in the room.

Kipling nodded at something her mother said, then turned her head to look at the young woman removing the blood pressure cuff from her arm. Her movements were slow, unfocused.

"I know." Grayson crossed his arms, watching his wife.

"I didn't ask her. Who shot who?"

"Patrícia, the woman there" — he tipped his head toward the prone, still body beside Lynne—"killed Mina, I presume outside based on conversation. And she did so in front of Kipling."

Greg swore.

"I don't know where Mina's body is now," Grayson continued. "Flannery is aware she needs to be located. Victor Barriero, Langdon Howell, and the first shot on Lynne…Kipling delivered."

"Damn. No wonder she's struggling to process."

"I'm still befuddled by her accuracy. They were not kill shots; however, they were very clearly debilitating. Whether that was by choice or by lack of skill, I didn't know—"

"She took gun safety certification," Greg provided. "When I was still John and you were back in London. I went to the range with her once. She wasn't a perfect shot, but she hit the target."

Grayson nodded. "I was aware she'd taken self-defense. I wasn't aware of…" He trailed off, his thoughts incomplete. With a sharp breath, he refocused to answer his cousin's question. "Moments after Kipling shot the three, Patrícia came from another part of the house. I had the gun by then — it was initially Lynne's weapon — and I stopped her. Lynne was not fully incapacitated and tried to retrieve the dropped weapon. She would not listen to my demand to stop. I gave her a chance."

"It's more than she would have given you, Ollie. Don't dwell on it. It's over now."

"I fear we aren't yet at the end." He looked around the room. Barriero was awake and moaning, fighting the restraints of the stretcher he'd been strapped to as he was escorted by an uniformed officer with the emergency personnel. Howell was still silent. He might yet succumb to his injuries, and Grayson was genuinely torn over which outcome he preferred. Death or justice. "But I hope we are past the danger."

Chapter Forty

Kip Branson is the sister the universe gave me. Jackson and Jane Branson were the bonus parents I needed. Mom Branson taught Kip and I everything we needed to know to grow up. All the things my dad didn't know how to talk about. Dad Branson invited us over so Dad had someone to watch the Sox with and to lament over the lean years when the Pats got nowhere near the Superbowl. Mom Branson sent me a care package twice a month, every month, all the way through school, even med school.

If something has happened to me, I want them to be the ones to take care of me. I want them to be the ones to be my family. They didn't know me when my mother took off, but they stood in the gap. When Dad died, they were all I had left and they were more than enough.

Kipling had to leave the stack of papers on the kitchen table, unable to hold the document and read because of the trembling in her hands. She could barely read the words through the haze burning her eyes. Her mother's stifled sniffle, sitting across the table from Kipling, made Kipling's chest tighten.

Despite what Mina had done, she was family. Mom struggled with it. Daddy struggled with it. Kipling struggled with it, even though she'd known what Mina had done well before her parents.

"Am I correct in assuming you weren't aware of Doctor Russo's final wishes, Mrs. Holmes?"

She blinked rapidly to clear her vision, the tears dripping from her chin to the edge of the paper. "Not specifically, no," she managed to answer, her voice nearly lost in the rough claw of sorrow. Kipling raised her head to look across the table to Attorney Donna Innes, Mina's estate planning lawyer. "Conversations here and there, especially after her father died, but never anything… formal. When did she draft this?"

"Two years ago."

Kipling nodded, struggling to process the new layer to her splintered and fractured reality. Mina had made her requests formal well before Kipling had even met Grayson. Well before Mina had…

She didn't know how to categorize the change in Mina.

"While she made her wishes clear to have you be the executor of her estate, I do need your confirmation that you are willing to accept the responsibility."

"I have to choose?"

"Well, yes. You are not obligated to accept. You can file a renunciation form and we will proceed with Ms. Russo's alternative instructions."

Kipling set her elbow on the table beside the papers and rested her forehead in her hand. She closed her eyes, more tears slipping free, and tried to breathe. It was so much. *Too much.*

"I understand the hesitation," Attorney Innes said. "Her death was sudden and tragic, and I'm sure you are still processing that loss.

I will add, in case this is a concern, the execution of her wishes can be managed from the UK if you have plans to leave the country."

Kipling nodded her head within her own hold. Much of the events in the last few weeks, especially the ones leading to Mina's death the week before, had been kept out of public knowledge. Since Attorney Innes was Mina's representative, Kipling didn't know how much truth the woman had been told and she didn't want to be the one to say too much. The investigation was still ongoing, which was one of the reasons she and Grayson hadn't yet been able to plan on going home. Later in the day they had to meet with Agent Flannery and Director Stanton to give final statements.

"You don't need to tell me today," Attorney Innes said, her tone softer. "I can check with you later this week. Do you have plans to return to London?"

"We will be." *Not soon enough.* "Not yet…" Kipling managed to say, opening her eyes again.

The front door opened, letting in the conversation between Grayson and her father. Daddy laughed at whatever had been said outside the house, and Grayson's low rumble followed. They had left the house an hour earlier to pick up some groceries with a promised swing by Dunks on the way home. Attorney Innes arrived within minutes of their departure.

"We're home," her dad called out as they approached the kitchen. "Oh, we have company. We should have picked up another coffee." He spoke over his shoulder to Grayson as he moved into the kitchen. "I told you the dozen donuts wouldn't go to waste."

Kipling scooted back her chair and stood, as did Attorney Innes, and turned to look at her husband and father. The shift in Grayson's demeanor was probably unnoticed by everyone else, but as much as she knew he sensed her emotions she also read his.

"This is Attorney Donna Innes," Kipling said, motioning toward the woman. "She's Mina's estate planning attorney. This is my father Jack Branson." Kipling indicated her father, then Grayson. "This is my husband Grayson Holmes."

Daddy realized, too, the strain in the room and moved around the table to set his Market Basket bags on the counter, stepping behind Mom's chair. Grayson reached past her to set the cardboard takeaway tray on the table with their coffees to free his hand before extending it to Attorney Innes.

"Nice to meet you," she said, "though the situation isn't ever the best. Mina told me so much about Kip I felt I almost knew her. She never told me anything about Kip's husband."

"Mina drew up a will two years ago," Kipling clarified, and Grayson met her gaze. "She named me her executor."

The slight shift in his eyes said he understood. Of course he did. Grayson slipped his arm behind her after shaking the woman's hand and pressed his palm to her back. "Kipling and I hadn't yet met two years ago," he said with what would likely seem a pleasant enough smile to anyone else, but the strain was obvious to Kipling.

"Well, that certainly explains things. I will leave you to your day," she said, bending to retrieve her bag from where it leaned against a table leg. "The document is your copy to review in your own time. If you have questions about any part, please reach out. My contact information is on the last page. Let me know your decision when you've made it. Have a good day."

Dad walked her to the door, and as soon as she was gone Grayson's hand left her back to rest at the base of her neck, his touch gently urging her to turn into him. Kipling did, pressing her forehead to his chest as his arms wrapped around her. She would explain everything soon enough, but for a minute she just needed his strength.

"Let me just give some marching orders, and I'll be right back. You need anything, chief? Greg?" Patrick Flannery asked, standing as he shifted his stack of papers in preparation for stepping out.

"I'm fine, thank you."

"I wouldn't say no to a coffee. As long as it's been brewed some-time since the crack of dawn," Greg joked.

"No promises. Kip? Some water maybe? I got juice, too."

Kipling smiled, or attempted to, and nodded. "Thank you."

"I need to see to something," Director Stanton said, walking to the door with Flannery. "Shouldn't be too long."

Director Stanton and Patrick Flannery left Grayson, Kipling, and Greg alone in the Bureau conference room where they had been with Patrick, Director Stanton, and two other agents for the last hour and a half detailing the events of days before. They had finally finished, and Director Stanton had assured them that any investigations into the deaths of Mina Russo, Lyana Guerreiro once known as Lynne Connelly, and Patrícia Henriqueta, and the shooting of Victor Barriero and Langdon Howell were now complete.

It had been eight days since the events in Roxbury, the town where the house of horrors had been. In those days, his wife had wavered between tears and laughter, silence and nightmares, calm and panic. Today was an unsettling silence after her heartbreaking visit that morning by Mina Russo's attorney.

Mina's formal instructions had been drawn up before the explo-sion that Howell had machinated, before he and Kipling had met, before they fell in love, before Mina's personality shifted, before their wedding. Before anything had changed.

It had been gutting for her. She wasn't surprised by the existence of the instructions but learning of them had left her devastated.

Once the initial shock had passed, she had slipped into with-drawn silence. He wished above all else to give his wife some level of peace again.

"How much longer do you think we'll be?" Kipling asked.

"Not long now, I should think. They have our statements which should conclude our portion of the investigation." Grayson flipped his hand to read his watch. "Should have plenty of time to make it home for dinner. Your mother promised a New England boiled dinner."

Greg hummed in appreciation. "I'm invited, right?"

Kipling smiled, genuinely this time. "Of course. Mom always makes plenty and always loves company."

"If I keep eating your mom's cooking, I'll gain ten pounds and Esther won't recognize me."

Kipling chuckled; a sound that lightened Grayson's heart. "She's just figuring out the face you've got. What's a few extra pounds?"

Greg hissed in feigned pain, clutching the front of his shirt. "Oh! You wound me greatly!"

Flannery came back to the conference room with a cup of coffee in one hand, two bottles of water and a bottle of juice held to his chest with the other arm. He paused to use his foot, kicked the door closed again before setting the cup in front of Greg. He handed the apple juice directly to Kipling and set the bottles of water on the table before spinning around the chair he'd occupied previously and sat with a huff as he adjusted his suit jacket.

"Okay," he said, finally settling. "Just wanted to give you some updates. The judge ruled on the Sheldon case. While your testimony, Kip, would have really been a big nail in his coffin, prosecution asked Judge Sauvage to allow the trial to move forward. There was plenty other evidence to get the guilty verdict. He was sentenced to life without ever having the chance of parole. Never got the evidence to pull Howell into the scheme, not enough anyway, but like I said…didn't need it. And any contempt of court charges that could have technically been brought against Kip are obviously not happening."

As Patrick spoke, Kipling focused on him but her hand moved toward Grayson under the table. He took his wife's hand and shifted the chair closer to her.

"Malcolm is proving to be not quite as solid a case. He's still being held without bail and investigators are workin' on building a better foundation for prosecution. The primary charge is murder of Burke DiMatto, but we'd sure as hell like to find a way to connect him to Howell."

"Have you talked to Sandi?" Greg asked. "She's a whiz at finding connections no one else can."

Flannery winked and clicked his cheek. "Sure have. Thus far, even she hasn't found anything strong enough to use. I don't think she's given up, but we've all been focused on other things the last few weeks."

Like finding Kipling.

The clarification wasn't needed for anyone in the room.

"We'll have to fish or cut bait soon. Defense is pushing for a speedy trial. Probably because they know the case is weaker than Malcolm's. Now about your buddy." Flannery laced his fingers and set his arms on the table, leaning forward a few degrees. "Barriero's been moved to Devens until his trial since he's up on federal charges. Howell has been moved outta Mass General after a couple surgeries. Nothing really life-threatening, but you sure did incapacitate him, Kip, if you don't mind me commending you on your aim."

"It's not something I think I'll ever find pride in," Kipling said in a small voice.

"Well, be that as it may, he's recoverin' just fine over in Shattuck. Lemuel Shattuck Hospital in Jamaica Plains. They got a secure correctional unit for the treatment and retention of criminals and the like from around Massachusetts and around the region. I hear he might be transferred to a cell in the next day or so while the powers that be here in the States argue with the powers that be on your side of the pond about who gets to keep him. I hear he'd already been sentenced for his bullsh—" He stopped, cleared his throat, and diverted his eyes away from Kipling. "Shenanigans this past spring in London. Sure do envy the speed of your courts compared to us. You book along while we're molasses going uphill in January. But, that's not my fight.

"Now, I did want to share some, I guess, *interesting* results that came out of the autopsy of Doctor Russo—"

"Autopsy?" Kipling interrupted. "Why would they need to do an autopsy?"

"Just routine," Flannery said, shaking his head. "I mean, not to be too cold about it, the actual cause of death isn't in question. But given the circumstances, the coroner did the usual stuff." He took a sheet of paper from the folder he'd left on the table unopened during the previous meeting. Flannery glanced at it, then turned it to face them and pushed it across the table.

"What am I looking at?" Kipling asked, glancing from Flannery to Grayson.

Grayson reached for the paper, holding it in one hand while still holding her fingers in the other. "It's a toxicology report," he answered, mentally processing the analysis.

"What does it say?"

Grayson scowled, finishing his scan of the full document. He then handed it down the table to Greg. "Mina had in her system the same drugs you did. This report indicates when the presence of drugs was confirmed in the blood and urine samples, they conducted tests on her hair. Was there a reason for the additional testing?" he asked, directing his attention to Flannery.

The man nodded, tapping his fingertips on the table. "We asked them to. Knowing what the doc found with Kip after she got away, it struck me as something to follow up on."

Grayson took a few moments to study Patrick Flannery. He'd long suspected the man was far more perceptive and intelligent than he preferred to let on. Grayson never questioned Patrick Flannery's intelligence, but in this case he may have been guided by a sense of empathy.

"What does it mean?" Kipling asked. "Are you saying Mina was taking the same drugs she forced on me?"

"The results say the same drugs were in her system," he said, focusing on his wife. "Hair toxicology is usually considered accurate for up to ninety days, and these tests indicate the drugs were in her system at least that long."

Kipling's eyes narrowed and she released his hand, reaching for the paper Greg had been reading. "What do *you* think it means?" she asked, looking up from the paper at Grayson.

"All that tells us is she had been under the same level of dosage as you, if not a higher dose, based on that information. The fact the hair test confirms a three-month period says to me the dosing began before that."

She didn't blink, her eyes shifting ever so slightly left to right as she processed the information. Then she took in a sharp breath. "Grayson...do you think they were — that she was being manipulated, too?"

"It's likely we will never know, but it's possible."

Her eyes brimmed before the tears fell free and she dropped her head forward, eyes closed.

Not for the first time, Grayson regretted not ending Langdon Howell when he had the opportunity. As he had promised.

Chapter Forty-One

"I won't keep you long, Grayson," Director Stanton said, motioning for Grayson to sit at the chair on the visitor side of his desk. "I'm sure you want to keep your time away from Kipling at a minimum."

Grayson pulled the chair away from the desk and sat. "I will admit I am reluctant, all things considered, and will likely feel so for a good time yet. But Greg is with her."

"How is she feeling? My wife had pretty rough starts to her pregnancies, but things seemed to level off second trimester. We didn't go anywhere without a bag of oyster crackers."

"She is fatigued in the afternoon and has on occasion felt ill especially if she has gone too long without eating, but all in all she is doing well. For that, I am thankful as she has suffered enough without the added insult of morning sickness. Or sickness at any other time of day or night. Because of timing of" — Grayson squinted and ticked his head to the side—"events and abuses, it's difficult to assign symptoms to either that or early pregnancy. Either way, now in her second trimester, she is doing well."

"Good." Stanton shifted his broad frame in his chair, folding his hands together on the desk. "Look, I'm going to just lay out my cards here and show my hand. I'm not expecting an answer right now. You and your wife have a lot going on. I feel like I've got to make the offer."

Grayson tipped his head in an acknowledging nod. He wasn't surprised by the subject; the conversation had taken place in his own mind more than once in the months since he'd learned his cousin was alive. And at least a few within Six knew it, orchestrated it, and hid Greg from his family. The deception was still very raw.

"I know you're not surprised," Stanton said, his smile lopsided. "You probably know the offer letter and benefits package."

"Not quite," Grayson said with a chuckle.

"So, here goes. Look, I've known since last winter about your dual citizenship — though I'm curious as all hell how you managed it — and all things considered, I'm positive we can get the same dispensation here. I mean, if the British Crown and SIS are cool with it, the federal government isn't about to let themselves look stupid."

"I have not frequently leveraged the presumptive power of my name, but Six wished to recruit me and while I am a proud British citizen, I am also my mother's son and I was not willing to relinquish that tie to her heritage. It was a sticking point on my part."

"Good for you, Holmes. I'm sure your mom is proud."

"She never asked me to take on the fight, but it pleased her when I was able to tell her I would remain, at least in documentation, an American citizen."

"Where are her people from?"

"New Hampshire, quite near the state border with Massachusetts."

Carl Stanton nodded, humming in affirmation. "So, last winter I soft pitched the idea of you joining us here in the Bureau. I didn't know for sure Kipling would end up being such an anchor to Boston for you, but I suspected, and maybe I thought I could leverage that. I don't want to leverage anything, Grayson. But, I do want to make it crystal clear that I would be ecstatic to have someone of your caliber, intelligence, and skill as part of my team."

Grayson shifted forward to rest his elbows on his thighs, meeting the man's eyes. "I appreciate your sincerity and your consideration. This is not a question I want to answer without discussing it with my wife. I am not saying no; I am not saying yes. But I will provide a clear answer when I have it."

"That's all I expect."

"I am thoroughly convinced your bookshelves harnessed the power of the TARDIS. There is no other feasible explanation as to how all these books fit on those shelves," Grayson teased, tilting his head toward the now mostly empty bookshelves in the corner of Kipling's apartment bedroom.

"When you have limited space and are an employee of a bookstore with the constant tease of a 30 percent discount, you have to get creative with book stacking."

She sat on the floor near one of the bookshelves so she could take the books and albums from the lower shelves, removing the last row of books at the front of the shelf to reveal the organized and stacked books behind them. They had already boxed the books and tchotchkes from the living room shelves and the boxes were neatly stacked in preparation of being picked up by the shipping company Grayson had contracted to move the remains of her life in Boston to her new life in England.

Grayson stood beside the now-stripped bed, the bare mattress waiting for pickup as well, but for discarding not shipping, with an open box he filled with books from the upper shelves.

"Is this a first edition?" he asked, slowly easing open the front cover of a hardbound book. The spine crackled, but he handled the book with reverence.

She looked up from her stack, recognizing the edition of *Perelandra* by C.S. Lewis. "It is," she answered, smiling at the expression of awe on her husband's face. "There should also be first edition copies of *Out of the Silent Planet* and *That Hideous Strength* in that stack.

Those never even made it to a shelf at the bookstore. I snatched them immediately and hid them until the end of the day so I could buy them."

He didn't answer and she smiled, watching his expression as his gaze skimmed the pages of the eighty-year-old book. He stopped reading, and his lips curled up in a smile.

"What did you just read?" she asked.

"A man who has been in another world does not come back unchanged," he read, then shifted his attention to her. "I would say such a simple sentence can be applied to many truths." He closed the book and put it in the box. "I see an extensive rearrangement of the Baker Street library will be in order once these precious boxes reach London. Though, now, I feel inclined to pack these books in our luggage to transport them personally."

Kipling chuckled, going back to her stack. "I don't think you realize how many antiquarian editions I have." To prove her point, she held out a copy of *The War of the Worlds*. It wasn't in the same pristine condition as many of her other books, but it was still in great shape if considered by any book collector.

Grayson took the step toward her and took the book. He ran his fingertips across the olive fabric cover. "I feel I should put on white gloves before touching any of these."

Kipling laughed again. "They've been in countless hands before ending up on my bedroom bookshelf. I think you're fine."

He eased open the cover. "Published in 1898. If we weren't already married, I would beg you to be my wife."

"You've been in it for the books the whole time."

Grayson laughed and returned to the bed to continue packing. With her shelves nearly empty, Kipling slid her hand along the wood to make sure she'd found everything. Her fingers brushed something and she pulled it out. Her heart dropped to her stomach and her chest immediately hurt. The small booklet was made from faded construction paper, once a bright blue and now blue gray at best, tied with yarn pulled through punched holes to keep it together. Glued on the front was a piece of thin, off-white paper like every elementary age kid had drawn pictures on for decades with two stick figures holding hands. Below each, written in a rough penmanship, were the names Kip and Mina.

Memories consumed her before she opened the book.

Inside the worn book, brittle and yellow cellophane tape struggled to hold a single picture in place. Two young girls stood shoulder-to-shoulder with their arms tossed around each other in front of the primate exhibit at the Franklin Park Zoo on their class field trip. Mina's Mediterranean and Spanish heritage made her suntanned skin a contrast to Kipling's paleness and freckles. Both girls wore ballcaps with the name of their elementary school on the front, Mina's in blue and Kipling's in orange. Mina's short-cut, dark hair hugged her cheeks and covered her ears, and even though Kipling's hair had been pulled back in a ponytail and pulled through the back of her cap, the breeze had lifted it so it created a flyaway mess behind her head. They wore matching t-shirts with their school name and lanyards around their necks with their names written in black marker.

Written in crayon, with each letter a different color, were the words Best Friends Forever, with Forever written beneath the picture.

Grayson crouched beside her, then pivoted on the balls of his feet and sat. He didn't say anything but rubbed his hand up and down her back.

"You were an absolutely adorable child."

"Third grade," Kipling managed to say, forcing the words from her tight throat. "We went to Franklin Park Zoo. It was almost the end of the school year so the school was filling the days with more fun than schoolwork. I didn't realize until I was an adult that was the reason we always had field trips in the spring," she said with a hoarse chuckle. "At eight or nine years old, it was just a fun trip. It was so hot. And humid. The outside exhibits smelled like hay and warm poop, but we had so much fun."

"I'd venture to say springtime field trips are common worldwide." His voice was gentle, soothing, and intentional. "I attended school in London through year five, and we moved back to Sussex for year six. That was the first time Greg and I attended school together. Until then we only spent time together on holidays and in the summer when we visited the country. I am sure it comes as no shock my mother and Aunt Hazel received phone calls from Headmaster Collins upon our return from Peveril Castle."

Kipling ran her thumb over the photo.

"I'm going to call the attorney tomorrow," she said, feeling sure of her choice for the first time since Attorney Innes handed her the executorship paperwork. "I don't know who she was these past few months, but the woman who asked me to take care of her after—"

Her voice cracked and she had to stop, pressing her tongue to the roof of her mouth as she swallowed hard. Grayson leaned into her and pressed a kiss to her temple. She closed her eyes and took several deep, slow breaths, focusing on his comfort.

"The woman who asked me to do this for her is the same girl from this picture. I want to remember this Mina, and maybe doing this for her will help me do that."

"You have my full support."

"Thank you," she managed to whisper.

They sat silent for a few minutes while Kipling grappled with the juxtaposition reality of the girl in the photo who had been her lifelong friend and the woman who had allowed her to be drugged and abused in some twisted attempt to help Kipling see some "truth" only Mina understood.

"Would you like to stay in Boston?"

The question surprised her, and she shifted away from Grayson to look at him. "What do you mean?"

"A great many things have happened in the last few months, and plans can and do change. I want you to know that if you now would like to stay here, in Boston, for the immediate future or on a more permanent basis, we will."

"But your family is in England—"

"And your family is in Boston," he interrupted, but gently.

"Did Director Stanton ask you again to work for the bureau?"

"He did. But staying in Boston is not contingent on his job offer. Nor is it contingent on any job offer. His offer did, however, inspire me to ask the question."

"Do you want to?"

"Please believe me when I say, because I am not avoiding commitment to an answer, but I will do whatever is in my power to make you happy. If that means staying here in Boston, we will cancel the shipment and we will go house shopping," he said with a smile. "My home is where you are, and where our baby will be."

"And my home is Baker Street," she said. "It's like that quote you just read from *Perelandra*. A man who has been in another world does not come back unchanged. I am changed, and I am happy for it. All I have wanted since the moment I shook off the haze of drugs and confusion and got away from that house of horrors, *all* I've wanted is to *go home*. Not here. Not Chelsea. Home."

"Then we shall go home," he promised, smoothing his thumb across her cheek, drying the tears she had let fall. "As soon as it can be arranged, we will go home."

Chapter Forty-Two

"I have just been in shock since we learned Mina was…gone."

Kipling struggled to grip her composure. She had been teeter-tottering between numb control and the painful edge of grief. For now, for at least today, she had shoved the heartache and rage at Mina's betrayal and the confusion of not knowing the woman with her best friend's name and face into a box and focused on the lifetime of friendship they had enjoyed. The Chelsea funeral home was intended to feel homey and less sterile, and she had chosen it because it was in the town where they had both grown up, but the stark contrast between the white of the walls and furniture and the crimson curtains and accents made her uneasy and anxious.

"It's been hard," she managed to say to Ashley McIver, a mutual friend between Kipling and Mina, a woman they'd known since high school and saw often since Ashley still lived in Boston. "It was… I'm still processing."

"Of course." Ashley's eyes pinched and she seemed to weigh her words before speaking again. "Kip, um, I don't know if there's a right way to ask this. Mina was *off* the last few months. Had you noticed?"

Kipling forced herself to swallow and looked down at the printed memorial booklet in her hands. How to answer? She didn't have to think twice about her decision not to share the full truth of Mina's death, especially once the Bureau offered the option to withhold details unnecessary to the general public. But it left her in an unfamiliar land of truth and lies. As far as most everyone was concerned, Mina had died in a terrible accident, which was also why her casket was closed. To avoid questions. Kipling hadn't seen her, but Grayson had, and said it was best she didn't.

"I don't think you need to answer. I just saw it in your eyes."

She released a long, slow breath through her lips and raised her chin to look at Ashley again. "Mina was having a hard time," she managed to say, latching on to the truth in the simplicity.

"She had a lot of opinions about you," Ashley continued, her expression apologetic, but she spoke anyway. "She said you—"

"I thought you might need a beverage, darling," Grayson said as he came to her side, holding a plastic cup of cool water the funeral home made available to the service attendees. As she took the cup, he stepped close to her side with his palm against her back, instantly calming her.

"This is Ashley McIver," Kipling provided. "We went to high school together and have stayed in touch since then."

Grayson extended his other hand. "Grayson Holmes," he said by way of introduction. "Kipling's husband. I'm doing my best to meet each person who has come to remember Mina."

Ashley's eyes widened for a moment, but she gathered her thoughts and smiled. "I'm sorry to look surprised."

Which answered the unasked question of what had Mina told people. Kipling strongly suspected Mina had been vocal and untethered with sharing her assumptions and conspiracy theories about Grayson. Revelations since Mina's death implied she may have been manipulated and influenced by "Patty," but her suspicions and anger toward Kipling had been the kindling to which Patty added gasoline and fire.

Grayson smiled, a schooled and outwardly cordial curl of his lips. His palm ran up and down her spine. "Apology accepted. It's an exceedingly difficult time for everyone."

"It's just — Mina kind of painted you, um, differently." Ashley smirked. "She said you claimed to be some kind of secret agent and you tricked Kipling and you were horrible. You don't exactly look the secret agent type, no offense."

Grayson chuckled. "None taken. After all, if we all looked like secret agents we wouldn't be very good at our jobs." He grinned, looked at Kipling, and winked. Ashley stared, wide eyed and mouth popping like a fish out of water. "Your mum and dad have found a quieter room to sit, should you wonder."

Kipling had all she could do not to laugh, pressing her lips together as she met her husband's mischievous eyes. "Thank you."

"Do you need anything?"

"I need to eat something soon."

He pulled the lapel of his suit jacket away from his chest and reached inside with the other hand, pulling out a small snack bag of oyster crackers and a small bag of sliced apples. The crackers were for when she went too long between eating and her stomach protested, and the apples were her current food obsession.

She smiled and took the bag, and he leaned in to kiss her forehead.

"I'm going to speak with the director to assure plans are set."

Grayson shifted into the small crowd, Kipling watching him for a moment before looking back at Ashley, whose eyes were still wide. It made her wonder what all Mina had said but decided it didn't matter. Nothing would change the past, but the now would shape the future.

"Mina didn't care much for Grayson," was all she said, hoping it would excuse any stories Ashley and others had heard as elaboration.

The less she said, the less she contradicted, hopefully the more people would make their own conclusions and let the topic go. Especially when the truth of everything was a secret to most, but she would balance the truth on a careful edge. Hoping to further avoid the conversation, she focused on opening the small bag of apple slices, a warm glow blooming in her chest at her husband's consideration.

Ashley started to say something, but whatever it was trickled off as she looked past Kipling. Curious, Kipling turned her head just enough to maybe see what Ashley reacted to and saw Greg coming toward them. Probably because Grayson had pointed him in her direction.

"John," Ashley called just loud enough to get his attention, raising her hand. "John Allen."

Greg looked up, held the show of recognizing them with a jut of his chin, and walked toward them with his hands pushed into his pockets. "Hey, Ashley. Good to see you, though not the reason why. Hey, Kip."

"Hi," Kipling said, playing along.

Greg as John had slid seamlessly into their small circle of friends, though after introducing himself tended to spend more time with Mina, and in retrospect, Kipling understood that had been intentional to keep himself close to Kipling. It was a strange shift, but at the same time, it was natural and easy to let Greg McQueen be John Allen again, especially when his already more muted accent was replaced by the natural-sounding accent he'd adopted while being John Allen.

What a weird life she lived. A year ago, she was a doctorate student working in a bookstore, single and happy, living in her Southie apartment. Now, she was married to a descendant of Sherlock Holmes, having a baby, and ready to leave Boston behind to build a life with him and begin her career as an university professor. Her husband and his cousin switched personas at a snap, and she no longer thought twice about it. Less than a year, and absolutely everything had changed.

Everything.

And as much as some moments caused smothering pain, she wouldn't change any decision she'd made. Not one. Especially not the moment she told Grayson Oliver Sherlock Holmes she loved him.

As much as Grayson would never begrudge Kipling a moment with her parents before they returned to London, he very much looked forward to sleeping in a bed better proportioned for the sleep of two adults. By staying with Kipling's parents, they were obligated to sleep in Kipling's childhood room with her compact bed. Not quite a single person size, but not much more.

The two small bedside lamps cast circles of light over the bed, leaving the rest of the room in shadows. The weather had cooled to Autumn temperatures, and since it seemed a tradition in New England to avoid turning on one's furnace until no earlier than November first, an extra afghan in a multicolored chevron pattern covered the yellow and white quilt. Despite the fact they were packed and their flight for London left mid-morning, sleep was evasive and they lay facing each other in the far too narrow and far too short bed.

"It was all I could do not to laugh out loud when you said that to Ashley," Kipling said with a laugh, her hands folded together beneath her cheek. "It was mean of you to do that to me."

Grayson chuckled, matching her position with his hands under his cheek so they were nose-to-nose, but he kept enough distance she could see his lips. She'd taken out her aids when she first laid down; her usual evening routine. "Then I was successful. I wanted to lift the weight for a moment or two."

"I thought you were going to say you were successful in being mean to me."

"No. Never."

She might have intended to say something, but instead she broke into a deep, jaw-stretching yawn.

"I suppose the answer is obvious, but how are you feeling?"

"Tired," she said, escaping the deep yawn. "It was an exhausting day. Physically and emotionally."

"Tomorrow will be equally exhausting."

"Yes, but a different kind. Travel is a whole lot of rushing followed by a whole lot of waiting and a whole lot of being stuck in a seat, but the final destination is worth it." She smiled, the expression genuine and sparking in her eyes. "We're going home."

"No hesitation?" he asked, taking a hand from beneath his cheek so he could brush his thumb across her jaw. "We can stay longer if you like."

Kipling shook her head before he finished. "No hesitation. I want to go home. And we'd have to go soon, either way. There will be a point where I shouldn't fly. I know it's still weeks off, but I'd rather not risk it. And I start at the university after the first of the year."

"You need not convince me, darling."

"Sorry," she said on a sigh, and shifted onto her back. She had to scoot closer to him to stay on the bed so he supported himself on his bent arm, fist at jaw, to look down at her. "You're trying to make sure you're not taking me away from where I want to be, and I'm trying to make sure you know the one thing I want is to be back home."

"Home is a name, a word, it is a strong one; stronger than magician ever spoke, or spirit ever answered to, in the strongest conjuration."

"Dickens had it right. It's a word, but it encompasses everything." She ran her hand over her stomach, looking up at the ceiling. "Home is the nicest word there is." She glanced at Grayson. "Laura Ingalls Wilder."

Grayson slipped his hand beneath the quilt and found the edge of her pyjama top, easing aside the hem to lay his palm on her stomach.

Kipling was barely into her second trimester, and her body had begun to show evidence of the baby but only to those who knew to look. In truth, Grayson was pleased she didn't yet appear pregnant to anyone who didn't know because that meant she had begun to regain the weight she had lost. As he'd told Director Stanton, he was so thankful she seemed to avoid the frequent sickness and nausea some women experienced. That would have been a cruel twist after everything else.

He knew her body.

Knew her curves and dips before they'd come back to Boston.

Knew the frightening waning of her body when she'd come back to him.

Knew the changes since as she returned to health.

And knew the ever-yet-so-slight bump of their child, loved and nourished by their mother.

"What would you like?" she asked, turning her head to look at him again. "A boy or a girl?"

"Either," he said, then added with a smirk, "Or both. Two of one, one of another."

Kipling's eyes widened, then narrowed as she squinted at him. "Grayson Holmes, do not put that out in the universe!"

He chuckled. "Don't you recall me telling you the Holmes family line has been greater with each generation?"

"Yes, but that doesn't mean we have to do it all in one shot!"

"Yes but consider the efficiency."

"Stop it," she ordered with a sparkle in her squinted eyes. Kipling looked up at the ceiling again, sighing as Grayson smoothed his hand over her waist. "I do feel better leaving now that it feels like things are better between you and my parents. I didn't like how they lashed out at you—"

"They were concerned parents, and for that I hold no judgment against them. I expect no less than utter devotion to you. I would likely feel exactly the same."

"I know, but…" She sighed, letting go the conversation they'd had more than once. She smiled, looking to him. "Having your parents invite them to stay at the cottage when they visit was wicked awesome. Not that she'd ever admit it, but I think Mom still is kind of in awe of the fact you're the great-grandson of the infamous Sherlock. Some people are starstruck by actors and celebrities; my mom is awestruck by literary rockstars. The only familial connection that would eclipse your family name would be if you were some descendant of Rudyard Kipling."

"Ah, but that would be rather awkward if you became Doctor Kipling Kipling."

His wife's laughter echoed off the angled ceiling and she slapped her hand over her mouth. Grayson chuckled and brought a finger to his lips, teasing her with a shush.

Chapter Forty-Three

"Esther says she's about done with airing out and cleaning up the place," Greg said, his head bent as he tapped at the screen of his phone with his thumbs. He paused and grinned.

"Somehow I don't think Esther just told him she'd cleaned out the fridge," Kipling said, teasing, as she leaned toward Grayson.

He chuckled. "I think that's definitely a dusting smile."

"Bugger off," Greg said, then lifted his head. "Look, I've had to watch the two of you for long enough. I get to enjoy coming home to my—"

He stuttered off and looked down again, his cheeks blooming red.

Kipling gasped and look at Grayson, dropping her jaw in shock. "Grayson, did you catch that? I think Greg has something to tell us."

"No, I do not." He tapped out a final message as they turned off Rossmore Road onto Baker Street. As he slid the phone into his shirt pocket, he grinned and winked. "But I'll let you know when I do."

Kipling's pulse raced and she was giddy. They had been away

from home for weeks — months — and she was almost home again. All she'd wanted was this. She squeezed Grayson's hand and glanced at him, noting the slow smile as he watched her. She felt like the first time she'd gone to Canobie Lake Park and they'd heard the clack-clack-clack of the wooden Yankee Cannonball rollercoaster when they got out of the car. Then the screams of the riders as it passed on the outer edge of the parking lot, circling back into the park again. She couldn't wait to ride it and know the thrill those riders had to have felt.

Giddy. Lightheaded. Flushed.

The cab stopped across the street from their door and the cabbie got out, heading to the back of the van to remove their luggage while Grayson processed payment on the small terminal inside the vehicle. Greg opened her door and offered his hand, and she stepped free. She knew she probably looked silly, but she couldn't both control her expression and control herself from running to her front door. With their luggage retrieved and their fare paid, Grayson took her hand with one of his, and pulled the largest of their bags with the other. Greg followed, dragging the rest, leaving Kipling only her pocketbook to carry.

Down the sidewalk from their door a group of students exited the Sherlock Holmes Museum, laughing and talking, bags of souvenirs swinging between them. She had a brief memory of coming out of that museum herself years before when she was still in high school, of feeling the excitement as a lover of literature that she was on the famous Baker Street. She'd known and understood even then the museum was a tourist location, but she had no idea the true Baker Street, the true home of Sherlock Holmes, was just a short walk away. Or that her future was so close and still so unknown. The students turned in the other direction toward the coffee and smoothie shop.

Grayson stepped beneath the lintel and into the stone archway protecting the door, the suitcase thumping on the single step behind him as he pushed open the door. Rather than continuing into the foyer, he stepped aside with a smile to allow Kipling to enter first. The tears hazing her vision neither surprised nor embarrassed her as she crossed through the short entry into the front parlor. The first time Kipling had entered Baker Street just over five months earlier, there had been two wingback chairs in shades of blue and white facing the white brick fireplace where a fire now crackled. She hadn't yet been home during cooler weather, and the sweet smell of whatever wood was stacked in the hearth mingled with the familiar aromas of bergamot and wood polish that always greeted them when they came home.

The chairs had been shifted to make space for the beautifully Erard piano Grayson had surprised her with when they returned home from their honeymoon. The lid was raised, and a small, round table Kipling thought she recognized as coming from the library sat within the curve of the case with a fragrant bouquet of white English roses and hydrangea.

Today, the mouthwatering temptation of cinnamon and nutmeg immediately won the undeclared battle and made Kipling's mouth water.

She resented the interruption of her stomach grumbling, demanding she eat. She wanted to absorb being home.

From the top of the stairs came the thundering run of four small, yet enthusiastic paws as their likely annoyed and ecstatic cat ran to greet them. It had been even longer since she'd seen Watson, and he her. Before the wedding. He seemed to fly down the last few steps, rather than run, and soared past his first owner to hit Kipling's leg with a headbutt so energized she nearly stumbled. Kipling laughed and crouched down, picking up the grey tabby. His purring was the loudest she'd ever heard, and he rubbed his head and face along her cheek, his claws finding purchase in her cardigan.

Kipling laughed. "Yes, I missed you, too."

"Ran past me like I haven't been feeding him for the last several years," Grayson mumbled begrudgingly, but came to her side to scratch the cat's head.

"Oh, he loves you, too."

"He loves you more. A sentiment I understand entirely."

"Hello!" Esther Mitchell called as she came through the back garden door. "Oh, it's good to see you!" Kipling barely managed to put Watson down before Esther enveloped her in a tight hug. She drew back and looked down at Kipling's still unobvious baby bump. "Everybody on board doing well? I baked oatmeal cookies with raisins and cranberries. Heard they're good for Mamas in progress. I see His Royal Highness heard you come home. He's been investigating every nook and cranny of this house searching for you. I think he suspected you were coming home as soon as I brought out his carrier, because he didn't give me a bit of trouble." She shot a glance to Grayson, a teasing smirk on her lips. "I don't know what you go on about with him. He's the sweetest little puss in the world and has gotten on just lovely with Roger."

"I still can't believe you talked me into naming that little furry hellion something like Roger," Greg mumbled, stepping around to come into view.

"Oh, shut up and kiss me hello."

Grayson feigned a desperation to get out of the way as Esther and Greg "said hello." Greg had been gone from London nearly as long as Grayson and Kipling, so she understood.

"I figured you would be hungry, but wouldn't want to cook, so I've got takeaway being delivered in about" — Esther slid her phone from her back pocket and looked at it—"four minutes. Had no idea what to get, what everyone would like, or what Mama would tolerate so I got everythin' on the small plate menu and a bi' of this and that otherwise."

"Thank you," Kipling said. "I'm starving."

"Good. We'll eat, catch up, and then get out of your hair."

They left the luggage at the bottom of the stairs to be taken up after eating, and the door chime sounded signaling the food delivery. With everything set out on the dining table, they all sat. The onslaught of aromas and spices tempted her to try everything.

It felt so good to be home. To be at their table. In their kitchen. Eating with their friends. Looking at their garden through their french doors.

Kipling paused, her fork loaded with a chicken and sesame dumpling before bringing it to her lips. The giddy, flushed feeling when they'd pulled up to the curb was replaced with the warm comfort of belonging. Laughter and conversation filled the space. She loved it. She loved every moment of it.

"Are you all right, my darling?"

She smiled and looked to her husband, seated beside her. "More than all right."

He lifted her hand to his lips and kissed her skin before returning to the meal and the conversation. Minutes later, both Greg's and Grayson's cellphones rang. It startled her because she knew at least Grayson had his ringer silenced except for very specific numbers calling. He and Greg looked at each other, a silent communication between them, and with a nod Grayson answered on his phone.

"We're both here, Sandra," Grayson said, setting the phone on the table between him and Greg on the other side with the screen up.

"Good. I only need to get this out once. I knew you were traveling today, but figured I'd catch one of you. Or both."

A cold chill skittered up Kipling's spine, smothering the warm calm of moments before as dread hit her. A call from Sandi wasn't necessarily unusual, but for her to reach out to both Grayson and Greg at the same time just didn't land well.

"What's wrong?"

Sandi sighed, a deep huff carrying over the line. "It's Director Cooper."

"We've been on English soil all of two hours, and I am still not interested in—"

"Grayson," Sandi interrupted. "He'd dead."

Grayson's head snapped up and he looked to Greg, who stared back with wide eyes. "When? How?"

"When is sometime in the last day. How is…" Her voice stuttered and tightened before she finished. "Self-inflicted gunshot. Where was in his home. He left a note. Mac and I haven't been privy to any specifics yet, which doesn't surprise me at all, but…he took the blame. For all of it."

"Thank you for coming in, Grayson," Director Bijan Shah said, extending his hand as Grayson and Greg entered his office. After shaking Grayson's hand, he extended to Greg. "Greg. The same."

He motioned toward an area away from his desk near a bank of windows where three chairs sat facing each other. Grayson mentally noted Director Shah's attempt at making the meeting less formal, less businesslike. Not effective, but the attempt was clear. They sat, Grayson and Greg in two chairs closest to each other with Shah facing them.

"I'm sure this isn't the kind of news you ever anticipated when returning from Boston," he said, unbuttoning his suit jacket as he sat. "I've of course read all the reports, including those shared by the FBI office in Boston. You made quite the impression on Director Stanton and Chief of Staff Suarez. Given the events...well, honestly, I don't know what I could possibly say."

"Given that, I would appreciate a concise explanation."

Director Shah nodded and stood again, returning to his desk to retrieve a folder from the corner where it obviously had been placed for easy access. He came back to them and handed the folder to Grayson. He opened it to face a photocopy of a handwritten letter in a penmanship he easily recognized: Jeffrey Cooper. He read quickly.

My guilt is overwhelming, my shame insurmountable. I will never escape the punishment for my crimes and as a coward, I choose not to face them.

I have been, at best, complicit with the machinations orchestrated by the Howell crime family, and at worst, a part of the execution within the structure of MI6. I have been aware of the influence and chokehold the

Howell family has had on our institution for well over three years and have been an active participant in the stratagem to discredit the name of Grayson Holmes and all associated with him.

This included following orders from those with more power within the institution to create the illusion of the death of Officer Gregory McQueen, to then force Officer McQueen to comply with orders to remain hidden, and to mislead the Holmes family to accept his death. Even as the scheme unfolded I knew our deception would not last. Grayson Holmes was far too invested in the truth. I have been anxiously awaiting the tumbling of this house of cards.

There is no justification. I did not participate because I was threatened or blackmailed. I did it purely out of malice and the promise of wealth. There is no ulterior motivation that might cast me in a better light. I am as much a criminal as Nelson or Langdon Howell or any other carrying the blood of the Howell legacy in their veins.

Having come to the end of the play, I have chosen to check myself out. The wealth is gone, and the malice remains. I am done. To which I offer no apology. I ask for no forgiveness.

Jeffrey Cooper

Grayson handed the folder to Greg to allow him to read, taking the moment to tamp down and harness the rage festering in his chest. He was very tired of being angry. So very tired of being deceived. So very tired of the weight and the darkness and the blood.

While Greg read, Grayson leveled his focus on Director Shah.

He didn't speak. He didn't ask or demand. He waited.

After a few moments, discomfort obvious in the lines of the man's face, Director Shah cleared his throat. "I felt you deserved the full extent of it. It serves no purpose to hide any of it." His smile twisted, not with animosity, but humility. "This brings to the fore-front a concern of our upper levels of leadership. It has been believed for a time now that certain actors have infiltrated MI6. Which is why I've asked you to meet with me."

Grayson maintained his silence. Greg cursed as he closed the folder.

Director Shah nodded, the embarrassment shifting to discomfit. "You have yet declared your intentions within Six, when or if you choose to return. That much was clear and I believe to be correct in the reports provided by Jeffrey Cooper. Am I correct?"

Grayson nodded, a single, slow motion of his head.

"I am not asking you return today. This week. This month. But I am asking you to consider returning to Six in a new capacity. As director, filling the gap left by Jeffrey Cooper. However, your primary duty would be a deep investigation of the extent of incursion the Howell family has managed into the institution. You would have at your disposal anyone you wanted. I know you and Mr. McQueen have a tight, efficient relationship with Sandra Sookoo and Angus Hennessey. You can have anyone you want. And this would be your assignment."

Grayson said nothing. He took the folder from Greg, stood, and headed for the door. Greg followed, without a word.

"Grayson—" Director Shah called.

He didn't stop.

Greg didn't say anything until they were out of the building and waiting on the kerb for a cab. Before he spoke, he cleared his throat and pushed his hands into his trouser pockets. "I'm guessing that's a no—"

"Quite likely, yes."

He nodded, Grayson catching the movement in his peripheral vision. "I mean, that's fine with me."

"You can do whatever you like regardless of my final decision."

"Nah," Greg said, scrunching his face. "You and me, Ollie, we're in this together. We stand together. We joined Six together, and despite their bullshit, we leave Six together." Greg sighed, long and dramatic, bouncing on the balls of his feet. "Now what to do with all this leisure time."

"You could get married and go on a six-month honeymoon."

"Hmm, that has possibilities."

"So, you're considering marriage?"

Greg turned his head to look at Grayson, winking. "I told you I'd let you know when I had something to tell you."

Grayson chuckled, some of the oppressive anger easing from his chest. "You do that. And when you do, I'll repeat this. I could not be happier for you. Esther Mitchell is good for you, and you for her. You're damn lucky she forgave you for being a twit."

"I am. I'm damn lucky. The universe gave me another chance when Kip and Esther somehow found each other in the middle of Howell's chaos."

"Yet another way he made an utter fool of himself. The more he tried, the more he cocked up."

A cab pulled up, and Greg opened the door first, sliding across the backseat. As Grayson followed, his mobile buzzed. "Baker Street," he told the cabbie and looked at the screen, his interest piqued. The actual call had gone to voicemail, and he tapped to open the message, bringing the mobile to his ear.

After listening, Grayson turned the phone to look at it in his hand.

"Who was that, Ollie?" Greg asked. "You look… I don't know. Can't be confused. You're never confused."

"Confused, no. But it would seem the universe is sending me a message as well." Without explaining, he tapped the message to connect back to the caller. It took only seconds for the call to be answered. "I just got your message. We should talk. May I come by now?"

Kipling finished hanging their clothes in the closet and tucked the now-empty luggage into the corner until they needed it again. Washing everything at home before putting it away made everything feel normal again. They smelled right again. One more step toward resetting the chaos that had taken over everything in the last few weeks.

She left the bedroom, but before going downstairs the rooms along the perpendicular landing drew her attention. Grayson's office she knew well, with his large desk and more bookshelves. The next door was the shared bathroom for the floor. And the door tucked at the far end was currently unused. Grayson had told her it had been his room as a child, and then where Greg slept when they both lived here, and briefly upon his return to London and life. Now, it was a guest room. She opened the door and looked inside. It was a decent sized room, large enough for a full bed, dresser, and other pieces of furniture. Sunlight from the window overlooking their garden showed off the dust motes set to flight by her entrance.

It would make a beautiful child's room.

Kipling smiled and closed the door as she left. From the floors below the sound of piano music rose up through the stairwell. Grayson was home. She didn't know how long he would be gone. Neither did he since the purpose of the meeting at Six was more mystery than not. She started down the stairs, joined by Watson when he bolted from their bedroom suddenly realizing she had escaped his immediate view. He'd stuck close for the last two days, barely letting her out of his sight.

And staring at Grayson with cold judgment, deeming him guilty of keeping her away for so long.

The music he played was the piano piece he'd first played for her on the night before their wedding, adding composer to his long list of accomplishments. It had expanded, developed, and grown into a much longer and intricate piece but the underlying composition hadn't changed. It made her think of the wind rustling leaves and steam from hot cups of tea. That probably would make no sense to someone who studied music, but it was the emotion she felt when she heard it. Peace. Calm. Safety. Love.

Grayson.

When she reached the ground floor, Grayson paused in playing only long enough to motion her toward him to sit on the bench by his side, then went back to playing. She joined him, watching his long fingers tap skillfully at the keys. He neared the end of the piece, letting the final notes linger before he set his hands in his lap.

"I hope you play this for me forever."

Grayson turned his head and leaned to her for a kiss. He pressed his palm against her cheek, smoothing her skin with his thumb. His unique eyes shifted as he studied her face.

"What are you thinking?" she asked.

He smiled. "Of how blessed I am. And how much better my life has become when I've let love guide me."

She gave a small chuckle. "That's quite a deep thought. And I do believe those are *your* words, not someone else's."

"For this, I must rely on my own bumbling abilities." She gave him a moment, sensing he was seeking words. Grayson drew in a long breath through his nose and released it again. "Six, and specifically Director Shah, has asked Greg and myself to return and head the investigation into how deeply in the institution the Howell family has been able to infiltrate and control. Sandra was right when Jeffrey Cooper took responsibility, though he also said he was following orders."

"That must be difficult to know."

He canted his head. "Yes, but more than anything it has reminded me I am not nearly as infallible as I once believed." His gaze shifted away from her eyes to her mouth. "And has made me understand I am no longer interested in spending my life seeking subterfuge and deception."

"Does that mean you're not accepting the offer?"

His eyes shifted up again. "No. But I have accepted a different offer."

"Okay," she said, tilting her head.

Grayson's lips spread and bowed into a pleased smile, and he took her hand to hold it on his lap. "Come January, you are looking at the newest professor at Westminster College. Save for Doctor Kipling Holmes, of course. However, we have adjusted what will likely be my course catalog. I received a call from Peter Rathborne, quite timely, and once again the universe has guided me. I stopped at his office on the way home. And I came clean," he said with a wink. "Peter knows I am not now, nor have I ever been, a commodities banker. While class names haven't been determined, I will likely be providing the opportunity to study criminal forensic and investigative science."

Kipling realized her mouth hung open and she shut it with a clack of her teeth, blinking at her husband. "You mean it?"

"Of course if you aren't willing to work at the same institution of higher learning as your husband—"

She squealed and wrapped her arms around him, and he laughed just before silencing the sounds of her excitement with a kiss.

Chelsea and Westminster
Hospital - April

"Our parents are here, my darling."

Grayson's voice wrapped around her and gently pulled her from her rest. She inhaled deeply and opened her eyes as she exhaled. Grayson sat in a chair beside the bed but leaned on the raised head portion, his cheek sharing her pillow, his fingers brushing her hair. Kipling smiled, feeling lethargic and heavy.

"Do you feel up to the visit?" he asked.

Kipling nodded and hummed, forcing her tired mind to engage. She tried to lick her lips, and Grayson moved away long enough to retrieve a cup with a straw. He held it for her and she took a long, satisfying drink of the juice. With her throat moistened, she let him take the cup away and tried to shift in her position. And was reminded in detail sharp enough to shove away any tendrils of sleep that she'd had a baby. She hissed and shifted again, relieving some of the ache.

"Do you need anything before I let them come?" he asked, his expression pinched with concern.

"I'm okay," she assured. "I need a kiss. And I need the baby."

He smiled, leaned to her to kiss her lips, then left her bedside to the open bassinet nearby. Her heart fluttered in giddy joy to see the tiny, swaddled baby. Grayson lifted the baby, speaking softly as he came back to the bed.

"Here you go, Mum. All bright eyed and ready to receive adoring guests." He gently laid the baby in the bend of her arm, kissed the wrinkled forehead beneath the beanie cap, and kissed Kipling's brow before he went to the door.

Kipling looked down at their baby, her heart swelling so much it made it hard to breathe and she had to blink to clear her eyes. Just like Holmes children for generations, eyes an imbalanced blend of blue and green blinked slowly, trying to bring her into focus, the sheen of the antibiotic still clinging to long lashes. Tiny, perfect lips opened, seeking, and tiny fingers of the only hand free of the swaddling curled and rubbed the blanket.

"You are perfect," she whispered. "And you are so loved. I don't know if there has ever been a baby so loved."

The door to her room opened and Grayson stepped in, holding it for their family to enter. Kipling looked up and smiled. Her mother and father led the way, and Mom gasped, covering her mouth to smother the sound as she blinked away the sheen.

"Oh, sweetheart," she whispered, coming around the side of the bed with Daddy — silent — beside her. She gently touched the beanie, studying the tiny face. "Perfect."

Grayson's mother and father followed, staying at the foot of the bed, Annalise mimicking Kipling's mother by keeping her hands over her mouth to stay quiet. Kipling smiled wider when Greg and Esther followed behind. Esther made no show of hiding her tears, sniffling and wiping her cheeks in contrast to the wide, happy smile on her face. She was Esther McQueen now. Once Greg proposed, they wasted no time and married just before Christmas.

"No one alert the nurses," Grayson said, easing the door closed again behind Greg. "I'm not sure we're allowed so many visitors at once, but I wasn't about to tell anyone no."

"Sweetheart, get on with it," his mother whispered, motioning toward Kipling and the baby. "The two of you have kept this secret long enough. We see a healthy baby and a healthy mum. Now, tell us who we've got."

Moving through the gathering of family, Grayson came back to Kipling's side, draping his arm across the top of the raised bed helping Kipling sit up. His fingers brushed along her hair and he looked down at them. In that moment, in all the moments she had seen love in her husband's eyes, none equaled now. She knew tears shined in her eyes, but seeing tears in his eyes as well made her fall in love with him all over again. Every day, she fell in love more.

"Everyone, we are ecstatically happy to introduce to you Jackson Gregory Sherlock Holmes."

About the Author

Gail R. Delaney is a multi-published, award-winning author of romance in multiple sub-genres, including contemporary romance, romantic suspense, and epic science fiction romance. She always wrote stories as a kid through her teens, but didn't decide to write 'for publication' until her early twenties after the death of her mother. While helping her father go through her mother's papers, she found a box her mother kept with everything Gail had ever written—from book reports to short stories. It was then she realized her mother saw her as a writer, and it was time to live up to her mother's vision.

You can find out more about Gail R. Delaney's body of work at:

http://www.GailDelaney.com

Also by Gail R. Delaney

Contemporary Romance

Something Better

Precious Things

Feel My Love

Fools Rush In

The Future Possible Saga

Book One: Revolution

Book Two: Outcasts

Book Three: Gaining Ground

Book Four: End Game

Book Five: Janus

Book Six: Triad

Book Seven: Stasis

Book Eight: Liber

www.ingramcontent.com/pod-product-compliance
Lightning Source LLC
Chambersburg PA
CBHW021232190726
48289CB00005B/1281